Henry Larkin

Carlyle and the open secret of his life

Henry Larkin

Carlyle and the open secret of his life

ISBN/EAN: 9783743306271

Manufactured in Europe, USA, Canada, Australia, Japa

Cover: Foto ©Raphael Reischuk / pixelio.de

Manufactured and distributed by brebook publishing software
(www.brebook.com)

Henry Larkin

Carlyle and the open secret of his life

CARLYLE

AND THE

OPEN SECRET OF HIS LIFE

"There where thou art, work, work; whatsoever thy hand findeth to do, do it,—with the hand of a man, not of a phantasm; be that thy unnoticed blessedness and exceeding great reward. Thy words, let them be few, and well ordered. Love silence rather than speech in these tragic days, when, for very speaking, the voice of man has fallen inarticulate to man; and hearts, in this loud babbling, sit dark and dumb towards one another."—*Latter-Day Pamphlets.*

CARLYLE

AND

THE OPEN SECRET OF HIS LIFE

BY

HENRY LARKIN

AUTHOR OF 'EXTRA PHYSICS, AND THE MYSTERY OF CREATION,' ETC.

LONDON

KEGAN PAUL, TRENCH & CO., 1, PATERNOSTER SQUARE

1886

CONTENTS.

CHAPTER I.

CHAPTER II.

√CHAPTER III.

CHAPTER IV.

CHAPTER V.

CHAPTER XV.

CHAPTER XVI.

CHAPTER XVII.

CHAPTER XVIII.

CHAPTER XIX.

CARLYLE,

AND

THE OPEN SECRET OF HIS LIFE.

CHAPTER I.

The unspoken secret of Carlyle's life—Far other than literary aims—His
Life in his Works—The chief elements deep below view or surmise—
The most private concerns of his life now public—Youthful misgivings
and aspirations—Journeyman's work : Essays and Magazine Articles
—German Transcendental Literature, and 'Philosophy of Clothes.'

Is the secret of Carlyle's life—namely, the hidden hopes,
aspirations and efforts, which gave to his character its
essential significance—a secret for ever impenctrable? Is
it possible that a man could have written so much and
so earnestly, and have made such a mark upon his
generation as he did, without revealing <u>his own practical</u>
aims, even to the most sympathetic of his readers? It
would almost seem so, judging from the way in which
his writings have from the beginning, and almost
universally, been received and commented on. But
surely there must be, and must long have been, a deeper
practical insight hidden in many hearts, than anything
that has yet found spoken utterance. What then was
it, throughout his life, that he was really trying to do?

Carlyle himself felt to the last that he had never been understood, that no one really believed him. People everywhere acknowledged his genius, but no one believed his report. He passionately assured them that he had 'far other than literary aims;' and they persisted in looking upon him as a mere eloquent writer, somewhat too frantic in the energy of his rhetoric. In short, it was, and still is, very generally believed that he had no real aim at all beyond that of startling, astonishing, and disconcerting all who listened to him. Of course there have always been manifold exceptions to such sheer perversity of judgment. And yet, even among the warmest of his sympathisers, how many are there who have not constantly lamented the absence of any definite constructive effort in all that he taught? He was a mighty puller-down, a disturber of sacred convictions, we are told on every hand; but he never seriously tried to build, or to bind together what was good amongst us. I hope, by following him step by step through his remarkable literary career, to show that all this is altogether a mistake. He said that his life was in his works. This is true in a far more practical sense than his readers are mostly aware of. Whatever he may have tried to do, or to become, throughout his earnestly struggling life, clearly his books were the main instruments he used in endeavouring to accomplish his purposes; and in those books, if only we know the circumstances which called them forth, and can penetrate to the spirit in which they were written, we shall inevitably find the indications we are seeking. But in order adequately to understand Carlyle's character, his life must be seen as a whole. For his character was no mere crystallised conventionality; but, from the beginning to the end of it, a most complex living growth : growing and ripening in Time, while its roots were deepening into Eternity. No mere summary of moral and intellectual qualities will in the least characterise him. If we cannot see his character, each with our own eyes, in what he did and what he tried to do, we shall never see it.

In his isolation and disappointment at the absence of any human recognition of his actual aims, he did not believe that any one would seriously try to understand him, or would have much success even if he did. In his private journal, December 29, 1848, three years after the publication of 'Cromwell's Letters and Speeches,' he made this remarkable entry :—

"Darwin (Erasmus) said to Jane the other day, in his quizzing serious manner, 'Who will write Carlyle's life ?' The word reported to me set me thinking how *impossible* it was, and would for ever remain, for any creature to write my 'life.' The chief elements of my little destiny have long lain deep below view or surmise, and never will nor can be known to any son of Adam. I would say to my biographer, if any fool undertook such a task, 'Forbear, poor fool! Let no life of me be written; let me and my bewildered wrestlings lie buried here and be forgotten swiftly of all the world. If thou write, it will be mere delusion and hallucination. The confused world never understood me nor will understand me and my poor affairs. Not even the persons nearest to me could guess at them; nor was it found indispensable; nor is it now (for any but an idle purpose) profitable, were it even possible. Silence, and go thy ways elsewhither.'" *

These words seem almost as solemnly prohibitory and final as the warning on Shakspeare's tomb, 'Good friend, for Jesus' sake forbeare!' And yet it is evident they

* 'Life in London,' 1834–1881, vol. i. p. 1.

were written more in sorrow at his own isolation, than in anger against any one who should make the attempt. Carlyle would have been the very last, even to wish to forbid any reader of his from searching his writings through and through, and wringing their last secret from them if it were possible. But besides this, the whole condition of the problem has become strangely widened since these words were written. Not only have we his own published works completely before us, but the most private concerns of his life have now become no less public property. Never was there such a total exposure of the most sacred privacies of a greatly interesting human heart. It is too late to talk about ' forbearing.' The most reticent of men has been fated to have his heart laid bare before the world, to be mocked at or reverenced, according to the world's good pleasure. Let those who still love him, with all his weaknesses and all his strength, at least try to understand him aright. But the secret of his life was not upon the surface. He was a mystery, even to himself; and much more so to those whom he tried to influence. 'The chief elements of my little destiny,' he says, 'never will nor can be known to any son of Adam.' So he gloomily thought, in the darkness of his own utter loneliness; but his whole strangely baffled, yet consistent life is now visible before us, and what once seemed to him so 'impossible' is impossible no longer.

I have no intention of adding another to the many biographies of Carlyle which have already been given to the world, nor yet of offering a detailed criticism of his works. My one aim is to try to make his character, and the purpose and meaning of his life, intelligible; and I shall only refer to, or offer for consideration, such facts of his life, and such portions of his writings, whether public or private, as seem to bear expressly upon the problem, and help to bring his extraordinary personality vividly before us.

The earliest utterances of his own personal aspirations which have as yet been made public are to be found in some interesting extracts from his early letters to the companions of his youth, which have been preserved by Mr. Alexander Ireland, and published with his consent by Mr. Moncure D. Conway in his recollections of Carlyle. The first extract is from a reply of his to a letter from his friend Thomas Murray, in which letter his young friend had prophesied that 'the name of Carlyle would be inseparably connected with the literary history of the nineteenth century :' a very remarkable prophecy for those young days. Carlyle's reply is dated 'August, 1814 ;' so he was between eighteen and nineteen when he wrote it. What can be more significant of his whole future life-struggle than the following words, in which he responds to his friend's hopeful prophecy with a foreboding no less prophetic of coming disappointment ; strangely grim and self-searching for a youth so gifted and so warmly appreciated ? He exclaims—

"But—O Tom! what a foolish, flattering creature thou art! To talk of future eminence in connection with the literary history of the nineteenth century to such a one as me! Alas! my good lad, when I and all my fancies and reveries and speculations shall have been swept over with the besom of oblivion, the literary history of no century will feel itself the worse. Yet think not, because I talk thus, that I am careless about literary fame. No, Heaven knows that ever since I have been able to form a wish, the wish of being known has been the foremost."

The wish of being known. Alas, yes ; and to the last he felt that he never had been known. He had been talked about enough, and far more than enough, for the more he was talked about, the more he seemed to be misknown.

Four years afterwards—November, 1818—we have another glimpse into the leaven of misery which was already working within him, showing how deeply he already felt himself a solitary sojourner among men.

"I have thought," he writes, "much and long of the irksome drudgery, the solitude, the gloom, of my condition. I have reasoned thus: These things may be endured, if not with a peaceful heart, at least with a serene countenance; but it is worth while to inquire whether the profit will repay the pain of enduring them,—a scanty and precarious livelihood constitutes the profit; you know me, and can form some judgment of the pain. But there is loss as well as pain. I speak not of the loss of health; but the destruction of benevolent feeling; that searing of the heart, which misery, especially of a petty kind, sooner or later will never fail to effect, is a more frightful thing. The desire which, in common with all men, I feel for conversation and social intercourse is, I find, enveloped in a dense, repulsive atmosphere, not of vulgar *mauvaise honte,* though such it is generally esteemed, but of deeper feelings, which I partly inherit from nature, and which are mostly due to the undefined station I have hitherto occupied in society.. . . . I have thought of writing for booksellers. *Risum teneas;* for at times I am serious in this matter. In fine weather, it does strike me that there are in this head some ideas, a few *disjecta membra,* which might find admittance into some one of the many publications of the day. To live by authorship was never my intention."

Thus was he, with evident premonitory shuddering, becoming gradually but surely driven and drawn into the stream of his destiny. With all his wish to

become honourably known, a life of literature clearly
was not the goal to which his heart aspired. But he
gradually found that his pen was the only weapon or
tool his untoward destiny had placed in his hand; and
with characteristic determination he cast about to discover how best to make it a means for the attainment
of some more distinctly human and personally effectual
career. Thus, March, 1821, he again writes,—

"I have tried about twenty plans this winter in the way
of authorship; they have all failed. I have about twenty
more to try; and if it does but please the Director of all
things to continue the moderate share of health now restored
to me, I will make the doors of human society fly open before
me yet, notwithstanding. My *petards* will not burst, or make
only *noise* when they do. I must mix them better, plant them
more judiciously; they shall burst and do execution, too."

I suppose no one will deny that he literally fulfilled
this promise of his youth. Whether, when the doors of
human society were flung open wide enough before him,
he was really any nearer to the attainment of his life's
hope will be seen better hereafter.

We must now pass over the long period which he
afterwards spoke of as little more than 'journeyman's
work:' the period of the Essays and Magazine Articles.
Many readers prefer those essays to anything he afterwards wrote; and, looking at them simply as literature,
there is some reason for the preference. The fact is they
were written without any immediate ulterior aims, and
were therefore more complete in themselves and more
entirely comprehensible. He was simply perfecting
himself in his craft; sounding the trumpet for the coming
battle, and at the same time trying to give honest work
for an honest livelihood. And assuredly few journey-

men, of any craft whatever, have ever worked more faithfully. But they were not the 'petards' which he was silently preparing and maturing to explode upon a moribund society; nor were they the beacons of hope which he longed to kindle upon the heights, as a sign to all men that a better day was about to dawn. It may seem little short of madness to many, to say that it was not till he had conceived the idea of 'Sartor Resartus' that he felt that the time had at length come when he was to make his mark in the world. Nevertheless such is actually the fact, as a careful study of that singularly pregnant book will sufficiently show. Of his disappointment at discovering his mistake we must speak afterwards.

It is admitted by all competent readers that 'Sartor Resartus' contains, in a highly condensed, suggestive, and symbolic form, an initial utterance of all Carlyle's intellectual or speculative convictions concerning God's Universe and *Man's* position therein. Some readers even go so far in their admiration of it as to pronounce it the greatest of Carlyle's works. Such exaggerative partiality, however, means little more than that they themselves have not yet passed beyond the splendours of speculative insight into the more vital realities of ethical and spiritual conviction. It is neither the greatest nor yet the highest of Carlyle's intellectual efforts; nor does it express his own most spontaneous intuitions, or his final ethical convictions. And yet it is undoubtedly the most brilliantly suggestive of his books, and contains the intellectual germs of all that he afterwards grew to. It is the seed-plot of the future harvest of his life. But essentially it is an importation from Germany; a wonderfully successful attempt to embody in a practically suggestive form, for the use of English readers, the entire German Transcendental Literature, which centred and culminated in Goethe, and which had for some years past absorbed Carlyle's earnest attention almost to the exclusion of everything else. No wonder it is so pregnant with meaning, and so teeming with soul-awakening thoughts. Carlyle's great merit for us lies in the fact that he was the first among us to discern the almost unspeakable social significance of that great uprising of speculative insight and passionate intuition; and that he brought home to us its practical issues with such a masterly incisiveness and freshness of utterance and of illustration, as not merely to stamp it with his own overpowering individuality, but to make it a direct appeal from his own heart to the intellects and hearts of his fellow-countrymen. But he no more originated the essential thoughts which it contains, than he originated the characters in the French Revolution which he so vividly portrayed. Without his German initiation and training, and the German platform from which he finally rose to his true intellectual stature and moral strength, it is impossible to imagine what he could have grown to. The Goethean ethics and transcendental intuition were to him the beginning of all practical light and hopeful effort in his generation.

The central idea of 'Sartor Resartus,' and of Goethe's 'Transcendent Realism,' is, that the physical universe does not stand for itself; that it is neither self-sufficient nor self-sustaining; but that it is the visible clothing and sensuous ultimatum of an invisible spiritual universe. That whatever we see with our eyes is a phantasmagoric projection of its own inner reality, thus made visible and tangible to our senses. That the Inner Universe is the real universe, and determines all the issues of seemingly physical existences. That the human body, especially, is a revelation to the physical senses of the presence of a human soul. And, as a corollary from this vast conception, that he who would vitally influence the physical sphere must work from the plane of realities, and not from the plane of mere visual appearances. This also was Swedenborg's great ontological conception of God's Universe.

Thus all visible or imaginable appearances are regarded as the covering or symbolic clothing of whatever reality may be hidden within them. It was this grand and pregnant thought which suggested to Carlyle his quaint notion of the ' Philosophy of Clothes,' which ' Sartor Resartus ' (the Tailor Re-tailored, or German Philosophy with a new application) professes to elucidate. Let us now take a rapid glance through the several chapters of this remarkable book, and see what we can cull from them in evidence of its origin and of its own earnestly practical purpose.

CHAPTER II.

The 'Clothes Philosophy' imported from Germany—An almost boundless problem—Carlyle's first impressions from German literature—
Richter and Goethe—Beginnings of German literary life—Aprons :
a digression—Middle-Age costumes and customs—A new and deeper
insight — Miraculous use of clothes and organised regulations —
Society impossible without social clothing—Nature, not an Aggregate but a Whole—Difficulties of transplanting foreign Thought into
a barren domestic soil.

Book I. Chap. I. Preliminary.—Carlyle begins his
great subject, which is ultimately to embrace the universe in the magnificent sweep of his speculations, by
calling attention to the singular but seemingly trivial
fact that, among all our scientific and philosophical
investigations, no one in this country has yet inquired
seriously into the meaning of the clothes we wear,—the
vestural tissue in which the whole man is included and
screened, in which his faculties work, and in which his
whole Self lives, moves, and has its being. In all speculations, he says, "they have tacitly figured man as a
Clothed Animal; whereas he is by nature a *Naked
Animal;* and only in certain circumstances, by purpose
and desire, masks himself in Clothes." And he professes to have received from Germany a most remarkable
treatise by Diogenes Teufelsdröckh opening up the
whole subject.

    Chap. II. Editorial Difficulties.—The first point

we have here to note is, that Carlyle speaks of 'Teufelsdröckh's Book,' the 'remarkable treatise' already spoken of, as "of boundless, almost formless contents, a very Sea of Thought."

"Directly on the first perusal," he says, "almost on the first deliberate inspection, it became apparent that here a quite new Branch of Philosophy, leading to as yet undescried ulterior results, was disclosed; farther, what seemed scarcely less interesting, a quite new human Individuality, an almost unexampled personal character, that, namely, of Professor Teufelsdröckh the Discloser."

Can any reader of Carlyle deliberately imagine that he was here speaking of his own thoughts and of himself? That his thoughts were the ' very Sea of Thought;' that he himself was the ' almost unexampled personal character,' which had struck him with such wonder? It is impossible to seriously imagine such a thing. The fact is, he was thinking of no single individual at all, but of the new insight and the new possibilities of human character and destiny which had dawned upon him as he became familiar with a whole literature, which he at least, to the end of his life, regarded as a new era in the history of human intelligence. But, he adds, as man is "emphatically a Proselytising creature," the new question arose : How might this " acquired good " be imparted to others ? " The first thought," he tells us, " naturally was, to publish Article after Article on this remarkable Volume, in such widely-circulating Critical Journals as the Editor might stand connected with." Did he not emphatically do this of German Literature ? The following list of articles published in the years immediately preceding the publication of ' Sartor Resartus ' will be a sufficient reply :—

'Jean Paul Friedrich Richter,' *Edinburgh Review,* 1827.

'State of German Literature,' *Edinburgh Review,* 1828.

'Goethe's Helena,' *Foreign Review,* 1828.

'Goethe,' *Foreign Review,* 1828.

'The Life of Heyne,' *Foreign Review,* 1828.

'Novalis,' *Foreign Review,* 1829.

'Signs of the Times,' *Edinburgh Review,* 1829.

'Jean Paul Friedrich Richter Again,' *Foreign Review,* 1830.

'Schiller,' *Fraser's Magazine,* 1831.

'The Nibelungen Lied,' *Westminster Review,* 1831.

'German Literature of the Fourteenth and Fifteenth Centuries,' *Foreign Quarterly Review,* 1831.

'Taylor's Historic Survey of German Poetry,' *Edinburgh Review,* 1831.

'Characteristics,' *Edinburgh Review,* 1831.

In this way he had earnestly striven to deliver himself of his newly acquired and as yet pent-up thoughts. But he soon found that thoughts would inevitably arise and demand utterance which, if uttered, 'might endanger the circulation of any journal extant.' Thus did he see himself, for a while, "shut out from all public utterance of those extraordinary Doctrines, and constrained to revolve them, not without disquietude, in the dark depths of his own mind."

But now comes a slight mystification of the outward sequence of events, in order to point to an important inward fact. We must suppose some at least of the foregoing Articles not as yet written; and that Carlyle, deeply as he had been interested with the original thinkers of Germany, was not as yet sufficiently familiar with German Literary History as a whole to enable him to trace its genesis and growth, which he says became, " in spite of all that memory and conjecture could do, more and more enigmatic." While thus at a loss for more detailed information on the subject, " altogether unexpectedly arrives a letter from Herr Hofrath Heuschrecke, our Professor's chief friend and associate in Weïssnichtwo." Carlyle here, and in what immediately follows, whimsically refers to another class of German writers,—the collectors, compilers, and commentators ; and more especially records his intellectual obligation to Franz Horn,, whose merits and grasshopper peculiarities are duly recorded in the Article, ' State of German Literature.' But the personal obligations indicated are no more to be taken as history, than the no less whimsical account of the offer of the book to Oliver Yorke of *Fraser's Magazine.*

One interesting fact, however, may here be dwelt upon. Carlyle seems to intimate—what was probably the truth — that it was after reading Horn's ' critical sketch of German Poets ' (four volumes in all) that the idea of a Clothes Philosophy and Philosopher arose in his mind. For he says,—

"Form rose out of void solution and discontinuity; like united itself with like in definite arrangement : and soon, either in actual vision and possession, or in fixed reasonable hope, the image of the whole Enterprise had shaped itself, so to speak, into a solid mass."

Carlyle elsewhere alludes to ' the first genesis of Sartor,' when the feeling of ' astonishment at *clothes* ' first struck him. Doubtless this was the fixed point around which the whole conception crystallised.—Clothes, he may have said to himself, which at once conceal and reveal: how strange that man alone among animals should seek to so shield and decorate, and thus distinguish and identify his person! It is because he alone has an ever-prolific Ideal hidden in his soul, which is continually striving to clothe itself with thoughts, words, acts, and outward symbols of itself. In this respect is not every clothed man or woman a type of the universe? Is not everything visible also the Clothing of an invisible Reality? Clothes, rightly seen through, are the type of a whole philosophy of Transcendent Realism. The net result of the teachings of Novalis, Richter, Goethe, Schiller, Fichte, Kant, and others,—what is it but a Philosophy of Clothes?

Accordingly Carlyle, 'emphatically a proselytising creature,' earnestly set himself to condense from that new strange 'Sea of Thought' whatever he had found practically profitable to his own life, so that 'this acquired good might be imparted to others.' For this purpose he chose to embody the whole subject in the form of the 'Life and Opinions of the Clothes Philosopher,' illustrated and intensified at every turn from his own varied reading and his own vivid experience. So much for his 'editorial difficulties,' which it must be admitted were neither few nor slight.

Chap. III. Reminiscences.—In this remarkable chapter we see Carlyle in his strength. Hitherto his humour was forced and heavy, as was generally the case whenever he tried to be merely whimsical. His genius was far too grimly earnest and sincere, either for mere whimsicalities or for fictitious imagination, and only found clear utterance when he had gained a clear basis of fact to work upon. We here have Carlyle's own reminiscences of his first acquaintance with German literature,

and of the feelings and new conceptions which it opened
out to him. But we also have a graphic bird's-eye picture
of life in Germany, while as yet her highest thought
was only struggling into existence,—nascent, inarticulate,
unrecognized, 'alone with the Stars.' This is quite after
the manner of Carlyle. No one knew better than he the
long silent preparation, and gathering together of vital
forces, which in any country must necessarily precede a
national outburst of genius.

Teufelsdröckh, it must be repeated, stands in Carlyle's
imagination for no individual man. He is a personation
of the German intellectual and passional ideal, as that ideal
presented itself to Carlyle's practical mind. But such is
Carlyle's invincible proclivity to fact, that he instinctively
seizes upon any trait or circumstance from whatever
source which he feels will give vigour and definiteness
to his description. Least of all, as we must continually
repeat, is Teufelsdröckh a portraiture of himself. No two
characters, sharing the same sentiments, could be more
strangely contrasted. Clearly Richter and Goethe, more
than any other, were continually in his mind as the basis
of his conception ; but even they were only portions of
the material that went to its formation. The graphic
description of the Professor's 'strange apartment' with
'old Lieschen' for general lion's-provider, is evidently
condensed from the experiences of many a poor German
student, struggling alone with his books, amid the inarticulate practical activity and industry by which he was
surrounded, and which made his life possible. It is also
curious to note that, referring to those struggling unrecognised days of German literature, Carlyle adds, "Few
strangers had admittance within : the only one we ever
saw there, ourselves excepted, was the Hofrath Heu-

schrecke." And then he deals out what seems to be rather hard measure to poor discursive Franz Horn, because he did not happen to be a genius among geniuses, but only a Boswell to his Johnson.

Chap. IV. Characteristics.— The characteristics here indicated are palpably those which he elsewhere recognises in the leading German writers; and especially those of Richter, to whom indeed the whole of this 'Book I.' more peculiarly belongs. The third, fourth, fifth, and sixth paragraphs are neither more nor less than a condensed sketch of Richter's characteristics as a writer,— his strange plainness of speech; his piercing insight into the essential facts of life, and his small respect for its upholsteries; his strange impartiality and scientific freedom, as of a man just dropped from the moon; his humour of looking at Matter and all material things as Spirit; his wonderfully cutting words, sheering down into the true centre of the matter in hand, intermixed with mere dawdling and dreaming; his omnivorous reading; in short, his

"rich idiomatic diction, picturesque allusions, fiery poetic emphasis, or quaint tricksy turns; all the graces and terrors of a wild Imagination wedded to the clearest Intellect,—but with sheer sleeping and soporific passages, circumlocutions, repetitions, touches even of pure doting jargon, so often intervening."

In the seventh paragraph Teufelsdröckh passes, 'without solution of continuity,' like a changing star, from Richter into Goethe, and perhaps Fichte and others, and so becomes lost to view in the unsounded depths of the German wonderland. The eighth is evidently put in for the sake of introducing a vivid recollection of what he elsewhere speaks of as the heartiest laugh he ever heard. And the ninth is simply a further statement of editorial difficulties, which would be a mere pointless exaggeration if they referred to anything less than a national literature.

Chap. V. The World in Clothes.—In this chapter, after a preliminary suggestion of the singular analogy between Customs and Costumes, between Architecture and Tailoring, and how in all 'cases " there is an incessant, indubitable, though infinitely complex working of Cause and Effect," Carlyle professes to quote from Teufelsdröckh a brief humorous sketch of the German literary world while yet its clothes or habitudes were serviceable and sufficient for it ; touching lightly on its old cause-and-effect philosophies, its omnivorous learning, its quaint mysticisms, and its inexhaustible ancient and modern researches of every conceivable kind. Then follow 'philosophical reflections' which read very much like Richter applied and condensed. Whether any, or how many of the thoughts were actually suggested by Richter I am unable to say ; or whether the German phrases in parentheses, here and elsewhere, are genuine quotations, or only mystifications ; but that the whole tone of thought in this and in the subsequent chapters is intentionally and emphatically Richter's is surely beyond question.

Chap. VI. Aprons.—Perhaps the whole of this short passage of sarcasm is mainly Carlyle's own, although the tone of thought is still evidently that of Richter. It has all the appearance of an interpolation ; it is more self-disparaging than any other part of the book, the sins pointed at are among Carlyle's most cherished animosities, the German phrases are without special significance, and the chapter altogether has no special reference to Germany. We may look upon it as a passing thrust of Carlyle's at sins nearer home. The Episcopal Apron, with the corner tucked in, as if the day's work were done; the enormous expansion of mere waste-paper literature, 'choking up the highways and public thoroughfares;' and the British Newspaper Press, a 'Satan's Invisible World Displayed,' are all unmistakably Carlylean.

Chap. VII. Miscellaneous - Historical. — This interesting chapter on German Middle-Age costumes and customs needs no comment. It is familiar to every reader of Carlyle; it has no recondite meanings which we have to struggle to make out; and however or wherever he culled his facts, he has condensed them into a picture of consummate skill and humour.

"Did we behold the German fashionable dress of the Fifteenth Century," he says, "we might smile; as perhaps those bygone Germans, were they to rise again, and see our haberdashery, would cross themselves, and invoke the Virgin!"

Chap. VIII. The World out of Clothes.—Carlyle's express work here fairly begins, what has preceded being merely historic and introductory. The *avowed* purpose, we may now say, of 'Sartor Resartus' is the introduction of German Transcendentalism, with its manifold practical applications, to the notice of the English reader. And accordingly, to this end, "readers of any intelligence are once more invited to favour him with their most concentrated attention." There is no whimsical equivocation or mystification of any kind now. All is serious as life and as death. And in all seriousness he points to Richter and to Goethe as the sowers of the seed which had taken such deep root in his own

soul.   It is also to be noted that in this matter he gives
Richter the precedence, making Teufelsdröckh his mouth-
piece.   Thus he begins :—

"With men of a speculative turn, writes Teufelsdröckh,
there come seasons, meditative, sweet, yet awful hours, when
in wonder and fear you ask yourself that unanswerable question: Who am *I*; the thing that can say 'I' (*das Wesen das
sich ICH nennt*) ? "

In like manner we find Richter saying, in a passage
quoted by Carlyle in his Essay, 'Jean Paul Friedrich
Richter Again,'—

"Never shall I forget that inward occurrence, till now
related to no mortal, wherein I witnessed the birth of my
Self-consciousness, of which I can still give the place and time.
One forenoon, I was standing, a very young child, in the outer
door, and looking leftward at the stack of firewood, when, all
at once, the internal vision,—'I am a Me (ich bin ein Ich),'
came like a flash from heaven before me, and in gleaming
light ever after continued."

The identity of thought in these two extracts is evident;
and they serve very well to illustrate what I mean
by supposing that many of the thoughts uttered by
Teufelsdröckh were suggested by Richter.   The grand
summary of transcendental insight which follows, beginning with this initial thought of Richter's, ends
with the 'thunder-speech of the Erdgeist' from Goethe.

But why is the chapter called, 'The World out of
Clothes'?   Hitherto Carlyle has been speaking of a
Clothed World; a world in which thinkers and workers
are alike moving in their old accustomed habitudes,
without misgiving or complaint.   But now in Germany,
he maintains, a New Era has been proclaimed, and a
new and deeper life revealed; experience, the touchstone

of truth, has quickened into spiritual activity, and insights which were once matters of mere intellectual speculation have become irresistible convictions of the heart and conscience. Man has once more discovered that he is more than raiment, and that life is more than all extraneous surroundings. "There is something great," Teufelsdröckh exclaims, "in the moment when a man first strips himself of adventitious wrappages ; and sees that he is indeed naked ; yet also a Spirit, and unutterable Mystery of Mysteries !"

Chap. IX. Adamitism.—In this chapter we have Carlyle himself in full vigour, and the method of it seems to be peculiarly his own ; a method which he turned to such effective account in his later writings. We may call it Carlyle's application of Richter's 'piercing insight' to the practical concerns of English life. The way in which he puts up Teufelsdröckh to utter, with the calmness of absolute conviction, the most searching and even paralysing truths ; and then argues and expostulates with him on behalf of timid readers, as if he were perhaps going a little too far, is in Carlyle's most characteristic style. It is wonderful the vividness with which he brings out the almost miraculous use of Clothes and appointed Customs in the construction and arrangements of society. But far more startling is the contrast to which he inexorably points between the significance of the Clothes, and the insignificance of the Man who sometimes hides within them. "Lives the man," he asks, "that can figure (even as a bare possibility) a naked Duke of Windlestraw addressing a naked House of Lords ? . . . And yet, why is the thing impossible ?" Why, indeed, 'did our stern fate so order it,' if the Man himself were what his Clothes proclaim him to be ? One conclusion drawn is that perhaps even the 'Scarecrow,' considering his importance as 'a defender of property,' might also be entitled to 'a certain royal Immunity and Inviolability.'

Chap. X.   Pure Reason.—And yet, 'speculative Radicals' as they all were, neither Carlyle, nor Richter, nor Goethe had the slightest faith in the actual existence of Society without Clothes; without laws, habitudes, limitations, and distinctions. "For our purposes," he says, "the simple fact that such a *Naked World* is possible, nay actually exists (under the Clothed one), will be sufficient." He then professes to quote a few suggestive thoughts from long disquisitions on the subject, and thus concludes :—

"Should some sceptical individual still entertain doubts whether in a world without Clothes, the smallest Politeness, Polity, or even Police, could exist, let him turn to the original Volume, and view there the boundless Serbonian Bogs of Sansculottism, stretching sour and pestilential, over which we have lightly flown."

For, he says, although 'to the eye of vulgar logic man is but an omnivorous biped that wears breeches, to the eye of pure reason he is a Soul, a Spirit and divine Apparition, clothed, swathed-in, manifoldly, wonderfully, inextricably.' "The beginning of all wisdom is to look fixedly on Clothes, till at last they become *transparent.*"

Chap. XI.   Prospective.—Having thus advanced from the conception of Clothes to a perception of the Man himself as an individual personality, we are now shown how wonderfully all things hang together; how 'Nature is not an Aggregate, but a Whole.'

" Detached, separated !—I say there is no such separation :
nothing hitherto was ever stranded, cast aside; but all, were
it only a withered leaf, works together with all; is borne
forward on the bottomless shoreless flood of Action, and lives
through perpetual metamorphosis." "Whatsoever sensibly
exists, whatsoever represents Spirit to Spirit, is properly a
Clothing, a suit of Raiment, put on for a season, and to be
laid off. Thus in this one pregnant subject of Clothes, rightly
understood, is included all that men have ever thought,
dreamed, done, been : the whole External Universe and what
it holds is but Clothing; and the essence of all Science lies in
the Philosophy of Clothes."

So closes the introductory account of the German
Transcendental Philosophy. But Carlyle is now preparing for a higher flight, namely, to give a kind of
symbolic embodiment of the genesis and growth, or
biography, of the Clothes Philosopher. Of course, if the
Philosophy be really Carlyle's version of German Transcendental teaching, the Philosopher must be equally
his version of the German Transcendental character.
Let us see how far this clue will lead us in attempting
to solve the further mystery of this seemingly inexplicable book.

Towards the end of our present chapter, Carlyle
gives a curiously quaint account of all the materials he
could gather for the biography in hand, and how he
came by them. The humour cannot be considered very
perfect, however we understand it. It is in what we
must call Carlyle's laboured style. But if we are to
deny it any basis in fact, I should hardly know what
to call it. He professes to have at last just received,
by the now 'expected aid of Hofrath Heuschrecke,' the
materials for the biography, in a 'bulky Weissnichtwo
packet.' Of course this only means that he was now

ready to use them. But the basis of fact I take to be, that he really had such materials in the shape of certain volumes on German Literary History, and that they arrived by some such mercantile conveyance as described. Perhaps they consisted primarily of Franz Horn's poor four volumes. And yet not by any means altogether so. For we know what an omnivorous reader Carlyle was; and there can be no doubt that he gathered his information from every source available to him. Thus he speaks of having to rely, after all said and done,—

"simply on the Diligence and feeble thinking Faculty of an English Editor, endeavouring to evolve printed Creation out of a German printed and written Chaos, wherein, as he shoots to and fro in it, gathering, clutching, piecing the Why to the far-distant Wherefore, his whole Faculty and Self are like to be swallowed up."

The whole account seems intelligible enough, and even grows in coherence as we read, if only we understand the subject to refer, not to any fictitious individual man, but to the birth and growth of a National Literature, with potentialities dating from Eternity, and experiences varied, far-reaching and world-embracing as the southern signs of the Zodiac.

That Carlyle, while writing it, clearly expected his book to be received and understood on the lines which I have thus far very imperfectly endeavoured to lay down, is, I think, sufficiently shown by the following words from the concluding paragraph of the chapter:—

"What work nobler than transplanting foreign Thought into the barren domestic soil; except indeed planting Thought of your own, which the fewest are privileged to do? Wild as it looks, this Philosophy of Clothes, can we ever reach its real meaning, promises to reveal new-coming Eras, the first dim rudiments and already-budding germs of a nobler Era, in Universal History."

All which will, of course, seem wild and fanciful enough to most readers; but it was evidently Carlyle's deliberate conviction; a conviction in which he has at least one earnest sympathiser and follower.

CHAPTER III.

Book II. Chap. I. Genesis.—If any intelligent student of Carlyle will recall, or re-read, the opening portion of the chapter on 'New Eras' in 'Chartism,' —showing how the successive generations of an appointed race hang together like an individual existence, or, to change the figure, how they flow continuously onward, wave after wave, like a stream of destiny, from the smallest beginnings to world-wide results,—he will easily realise Carlyle's conception as to the personality of Teufelsdröckh. Teufelsdröckh stands for the transcendental element in the German literary character; to Carlyle an altogether new revelation of the possibilities of human life, and a prophecy of wide changes and developments in human thoughts, and in the relations of men to each other. The question is not at present, whether the reader agrees with Carlyle in his extraordinary estimate of the teachings of Richter, Goethe, and the rest of them. In all probability he entirely disagrees. Be that as it may. All I now ask of him is to try and realise the fact that Carlyle himself most strenuously believed it: believed it with a depth of conviction which swallowed up every intellectual misgiving, and gradually made an altogether 'new man' of him. Upon him, in his darkness, the new revelation of thought and purpose shone like the morning sun upon the mountain-tops ; and, whatever we owe to Carlyle, we owe, primarily, through him, to Germany. The reader who cannot take this fact with him, will never realise the meaning and burden of 'Sartor Resartus.'

The beginnings of German literary genius, we are told, under the figure of the birth of Teufelsdröckh, were too insignificant to have left any distinct record of themselves in history. They can only be vaguely traced to the breaking-up of old habitudes following upon the wars of Frederick the Great; Frederick himself treating them with contemptuous indifference. It is curious to note that this date, the end of the Seven Years' War, 1763, was also the date of Richter's birth : Schiller was born in 1759, and Goethe in 1749. 'But even this Genesis can properly be nothing but an Exodus.' Whence came the seed which then first began to put forth tiny leaves of growth among the humble homesteads of the peasantry, and of the remnants of the disbanded army then settling among them? The answer is lost in the dimness of the past. Accordingly, as there are no "authentic lineaments of Fact," Carlyle quaintly admits that he is driven to the "forged ones of Fiction." He imagines a mysterious Stranger coming from afar with "a Basket, overhung with green Persian silk;" evidently suggesting a far-off connection with the Nature-loving mysticism of Persia.* This basket is silently left with a 'grenadier sergeant,' who once served under

---

* Carlyle says, in his Introduction to the Richter Translations,—"By a critic of his own country, Richter has been named a Western Oriental, an epithet which Goethe himself is at the pains to reproduce and illustrate in his *West-östlicher Divan.*"

Frederick; and it is found to contain—what shall we say?—the mysterious germs of a whole Transcendental Philosophy, in the shape of 'a little sleeping red-coloured Infant,' already named, as if from Eternity, and appointed to its work! "The little green veil," says Teufelsdröckh in after life, "I yet keep; still more inseparably the name." The tenderly picturesque setting of this quaint little myth is in Carlyle's happiest manner.

Chap. II. Idyllic.—Here we have a further phase of the German transcendental character illustrated; already struggling into consciousness, but in a homely, incipient, and altogether inarticulate condition. Such a stage of development must necessarily have existed, in Germany as elsewhere; but as there are still no 'authentic lineaments of Fact' to rely on, Carlyle is again thrown upon the resources of his own imagination, and the recollections of his own healthy spiritually aspiring childhood. Nothing of its kind can be more skilful or more intrinsically real, than the picture which he thus by sympathetic intuition brings before us of that old simple-hearted German life. In trying to understand Carlyle's own life, it is clearly of great interest to know which parts of this, or of any other chapter, are strictly autobiographic; and no biography of him could be complete in which they were not approximately indicated. But for our present purpose all such peeps behind the curtain rather tend to disturb the illusion. If we wish to realise the full power and meaning of 'Sartor,' we should try to understand it as its author intended and expected it to be understood: and undoubtedly Carlyle intended this chapter to be an ideal picture of early Germany inarticulate home-life.

Chap. III.   Pedagogy.—Our remarks on the autobiographic element apply also specially to this chapter. What Carlyle proposed to himself in writing it, was to give a suggestive picture of student-life in Germany; and, on the whole, it seems to me that he has fairly succeeded. But his recollections of his own student experiences were so vivid, that they evidently overpowered every other consideration. This is a serious imperfection in art, however interesting it may be in other respects, for it was not what he aimed at doing. The following passage, however, will sufficiently show the editorial difficulties he still had to struggle with; and which surely were enough to throw him once more on his own personal resources :—

"In the Bag *Sagittarius*," he says, "as we at length discover, Teufelsdröckh has become a University man; though how, when, or of what quality, will nowhere disclose itself with the smallest certainty. Few things in the way of confusion and capricious indistinctness can now surprise our readers; not even the total want of dates, almost without parallel in a Biographical work. So enigmatic, so chaotic we have always found, and must always look to find, these scattered Leaves. In *Sagittarius*, however, Teufelsdröckh begins to show himself even more than usually Sibylline: fragments of all sorts; scraps of regular Memoir, College-Exercises, Programs, Professional Testimoniums, Milkscores, torn Billets, sometimes to appearance of an amatory cast; all blown together as if by merest chance, henceforth bewilder the sane Historian. To combine any picture of this University, and the subsequent years; much more, to decipher therein any illustrative primordial elements of the Clothes-Philosophy, becomes such a problem as the reader may imagine."

If we look upon this passage,—prefiguring as it does his future struggles with Dryasdust,—as a brief sketch of the intolerable, and perhaps bootless labour that he would have taken upon himself had he tried to make the chapter, with any strictness of fact, historically true, we may accept it as his apology and justification for not making the attempt. Nevertheless, I maintain, this chapter can only be viewed as artistically related to the rest of the work, by trying to forget the autobiographical element, and reading it as a condensed symbolic account of student-life in Germany in those old days.

Chap. IV. Getting under Way.—Here again, in 'the subsequent years,' Carlyle's own personal experiences gradually get the better of his artistic judgment. He begins with eyes steadily fixed on the struggling aspirations of what might then have been called 'Young Germany;' evidently taking Richter and Schiller as types of that eager restless spirit, striving to work itself into free activity, which once made Germany a portent on the spiritual horizon. Take, for example, the following extract, which reads almost like a passage from Richter himself, known to Germany as *Jean Paul der Einzige :*—

"Thus nevertheless was there realised Somewhat; namely, I, Diogenes Teufelsdröckh : a visible Temporary Figure (*Zeitbild*), occupying some cubic feet of Space, and containing within it Forces both physical and spiritual; hopes, passions, thoughts; the whole wondrous furniture, in more or less perfection, belonging to that mystery, a Man. Capabilities there were in me to give battle, in some small degree, against the Empire of Darkness. . . . Truly a Thinking Man is the worst enemy the Prince of Darkness can have; every time such a one announces himself, I doubt not, there runs a shudder through the Nether Empire; and new Emissaries are trained, with new tactics, to, if possible, entrap him, and hoodwink and handcuff him."

Again, who can doubt that the following is a sketch of Schiller, desperately breaking loose from his entanglements ?—

"A young man of high talent, and high though still temper, like a young mettled colt, breaks off his neck-halter, and bounds forth, from his peculiar manger, into the wide world; which, alas, he finds all rigorously fenced-in. Richest clover-fields tempt his eye; but to him they are forbidden pasture: either pining in progressive starvation, he must stand; or, in mad exasperation, must rush to and fro, leaping against sheer stone-walls, which he cannot leap over, which only lacerate and lame him; till at last, after thousand attempts and endurances, he, as if by miracle, clears his way; not indeed into luxuriant and luxurious clover, yet into a certain bosky wilderness where existence is still possible, and Freedom though waited on by Scarcity is not without sweetness."

But Carlyle had felt too deeply the bitterness of his own restless struggle, to be able to continue to the end as a mere impartial historian; and his own personal exasperations come out in scorching sarcasms, which should perhaps have belonged to 'The Everlasting No,' rather than to 'Getting under Way.'

Chap. V. Romance.—Why need we waste words where facts speak for themselves? It must be clear to every manner of reader, that no symbolic portraiture of the German literary genius of that period could be anything better than a poor figure of clothed sawdust, which did not embrace some passionate expression of that new ideal of first, utter, romantic Love, which then dominated all other emotions, and gave the world its most brilliant chapter of ideal romance. How has Carlyle worked out this phase of his hero's experiences? Perhaps more artistically than any other portion of his passionate career. He begins, in the happiest strain of Richter (surely one of the most lovable of modern Literary Men), with quaint discoursings on Ideal Love. Then, after indicating the dangerous, gunpowdery composition of his hero, he says,—

"From multifarious Documents in this Bag *Capricornus*, and in the adjacent ones on both sides thereof, it becomes manifest that our philosopher, as stoical and cynical as he looks, was heartily and even frantically in Love." "In more recent years," he remarks, with a quiet thrust at Goethe, "to the Professor, women are henceforth Pieces of Art; of Celestial Art, indeed; which celestial pieces he glories to survey in galleries, but has lost thought of purchasing."

But now follows the highly wrought German melodrama we all so well know, of unutterable joys, hests of necessity, skyey portents, lips joining, and two souls, like two dewdrops melting into one,—for the first time, and for the last! And this inimitable picture of the Love portion of the German Stress-and-Storm Period, has been seriously taken to be a more or less authentic record of Carlyle's own almost blighted existence! Surely those who have so read it, must have borrowed for the occasion the 'green spectacles' which Carlyle gravely assures us he himself used in 'deciphering these unimaginable Documents.'

Of course, in this case, as in all others, Carlyle freely used any pigments from his own palette which would heighten the colours, or help to give his picture a touch of reality. For instance, he naturally enough gives his own bright young Wife the place of honour as the proto-type of his celestial Blumine.

"Blumine's was a name well known to him; far and wide was the fair one heard of, for her gifts, her graces, her caprices: from all which vague colourings of Rumour, from the censures no less than from the praises, had our friend painted for himself a certain imperious Queen of Hearts, and blooming warm Earth-angel, much more enchanting than your mere white Heaven-angels of women, in whose placid veins circulates too little naphtha-fire. Herself also he had seen in public places; that light yet so stately form; those dark tresses, shading a face where smiles and sunlight played over earnest deeps."

This is the sketch given to us by way of portraiture of Blumine; and I confidently assert it is the living portrait of his Wife, as she appeared to him in those early golden-tinted days. The vivid description of the growing interest and intimacy between Blumine and his hero is also probably little more than a daintily rhetorical rendering of his own sunniest recollections. But unfortunately for the exigencies of art the real Blumine did not ruthlessly leave him to banishment and the crash of doom. On the contrary, she prosaically married him, and made him one of the most self-devoted Wives that ever fell to the lot of a struggling man of genius. Here was a fix for the biographer of a Teufelsdröckh to be placed in! But a Clothes-Philosopher has many resources. Clearly he had used up his Wife from an Artist's point of view; and, as he still required a few sharp lines to complete his picture, he recollected that he had not always been so prosperous with the 'Enchantresses of mankind;' and, strange to say, he deliberately mixed up one personality with another; the 'mere white Heaven-angel' with the 'blooming warm Earth-angel;' and thus very cleverly succeeded in at once mystifying his biographers, and putting the last tragic artistic touch to his canvas. I need hardly say that all the passionate circumstances about lips joining, and two souls melting into one, only to part for ever, belong exclusively to Teufelsdröckh.

Chap. VI. Sorrows of Teufelsdröckh.—The chapter headed 'Romance,' beginning with the auroral splendours of Richter, and suddenly ending in the blackness of night, introduces the reader at once to the portentous Stress-and-Storm development of German Literature. Of this unparallelled upheaval of restless, reckless, despairing energy, Goethe's 'Sorrows of Werter' has always been considered the most perfect utterance. This period had now to be symbolically represented, and Carlyle has of course sketched it in his own way; which was to make Teufelsdröckh "write his sorrows in footprints over the surface of the Earth, even as the great Goethe had to write his in passionate words." But while the form is Carlyle's, the tone of thought is specifically Goethe's; even as the tone and teaching has hitherto been mainly that of Richter. In fact, the 'Sorrows of Teufelsdröckh,' as here represented, are little more than a paraphrase of the corresponding Sorrows of Goethe.

" A nameless Unrest," says ,Teufelsdröckh, "urged me forward; to which the outward motion was some momentary lying solace. Whither should I go? My Loadstars were blotted out; in that canopy of grim fire shone no star. Yet forward must I; the ground burnt under me; there was no rest for the sole of my foot. I was alone, alone! Ever too the strong inward longing shaped Fantasms for itself: towards these, one after the other, must I fruitlessly wander."

So also, in his Essay on 'Goethe,' Carlyle had already said,—

" That nameless Unrest, the blind struggle of a soul in bondage, that high and longing Discontent, which was agitating every bosom, had driven Goethe almost to despair. All felt it; he alone could give it voice. And here lies the secret of his popularity; in his deep, susceptive heart, he felt a thousand times more keenly what every one was feeling; with the creative gift which belonged to him as a poet, he bodied it forth into visible shape, gave it a local habitation and a name; and so made himself the spokesman of his generation. *Werter* is but the cry of that dim, rooted pain, under which all thoughtful men of a certain age were languishing: it paints the misery; it passionately utters the complaint; and the heart and voice, all over Europe, loudly and at once respond to it."

Chap. VII. The Everlasting No.—In this chapter, for the first time in the book, we seem to have intense, unmitigated Carlyle.. I do not suppose there is another piece of writing like it in existence. He is still striving to represent the great Unrest of the German Stress-and-Storm Period; but, in doing so, he probes the gnawing cancer to its deepest core, and his own heart cries out, irrepressible, in its bitter anguish. Not that this chapter, more than others, is to be taken as autobiographically true in its details; but symbolically it is unquestionably true to the very life. Carlyle was not the man to have his most earnest hopes suddenly blotted out in a passion of disappointed, unrequited love. His heart was made of far sterner and more impenetrable stuff. Neither was he ever so alone in the world, while his good Mother lived, as to have no true bosom he could press trustfully to his own. Nor have we yet been enlightened as to the special circumstances of that wonderful imperturbability so often exhibited in sea-storms and sieged cities. In fact, 'imperturbability' is the exact opposite of what would have been evinced by him in any such emergencies. The imperturbability, here and elsewhere so impressively described, is Richter's and Goethe's, not Carlyle's. The 'bitter protracted death-agony' was alone in this case specially his, ending in fierce 'fire-eyed defiance,' which he strangely and tragically mistook for victory. The 'Baphometic Fire-baptism' which, he says, this 'death-agony' and 'victory' were to him, is a fanciful allusion to the most sacred ordinance by which the Gnostics introduced a novitiate to their hidden mysteries ; and so, he thought, had he now become admitted into the darker meanings of life.

Chap. VIII. Centre of Indifference.—These discoursings from the Centre of Indifference form a magnificent instance of Carlyle's method of working out his subject. The quaint, searching, kindly realistic pictures and comments, as if from one who never even knew what conventionality meant, are all strangely suggestive of Richter ; while the concluding and more earnest portion, telling us 'how prospered the inner man of Teufelsdröckh under so much outward shifting,' seems to point no less significantly to the more sombre experiences of Goethe. Not, I must emphatically repeat, that Carlyle merely appropriated their thoughts, and wove them into his own design. I should say there is very little of such formal appropriation, without express acknowledgment, in all the pages of this singular book. If 'Sartor Resartus' is not a spontaneously creative effort on the part of Carlyle, it is at least sufficiently and characteristically original. There is much nonsense often talked about originality. The man who with his whole heart strives to be *true*—true to himself, and to the facts he strives to elucidate—must necessarily be original to the full extent of his ability ; but the man who consciously aims at originality will generally succeed in becoming a spinner of cobwebs and a weaver of moonshine. What Carlyle proposed to himself was, not to spin a web of new speculative ideas (however perfect in symmetry or sparkling with dewdrops), all out of his own conceit; but, first of all, to try to understand the practical purport of the German teaching; and then to embody the wisdom he had thus gained, in a form which would bring it home to English experiences and needs. It seems to me that he has done this in a manner as strikingly original as it has been practically effective. What better originality could we wish for? Richter and Goethe did not *invent* the truths they taught, any more than Carlyle did. They simply *saw* them. Saw them here and there, in all the wise books they had ever read; saw them in the experiences of their own lives; saw them in the needs and the failures and successes of others. Their originality consisted, not in starting spontaneously in new directions 'with no past at their back,' but in seeing just a little further, a little wider, and therefore a little more clearly than they had been expressly taught; and the wisest man can have no better said of him. Happy is he who can have as much. This note of originality and wisdom I claim for Carlyle in all that he has written, and pre-eminently in the work we are now considering.

Chap. IX. The Everlasting Yea.—In the Everlasting Yea we have, with hardly an attempt at equivocation or disguise, a very strenuous embodiment of Goethe's most characteristic ethical insight :—Annihilation of Self: Nature the Living Garment of God: The poor Earth our needy Mother: Man's misery the shadow cast upon him by his own Self: Freedom only to be attained in well-doing: Blessedness, not Happiness, the true aim of life: The 'Worship of Sorrow,' a sacred lamp perennially burning: All History a Bible: Doubt to be removed only by action: Our America *here,* or nowhere. The beginning of Creation is Light. These highest principles in Goethe's ethics, or revelation of what he saw of God's purposes in the world, are here given as the highest stage of development attained by Teufelsdröckh. Can there any longer be a doubt in the mind of any thoughtful reader, that Teufelsdröckh himself was intended, and expected to be understood, as a symbolic embodiment of the essential Literary Life of Germany, beginning, unrecognized, in the times of Frederick the Great, and culminating in the maturest world-wide wisdom of Goethe ?

The following may be taken as the moral of Teufelsdröckh's life, and of Goethe's :—

" May we not say that the hour of Spiritual Enfranchisement is even this : When your Ideal World, wherein the whole man has been dimly struggling and inexpressibly languishing to work, becomes revealed, and thrown open ; and you discover, with amazement enough, like Lothario in *Wilhelm Meister*, that your 'America is here or nowhere' ? The Situation that has not its Duty, its Ideal, was never yet occupied by man. . . . The Ideal is in thyself, the impediment too is in thyself: thy Condition is but the stuff thou art to shape that same Ideal out of : what matters whether such stuff be of this sort or that, so the Form thou give it be heroic, be poetic ? O thou that pinest in the imprisonment of the Actual, and criest bitterly to the gods for a kingdom wherein to rule and create, know this of a truth : the thing thou seekest is already with thee, 'here or nowhere,' couldst thou only see ! It is with man's Soul as it is with Nature : the beginning of Creation is —Light."

Chap. X. Pause.

" Thus have we, as closely and perhaps satisfactorily as, in such circumstances, might be, followed Teufelsdröckh through the various successive states and stages of Growth, Entanglement, Unbelief, and almost Reprobation, into a certain clearer

state of what he himself seems to consider as Conversion. . . . .
It is here then that the spiritual majority of Teufelsdröckh
commences: we are henceforth to see him 'work in well-
doing,' with the spirit and clear aims of a Man."

The remarks on Tools, and that mightiest of wonder-
working tools, the Pen, need no comment. Nor need we
dwell on the sarcastic reflections concerning the 'Con-
servation of Property:' how at a time when religion
and all that is sacred seems tumbling into wreck, this
is the one thought that anywhere rises into articulate
expression: 'Property, property, property,' is all he can
hear them say.

What more especially concerns us is, the little bit of
suggestive mystification with which the chapter closes.
I believe it is a fact that, during the publication of the
several chapters from month to month in *Fraser*, more
than one excited reader mistook Teufelsdröckh for an
actual German Professor; even as some less excited
readers now take that mysterious personage almost for
Carlyle himself; and protested against the insertion of
any more of his outrageous communications. Perhaps
partly to still more perplex those troubled minds, and
partly to have an easy laugh at their expense, Carlyle
here gravely ventures to doubt whether these autobiographical documents may not after all be partly a mystification which had been practised upon him.

"What," he says, "if we have here no direct Camera-
obscura Picture of the Professor's History; but only some
more or less fantastic Adumbration, symbolically, perhaps
significantly enough, shadowing forth the same! . . . . His outward Biography, therefore, which, at the Blumine Lover's-
Leap, we saw churned utterly into spray-vapour, may hover in
that condition, for aught that concerns us here. Enough that
by survey of certain 'pools and plashes,' we have ascertained

its general direction ; do we not already know that, by one way and other, it *has* long since rained down again into a stream ; and even now, at Weissnichtwo, flows deep and still, fraught with the *Philosophy of Clothes*, and visible to whoso will cast eye thereon ? Over much invaluable matter that lies scattered, like jewels among quarry-rubbish, in those Paper-catacombs, we may have occasion to glance back, and somewhat will demand insertion at the right place : meanwhile be our tiresome diggings therein suspended."

All this is quite in Carlyle's way : to give the clue plainly enough to those who can see it ; but so that it shall slip through the fingers of all who can neither see it, nor make any wise use of it even if they could. So closes the Biography of Teufelsdröckh. We now pass on to the book of practical applications.

CHAPTER IV.

Carlyle's method—Individual independence of effort—The body-social an organic whole—Silence and Speech—True nobility of Work—From Old to New—Worship of Clothes—Beginnings of new life and order—Intrinsic Facts of Existence—Transcendent Realism—Social Dandies and Social Drudges—True formers and re-formers of Society —Passionate hopes and indications.

Book III. Chap. I. Incident in Modern History.— The sorrows of Teufelsdröckh are now ended. The seven thunders have uttered their voices, within him and around him; but he still stands before us with a 'little book open' in his hand. Let us take the little book, and try what we can make of it; even though it should be sweet in the mouth, but bitter to digest.

In the succeeding chapters, Carlyle, as interpreter of the German message to the world, gives his own intensely practical elucidations of the changes immanent in social life; of the passing away of the Old, and the coming in of the New; casting his German 'Greek-fire into the general Wardrobe of the Universe.' He no longer sets himself to merely elucidate the thoughts of others; but speaks forth freely what is in his own heart; what he feels that 'God has given him, and the devil shall not take away.' But he still speaks in the name of Teufelsdröckh, because it is still Goethe's teaching and the Goethean Ideal of Life which inspires his thoughts, and which he seeks to embody in the actual life of England. There is also a great practical convenience, as we have said, in this favourite method of his ; for it enables him, not only to speak freely his utter thought and conviction, but also to be his own critic, and even devil's advocate ; leaving nothing for the disconcerted reader to urge against him which he has not already anticipated, and even put into his mouth. These chapters, if wisely read, throw an interesting light upon all Carlyle's subsequent efforts as a social reformer. We can only here glance very hastily at the leading thoughts pointing expressly in that direction.

The 'Incident in Modern History,' notwithstanding the exaggerated importance rhetorically given to it, presents a really pregnant symbol of the minimum of all that is essential in 'clothes,' with a maximum in its kind of spiritual result. Here was a man who resolutely took the lowest place at the banquet of life, in order that he might rid himself of all extraneous seductions, and be free to minister to what he believed to be the highest good. Of course Carlyle was the last person to wish to see such an example literally followed. But followed in spirit it must be by every one who would be spiritually free ; and 'from the lowest depth find a path to the loftiest height.' This was the constant tenor of Carlyle's teaching. 'He that cannot do without Paradise,' he says elsewhere, 'let him go his ways : suppose we tried *that* for a time !'

Chap. II.　Church-Clothes.

"These are," says Carlyle, "unspeakably the most important of all the vestures and garnitures of Human Existence." But "by Church-Clothes, it need not be premised, that I mean infinitely more than Cassocks and Surplices ; and do not at all mean the mere haberdasher Sunday Clothes that men go to Church in. Far from it! Church-Clothes are, in our vocabulary, the Forms, the *Vestures*, under which men have at various periods embodied and represented for themselves the Religious Principle; that is to say, invested the Divine Idea of the World with a sensible and practically active Body, so that it might dwell among them as a living and life-giving Word. . . . Mystical, more than magical, is that Communing of Soul with Soul, both looking heavenward: here properly Soul first speaks with Soul; for only in looking heavenward, take it in what sense you may, not in looking earthward, does what we can call Union, mutual Love, Society, begin to be possible. How true is that of Novalis: ' It is certain, my Belief gains quite *infinitely* the moment I can convince another mind thereof!' . . . Society becomes possible by Religion."

Thus 'Society' is, or rather should be, to the human souls gathered together in mutual helpfulness and love, which constitute it, what the human Body is to its own Soul : that is, Society should be the practical and organised expression, and ultimate embodiment, of the harmonious activities of all the Souls so gathered together. This, and only this, can properly be called 'Society;' of which body-social religion is the life-blood and nervous tissue. But how if Religion have ceased to be the life of society? "Then," says Carlyle, "men were no longer Social, but Gregarious; which latter state also cannot continue." This, we are told, is now the condition of the world; but that "in unnoticed nooks is Religion weaving for herself new Vestures, wherewith to reappear, and bless us, or our sons or grandsons."

Chap. III. Symbols.—"Man, though based, to all seeming, on the small Visible, does nevertheless extend down into the infinite deeps of the Invisible, of which Invisible, indeed, his life is properly the bodying forth."

This is the key-note of all Carlyle's ideas of 'the benignant efficacies' of Symbols and of Silence. No part of his teaching has been the subject of more frequent comment, both wise and foolish, than his great doctrine that Silence is greater and more fruitful than Speech. Yet the matter is really simple, although it reaches to the deepest foundations of our being. Speech, as Carlyle says, is like Light. But what would be the value of light to us, if there were no seeing-eye and nothing for the light to reveal? The value of light depends wholly on the wonders and the splendour of the Facts it illuminates. Therefore is the Universe greater even than the Light which reveals it to us. Again, 'wise speech' is humanly uttered truth; but 'the Divine Silence' stands for all the unuttered, and even unutterable truth in God's entire Universe. Well then might Carlyle say, 'Speech is of Time, Silence of Eternity.' So, in like manner, is it with each one of us. Wise speech is that portion of our wisdom, be it much or little, which we can put into intelligible words; while Silence stands for, and covers as with a mystic veil of reverence, all the insights, aspirations, accumulating experiences, formed and half-formed purposes, and all the as yet unconscious infinite possibilities, which in their totality form the sum of our character. Who then shall say that wise Silence is not infinitely greater than the wisest Speech? But once more, speech is of two kinds, superficial and symbolic. Superficial speech is easily understood, and its interest is soon exhausted; for it tells only of sensuous things to the sensuous intellect. But symbolic speech, as in the Divine Parables, although still uttering itself in sensuous · images, contains meaning within meaning, inexhaustible and ever new; and deepening in interest as the inner sight becomes more and more open to discern its inner and profounder significance; and thus connects the lowest with the Highest in one ever-living sacramental thought. This is for ever true of all intrinsic symbols, and of all extrinsic symbols while life is in them: for in every real Symbol, Speech and Silence walk hand in hand together, even though, as so often happens, the one be taken and the other left.

Chap. IV. Helotage.—Perhaps no sterner or more practical appeal than that contained in this chapter was ever before made to an Idle Dominant Class in any country. The picture of the Two Men, *and no third,* worthy of honour, is too well known, and has made too deep an impression on all impressionable hearts and consciences, to need comment here.

" It is not because of his toils," Carlyle exclaims, " that I lament for the poor : *we must all toil, or steal* (howsoever we name our stealing), which is worse ; no faithful workman finds his task a pastime. . . . What I do mourn over is, that the lamp of his soul should go out; that no ray of heavenly, or even earthly knowledge, should visit him : but only, in the haggard darkness, like two spectres, Fear and Indignation bear him company."

Education, of the rate-paid School-board kind, and Emigration, in a scrambling reckless sort of way, we have at last got. But who yet believes that " a white European Man, standing on his two Legs, with two five-fingered Hands at his shacklebones, and miraculous Head on his shoulders, is worth from fifty to a hundred Horses ? "

" A full-formed Man is still worth nothing in this world ; but the world could still afford him a round sum would he simply engage to go and hang himself. . . . Too crowded indeed! Meanwhile, what portion of this inconsiderable terra-queous Globe have ye actually tilled and delved, till it will grow no more?   How thick stands your Population in the Pampas and Savannas of America; round ancient Carthage, and in the interior of Africa; on both slopes of the Altaic chain, in the central Platform of Asia; in Spain, Greece, Turkey, Crim Tartary, the Curragh of Kildare?   One man, in one year, as I have understood it, *if you lend him Earth*, will feed himself and nine others.   Alas, where now are the Hengsts and Alarics of our still-glowing, still-expanding Europe; who, when their home is grown too narrow, will enlist, and, like Fire-pillars, guide onwards those superfluous masses of indomitable living Valour; equipped, not now with the battle-axe and war-chariot, but with steam-engine and ploughshare?   Where are they?—Preserving their Game!"

Chap. V.   The Phœnix.

"Call ye that a Society, where there is no longer any Social Idea extant; not so much as the Idea of a common Home, but only of a common overcrowded Lodging-house? Where each, isolated, regardless of his neighbour, turned against his neighbour, clutches what he can get, and cries 'Mine!' . . . The World," in such a case, Carlyle says, "as it needs must, is under a process of devastation and waste, which, whether by silent assiduous corrosion, or open quicker combustion, as the case chances, will effectually enough anni-hilate the past Forms of Society; replace them with what it may."

In this chapter he gives a vivid picture of a few of the more evident disintegrating forces then widely work-ing; and now rushing with accelerated and wide-spreading velocity, 'inevitable and inexorable,' to their appointed goal.   Nevertheless, he adds,—

"Society is not dead: she herself, through perpetual meta-morphosis, in fairer and fairer development, has to live . . .

for, wheresoever two or three Living Men are gathered together, there is Society; or there will be!"

The reader may, if he please, take this hint in connection with what Carlyle said, in Book I. Chap. II., of the emphatically proselyting purpose of his work. He already thought, if only two or three 'Living Men' could have been gathered together, good might have come of it.

Chap. VI. Old Clothes.

"Shall Courtesy," he says, "be done only to the rich, and only by the rich? In Good-breeding,—which differs, if at all, from High-breeding, only as it gracefully remembers the rights of others, rather than gracefully insists on its own rights,—I discern no special connection with wealth or birth: but rather that it lies in human nature itself, and is due from all men towards all men. Of a truth, were your Schoolmaster at his post, and worth anything when there, this, with much else, would be reformed. Nay, each man were then also his neighbour's schoolmaster; till at length a rude-visaged, un-mannered Peasant could no more be met with, than a Peasant unacquainted with botanical Physiology, or who felt not that the clod he broke was created in Heaven."

Then follows a sternly ironical picture, symbolically worked out, of reverence paid, not at all to the character and worth of the man himself, but exclusively to the decorations and distinctions, clerical or secular, by which his body is covered; and by which his own intrinsic insignificance puts on a factitious dignity and impor-tance. If this be the real quality of your 'reverence,' exclaims Teufelsdröckh bitterly, let us walk through Monmouth Street (the Jewish Old-Clothes Market in the east of London), and with awe-struck hearts worship there! There we shall see the Sacred Clothes them-selves, which actually fluttered through 'the Pageant of Existence;' no longer profaned by the 'straddling animal with bandy legs' who once got into them, and feloniously appropriated their significance to himself.

Perhaps many of Carlyle's readers may never have seen the innumerable grey-bearded Jews, alluded to in this chapter, who once perambulated the streets of London, with their unceasing 'Ou' Clo';' and with perhaps a couple of black calico bags thrown over their shoulders, containing old clothes of every kind; and with two or three hats slung or stuck anywhere about them for convenience of carriage. Hats were made of beaver-skin in those days, and were specially prized by that symbolic fraternity, now to be seen and heard no more. Field Lane also, with its long fluttering rows of silk handkerchiefs (the prizes of successful pocket-picking), where victims sometimes purchased, on cheap terms, in the morning, handkerchiefs they had lost over-night,—Field Lane also has been swept from existence by the new times; but both it, and what were called the 'Ou' Clo' Men,' were once familiar enough to the inhabitants of London. The weird look of those Wandering Jews, and their bodeful, perpetual cry—'Ou' Clo'—Ou' Clo',' through all streets, seem to have stirred strange feelings of coming doom in Carlyle's mind, for he refers to them again many years afterwards in the 'Latter-day Pamphlets.'

Chap. VII.   Organic Filaments.

"For us, who happen to live while the World-Phœnix is burning herself, and burning so slowly that, as Teufelsdröckh calculates, it were a handsome bargain would she engage to have done 'within two centuries,' there seems to lie but an ashy prospect. Not altogether so, however, does the Professor figure it. 'In the living subject,' says he, 'change is wont to be gradual : thus, while the serpent sheds its old skin, the new is already formed beneath.   Little knowest thou of the burning of a World-Phœnix, who fanciest that she must first burn out, and lie as a dead cinereous heap ; and therefrom the young one start up by miracle, and fly heavenward.   Far otherwise !"

In all which, and in what follows, it is curious, and even pathetic, to note how hopefully at this time Carlyle regarded the World-crisis, in the midst of which he was trying to find his true work.   All Mankind, past and present, were grouped and personally related in his imagination as one complex Spiritual Existence or Whole (what Swedenborg called the *Maximus Homo*) ; the units and succeeding generations of which are held inevitably in mysterious union, 'whether by the soft binding of Love, or the iron chaining of Necessity, as we like to choose it :' which immense spiritual Complexity-in-Unity is the invisible, but eternal Fact, of which all Time-Pictures are but the temporary expression and embodiment.

"It is thus that the heroic Heart, the seeing Eye of the first times, still feels and sees in us of the latest ; that the Wise Man stands ever encompassed, and spiritually embraced, by a cloud of witnesses and brothers ; and there is a living, literal *Communion of Saints,* wide as the World itself, and the History of the World ! . . . Thus all things wax, and roll onwards ; Arts, Establishments, Opinions, nothing is completed, but ever completing. . . . The Phœnix soars aloft, hovers with outstretched wings, filling Earth with her music ; or, as now, she sinks, and with spheral swan-song immolates herself in flame, that she may soar the higher and sing the clearer."

This deep faith in an actual World-crisis, amid all the disappointments and contradictions of his time, Carlyle never lost ; but declared it, now in sunshine, and now in fierce thunderstorm, to the very end of his teaching.

E

Among the 'organic filaments' indicated as already 'mysteriously spinning themselves,' are the perennial nature of Kingship, or *guidance* by the Wisest; and of Hero-worship, or heartfelt *reverence* for the Wisest. "A Preaching Friar also," he says, "settles himself in every village; and builds a pulpit, which he calls Newspaper:" and even the "immeasurable froth-ocean we name Literature" contains fragments of a genuine Church-*Homiletic;* nay, even of a *Liturgy.* But, he exclaims,—

"Be of comfort! Thou art not alone, if thou have Faith. Spake we not of a Communion of Saints, unseen, yet not unreal, accompanying and brother-like embracing thee, so thou be worthy? Their heroic Sufferings rise up melodiously together to Heaven, out of all lands, and out of all times as a sacred *Miserere;* their heroic Actions also, as a boundless everlasting Psalm of Triumph. Neither say that thou hast now no Symbol of the Godlike; is not Immensity a Temple; is not Man's History, and Men's History, a perpetual Evangel? Listen, and for organ-music thou wilt ever, as of old, hear the Morning Stars sing together."

Chap. VIII.   Natural Supernaturalism.

"It is in his stupendous Section, headed 'Natural Supernaturalism,' that the Professor first becomes a Seer; and, after long effort, such as we have witnessed, finally subdues under his feet this refractory Clothes-Philosophy, and takes victorious possession thereof. . . . Nay, worst of all, two quite mysterious, world-embracing Phantasms, TIME and SPACE, have ever hovered round him, perplexing and bewildering: but with these also he now resolutely grapples, these also he victoriously rends asunder. In a word, he has looked fixedly on Existence, till, one after the other, its earthly hulls and garnitures have melted away; and now, to his rapt vision, the interior celestial Holy of Holies lies disclosed."

What are we to understand by a 'Seer'? A Seer is properly one who *sees through the illusions of the senses,* to the intrinsic Facts of Existence, as they stand, clothed in Eternity, around the Throne of God. But there are many degrees of seership, as there are many altitudes of Wisdom and of Life; vesture within vesture, meaning within meaning, and life within life; until we reach the 'Great White Throne' itself, before which all books are open, and every secret stands revealed. Carlyle indeed pierced through the illusions of what we may call 'physical existence,' with flashes of insight which sometimes amounted almost to spiritual discernment; but his eye as yet rested only on a Sacred Immensity and Eternity, and 'Silence,' not yet named 'Divine,' was the highest and most reverent word then given him to utter. His flashes of intuition into the meaning of Miracles, and into the blinding influence of Time and Space upon our souls, are in his highest style of symbolic suggestiveness: but, alas, they are far from disclosing the 'Holy of Holies,' as he thought. But no one can complain that his conception of Nature, as Nature, was not miraculous and supernatural enough, and, what is still better, profoundly true.

" System of Nature!" he says. " To the wisest man, wide as is his vision, Nature remains of quite *infinite* depth, of quite infinite expansion; and all Experience thereof limits itself to some few computed centuries and measured square-miles. The course of Nature's phases, on this our little fraction of a Planet, is partially known to us: but who knows what deeper courses these depend on; what infinitely larger Cycle (of causes) our little Epicycle revolves on? To the Minnow every cranny and pebble, and quality and accident, of its little native Creek may have become familiar: but does the Minnow understand the Ocean Tides and periodic Currents, the Trade-winds and Monsoons, and Moon's Eclipses; by all which the condition of its little Creek is regulated, and may, from time to time (*un*-miraculously enough), be quite overset and reversed? Such a minnow is Man; his Creek this Planet Earth; his Ocean the immeasurable All; his Monsoons and periodic Currents the mysterious Course of Providence through Æons of Æons."

Chap. IX. Circumspective.—This chapter is Carlyle's proselyting Roll-Call to the very few readers (for he still hopes there may be 'here and there one of a thousand') who have continued to the end; and who have struggled with him until they have at last fairly gained the New Conception of God's Universe, which he has been striving in so many symbolic ways to make spiritually tangible to their thoughts. No mere universe in a nutshell which a philosophic squirrel might crack. Not Idealism, or the essential nothingness of Creation; nor yet Pantheism, with its essential Nothing for Creator: but Transcendent Realism, in which the Immutable Creator, and His infinitely inexhaustible Creation, are Two coefficient Realities; each utterly unimaginable without the other.

But, again we ask, what then is Visible Nature? In its physical manifestation, of Time and Space and all that holds to them, it is 'such stuff as dreams are made of,'— a Vision of the Senses. In its hidden Reality, it is the 'Living Garment of God;' a symbolic adumbration of His Glory and ministering Helpfulness; actually existing, as the Power which sustains it exists, and exhaustless in its significance as the Wisdom from which it momently flows. Withdraw the creative spirit, and the Whole Universe would instantly be blank nothingness, like a 'dissolving view' when the lamp is extinguished: with the creative spirit as the immutable basis of existence, Nature is, in Goethe's words, the 'Mighty Mother' of us all, and Man, her child, a revelation or 'image' of the Creator, struggling through his own personal entanglements, until he bring himself into · voluntary harmony with the perfect Whole. This, in brief, is Goethe's highest ethical conception of God's Universe, and of human Culture in it; and this is the German Transcendent Message which came to Carlyle's heart as a 'revelation from Heaven;' which saved him from the dark horrors of materialism and spiritual death; and which it was the highest purpose of 'Sartor Resartus' to elucidate and apply. All that is visible, whether in Nature or in Society, will wax old and pass away, like a poor garment that is done with; but the hidden Reality, which dwells in Eternity, and which the time-garment had clothed, and revealed to the seeing, can never pass away; but will clothe itself, ever anew, in higher and more perfect embodiments, 'till Time itself melt into Eternity.'

"Here, then," says Carlyle, "arises the so momentous question: Have many British Readers actually arrived with us at the new promised country; is the Philosophy of Clothes now at last opening around them? Long and adventurous has the journey been. . . . Along this most insufficient, unheard-of Bridge, which the Editor, by Heaven's blessing, has now seen himself enabled to conclude, if not complete, it cannot be his sober calculation, but only his fond hope, that many have travelled without accident. No firm arch, overspanning the Impassable with paved highway, could the Editor construct; only, as was said, some zigzag series of rafts floating tumultuously thereon. Alas, and the leaps from raft to raft were too often of a break-neck character; the darkness, the nature of the element, all was against us.

"Nevertheless, may not here and there one of a thousand, provided with a discursiveness of intellect rare in our day, have cleared the passage, in spite of all? Happy few! little band of Friends! be welcome, be of courage. By degrees, the eye grows accustomed to its new Whereabout; the hand can stretch itself forth to work there: it is in the grand and indeed highest work of Palingenesia that ye shall labour, each according to ability. New labourers will arrive; new Bridges will be built; nay, may not our own poor rope-and-raft Bridge, in your passings and repassings, be mended in many a point, till it grows quite firm, passable even for the halt ? Meanwhile . . . the most have recoiled, and stand gazing afar off in unsympathetic astonishment, at our career; not a few pressing forward with more courage, have *missed footing,* or *leaped short;* and now swim weltering in the Chaos-flood, some towards this shore, some towards that."

Chap. X.   The Dandiacal Body.—In this graphic description of the Dandies and Drudges of British social life, we have a specimen of Carlyle's grimmest and most finished irony.   He has already taken us through Monmouth Street, and given us in symbol a grimly ironical picture of those who worship the ' Old Clothes ' of our social existence, after all the human life has died out of them ; and he now gives us in the Dandies a corresponding picture of those whose whole lives are given to their clothes, appearances, and outward observances.   After some pungent ironical remarks on the Ideal Dandy, ' a witness and living martyr to the eternal Worth of Clothes,' he glances contemptuously at what may be called religious or Clerical Dandyism, probably little thinking then what it was yet to grow to ; and then passes on to consider the more inclusive subject of Social Dandyism, with its fashionable novels, fashionable dressings and adornments, fashionable nothingness clothed in curses of debasing luxury and self-indulgence ; bitterly contrasting with it the utter destitution and self-abasement of the poor Rag-clothed Drudges, who form the other extreme of our civilized existence.   These two extremes, he says, are far apart at present, but it 'seems probable they will one day part England between them;' and then,—'we have the true Hell of Waters, and Noah's Deluge out-deluged!'

Chap. XI. Tailors.—Under the symbol of Tailors, or Clothes-makers, Carlyle here gives a brief but vivid picture of the neglect and contumely with which the best moral teachers and Formers and Re-formers of Society have hitherto been treated :—

"For, looking away from individual cases, and how a Man is by the Tailor new-created into a Nobleman, and clothed not only in Wool but with Dignity and a Mystic Dominion,—is not the fair fabric of Society itself, with all its royal mantles and pontifical stoles, whereby, from nakedness and dismember-ment, we are organised into Polities, into nations, and a whole coöperating Mankind, the creation, as has here been often irrefragably evinced, of the Tailor alone.

"Upwards of a century must elapse, and still the bleeding fight of Freedom be fought, whoso is noblest perishing in the van, and thrones be hurled on altars like Pelion on Ossa, and the Moloch of Iniquity have his victims, and the Michael of Justice his martyrs, before Tailors can be admitted to their true prerogatives of manhood, and this last wound of suffering Humanity be closed."

Chap. XII. Farewell.—He now says distinctly,—

"So have we endeavoured, from the enormous, amorphous Plum-pudding, more like a Scottish Haggis, which Herr Teufelsdröckh had kneaded for his fellow-mortals, to pick out the choicest Plums, and present them separately on a cover of our own."

What more explicit acknowledgment could Carlyle make as to the essential character of this Book ? Well might he say, "in a Symbol there is concealment and yet revelation : " it is a sentence which strikes the key-note of almost everything he has written.   In his most metaphorical utterances there is always meaning, clear as day and practical as light on our path, to those who can follow his thought ; but bewildering as a torch-dance in a fog to all others. —

The whole of this singular chapter, if well read, will be found to throw much unexpected light on Carlyle's inner man.   But the reader must bear in mind that 'concealment and yet revelation' is the symbolic law under which it was written.   Here, however, is a small bit of revelation and acknowledgment, without any attempt at concealment.   "Has not," he says, "the Editor himself, working over Teufelsdröckh's German, lost much of his own English purity, even as the smaller whirlpool is sucked into the larger, and made to whirl with it ?"   In after-life he was wont to say that it was his own native rugged Annandale dialect which formed the basis of his style ; and that he owed it mainly to his Father.   This is undoubtedly the essential truth, for his style was as native to him as the spirit in which his words were uttered ; but it was Annandale energy and directness, wedded to German luxuriance of thought and expression.   There is hardly a trace of his own peculiar style until he became saturated with German thought ; and after that it never really left him, for he had found, or rather, had thus unconsciously developed, his wondrously rich metaphorical dialect into which he could pour the whole energy of his Annandale im-petuosity.

We have already noticed several significant allusions to 'the universal feeling, a wish to proselytise ;' indi-cating pretty clearly a constant secret longing on Carlyle's part for human sympathy and communion of thought and deed, in connection with the new ideas and hopes which had taken so strong a hold of his whole spiritual nature. We have here one more emphatic and final appeal, pointing, very covertly, but all the more significantly and wistfully in this direction.

"How," he asks quite abruptly, "were Friendship possible? In mutual devotedness to the Good and True: otherwise impossible; except as Armed Neutrality, or hollow Commercial League. A man, be the Heavens ever praised, is sufficient for himself; yet were ten men, united in Love, capable of being and doing what ten thousand singly would fail in. Infinite is the help man can yield to man. . . . It is the Night of the World, and still long till it be Day; we wander amid the glimmer of smoking ruins, and the Sun and Stars of Heaven are as if blotted out for a season; and two immeasurable Phantoms, HYPOCRISY and ATHEISM, with the Gowl SENSUALITY, stalk abroad over the Earth, and call it theirs: well at ease are the Sleepers for whom Existence is a Shallow Dream.

"But what of the awestruck Wakeful who find it a Reality? *Should not these unite;* since even an authentic Spectre is not visible to Two?—In which case were this enormous Clothes-Volume properly an enormous Pitchpan, which our Teufelsdröckh in his lone watch-tower had kindled, that it might flame far and wide through the Night, and many a disconsolately wandering spirit be guided thither to a Brother's bosom!—We say as before, with all his malign Indifference, who knows what mad Hopes this man may harbour?"

Surely this is pretty plain speaking for one so proudly shy and enigmatic. What reader, believing with Lord Jeffrey that Carlyle was even 'too terribly in earnest,' can doubt that, when he came to London with this book in his hand, he was secretly yet passionately hopeful of gathering around him a few kindred spirits, to co-operate with him in something better and more practical than mere book-writing ? Perhaps some of my readers will be surprised to find, as we proceed with our examination of his several works, how this secret passionate hope, constantly deferred and never realised, grew and deepened within him, until, in its utter disappointment, his whole life seemed to him the miserablest failure.

Towards the end of the chapter there is a singularly enigmatic allusion to Goethe's death, and to several incidental signs of the passing time ; ending with the following significant words :—

"So that Teufelsdröckh's public History were not done, then, or reduced to an even, unromantic tenor ; nay, perhaps *the better part thereof were only beginning?* We stand in a region of conjectures, where substance has melted into shadow, and one cannot be distinguished from the other. May Time, which solves or suppresses all problems, throw glad light on this also ! Our own private conjecture, now amounting almost to certainty, is that, safe-moored in some stillest obscurity, *not to lie always still*, Teufelsdröckh,"—or he upon whom his mantle had fallen,—"is actually in London !"

Alas for human hopes and struggles, if there were no God in Heaven to guide all things to a more perfect issue than human hearts ever longed for, or human energies ever struggled to achieve !

CHAPTER V.

Goethe the intellectual centre of a great Teutonic outbirth—Carlyle's
   great indebtedness to him—Baffled aspirations—Not a puller-down—
   His stern warning in the Great French Revolution—The living Past
   made vividly present—Prophetic earnestness and tremulous despair.

I HAVE endeavoured to show that ' Sartor Resartus ' was
essentially Carlyle's earnest announcement to English
readers that a veritable New Era of human life and
thought had dawned upon the world in that wonderful
outburst of splendour, insight, energy, and rainbow-
tinted hope, of which Richter and Goethe were the
crowning expression.   But he never seems to have
adequately realised that our own Byron, Scott, Shelley,
Wordsworth, Coleridge, and all the lesser lights which
followed in their train, belonged essentially, and with
even a profounder emphasis, to the same great spiritual
awakening of the Teutonic race.   He recognised the
new birth in Germany, mainly because he fully recognised Goethe ; who was not only essentially intellectual,
like himself, but was in fact the intellectual centre of the
whole wonderful movement, here hardly less than in
Germany itself.   Byron frankly acknowledges Goethe as
his "Liege Lord, the first of existing Writers, who had
created the literature of his own country, and illustrated
that of Europe ; " Scott drew his first inspiration from

Goethe's pages ; Shelley was no less openly indebted to
him ; and Wordsworth and Coleridge owed him more
than perhaps they clearly knew. All around him was
a spiritual chaos of impassioned intuitions and un-
governed aspirations, as of souls just awakened from
the sleep of death. Goethe alone kept his intellectual
crown, and remained clear-seeing, wisely discriminating,
and organically constructive. If his ethical intuitions
were not the highest, they were, for the time, the most
immediately practical ; and he had the wise poetic
insight that could reverence and appreciate in others,
a higher life, when sincerely lived, even than he could
realise in his own experience. This indeed is one of
Goethe's most remarkable gifts. But, on the other
hand, he could also look with impassive tolerance on the
most degrading passions that corrupt the human heart.
Whatever he could not realise in his own life, whether
good or not good, he quietly kept outside himself, and
scientifically investigated at a distance, as through the
telescope of his keenly inquiring intellect. He quarrelled
with nothing ; but strove to find a place for all things,
and to put each thing in its place. Order was the
necessity of his life ; and Beauty, the visible form of
Order, his ideal excellence.

Shall we quarrel with Goethe, because he occupied
and wisely cultivated the lowest ground of ethics ;
and only pointed, symbolically and from afar off, to
the highest ? He did what he could—what was given
him to do—thoroughly, wisely, and well. He gave
us the first firm outline of a human cosmos rising out
of chaos. He taught us self-renunciation : to look for
freedom, not in mere self-development, and still less
in mutual indulgence ; but in mutual service, and the

voluntary and glad devotion of the individual to the universal. He showed us that the universe is a wisely guided and governed Whole ; and that no most solitary-looking unit is left out of the reckoning : that for the wise man every circumstance of his life is, for the time passing, the ideal and actual best for him ; that no moment of his life is without its duty, and that the duty there and then possible for him is exactly the duty there and then required of him ; that all doubt and discontent with our position is a mere sickness of the soul, which can only be cured by faithfully working through the obstructions prescribed ; and that every smallest duty so done, is an open doorway leading to the infinite possibilities of each one of us. These ethical maxims, and a thousand others on the same practical level, Goethe explained, enforced, illustrated, and lived up to, with all the strength that was in him. If any one would do better, let him at least begin by doing as well.

This is the man of whom Carlyle said, in a letter to Sterling (December 25, 1837),—

"The sight of him was to me a Gospel of Gospels, and did literally, I believe, save me from destruction outward and inward. We are far parted now, but the memory of him shall be ever blessed to me as that of a deliverer from death."*

All this we must distinctly carry with us, if we care to understand Carlyle aright : what he accomplished, and what he earnestly hoped to accomplish. He actually believed what Germany had taught him, that we had entered upon a New Era of the World, unparalleled since the time of Luther, or even since the birth of Christianity : a new era of human life and thought, of

* 'Life in London,' 1834–1881, vol. i. p. 123.

individual and social activity. He believed that the world-wide disintegration of society, and the crumbling to ruin of old institutions, then and now going on, was but one aspect of the signs of the times ; and that by far the more important half consisted in the new insights and activities already busily at work fashioning new garments to take the place of those which were everywhere falling away. Here was a work which, once fairly realised in his heart, kindled all his crushed enthusiasm into life. He was no longer doomed ' to enact that stern Monodrama, *No Object, and no Rest.*' All life had, in moments of hopeful insight, become radiant to him with auroral splendour. But how could he make others see what to him was as evident as the risen sun ? He tried to do so with the earnestness of his whole heart, even while hiding the tremulous intensity of his feelings under a veil of symbol and humorous extravagance. He, also, as he says of Teufelsdröckh, kindled his high-flaming Pitchpan in his lonely watch-tower, that haply ' some disconsolately-wandering spirit might be guided thither to a Brother's bosom.' We know too well what came of it. His spiritual Pitchpan was only mocked at ; and, even at the last and best, was looked upon as little more than a brilliant display of intellectual pyrotechnics. He was thrown ruthlessly back upon himself, to chew the bitter cud of his own reflections. He had mixed his ingredients and planted his ' petard ' with his utmost skill ; and had said to himself, ' It shall burst, and shall do execution too ! ' And, so far as he could see, it had produced no more effect than a handful of children's crackers.

It was years before he fairly rallied from this first great disappointment of his hopes. He continued to labour steadily and wearily for his daily bread. His writings were admired, and he was everywhere courted for the brilliance of his conversational powers. He had friends and admirers in abundance, eager to help him in their several ways. But ' no one believed him ; ' or, if they did, they looked upon the disintegration of society to which he warningly pointed, as itself the thing to rejoice at. But that was not the execution at which he had aimed. Carlyle has been called a mere puller-down and destroyer ; but what he tried to destroy was, the delusions which were fast eating into the very constitution and possible life of society. It would be truer to call him the only real Conservative since Goethe. If he saw that a tree was dead, he said it was dead ; and earnestly warned those who, unwittingly, were sheltering beneath its crumbling branches from the approaching storm. But this was very different from recklessly cutting the tree down, leaving the deluded shelterers to take the consequences. And so of any social institution. If it was no longer a living reality, he called upon all who were wise to recognise the fact, and no longer rely on it for safety ; but by no means to pull it down while it served any useful purpose, or until they had prepared something better to take the place of it. This ' something better to take the place of it ' was the constant cry of Carlyle's heart. I am far enough from wishing to defend all his convictions and utterances, for I know too well that upon the highest of all subjects he was sometimes impatiently and tragically insufficient. But that, throughout his whole life, he was passionately eager to build up, and absolutely shuddered at every kind of pulling down, really ought not to need emphatic assertion.

And yet there is one book of his,—and, as a transcendent effort of imaginative genius, beyond question the most wonderful book he has written,—which is essentially one terrible Apocalyptic Vision of the most tremendous pulling down and trampling underfoot that the modern world has yet witnessed. How was it that Carlyle, with his shrinking horror of rebellion and revolution, deliberately set himself, with all the desperate energy that was in him, to such a task as that?

As I read the indications the answer is plain enough. He had now, for some seven years, been brooding in utter isolation and despair over the many social problems which he had suggested and illustrated in 'Sartor Resartus.' Meanwhile he had come in personal contact with some of the most earnest thinkers in England; men who had really taken the welfare of England deeply to heart; 'speculative Radicals' most of them. They all admired his genius, and many of them anxiously looked up to him as a leader. But he could get none of them to see what he saw: his hopes and his fears were alike incredible to them. That many of the laws, customs, and institutions of the country had become practically effete, and intolerably unsuitable to the new times, he and they were perfectly agreed. In these circumstances, their hearts' wish was, to sweep away every unrighteous encumbrance, and thus make a grand clearance for what was to follow. Carlyle, with his whole heart and strength, said in effect,—Not so: many of these things, now grown so oppressively cumbersome and even tragically unjust, were once of priceless value; and even now, with all their insufficiencies and intolerabilities, they do somehow hold society together, and save it from the abyss of Open Revolution. Leave them to their doom, which is coming swiftly enough upon them, inexorable as death ; and let those who are wise look strenuously to the new practical needs of society, and try what can be gradually devised and built up to take their place. This once well done, all that is uselessly effete will crumble into dust, and be blown away, almost unnoticed, by the first passing breeze.

This was Carlyle's contention with his Radical friends. We are not now discussing its wisdom or its validity ; it is enough for the present if we distinctly realise how it was that Carlyle, surrounded by warm admirers, felt himself so isolated and paralysed. He could make no way with them. The stormful breakdown of the institutions of the country at which he shuddered, some of them flatly disbelieved in, and others looked upon as the very thing to be hoped for. "Good Heavens," he must often have exclaimed to himself, as in later years he exclaimed to his readers, "have men computed what a game that of trying for cure in the Medea's-cauldron of Revolution is !" The result was that, after many heart-breaking misgivings, shudderings, and compunctions, it gradually settled on his conscience that the next work he had got to do, cost him what it might, was literally to *show them a Revolution*, in all its celestial-infernal splendour and terror ; and let each reader judge for himself how he would like a corresponding development of universal liberty in such a country as this, where the materials for a national conflagration are piled so much higher and more temptingly than ever they were in France.

Such I take to be the true genesis of Carlyle's ' French Revolution,'—a work which formed the flaming background of his subsequent social efforts in 'Chartism,' 'Past and Present,' and the 'Latter-Day Pamphlets.' It was written with nerves strung to an almost frenzied pitch of intensity, by no means of a triumphant nature ; and when finished, was flung from him with a kind of scathed feeling that even Providence might have spared him such an experience as that. Writing to Sterling at the time, he says—

"It is a wild savage book, itself a kind of French Revolution ; which perhaps, if Providence have so ordered, the world had better not accept when offered it. With all my heart. What I do know of it is, that it has come hot out of my own soul, born in blackness, whirlwind and sorrow; that no man for a long while has stood, speaking so completely alone under the eternal azure, in the character of man only, or is likely for a long while so to stand." *

This book at once placed Carlyle in a position second to none of living writers. Here was a History which was altogether a new thing in literature : an inspired poem, not of ancient legends, but of actual modern Facts. Not 'Achilles' wrath,' but 'Sansculottic wrath,' was the burden of the verseless Epic. To those who cared to look, it was as if the curtains of Time had become suddenly lifted, and the living Past were visibly present before them. But, alas, it was not easy reading ; it required the active co-operation of the reader's imagination with that of the writer, as in every other high poem, before it could be fitly appreciated ; and it was only here and there, with a few thoughtful readers, that it made any deep and lasting impression.

What the net value of the impression produced may have been, we have small means of judging. But it brought no deliverance to Carlyle. He did not care for

* 'Life in London,' 1834–1881, vol. i. p. 85.

admiration : he wanted to be believed. People said,
—Yes, it is a wonderful picture of French oppression,
exasperation, heroism, and madness; but what have *we*
specially to do with it ? We are a different sort of
people altogether. Things could never come to such a
pitch in this free country ! And so, as always, because
history never repeats itself in the same circumstantial
form, the spirit of its teaching is disregarded, and its
most solemn lessons set at nought. This, at least, was
what Carlyle felt. Right or wrong, no one can doubt
that he suffered a martyrdom in his convictions. No
prophet Elijah or Ezekiel ever mourned more bitterly
over their country's woes and wrong-doing than Carlyle
did over England's. But the heavens were as brass
above him, and men's hearts were closed against his
message as if with walls of stone. He tried lecturing,
and moved his hearers with wondering delight, and
sometimes even with a touch of sympathetic awe, at
the abundance and splendour of his thoughts, but most
of all at the tremulous, almost bashful intensity of his
strange convictions. What could such a man make of
a fashionable audience of mere admirers ? He felt that
he stood in a false position, that he was sacrificing his
soul to idols; "detestable mixture of prophecy and
play-actorism," he afterwards called it; and, even though
his daily bread seemed to depend on its continuance, he
turned away from an idle admiration which could never
have ripened into sincere belief.

CHAPTER VI.

A new series of practical lessons and encouragements—Hero as Divinity
—Old Norse Mythology—Odin the Supreme Deity—An inconclusive
argument—Hero-worship, or reverence for human worth—Hero as
Prophet—Inspiration of the Almighty—Mahomet and Carlyle—
Sympathetic self-revelation.

THE only series of his Lectures which Carlyle thought of
sufficient importance to publish in the form of a book was
the last he delivered : that on Heroes and Hero-Worship.
These Lectures were an earnest attempt to carry out and
further illustrate some of the leading ideas in 'Sartor
Resartus ;' but the tone of banter and enigma which runs
through that work, and as it were floods it from beginning
to end, was now entirely dropped. He had found, to
the mortification of his hopes, that the grim banter in
which he had shrouded the sensitive intensity of his
feelings, had in effect so baffled his readers that the
whole thing was looked upon, even by the more thoughtful of them, as a brilliant yet cumbrous sport of a genius
overflowing with ideas and wild suggestions too crude
for articulate utterance. Perhaps some of his admirers
even accepted his most earnest thoughts as the best part
of the elaborate joke : if so, they must have been a little
disconcerted at the solemn sincerity, and almost prophetic fervour, with which he restated them in the first
of these lectures.

This first lecture is in many respects the most magnificent of the series ; and yet, in the express purpose of it, it is the most inconclusive and disappointing. Nothing can be grander of its kind than the introductory portion ; mainly embodying the transcendental ideas of ' Sartor,' but with the now added emphasis of his own personal endorsement. No less satisfactory is the light he throws upon the old Norse Mythology, still living amongst us in strange, unexpected ways.

"The primary characteristic," he says, "of this old North-land Mythology I find to be Impersonation of the visible workings of Nature. Earnest simple recognition of the workings of Physical Nature, as a thing wholly miraculous, stupendous and divine. What we now lecture of as Science, they wondered at, and fell down in awe before, as Religion. The dark hostile Powers of Nature they figure to themselves as *Jötuns*, Giants, huge shaggy beings of a demonic character. Frost, Fire, Sea-tempest ; these are Jötuns. The friendly Powers again, as Summer-heat, the Sun, are Gods. The empire of this Universe is divided between these two ; they dwell apart, in perennial internecine feud. . . . Curious all this ; and not idle or inane, if we will look at the foundation of it !

"The power of *Fire*, or *Flame*, for instance, which we designate by some trivial chemical name, thereby hiding from ourselves the essential character of wonder that dwells in it as in all things, is with these old Northmen, Loke, a most swift subtle *Demon*, of the brood of the Jötuns. . . . From us too no Chemistry, if it had not Stupidity to help it, would hide that Flame is a wonder. What *is* Flame ?—*Frost* the old Norse Seer discerns to be a monstrous hoary Jötun, the Giant *Thrym*, *Hrym ;* or *Rime*, hoar-frost. *Rime* was not then as now a dead chemical thing, but a living Jötun or Devil ; the monstrous Jötun *Rime* drove home his Horses at night, sat 'combing their manes,'—which Horses were *Hail-Clouds*, or fleet *Frost-Winds*. . . . Thunder was not then mere Electricity, vitreous or resinous ; it was the God Donner (Thunder) or Thor,—God also of beneficent Summer-heat. The thunder was his wrath ;

the gathering of the black clouds is the drawing-down of Thor's angry brows; the fire-bolt bursting out of Heaven is the all-rending Hammer flung from the hand of Thor: he urges his loud chariot over the mountain tops,—that is the peal; wrathful he 'blows in his red beard,'—that is the rustling stormblast before the thunder begins. Balder, again, the White God, the beautiful, the just and benignant (whom the early Christian Missionaries found to resemble Christ), is the Sun,— beautifullest of visible things; wondrous too, and divine still, after all our Astronomies and Almanacs!"

In all this Carlyle carries the reader with him, with clear conviction and illumination. But the moment he comes to his special subject, the Hero as Divinity, or rather, the Divinity as Hero, we feel that we are leaving the solid basis of evident fact for the merest guesswork. It was his express business,—not merely to suppose for us,—but to show us, how a great original man came to be regarded by his fellow-men, not merely as *a* Divinity, but as The Divinity; the Supreme Lord of all the stupendous Powers of the Universe. Every great mythology has inevitably assumed the existence of such a Being, and the mythology of those old Norsemen forms no exception. Odin was the name of their Highest God: of all the Impersonated Powers of the Universe, He was the chief. And yet, altogether ignoring the far more plausible claims upon humanity of Balder and Thor, Carlyle asks us to believe, upon a mere casual statement of Snorro, that 'Odin was a heroic Prince, in the Black-Sea region.' It is true that 'Grimm, the German Antiquary, goes so far as to deny that any man Odin ever existed;' but, exclaims Carlyle, "Cannot we conceive that Odin was a reality?" Undoubtedly we can; and, to the wild Norse imagination, he must have been an overpowering reality. Were not Thor and Balder

also, in those simple earnest days, very palpable realities ?
What comes of the Norse Nature-worship if they were
not ?   We can easily conceive that there may have been
a man, or even many men, named Odin, if that would
help ; but we have only Carlyle's imaginative assurance
that he, or any one of them, was ever believed to be the
supreme deity.   He says—

"We will fancy him to be the Type Norseman; the finest
Teuton whom that race had yet produced. The rude Norse
heart burst-up into *boundless* admiration round him; into
adoration. . . . He was the Chief God to all the Teutonic
Peoples."

I have always felt, since I first read these Lectures,
that this exaggerated and wholly imaginative illustration
of the highest splendour of Hero-worship forms a most
remarkable exception to Carlyle's otherwise sturdy adherence to, and almost worship of, the hard concrete
facts of any subject he took in hand. That it seriously
prejudiced many earnest hearts against his teaching, I
have no doubt whatever. How could it have been
otherwise ? With 'Hero-worship,' rightly understood,
no truest Christian need have any quarrel: and they
know well where to look for their Perfect Hero. I
entirely agree with Carlyle that, in its true meaning,
Hero-worship is the living bond and sanction of every
sincere social relation. He himself saw far more deeply
into the meaning of it as his ethical insight deepened ;
but, as here so rhetorically set forth, it reads like little
more than worship of brilliant success ; perhaps capable
of becoming the most insidious and baleful idolatry of
which the human heart is capable. Hero-worship, as
Carlyle afterwards very clearly and continuously ex-
pounded it, means simply faithful and heartfelt reverence

for human worth wherever we can find it, whether in high or low, in great or small; and the more down-trodden, and crushed by seeming defeat (as in Carlyle's own case), the more worthy of the heart's most reverent sympathy.

Hero as Prophet.—If the first lecture was in transcendent eloquence the most magnificent of this series, we may say of the second that it must certainly have been the most startling and impressive.

"It was a rude gross error," Carlyle admits, "that of counting the Great Man a god. . . . The worship of Odin astonishes us,—to fall prostrate before the Great Man, into *deliquium* of love and wonder over him, and feel in their hearts that he was a denizen of the skies, a god! This was imperfect enough:"

but even this he thinks was immeasurably better than not believing in him at all.

He now speaks of 'the second phasis of Hero-worship: the first or oldest having passed away never to return.' But neither is this phasis, that of the Hero as Prophet, regarded by him as entirely credible: this also is a 'product of the old ages; not to be repeated in the new.' Such an assertion, thus broadly made, may well give rise to reflections. What is it in the old conception of a prophet, that has now become incredible? I do not know that Carlyle anywhere expressly tells us. Perhaps, if we could see to the bottom of his thought, we should find that it was really the old conception he was en-deavouring to restore; and that it was the comparatively modern shallow speculations which had gathered round it, which had at last become incredible. One thing he does with his whole heart and conscience believe, namely, that all *wisdom* is 'the inspiration of the Almighty,' and

the *highest wisdom* the most expressly so. But he did
not believe · that every inspired man was - therefore
infallible ; for even the most truly inspired prophet could
speak only according to the measure of wisdom given
him. It was partly to enforce this truth, without offence
to religious feelings, that he chose Mahomet as the
subject of his discourse.

"We have chosen Mahomet," he says, "not as the most
eminent Prophet ; but as the one we are freest to speak of.
He is by no means the truest of Prophets ; but I do esteem
him a true one. Farther, as there is no danger of our becoming, any of us, Mahometans, I mean to say all the good of him I
justly can. It is the way to get at his secret : let us try to
understand what *he* meant with the world."

But our business is not now with Mahomet, it is with
Carlyle. Let us, then, on the same terms, try to get at
what Carlyle meant with the world. He evidently
believed a man might actually be a prophet, and even
' a true prophet.' He himself has often been called a
prophet ; and, as I estimate his work in the world, no
title seems to me so exactly appropriate. But I imagine
that in his own heart he always rather shrank from such
an interpretation of his character and work : partly from
a deep sense of his own insufficiency and even unworthi-
ness ; but perhaps still more because such a thought
diverted the attention of his readers from the more practical and secular issues towards which he was constantly
striving. As I read the indications throughout his
writings, I should say that he always consciously felt
himself far more of a Saul than a Samuel. Little as
some of his critics imagine it, his heart was sick of per-
petually exhorting and admonishing. He longed to be
doing something, instead of, as he says, eloquently writing

and talking about it: to be a kind of king or leader
in the practical activities of life; not a mere prophet,
for ever and for ever prophesying. This was the stern
burden laid upon him from the beginning. He felt that
he had been commissioned to *do* something effectual for
the world; and he could find no practical outlet for
what he believed to be his God-given powers and energy.
If any of my readers can realise in their hearts that this
was the pent-up secret of Carlyle's life, I think that
much that has hitherto seemed contradictory and inexplicable will begin to gather into a kind of pathetic
coherence; and that they will see in Carlyle, not the
monster of contradictions he has been represented to be,
but a heavily laden human brother, whom we can gratefully love and revere, even while we sorrow over his
passionately confessed shortcomings.

It seems to me that we have more self-revelation in
this sketch of the Hero as Prophet, than in all 'Sartor
Resartus' put together. We cannot call it altogether
unconscious self-revelation. How could he have been
unconscious that he was speaking of a far-off, inarticulate brother-soul? He once called himself, in a letter
to Emerson, 'a grim Ishmaelite;' and the passionate
colours in which he has sketched Mahomet may even be
truer of himself than of any Mahomet that ever lived.
For instance: let us read with human sympathy the
following passage, singularly applicable as it is to our
recent overpowering dispensation of scandals and small
criticisms, little as he could have anticipated that it
would ever be used for such a purpose.

"On the whole, we make too much of faults; the details
of the business hide the real centre of it. Faults? The
greatest of faults, I should say, is to be conscious of none.

Readers of the Bible above all, one would think, might know better. Who is called there 'the man according to God's own heart'? David, the Hebrew King, had fallen into sins enough; blackest crimes; there was no want of sins. And thereupon the unbelievers sneer and ask, Is this your man according to God's heart? The sneer, I must say, seems to me but a shallow one. What are faults, what are the outward details of a life; if the inner secret of it, the remorse, temptations, true, often-baffled, never-ended struggle of it, be forgotten? 'It is not in man that walketh to direct his steps.' Of all acts, is not, for a man, *repentance* the most divine? The deadliest sin, I say, were that same supercilious consciousness of no sin;—that is death; the heart so conscious is divorced from sincerity, humility and fact; is dead: it is 'pure' as dead dry sand is pure. David's life and history, as written for us in those Psalms of his, I consider to be the truest emblem ever given of a man's moral progress and warfare here below. All earnest souls will ever discern in it the faithful struggle of an earnest human soul towards what is good and best. Struggle often baffled, sore baffled, down as into entire wreck; yet a struggle never ended; ever, with tears, repentance, true unconquerable purpose, begun anew. Poor human nature! Is not a man's walking, in truth, always that: 'a succession of falls'? Man can do no other. In this wild element of a Life, he has to struggle onwards; now fallen, deep-abased; and ever, with tears, repentance, with bleeding heart, he has to rise again, struggle again still onwards. That his struggle *be* a faithful unconquerable one: that is the question of questions."

Let us again take the following utterances of his own deep heart, as to Mahomet's so-called 'ambition':—

"Ah no: this deep-hearted Son of the Wilderness, with his beaming black eyes, and open social deep soul, had other thoughts in him than ambition. A silent great soul; he was one of those who cannot *but* be in earnest; whom Nature herself has appointed to be sincere. While others walk in formulas and hearsays, contented enough to dwell there, this man could not screen himself in formulas; he was alone with his own soul and the reality of things. The great Mystery of Existence, as I said, glared-in upon him ; with its terrors and its splendours ; no hearsays could hide that unspeakable fact, 'Here am I !' Such *sincerity*, as we named it, has in very truth something of divine. The word of such a man is a Voice direct from Nature's own Heart. Men do and must listen to that as to nothing else ;—all else is wind in comparison. From of old, a thousand thoughts, in his pilgrimings and wanderings, had been in this man ; What am I ? What *is* this unfathomable Thing I live in, which men name Universe ? What is Life ; what is Death ? What am I to believe ? What am I to do ? The grim rocks of Mount Hara, of Mount Sinai, the stern sandy solitudes answered not. The great Heaven rolling silent overhead, with its blue-glancing stars, answered not. There was no answer. The man's own soul, and what of God's inspiration dwelt there, had to answer !"

This too, of Mahomet's Wife, must have had a very pathetic meaning both to his own Wife and to himself,—

"The good Kadijah, we can fancy, listened to him with wonder, with doubt : at length she answered : Yes, it was *true* this that he said. One can fancy too the boundless gratitude of Mahomet ; and how of all kindnesses she had done him, this of believing the earnest struggling word he now spoke was the greatest. 'It is certain,' says Novalis, 'my Conviction gains infinitely, the moment another soul will believe in it.' It is a boundless favour."

What a window do these passionate utterances open into Carlyle's own heart !

CHAPTER VII.

Hero as Poet—Could a great man become ' all sorts of men ' ?—Distinction in gifts—Real intellect and Sham intellect—Intellect not the greatest —Clever scoundrels—Shakspeare a bond of union to all Saxondom— Hero as Priest—Luther the central figure in Modern European History—Liberty of private judgment—Knox and Puritanism—A whole ' nation of heroes.'

Hero as Poet.—The brilliant flashes of insight into the characters, and into the worth of Dante and Shakspeare, which irradiate this lecture, are too well known and generally appreciated to need comment here. I will therefore content myself with asking the serious attention of my readers to the leading practical thought and purpose which runs through it. This thought I will give in Carlyle's own words. He says—

" I confess, I have no notion of a truly great man that could not be *all* sorts of men. The Poet who could merely sit in a chair, and compose stanzas, would never make a stanza worth much. He could not sing the Heroic warrior, unless he himself were at least a Heroic warrior too. I fancy there is in him the Politician, the Thinker, Legislator, Philosopher ;— in one or the other degree, he could have been, he is all these."

In one or the other degree, undoubtedly ; but alas, in the practical activities of life, the degree which a man is specially gifted to attain, is the crucial question, for him and for those with whom he stands related. A really wise man, great or small, has truly the living

germs of infinite possibilities in the unconscious depths
of his soul, which through all the evolutions of Eternity
can never be exhausted. But what he can actually best
do in this world, is a tragically limited possibility in
comparison. That 'Shakspeare is the chief of all Poets
hitherto; the greatest intellect who, in our recorded
world, has left record of himself in the way of Literature,' affords no guarantee that he could have acquired
in any really high degree the constructive skill of an
Architect, or the correct eye and manipulative dexterity
of a Painter or Sculptor; or that he could have equalled
Beethoven or Mendelssohn as musical composers, or even
Newton or Faraday as physical explorers. All these
things require, not only the potential insights, sympathies,
and yearnings, which are the living germs from which
they spring, and which give them all their human significance; but they also require each its own special gift
of expression or utterance: and a well-pronounced gift,
which is free to pass to the loftiest heights of excellence
in one direction, may render every other path in life an
irksome and disastrous futility. I should say that a
great man was least of all able to become 'all sorts of
men;' that he achieved greatness by having been
specially fitted for a great work; and, when he had
found the work he could do best, by keeping to it. No
one knew practically the value and necessity of such
concentration of energy better than Carlyle; but he
thought that a man of real intellect could equally take
in hand any real work that came honestly within his
reach; and the sirens sang to him of what he himself
could do, if the stern destinies and the world would but
permit him the chance. Intellect, to him, was one,
indivisible, all-inclusive; it was the measure of the man.

"If," he says, "called to define Shakspeare's faculty, I should say superiority of Intellect, and think I had included all under that. What indeed are faculties? We talk of faculties as if they were distinct, things separable; as if a man had intellect, imagination, fancy, etc., as he has hands, feet and arms. That is a capital error."

To me, on the contrary, it is, and always has been, a fundamental truth. He admits that the "necessities of language do perhaps prescribe such forms of utterance ; we must speak, I am aware," he says, "in that way, if we are to speak at all." But surely the necessities of thought require it, no less than the necessities of language. Carlyle worshipped Intellect ; but even he had to divide it into real intellect and sham intellect. Real intellect is that which is cognisant of facts ; sham intellect, that which is cognisant only of illusions and abstractions. The one is based on morality, sincerity, faithful discernment ; the other on 'formulas,' make-believe, subterfuge, and all manner of short-cuts. Here at once we have distinctions, separations, and diverse elements, mingling and struggling in the same mind ; for even Carlyle would not say that any one intellect was altogether real, and another intellect altogether sham. Again, he admits that the very Fox has a sort of vulpine morality and intellect, or 'he could not even know where the geese were, or how to get at the geese.' And of course, what Carlyle calls a human Phantasm, must also have a kind of morality and intellect, or he could not even believe in his own poor life of abstract perfection. That there are many kinds of intellect, as there are many kinds of light, is evident enough ; but what makes the difference ? Intellect, considered in itself, is like the sight of the eye ; penetrating or dim, limited or wide-embracing, as the case may be, but neither moral nor immoral, neither good nor bad. It is the end for which it works, the use that is made of it, which determines its quality. Not the mere intellect, common to men, foxes, and phantasms; but that which gives colour to it, that which lies behind it, and shines through it : the ideal of his life ;—this gives the true measure of the man, and of the woman too. Of course Carlyle meant all this when speaking of the intellect of Shakspeare ; he meant his intellect, and all that it contained. Nevertheless, I could not label the mind of Shakspeare 'Intellect,' and think I had included all under that term. Intellect may be great, but it is not the greatest.

I have dwelt somewhat earnestly on this point, because I have long felt that the stress which Carlyle sometimes laid upon mere intellect, was the one entirely false note in his teaching. In this very lecture he quotes with approval "the crabbed old Schoolmaster who used to ask, when they brought him a new pupil, 'But are ye sure he's *not a dunce ?* '" and adds, partly in serious-ness, but partly also in grim banter, "really one might ask the same thing in regard to every man, and consider it the one inquiry needful. There is, in this world, no other entirely fatal person." Nay, there is one other, even more fatal ; of whom the crabbed old Schoolmaster may stand as the type ; a man of intellect, without pity and without conscience. The question he had a right to ask was, 'Are ye sure he'll *do his best ?* '

Carlyle had small patience with either bores or dunces ; but he never really preferred a scoundrel, as his words might sometimes seem to imply. A clever scoundrel he looked upon as the completest and most detestable dunce of them all. Carlyle's great Gospel

of Intellect is not a thing to execrate, or even altogether
to disparage. It is the first indispensable half of the
still greater Gospel of Love. 'The people which sat in
darkness saw a great light:' but we should never forget
that light by itself is neither moral nor immoral; it
simply gives us a choice of roads.

One more extract must close our consideration of the
present lecture. We hear a great deal in these days
about the 'Greater Britain' which is rapidly extending
itself over the hitherto uncultivated spaces of the earth.
Perhaps few of Carlyle's readers have adequately realised
how vividly this vast conception had presented itself to
Carlyle's imagination nearly half a century ago. It is
a conception which he repeatedly dwells upon with hopeful solicitude. We have already quoted from 'Sartor
Resartus' his stirring appeal to our new 'Hengsts and
Alarics' who should be leading and guiding vast streams
of Emigration to new homes in the wide world. He
now takes up the same great thought from another point
of view. He is already looking forward to some kind of
united Saxondom, as among the possible developments
of history; and he thinks Shakspeare, in addition to his
other inestimable services to us as Englishmen, may well
lend a helping hand.

"England," he says, "before long, this Island of ours, will
hold but a small fraction of the English: in America, in New
Holland, east and west to the very Antipodes, there will be
a Saxondom covering great spaces of the Globe. And now,
what is it that can keep all these together into virtually one
Nation, so that they do not fall-out and fight, but live at
peace, in brotherlike intercourse, helping one another? This
is justly regarded as the greatest practical problem, the thing
all manner of sovereignties and governments are here to
accomplish: what is it that will accomplish this? Acts of

Parliament, administrative prime-ministers cannot. America is parted from us, so far as Parliament could part it. Call it not fantastic, for there is much reality in it: Here, I say, is an English King, whom no time or chance, Parliament or combination of Parliaments, can dethrone! This King Shakspeare, does not he shine, in crowned sovereignty, over us all, as the noblest, gentlest, yet strongest of rallying-signs; *indestructible*; really more valuable in that point of view, than any other means or appliance whatsoever? We can fancy him as radiant aloft over all the Nations of Englishmen, a thousand years hence. From Paramatta, from New York, wheresoever under what sort of Parish-Constable soever, English men and women are, they will say to one another: 'Yes, this Shakspeare is ours; we produced him, we speak and think by him; we are of one blood and one kind with him.' The most common-sense politician, too, if he pleases, may think of that."

Hero as Priest.—In his masterly sketch of the life and work of Luther, Carlyle for the first time descends from the prophetic and poetic splendours, to what we may call the simpler and more sacred veracities of human existence. His subject was in itself so simple, yet so unspeakably great, that he evidently felt no utmost eloquence of his could magnify its significance. He had found a man, a Great Man after his own heart, whose sincerity was deeper, and even truer than his own; and in heartfelt reverence his soul humbled itself before him. He shook the winged sandals from his feet, for he felt that he was already standing on holy ground. I know nothing in Carlyle's life more touchingly sacred than his entire, heartfelt reverence for the character of Luther. Not only does he here so speak of him, but, in his last great work, his account of Luther is almost the only clear outburst of heavenly radiance that illumines its pages; and when, in looking over Frederick's battle-fields, he took occasion to visit Luther's home and the place of his solitary exile, his feelings were those of an old devout Crusader visiting the goal of his earthly pilgrimage. How many, among all Carlyle's readers, have yet realised the pregnant significance of the following deliberate averment ?—

"The Diet of Worms, Luther's appearance there on the 17th of April, 1521, may be considered as the greatest scene in Modern European History; the point, indeed, from which the whole subsequent history of civilisation takes its rise."

Carlyle has been charged, by those who should have known better, with having no better hope for the world, than abject, unquestioning submission to superior intellect and strength. Let us read what he himself here says on this matter :—

"Liberty of private judgment, if we will consider it, must at all times have existed in the world. . . . Liberty of Judgment ?   No iron chain, or outward force of any kind, could ever compel the soul of a man to believe or to disbelieve : it is his own indefeasible light, that judgment of his ; he will reign, and believe there, by the grace of God alone !"   "In all this wild revolutionary work, from Protestantism downwards, I see the blessedest result preparing itself : not abolition of Hero-worship, but rather what I would call a whole World of Heroes.   If Hero mean *sincere man*, why may not every one of us be a Hero ?   A world all sincere, a believing world : the like has been ; the like will again be,—cannot help being."

In the brief but emphatic account of Knox, ' the Chief Priest and founder of Puritanism,' Carlyle gives his first light-flash into that great struggle which afterwards became so full of deep and earnest significance to him.

"We may censure Puritanism as we please ; and no one of us, I suppose, but would find it a very rough defective thing. But we, and all men, may understand that it was a genuine thing; for Nature has adopted it, and it has grown, and grows. I say sometimes, that all goes by wager-of-battle in this world; that *strength*, well understood, is the measure of all worth. Give a thing time; if it can succeed, it is the right thing. Look now at American Saxondom; and at that little Fact of the sailing of the Mayflower, two-hundred years ago, from Delft Haven in Holland! Were we of open sense as the Greeks were, we had found a Poem here; one of Nature's own Poems, such as she writes in broad facts over great continents. For it was properly the beginning of America."

We may here note a curious initial utterance of that favourite maxim of Carlyle's, 'that *strength*, well understood, is the measure of all worth.' As we shall have occasion hereafter to quote his own more express words on this subject, I will only now say that the maxim is perfectly true, *if* 'well understood;' but that, for myself, I should prefer to put the same truth in the converse form, and say, 'that *worth*, if understood, is the measure of all strength.' It really means, as he himself says elsewhere, that, in the long run, worth and strength are identical. The fact is, strength is really the measure of worth, after the event; but worth is both the measure and giver of strength from the beginning.

" In the history of Scotland too," Carlyle continues, " I can find properly but one epoch: we may say, it contains nothing of world-interest at all but this Reformation by Knox. A poor barren country, full of continual broils, dissensions, massacrings; a people in the last state of rudeness and destitution. . . . It is a country as yet without a soul: nothing developed in it but what is rude, external, semi-animal. And now at the Reformation, the internal fire is kindled, as it were, under the ribs of this outward material death. A cause, the noblest of causes kindles itself, like a beacon set on high; high as Heaven, yet attainable from Earth;—whereby the meanest man becomes not a Citizen only, but a Member of

Christ's visible Church; a veritable Hero, if he prove a true man!

"Well; this is what I mean by a whole 'nation of heroes;' a *believing* nation. There needs not a great soul to make a hero; there needs a God-created soul which will be true to its origin; that will be a great soul! The like has been seen, we find. The like will be again seen, under wider forms than the Presbyterian: there can be no lasting good done till then."

This is Carlyle's own definition of his hopes and purposes; and, with all deference to Mr. Froude, I unhesitatingly assert, '*this* was the principle which he proposed especially to illustrate throughout these discourses:' how to become a Nation of heroes.

CHAPTER VIII.

Hero as Man of Letters—A product of these new ages—Practical appeal
to the thinkers and writers of England—The Roll-Call too inclusive—
Rousseau the Evangelist of the French Revolution—Hero as King—
Carlyle's hope that the French Revolution was the final act of our
modern insurrectionary drama—New Spiritual Sansculottism—True
Ambition—The ideal King.

HITHERTO Carlyle has been speaking of forms of heroism
more or less remote from our own times and circumstances ; and the lessons he deduces from them are rather
of moral and individual application than socially organic
and constructive.   We shall now see practically what it
is that he suggests as the first step possible towards
bringing about what, in 'Sartor Resartus,' he calls 'the
Palingenesia or New-birth of Society.'

"The Hero as Man of Letters," he says, "is altogether a
product of these new ages; and so long as the wondrous art of
Writing, or of Ready-writing which we call *Printing,* subsists,
he may be expected to continue."   Moreover, "since it is the
spiritual always that determines the material, this same Man-
of-Letters Hero must be regarded as our most important
modern person.   He, such as he may be, is the soul of all.
What he teaches, the world will do and make. . . . There are
genuine Men of Letters, and not genuine; as in every kind
there is a genuine and a spurious.   If *Hero* be taken to mean
genuine, then I say the Hero as Man of Letters will be found
discharging a function for us which is ever honourable, ever

the highest, and was once well known to be the highest. He is uttering-forth, in such way as he has, the inspired soul of him; all that a man, in any case, can do. I say *inspired;* for what we call 'originality,' 'sincerity,' 'genius,' the heroic quality we have no good name for, signifies that. . . . Intrinsically it is the same function which the old generations named a man Prophet, Priest, Divinity for doing; which all manner of Heroes, by speech or by act, are sent into the world to do."

This, in brief, is Carlyle's definition of the genuine Man of Letters, and of the high work to which he is called in these new times. I shall be obliged to continue my extracts (for we have now come to the real push of business), keeping them as brief as possible, until we arrive at the issue to which he is gradually but steadily leading us: and I must request the reader's patient attention, if he has any care to understand clearly the spirit in which Carlyle constantly worked ; and the disappointment which as constantly attended his most strenuous efforts. In whatever he wrote, he steadily kept a definite aim before him—a 'load-star,' as he so often calls it—beyond that of mere literature, however excellent. We have seen his notion of the essential function of the genuine literary hero, the express product of these present ages.

" Our pious Fathers," he now says, " feeling well what importance lay in the speaking of man to men," founded pulpits, churches, universities. " It was a right pious work, that of theirs; beautiful to behold ! But now with the art of Writing, with the art of Printing, a total change has come over that business. The Writer of a Book, is not he a Preacher preaching not to this parish or that, on this day or that; but to all men, in all times and places ?" " Universities arose while there were yet no Books procurable; while a man, for a single Book, had to give an estate of land. That, in those circumstances, when a man had some knowledge to communicate, he should do it by gathering the learners round him, face to face, was a necessity for him. . . . It is clear, however, that with this simple circumstance, facility of getting Books, the whole conditions of the business from top to bottom were changed. Once invent Printing, you metamorphosed all Universities, or superseded them! The Teacher needed not now to gather men personally round him, that he might *speak* to them what he knew; print it in a Book, and all learners far and wide, for a trifle, had it each at his own fireside, much more effectually to learn it."

"Or turning now to the Government of men. Witenage-mote, old Parliament, was a great thing. The affairs of the nation were there deliberated and decided; what we were to *do* as a nation. But does not, though the name Parliament subsists, the parliamentary debate go on now, everywhere and at all times, in a far more comprehensive way, *out* of Parliament altogether? . . . Whoever can speak, speaking now to the whole nation, becomes a power, a branch of government, with inalienable weight in law-making, in all acts of authority. . . . I say, of all Priesthoods, Aristocracies, Governing Classes at present extant in the world, there is no class comparable for importance to that Priesthood of the Writers of Books. This is a fact which he who runs may read—and draw inferences from. 'Literature will take care of itself,' answered Mr. Pitt, when applied to for some help for Burns. 'Yes,' adds Mr. Southey, 'it will take care of itself; *and of you too, if you do not look to it!*'

"The result to individual Men of Letters is not the moment-ous one; they are but individuals, an infinitesimal fraction of the great body; they can struggle on, and live or else die, as they have been wont. But it deeply concerns the whole society, whether it will set its *light* on high places, to walk thereby; or trample it underfoot, and scatter it in all ways of wild waste (not without conflagration), as heretofore! Light is the one thing wanted for the world. Put wisdom in the head of the world, the world will fight its battles victoriously, and be the best world man can make it. I call this anomaly of a disorganic Literary Class the heart of all other anomalies, at once product and parent; some good arrangement for that would be as the *punctum saliens* of a new vitality and just arrangement for all."

Surely all this is sufficiently indicative of what Carlyle was aiming at; and a clear enough challenge to the best thinkers in England. Can any reader seriously doubt that Carlyle, however he may have shrouded his own personal feelings, was desperately in earnest in making it? To me it is perfectly clear that this series of lectures forms the promised 'Second Volume' of 'Sartor Resartus,' to which there are so many mysterious allusions in that work, and with which it is now bound; that he still hoped 'two or three Living Men might be gathered together;' and that he still looked for them especially from the Men of Letters of his day. Of course nothing practical came of it; not even the Editorship of a radical Review; only one more personal disappointment, and a remarkable and perhaps rather deep leavening in the thoughts of many young and enthusiastic minds.

The fact is Carlyle's Roll-Call was too inclusive. He demanded only intellect and sincerity, and had yet to learn that men might have both, and yet be opposite as night and day. He partly felt that it was so, but would hardly admit it even to himself. This is sufficiently evident in his sketch of Rousseau, which, coming as it does between those of Johnson and Burns, is like a glimpse into the lurid hungry flames of Gehenna. He tried his best to work him into his list of heroes, for he says of him, "he has the first and chief characteristic of a Hero: he was heartily in *earnest.* In earnest, if ever man was." And yet this is his final verdict on him:—

"It was expedient, if anyway possible, that such a man should *not* have been set in flat hostility with the world. He could be cooped into garrets, laughed at as a maniac, left to starve like a wild-beast in his cage;—but he could not be hindered from setting the world on fire. The French Revolution found its Evangelist in Rousseau. . . . Difficult to say what the governors of the world could do with him! What he could do with them is unhappily clear enough,—*guillotine* a great many of them!"

Hero as King.—There is little in this concluding lecture which seems to be specially addressed to 'the two or three Living Persons' whom he hoped might some day be gathered together. The Hero as King, although a favourite subject with Carlyle, is treated throughout as one of general interest, rather than as one of special or immediate application. In fact, the whole stream of practical purpose which runs through these discourses, centres and almost terminates in his earnest call to the Men of Letters; 'some good arrangement for whom would,' he thought, 'be the *punctum saliens* of a new vitality and just arrangement for all.' The present lecture, which, strictly speaking, treats only of the King as Revolutionary Hero, is more than anything else a stern warning, like his 'French Revolution' itself, of what might hereafter come upon us, if the Literary Heroes shirked their work, and left the country to drift into open anarchy. In this sense we may perhaps now look upon it as prophetic and practical enough. But it is remarkable, and should by no means be forgotten, that Carlyle himself, at this time, regarded the great French Revolution as the final act in the great modern insurrectionary drama.

"The beginning of it," he says, "was not the French Revolution; that is rather the *end*, we can hope. It were truer to say, the *beginning* was three centuries farther back: in the Reformation of Luther. . . . From that first necessary assertion of Luther's, ' You, self-styled *Papa*, you are no Father in God at all; you are—a Chimera, whom I know not how to name in polite language!' from that onwards to the shout which rose round Camille Desmoulins in the Palais-Royal, ' *Aux armes!* ' when the people had burst-up against *all* manner of Chimeras, I find a natural historical sequence. That shout too, so frightful, half-infernal, was a great matter. Once more the voice of awakened nations;—starting confusedly, as out of nightmare, as out of death-sleep, into some dim feeling that Life was real; that God's world was not an expediency and diplomacy! Infernal; yes, since they would not have it otherwise.

"Truly, without the French Revolution, one would not know what to make of an age like this at all. . . . A true Apocalypse, though a terrible one, to this false withered artificial time; testifying once more that Nature is *preter*natural; if not divine, then diabolic; that Semblance is not Reality; that it has to become Reality, or the world will take fire under it,—burn *it* into what it is, namely, Nothing! Plausibility is ended; empty Routine has ended; much has ended. This, as with a Trump of Doom, has been proclaimed to all men. They are the wisest who will learn it soonest. . . . It is properly the third and final act of Protestantism; the explosive confused return of mankind to Reality and Fact, now that they were perishing of Semblance and Sham. We call our English Puritanism the second act: ' Well then, the Bible is true; let us go by the Bible!' 'In Church,' said Luther; ' In Church and State,' said Cromwell, ' let us go by what actually *is* God's Truth.' Men 'have to return to reality; they cannot live on semblance. The French Revolution, or third act, we may well call the final one; for lower than that savage *Sansculottism* men cannot go."

What Carlyle afterwards thought we shall see clearly enough in his later writings. There is a depth of *Spiritual Sansculottism* (compared with which the French infatuation was but a superficial business), which he never actually sounded; and which his own gospel of intellect and sincerity helped to awaken into life. In later days he saw it looming in the distance, stark and bodeful; and, more than anything else, it filled him with despair. But we must leave all that for the present. At this time it is evident Carlyle thought one such revolution was didactic enough; that the wiser among his readers and listeners would take warning in time; and that, by wise forethought and wise co-operation, the omens might yet be averted. I cannot too often repeat that the constantly deferred, but inextinguishable hope which urged him onward, even to the meridian of his working life, was that of seeing a few wise men gather together, wise enough and silently strong enough to initiate a new vitality in our social relations, and help in every beneficent reform; and thus strive to bring about the immense, inevitable, indispensable changes in our social life,—' without solution of continuity,' and without a reckless and disastrous break-down of the existing social edifice. Carlyle was as far as any man that ever lived from any petty dreams of mere self-advancement; and as little was he a man to encourage such thoughts in others. But he did earnestly call upon every man to look his own duties and practical possibilities frankly in the face; and, without turning to the right hand or the left, follow them honestly, and even with a firm personal grip, wheresoever they might honestly lead. We will read what he says on the subject of Ambition.

"The noble silent men, scattered here and there, each in his department; silently thinking, silently working; whom no Morning Newspaper makes mention of! They are the salt of the Earth. A country that has none or few of these is in a bad way. Like a forest which had no *roots;* which had all turned into leaves and boughs;—which must soon wither and be no forest. Woe for us if we had nothing but what we can *show*, or speak. Silence, the great Empire of Silence; higher than the stars; deeper than the Kingdoms of Death! It alone is great; all else is small.—I hope we English will long maintain our *grand talent pour le silence.* Let others that cannot do without standing on barrel-heads, to spout, and be seen of all the market-place, cultivate speech exclusively,—become a most green forest without roots! Solomon says, There is a time to speak; but also a time to keep silence. Of some great silent Samuel, not urged to writing,— as old Samuel Johnson says he was, by *want of money*, and nothing other,—one might ask, 'Why do not you too get up and speak; promulgate your system, found your sect?' 'Truly,' he will answer, 'I am *continent* of my thought hitherto; happily I have yet had the ability to keep it in me, no compulsion strong enough to speak it. My "system" is not for promulgation first of all; it is for serving myself to live by.'

"But now, by way of counterpoise to this of Silence, let me say that there are two kinds of ambition; one wholly blamable, the other laudable and inevitable. Nature has provided that the great silent Samuel shall not be silent too long. The selfish wish to shine over others, let it be accounted altogether poor and miserable. 'Seekest thou great things, seek them not:' this is most true. And yet, I say, there is an irrepressible tendency in every man to develop himself according to the magnitude which Nature has made him of; to speak out, to act out, what Nature has laid in him. This is proper, fit, inevitable; nay, it is a duty, and even the summary of duties for a man. The meaning of life here on earth might be defined as consisting in this: To unfold your self, to work what thing you have the faculty for. It is a necessity for the human being, the first law of our existence."

"Fancy, for example, you had revealed to the brave old Samuel Johnson, in his shrouded-up existence, that it was possible for him to do priceless divine work for his country and the whole world. That the perfect Heavenly Law might be made Law on this Earth; that the prayer he prayed daily, 'Thy kingdom come,' was at length to be fulfilled! If you had convinced his judgment of this; that it was possible, practicable; that he the mournful silent Samuel was called to take a part in it! Would not the whole soul of the man have flamed-up into a divine clearness, into noble utterance and determination to act; casting all sorrows and misgivings under his feet, counting all affliction and contradiction small,—the whole dark element of his existence blazing into articulate radiance of light and lightning? It were a true ambition this! And think now, how it actually was with Cromwell."

Here we have another open window into Carlyle's very soul. This was the kind of 'Ambition' he himself passionately felt, and strove to awaken in every thinking head and earnest heart amongst us. A career for every man and woman, according to their honest ability and worth. What can the stoutest democrat wish for better than this? An anarchist may wish for something widely different.

On Carlyle's notions about Kingship we need not now dwell. We shall have ample opportunity hereafter of seeing from top to bottom of that matter. His ideal king or leader of any community is its Ablest Man; which, he says, 'means also the truest-hearted, justest, the Noblest Man.' Were the perfect king at the head of affairs, we should all find our best interest and truest freedom in intelligent, independent yet heartfelt obedience. But in actual life all goes by approximation: with the approximate king there can be but approximate obedience; and with the sham king, only judicious disobedience, and at last defiance. In what Carlyle called 'a whole nation of heroes,' each individual member would be, veritably, 'a king by the grace of God,' according to his ability; all working together in due subordination and mutual helpfulness or organic co-operation; and the whole body-social would be full of light. With us all this may seem 'impossible' enough. I now only repeat, that however impossible, or even humdrum, it may look to us, *this* was Carlyle's Ideal of a Nation throughout these discourses on 'Heroes, Hero-Worship, and the Heroic in History.'

CHAPTER IX.

Carlyle as a Social Reformer—Condition of the Working Classes—
Statistics—The New Poor-Law—Awful transition-period of English
Industry—Rights and Mights—Who are to blame?—What can be
done?—Grand destiny of the English-speaking race—Behold, our
lot is unfair!—Impossible—Universal Education and World-wide
Emigration.

'CHARTISM,' Carlyle's next book, is the briefest, and also
the most simple, direct, and business-like of any of his
works. The splendours of diction which characterised
his previous efforts were now, as in his account of
Luther, rigorously laid aside, as if he had resolved that
he would have practical belief, or nothing. No one
could read this little book with any intelligence, and
think of it as a mere literary performance: it is his
first distinct effort as a Social Reformer. German Transcendentalism retires into the Divine Silences, and
English practicality comes to the front. It must be
understood that 'Chartism' was published long before
the Corn Laws were repealed, and that it made a very
deep impression at the time of its appearance. How
much of the subsequent practical legislation may have
been directly or indirectly influenced by it, it is perhaps
impossible now to determine. All we can say is, that
from this time legislation did begin, in various directions,
to take the practical tone Carlyle here strove to initiate.

The chief measure, affecting the substantial interests of the labouring classes, which had been carried through the Reformed Parliament previous to this time, was the New Poor-Law, of which we shall hear. Let us, with as little comment as possible, glance swiftly at the chief points offered for consideration ; and we may then seriously ask ourselves what we conscientiously think of Carlyle's notions of social reform, and of the duties of all Governments.

Condition-of-England Question. — He begins by calling attention to the practical condition of England. Chartism had (for the time) been ' put down,' but the discontent, of which it was the expression, remained. What meant this bitter discontent of the Working Classes ? he asks. Why did Parliament throw no light on the condition or disposition they were in ? We had got our Reformed Parliament, but what had it yet done to improve the practical condition of the bulk of the nation, the labouring classes ? What had it even tried to do ? Had it even strenuously tried to ascertain what their practical condition was ? Surely, he says, among the questions which agitate a Reformed Parliament, " Honourable Members ought to speak of the Condition-of-England question too."

Statistics.—And yet we had ' statistics ' in abundance ; but, as Carlyle says, ' with as good as no result.' Assertion swallowing assertion, ' according to the proverb, " as the *statist* thinks, the bell clinks." '

" A witty statesman said, you might prove anything by figures. . . . A judicious man looks at Statistics, not to get knowledge, but to save himself from having ignorance foisted on him !"—" The condition of the working man in this country, what it is and has been, whether it is improving or retrograding,—is a question to which from statistics hitherto no solution can be got. . . . What constitutes the well-being of a man ?　Many things ; of which the wages he gets, and the bread he buys with them, are but one preliminary item. Grant, however, that the wages were the whole ; that once knowing the wages and the price of bread, we know all ; then what are the wages ? . . . And then, given the average of wages, what is the constancy of employment ; what is the difficulty of finding employment ; the fluctuation from season to season, from year to year ?　Is it constant, calculable wages ; or fluctuating, incalculable, more or less of the nature of gambling ?　This secondary circumstance, of quality in wages, is perhaps even more important than the primary one of quantity.　Farther we ask, Can the labourer, by thrift and industry, hope to rise to mastership ; or is such hope cut off from him ?　How is he related to his employer ; by bonds of friendliness and mutual help ; or by hostility, opposition, and chains of necessity alone ?　In a word, what degree of contentment can a human creature be supposed to enjoy in that position ? "

"These are inquiries on which, had there been a proper 'Condition-of-England question,' some light would have been thrown, before 'torch-meetings' arose to illuminate them ! Far as they lie out of the course of Parliamentary routine, they should have been gone into, should have been glanced at, in one or the other fashion.　A Legislature making laws for the Working Classes, in total uncertainty as to these things, is legislating in the dark ; not wisely, nor to good issues.　The simple fundamental question, Can the labouring man in this England of ours, who is willing to labour, find work, and subsistence by his work ? is matter of mere conjecture and assertion hitherto."

I am compelled to make somewhat lengthy extracts from this little book, not only because it forms a most important epoch in Carlyle's intellectual and moral development, but because it shows so explicitly the kind of change which he, more than any one else, helped to bring about in our legislative ideas. And surely the significance of his practical suggestions as a Social Reformer, and the urgent appositeness of his exhortations and warnings are still far enough from being exhausted.

New Poor-Law.—Carlyle had no special quarrel with the 'Poor-Law Amendment Act' in itself. In fact, he looked upon it as, under the circumstances, an almost necessary preliminary to any effectual help for the really deserving. But that Parliament, in the plenitude of its conviction that every one must take care of himself, should have stopped short there, and have left the really helpless and deserving poor more outcast and helpless than ever, and that this should have been regarded as ' the " chief glory " of a Reform Cabinet,' he thought betokened 'rather a scarcity of glory there.'

"To read the Reports of the Poor-Law Commissioners, if one had faith enough, would be a pleasure to the friend of humanity. One sole recipe seems to have been needful for the woes of England : 'refusal of out-door relief.' England lay in sick discontent, writhing powerless on its fever-bed, dark, nigh desperate, in wastefulness, want, improvidence, and eating care, till, like Hyperion down the eastern steeps, the Poor-Law Commissioners arose, and said : Let there be workhouses, and bread of affliction and water of affliction there ! It was a simple invention ; as all truly great inventions are. . . . If paupers are made miserable, paupers will needs decline in multitude. . . . That misery and unemployed labour should ' disappear ' in that case is natural enough ; should go out of sight,—but out of existence ? "—" To believe practically that the poor and luckless are here only as a nuisance to be abraded and abated, and in some permissible manner made away with, and swept out of sight, is not an amiable faith. To button your pockets and stand still is no complex recipe. . . . And yet, as we said, Nature makes nothing in vain ; not even a

Poor-Law Amendment Act. . . . Any law, however well meant as a law, which has become a bounty on unthrift, idleness, bastardy and beer-drinking, must be put an end to. In all ways it needs, especially in these times, to be proclaimed aloud that for the idle man there is no place in this England of ours. He that will not work, and save according to his means, let him go elsewhither; let him know that for *him* the Law has made no soft provision, but a hard and stern one. . . . Work is the mission of man in this Earth. A day is ever struggling forward, a day will arrive in some approximate degree, when he who has no work to do, by whatever name he may be named, will not find it good to show himself in our quarter of the Solar System. . . . He that can work is a born king of something; is in communion with Nature, is master of a thing or things, is a priest and king of Nature so far. He that can work at nothing is but a usurping king, be his trappings what they may; he is a born slave of all things. Let a man honour his craftmanship, his *can-do;* and know that his rights of men have no concern at all with the Forty-third of Elizabeth."

Finest Peasantry in the World.—Truly Carlyle was no flatterer, either of the poor man or of the rich. He held that the one law, of faithful ungrudging work, each according to his ability, was alike imperative upon us all. But what appealed to his compassion more sorrowfully than almost any other sorrow, was, that a poor man in his utter guidelessness should be eagerly seeking for work, and have no one, anywhere, to help him to find it.

"A man willing to work, and unable to find work, is perhaps the saddest sight that Fortune's inequality exhibits under this sun. Burns expresses feelingly what thoughts it gave him: a poor man *seeking work;* seeking leave to toil that he might be fed and sheltered! That he might be put on a level with the four-footed workers of the Planet which is his! . . . There is one fact which Statistic Science has communicated, and a most astonishing one; the inference from which is pregnant as to this matter. Ireland * has near seven millions of working people, the third unit of whom, it appears by Statistic Science, has not for thirty weeks each year as many third-rate potatoes as will suffice him. It is a fact perhaps the most eloquent that was ever written down in any language, at any date of the world's history. . . . A government and guidance of white European men which has issued in perennial hunger of potatoes to the third man extant,—ought to drop a veil over its face, and walk out of court under conduct of proper officers; saying no word; expecting now of a surety sentence either to change or die. All men, we must repeat, were made by God, *and have immortal souls in them.* The Sanspotatoe is of the selfsame stuff as the superfinest Lord-Lieutenant. Not an individual Sanspotatoe human scarecrow but had a Life given him out of Heaven, with Eternities depending on it; for once and no second time. With Immensities in him, over him and round him; with feelings which a Shakspeare's speech would not utter; with desires illimitable as the Autocrat's of all the Russias! Him various thrice-honoured persons, things and institutions have long been teaching, long been guiding, governing: and it is to perpetual scarcity of third-rate potatoes, and to what depends thereon, that he has been taught and guided. Figure thyself, O high-minded, clear-headed, clean-burnished reader, clapt by enchantment into the torn coat and waste hunger-lair of that same root-devouring brother man!"

Then follows a fearful picture of the destitution, misery, and degradation of Ireland during that trying time, and how the English labour-market was being literally drowned in the widespread flood of Irish beggary and starvation everywhere flowing into it. Those were indeed trying times, even had the Government been doing its best to ameliorate them. But with a Government doing practically nothing; not even, as Carlyle

---

* This was written in 1839.

says, seriously inquiring into the condition of the people, they were appalling. But it was not of Ireland only that he spoke. This was the awful transition-period of English industry, when hand-work was everywhere rapidly changing into machine-work, without any thought or care for the hardworking hands which were daily in thousands being pushed out of their accustomed employments.

"Half-a-million handloom weavers, working fifteen hours a day, in perpetual inability to procure thereby enough of the coarsest food; English farm-labourers at nine shillings and at seven shillings a week; Scotch farm-labourers who, 'in districts the half of whose husbandry is that of cows, taste no milk, can procure no milk:' all these things are credible to us; *several of them are known to us by the best evidence, by eyesight.* With all this it is consistent that the wages of 'skilled labour,' as it is called, should in many cases be higher than they ever were: the giant Steam-engine in a giant English Nation will here create violent demand for labour, and will there annihilate demand. But, alas, the great portion of labour is not skilled: the millions are and must be skilless, where strength alone is wanted; ploughers, delvers, borers; hewers of wood and drawers of water; menials of the Steam-engine, only the *chief* menials and immediate *body*-servants of which require skill. English Commerce stretches its fibres over the whole earth; sensitive literally, nay quivering in convulsion, to the farthest influences of the earth. The huge demon of Mechanism smokes and thunders, panting at his great task, in all sections of English land; changing his *shape* like a very Proteus; and infallibly at every change of shape, *oversetting* whole multitudes of workmen, and as if with waving of his shadow from afar, hurling them asunder, this way and that, in their crowded march and course of work or traffic; so that the wisest no longer knows his whereabout."

Rights and Mights.—A man's 'rights,' Carlyle thought, are of somewhat too intricate and abstruse a nature to be dealt with by mere statistics, or any pecuniary balances of profit and loss.

"It is not what a man outwardly has or wants that constitutes the happiness or misery of him. Nakedness, hunger, distress of all kinds, death itself have been cheerfully suffered, when the heart was right. It is the feeling of *injustice* that is insupportable to all men. . . . The real smart is the soul's pain and stigma, the hurt inflicted on the moral self. The rudest clown must draw himself up into attitude of battle, and resistance to the death, if such be offered him. He cannot live under it; his own soul aloud, and all the Universe with silent continual beckonings, says, It cannot be. He must revenge himself; *revancher* himself, make himself good again, —that so *meum* may be mine, *tuum* thine, and each party standing clear on his own basis, order be restored."

And so also of man's ' mights.'

"Conquest, indeed, is a fact often witnessed; conquest, which seems mere wrong and force, everywhere asserts itself as a right among men. Yet if we examine, we shall find that, in this world, *no conquest could ever become permanent, which did not withal show itself beneficial to the conquered as well as the conquerors.* . . . The Romans, having conquered the world, held it conquered, *because* they could best govern the world; the mass of men found it nowise pressing to revolt; their fancy might be afflicted more or less, but in their solid interests they were better off than before. So too in this England long ago, the old Saxon Nobles, disunited among themselves, and in power too nearly equal, could not have governed the country well; Harold being slain, their last chance of governing it, except in anarchy and civil war, was over: a new class of strong Norman Nobles, entering with a strong man at the head of them, and not disunited, but united by many ties, by their very community of language and interest, had there been no other, *were* in a condition to govern it; and did govern it, we can believe, in some rather tolerable manner, or they would not have continued there. . . . How *can-do*, if we will well interpret it, unites itself with *shall-do* among mortals; how strength acts ever as the right-arm of justice; how might and right, so frightfully discrepant at first, are ever in the long-run one and the same,—is a cheering consideration, which always in the black tempestuous vortices of this world's history, will shine out on us, like an everlasting polar star."

"But indeed the 'rights of man,' as has been not unaptly remarked, are little worth ascertaining in comparison to the *mights* of man,—to *that portion of his rights he has any chance of being able to make good!*   The accurate final rights of man lie in the far deeps of the Ideal, where 'the Ideal weds itself to the Possible,' as the Philosophers say.   And yet that there is verily a 'rights of man' let no mortal doubt.   An ideal right does dwell in all men, in all arrangements, pactions and procedures of men; it is to this ideal of right, more and more developing itself as it is more and more approximated to, that human Society for ever tends and struggles.   We say also that any given thing either *is* unjust or else just; however obscure the arguings and strugglings on it be, the thing in itself there as it lies, infallibly enough, *is* the one or the other. To which let us add only this, the first, last article of faith, the alpha and omega of all faith among men, *That nothing which is unjust can hope to continue in this world.*"

Surely all this is very different from the popular notion that Carlyle's idea was—Might *makes* Right!

Laissez-Faire.—Let us now read very seriously what, in those 'hard times,' harder even than our own, he had to say as to the heavy, and even perilous responsibility laid upon all Governments, and all guides and leaders of men.

"A government of the under classes by the upper on a principle of *Let alone* is no longer possible in England in these days. . . . For, alas, on us too the rude truth has come home.   Wrappages and speciosities all worn off, the haggard naked fact speaks to us: Are these millions taught?   Are these millions guided?   We have a Church, the venerable embodiment of an idea which may well call itself divine; which our fathers for long ages, feeling it to be divine, have been embodying as we see : it is a Church well furnished with equipments and appurtenances; educated in universities; rich in money; set on high places, that it may be conspicuous to all, honoured of all. We have an Aristocracy of landed wealth and commercial wealth, in whose hands lies the law-making and law-administering; an Aristocracy rich, powerful, long secure in its place; an Aristocracy with more faculty put free into its hands than was ever before, in any country or time, put into the hands of any class of men. This Church answers: Yes, the people are taught. This Aristocracy, astonishment in every feature, answers: Yes, surely the people are guided! Do we not pass what Acts of Parliament are needful; as many as thirty-nine for the shooting of the partridges alone? Are there not treadmills, gibbets; even hospitals, poor-rates, New Poor-Law? So answers Church; so answers Aristocracy, astonishment in every feature."

"Surely of all 'rights of man,' this right of the ignorant man to be guided by the wiser, to be, gently or forcibly, held in the true course for him, is the indisputablest. Nature herself ordains it from the first; Society struggles towards perfection by enforcing and accomplishing it more and more. If Freedom have any meaning, it means enjoyment of this right, wherein all other rights are enjoyed. It is a sacred right and duty, on both sides; and the summary of all social duties whatsoever between the two. Why does the one toil with his hands, if the other be not to toil, still more unweariedly, with heart and head? The brawny craftsman finds it no child's-play to mould his unpliant rugged masses; neither is guidance of men a dilettantism: what it becomes when treated as a dilettantism, we may see!"

"What is an Aristocracy? A corporation of the Best, of the Bravest. To this joyfully, with heart-loyalty, do men pay the half of their substance, to equip and decorate their Best; to know no limits in honouring them. Whatsoever Aristocracy *is* still a corporation of the Best, *is safe from all peril*, and the land it rules is a safe and blessed land. Whatsoever Aristocracy does not even attempt to be that, but only

to wear the clothes of that, is not safe; neither is the land
it rules safe ! For this now is our sad lot, that we must find
a *real* Aristocracy, that an apparent Aristocracy, how plausible
soever, has become inadequate for us. One way or other, the
world will absolutely need to be governed; if not by this
class of men, then by that."

Not Laissez-Faire.—If our leading' classes deliberately shirked the duties of their exalted position,—
letting things take their own course around them, and
preferring, like the idle pauper, ease and self-indulgence
to strenuous effort and real work for the common good,
—Carlyle warned them that neither was there any perpetual 'Forty-third of Elizabeth' provided for them.
But he also warned them that it was very real work that
would have to be grappled with,—reserving all details
for future, and, as we shall see, very explicit elucidation.

"How an Aristocracy, in these present times and circumstances, could, if never so well disposed, set about governing
the Under Class ? What they should do; endeavour or
attempt to do ? That were even the question of questions :—
the question which *they* have to solve ; which it is our utmost
function at present to tell them, lies there for solving, and
must and will be solved.

"Insoluble we cannot fancy it. One select class Society
has furnished with wealth, intelligence, leisure, means outward
and inward for governing ; another huge class, furnished by
Society with none of those things, declares that it must be
governed: Negative stands fronting Positive ; if Negative
and Positive *cannot* unite,—it will be worse for both ! Let
the faculty and earnest constant effort of England combine
round this matter ; let it once be recognised as a vital matter.
Innumerable things our Upper Classes and Lawgivers might
'do;' but the preliminary of all things, we must repeat,
is to know that a thing must needs be done. We lead them
here to the shore of a boundless continent; ask them, Whether
they do not with their own eyes see it, see strange symptoms

of it, lying huge, dark, unexplored, inevitable; full of hope, but also full of difficulty, savagery, almost of despair? Let them enter; they must enter; Time and Necessity have brought them hither; where they are is no continuing! Let them enter; the first step once taken, the next will have become clearer, all future steps will become possible. It is a great problem for all of us; but for themselves, we may say, more than for any. On them chiefly, as the expected solvers of it, will the failure of a solution first fall.

"True, these matters lie far, very far indeed, from the 'usual habits of Parliament,' in late times; from the routine course of any Legislative or Administrative body of men that exists among us. Too true! And that is even the thing we complain of: had the mischief been looked into as it gradually rose, it would not have attained this magnitude. That self-cancelling Donothingism and *Laissez-faire* should have got so ingrained into our Practice, is the source of all these miseries. It is too true that Parliament, for the matter of near a century now, has been able to undertake the adjustment of almost one thing alone, of itself and its own interests; leaving other interests to rub along very much as they could and would. . . . Parliament will absolutely, with whatever effort, have to lift itself out of those deep ruts of donothing routine; and learn to say, on all sides, something more edifying than *Laissez-faire*. If Parliament cannot learn it, what is to become of Parliament?"

New Eras.—As I have said, Carlyle believed that we are living in a New Era of the World; an era more critical in its issues, and of more world-wide significance than any era since the Birth of Christianity; and I repeat that, unless we carry this thought steadily with us, we shall never get into the real secret of his work. He had high, almost inexpressible hopes of the destiny of the English-speaking race. He even thought that perhaps there had never been a race of men in this world so palpably prepared by the Great Providence of the World, and so appointed from afar off, for a heroic work, not of military conquest, but of world-embracing social development and wisely organised industry. Carlyle a mere puller-down? He had one of the grandest dreams of social building-up that ever kindled a prophetic imagination; and he believed the united Anglo-Saxon race were destined to accomplish it. He points to this great thought in pregnant hints throughout his works, and each fresh time with clearer emphasis. We have already seen two instances. But nowhere does he lay the foundations of his hope in the destiny of our race so deeply and thoroughly as in this chapter on 'New Eras.' As is usual with him when giving utterance to his most intense and most glowing convictions, he professes to quote from a German Author, thus leaving his readers free to think as they please or can. In this case it is Professor Sauerteig who writes. I look upon the whole chapter as the most significant and condensed picture of English organic history that even Carlyle has written. Sauerteig thus begins,—

"Who shall say what work and works this England has yet to do? For what purpose this land of Britain was created, set like a jewel in the encircling blue of Ocean; and this Tribe of Saxons, fashioned in the depths of Time, 'on the shores of the Black Sea' or elsewhere, 'out of Harzgebirge rock' or whatever other material, was sent travelling hitherward? No man can say: it was for a work, and for works, *incapable of announcement in words.* Thou seest them there; part of them stand done, and visible to the eye; even these thou canst not *name:* how much less the others still matter of prophecy only!—They live and labour there, these twenty million Saxon men; they have been born into this mystery of life out of the darkness of Past Time:—how changed now since the first Father and first Mother of them set forth, quitting the tribe of *Theuth,* with passionate farewell, under questionable auspices; on scanty bullock-cart, if they had even bullocks and a cart; with axe and hunting-spear, to subdue a portion of our common Planet! This Nation now has cities and seedfields, has spring-vans, dray-wagons, Long-Acre carriages, nay railway trains; has coined-money, exchange-bills, laws, books, war-fleets, spinning-jennies, warehouses and West India Docks: see what it has built and done, what it can and will yet build and do! These umbrageous pleasure-woods, green meadows, shaven stubble-fields, smooth-sweeping roads; these high-domed cities, and what they hold and bear; this mild Good-morrow which the stranger bids thee, equitable, nay forbearant if need were, judicially calm and law-observing towards thee a stranger, what work has it not cost? How many brawny arms, generation after genera-tion, sank down wearied; how many noble hearts, toiling while life lasted, and wise heads that wore themselves dim with scanning and discerning, before this waste *White-cliff*, Albion so-called, with its other Cassiterides *Tin Islands*, became a BRITISH EMPIRE! The stream of World-History has altered its complexion; Romans are dead out, English are come in. The red broad mark of Romanhood, stamped in-effaceably on the Chart of Time, has disappeared from the present, and belongs only to the past. England plays its part; England too has a mark to leave, and we will hope none of the least significant. Of a truth, whosoever had, with the bodily eye, seen Hengst and Horsa mooring on the mud-beach of Thanet, on that spring morning of the Year 449; and then, with the spiritual eye, looked forward to New York, Calcutta, Sidney Cove, across the ages and the oceans; and thought what Wellingtons, Washingtons, Shakspeares, Miltons, Watts, Arkwrights, William Pitts and Davie Crocketts had to issue from that business, and do their several taskworks so, —*he* would have said, those leather-boats of Hengst's had a kind of cargo in them!"

"To this English People in World-History, there have been, shall I prophesy, Two grand tasks assigned? Huge-looming through the dim tumult of the always incommensur-able Present Time, outlines of two tasks disclose themselves: the grand Industrial task of conquering some half or more of this Terraqueous Planet for the use of man; then, secondly, the grand Constitutional task of *sharing*, in some pacific endurable manner, the fruit of said conquest, and showing all people how it might be done.   These I will call their two tasks, discernible hitherto in World-History: in both of these they have made respectable though unequal progress.   Steam-engines, ploughshares, pickaxes; what is meant by conquering this Planet, they partly know.   Elective franchise, ballot-box, representative assembly; how to accomplish *sharing* of that conquest, they do not so well know.   Europe knows not; Europe vehemently asks in these days, but receives no answer, no credible answer."

But, lest his glowing hope should seem utterly base-less and extravagant, Carlyle shows us what strange Eras have already burst up unexpectedly in England's history.   Among them are the following :—

"Long stormy spring-time, wet contentious April, winter chilling the lap of very May; but at length the season of summer does come.   So long the tree stood naked; angry wiry naked boughs moaning and creaking in the wind: you would say, Cut it down, why cumbereth it the ground ?   Not so; we must wait; all things will have their time.—Of the man Shakspeare, and his Elizabethan Era, with its Sydneys, Raleighs, Bacons, what could we say ?   That it was a spiritual flower-time.   Suddenly, as with the breath of June, your rude naked tree is touched; bursts into leaves and flowers, *such* leaves and flowers.   The past long ages of nakedness, and wintry fermentation and elaboration, have done their part, though seeming to do nothing.   The past silence has got a voice, all the more significant the longer it had continued silent.   In trees, men, institutions, creeds, nations, in all things extant and growing in this Universe, we may note such vicissitudes and budding-times.   Moreover there are spiritual budding-times; and then also there are physical, appointed to nations.

"Thus in the middle of that poor calumniated Eighteenth Century, see once more ! Long winter again past, the dead-seeming tree proves to be living, to have been always living ; after motionless times, every bough shoots forth on the sudden, very strangely :—it now turns out that this favoured England was not only to have had her Shakspeares, Bacons, Sydneys, but to have her Watts, Arkwrights, Brindleys ! We will honour greatness in all kinds. The Prospero evoked the singing of Ariel, and took captive the world with those melodies ; the same Prospero can send his Fire-demons panting across all oceans ; shooting with the speed of meteors, on cunning high-ways, from end to end of kingdoms ; and make Iron his missionary, preaching *its* evangel to the brute Primeval Powers, which listen and obey : neither is this small. . . . Hast thou heard, with sound ears, the awakening of a Manchester, on Monday morning, at half-past five by the clock ; the rushing off of its thousand mills, like the boom of an Atlantic tide, ten-thousand times ten-thousand spools and spindles all set humming there,—it is perhaps, if thou knew it well, sublime as a Niagara, or more so. Cotton-spinning is the clothing of the naked in its result ; the triumph of man over matter in its means. Soot and despair are not the essence of it ; they are divisible from it,—at this hour, are they not crying fiercely to be divided ? "

" On the whole, were not all these things most unexpected, unforeseen ? As indeed what thing is foreseen ; *especially what man, the parent of things !* Robert Clive in that same time went out, with a developed gift of penmanship, as writer or superior book-keeper to a trading factory established in the distant East. With gift of penmanship developed ; with other gifts not yet developed, which the calls of the case did by and by develop. Not fit for book-keeping alone, the man was found fit for conquering Nawaubs, founding kingdoms, Indian Empires ! In a questionable manner, Indian Empire from the other hemisphere took up its abode in Leadenhall Street, in the City of London.

" Accidental all these things and persons look, unexpected every one of them to man. Yet inevitable every one of them ; foreseen, not unexpected, by Supreme Power ; prepared, appointed from afar. Advancing always through all centuries, in the middle of the eighteenth they *arrived.*"

Does the reader think there was no other man, ' the parent of things,' besides Robert Clive, ' with gift of penmanship developed ; with other gifts not yet developed ' ?

Parliamentary Radicalism.—Thus Carlyle, with his accustomed wariness, chose to treat his grand ultimate hope as a mere pregnant hint and suggestion of Sauerteig's; knowing well that even his most sympathising and admiring readers would, as Regent Murray is said to have done to John Knox, simply have shrugged their shoulders and exclaimed, ' It is a devout Imagination.' He thus quietly leaves it to make what impression it may.

"To us," he adds, "looking at these matters somewhat in the same light, Reform-Bills, French Revolutions, Louis-Philippes, Chartisms, Revolts of Three Days, and what not, are no longer inexplicable. Where the great mass of men is tolerably right, all is right; where they are not right all is wrong."

"Parliamentary Radicalism, while it gave articulate utterance to the discontent of the English people, could not by its worst enemy be said to be without a function. If it is in the natural order of things that there must be discontent, no less so is it that such discontent should have an outlet, a Parliamentary voice. Here the matter is debated of, demonstrated, contradicted, qualified, reduced to feasibility;—can at least solace itself with hope, and die gently, convinced of *un*feasibility. The New, Untried ascertains how it will fit itself into the arrangements of the Old ; whether the Old can be compelled to admit it ; how in that case it may, with the minimum of violence, be admitted. Nor let us count it an easy one, this function of Radicalism; it is one of the most difficult. The pain-stricken patient does, indeed, without effort groan and complain; but not without effort does the physician ascertain what it is that has gone wrong with him, how some remedy may be devised for him. And above all, if your patient is not one sick man, but a whole sick nation ! Dingy dumb millions, grimed with dust and sweat, with darkness, rage and sorrow, stood round these men, saying, or struggling as they could to say : Behold, our lot is unfair ; our life is not whole but sick ; we cannot live under injustice ; go ye and get us justice ! "

"How Parliamentary Radicalism has fulfilled this mission, entrusted to its management these eight years,* is known to all men. The expectant millions have sat at a feast of the Barmecide ; been bidden fill themselves with the imagination of meat. What thing has Radicalism obtained for them ; what other than shadows of things has it so much as asked for them ? . . . There is a class of revolutionists named *Girondins,* whose fate in history is remarkable enough ! Men who rebel, and urge the Lower Classes to rebel, ought to have other than Formulas to go upon. Men who discern in the misery of the toiling complaining millions not misery, but only a raw-material which can be wrought upon, and traded in, for one's own poor hidebound theories and egoisms ; to whom millions of living fellow-creatures, with beating hearts in their bosoms, beating, suffering, hoping, are ' masses,' mere 'explosive masses for blowing down Bastilles with,' for voting at hustings for *us* : such men are of the questionable species ! "

Impossible.—Carlyle tells us 'there is a phenomenon which one might call Paralytic Radicalism, in these days,' rather frequent among ' those Statistic friends of ours ; ' and ' one of the most afflictive phenomena the mind of man can be called to contemplate.' These are men, and there are many branches of the family, to whom nothing is possible until it has been done. And yet, as every earnest heart well knows, there are emergencies in life when we must passionately resolve, as Goethe puts it, to—'*Do what is impossible ;*' and thus only find out how possible it was.

"'But what are we to do ?' exclaims the practical man,

* Written in 1839.

impatiently on every side : ' Descend from speculation and the safe pulpit, down into the rough market-place, and say what can be done !'—O practical man, there seem very many things which practice and true manlike effort, in Parliament and out of it, might actually avail to do. But the first of all things, as already said, is to gird thyself up for actual doing; to know that thou actually either must do, or, as the Irish say, ' come out of that !'

"It is not a lucky word this same *impossible:* no good comes of those that have it so often in their mouths. Who is he that says always, There is a lion in the way? Sluggard, thou must slay the lion then; the way has to be travelled ! In Art, in Practice, innumerable critics will demonstrate that most things are henceforth impossible; that we are got, once for all, into the region of perennial commonplace, and must contentedly continue there. Let such critics demonstrate; it is the nature of them : what harm is in it ? Poetry once well demonstrated to be impossible, arises the Burns, arises the Goethe. Unheroic commonplace being now clearly all we have to look for, comes the Napoleon, comes the conquest of the world. It was proved by fluxionary calculus, that steamships could never get across from the farthest point of Ireland to the nearest of Newfoundland : impelling force, resisting force, maximum here, minimum there ; by law of Nature, and geometric demonstration :—what could be done ? The Great Western could weigh anchor from Bristol Port ; that could be done. The Great Western, bounding safe through the gullets of the Hudson, threw her cable out on the capstan of New York, and left our still moist paper-demonstration to dry itself at leisure. ' Impossible ? ' cried Mirabeau to his secretary, ' *Ne me dites jamais ce bête de mot,* Never name to me that blockhead of a word !' "

"Two things, great things," Carlyle says, "dwell for the last ten years, in all thinking heads in England; and are hovering, of late, even on the tongues of not a few. With a word on each of these, we will dismiss the practical man, and right gladly take ourselves into obscurity and silence again. Universal Education is the first great thing we mean ; general Emigration is the second."

Then follows an urgent appeal on behalf of Universal Education. It is a thing, Carlyle tells us, which should need no advocating.

"To impart the gift of thinking to those who cannot think, and yet who could in that case think : this, one would imagine, was the first function a government had to set about discharging. Were it not a cruel thing to see, in any province of an empire, the inhabitants living all mutilated in their limbs, each strong man with his right arm lamed? How much crueller to find the strong soul, with its eyes still sealed, its eyes extinct so that it sees not! Light has come into the world, but to this poor peasant it has come in vain. For six thousand years the Sons of Adam, in sleepless effort, have been devising, doing, discovering; in mysterious infinite indissoluble communion, warring, a little band of brothers, against the great black empire of Necessity and Night; they have accomplished such a conquest and conquests; and to this man it is all as if it had not been. . . . Heavier wrong is not done under the sun. It lasts from year to year, from century to century; the blinded sire slaves himself out, and leaves a blinded son; and men, made in the image of God, continue as two-legged beasts of labour. . . . These Twenty-four million labouring men and their affairs cannot remain unregulated, chaotic; but must be regulated, brought into some kind of order. What intellect were able to regulate them? The intellect of a Bacon, the energy of a Luther, if left to their own strength, might pause in dismay before such a task; a Bacon and Luther added together, to be perpetual prime minister over us, could not do it. No one great and greatest intellect can do it. What can? *Only Twenty-four million ordinary intellects, once awakened into action ; these well presided over, may.*"

Surely this should be enough to show how little Carlyle's notion of Government was that of intellect and force on the one hand, and servile blind obedience on the other. And yet that charge is continually laid against him, even by those who ought to know better, as if it were one of those things which no one could dispute. These words are no exceptional utterance of Carlyle's. The thought which they express forms the practical basis of his great hope for the world : the intelligent and conscientious co-operation of all effective heads and hands throughout the entire social organism. On no other terms, he always knew, and rejoiced to know, could such a dream as his by any possibility become realised as a working fact. It is evident that he still looked forward to what he called 'a whole nation of heroes;' but it is further evident that he still looked upon Intellect as the one thing needful, and upon Ignorance, with its consequent misunderstandings, as the one deadliest enemy to be fought against. If this were so, how is it that the educated, and what we call the intellectual classes, are not also in all cases intrinsically and inevitably the *best ?* We all know that it is not so ; but that, class for class, there is as much actual human worth in the lowest as in the highest. Carlyle himself saw this insufficiency of light alone, clearly enough in his after-life ; and emphatically declared that the bigger light you kindled in a bad man, the more hideous and dangerous he became ; this it was which compelled him to discriminate very sternly between what he called 'real intellect' and 'sham intellect.' But, of course, all this is no argument against universal Education ; it only shows that it is not all-sufficient. All have equal claim to education, with all its advantages ; and only on such terms can the great battle between Good and Evil, between Faithfulness and Unfaithfulness, ever be effectually fought out. Intellect is not the greatest, but it gives us, as already said, a choice of sides, a choice of roads.

Carlyle's extraordinary Emigration Scheme, to which he again and again returns in after years, and which is enough to strike a Colonial Secretary blank with astonishment, points also unmistakably in the same direction as his urgent demand for universal education; namely, to a nation of heroes, and even to a world of heroes !

"But now," he says, "we have to speak of the second great thing : Emigration. It was said above, all new epochs, so convulsed and tumultuous to look upon, are 'expansions,' increase of faculty not yet organised. It is eminently true of the confusions of this time of ours. . . . Over-population is the grand anomaly, which is bringing all other anomalies to a crisis. Now once more, as at the end of the Roman Empire, a most confused epoch and yet one of the greatest, the Teutonic Countries find themselves too full."

"The controversies on Malthus and the 'Population Principle,' with which the public ear has been deafened for a long while, are indeed sufficiently mournful: dreary, stolid, dismal, without hope for this world or the next. . . . And all this is in a world where Canadian Forests stand unfelled, boundless Plains and Prairies unbroken with the plough; on the west and on the east green desert spaces never yet made white with corn ; and to the overcrowded little western nook of Europe, our Terrestrial Planet, nine-tenths of it yet vacant or tenanted by nomades, is still crying, Come and till me, come and reap me ! And in an England with wealth, and, means for moving, such as no nation ever before had. With ships; with war-ships rotting idle, which, but bidden move and not rot, might bridge all oceans. With trained men, educated to pen and practice, to administer and act; briefless Barristers, chargeless Clergy, taskless Scholars, languishing in all court-houses, hiding in obscure garrets, besieging all antechambers, in passionate want of simply one thing, Work;—with as many Half-pay Officers of both Services, wearing themselves down in wretched tedium, as might lead an Emigrant host larger than Xerxes' was ! Is it not as if this swelling, simmering, never-resting Europe of ours stood, once more, on the verge of an expansion, this time without parallel ; struggling. struggling like a mighty tree again about to burst in the embrace of summer, and shoot forth broad frondent boughs which would fill the whole earth ?　A disease ; but the noblest of all,—as of her who is in pain and sore travail, but travails that she may be a mother, and say, Behold, there is a new Man born ! "

Such was Carlyle's grand conception of what might be possible to a Nation of Heroes, furnished with all our modern equipments of world-embracing industry and enterprise.　Surely we may well acquit him of being a mere destructive ; and at least exclaim with wistful sympathy, ' It is a devout Imagination ! '

CHAPTER X.

How find our Able Man?—An example from the Past : Abbot Samson—
Not Men of Letters—True Captains of Industry—Organisation of
Labour—Mammonism—No noble task was ever easy—Land question — An Idle Aristocracy—Noble exceptions—A priceless breath-
ing-time—A Future, wide as the world—Personal aspirations, and
struggles with despair.

I HAVE always felt 'Past and Present' to be the most
hopeful and even triumphant in tone of any book that
Carlyle has written. In it, for the first time, he seems to
fling away all reserve, and to speak, straight out from
the fulness of his heart, the thoughts and aspirations
which had so long been growing to their maturity in
him. It is essentially an expansion of 'Chartism;' but
with many new illustrations, and direct applications to
the social condition of England, into which, however, it
will not now be necessary to follow him. But what is
more specially significant for our present purpose, namely,
the elucidation of Carlyle's personal character and aims,
is the fact, that here for the first time he distinctly takes
his position, not merely as a writer with 'a developed
gift of penmanship,' but as a man, a Leader of men,
the parent of things. And why should he not, if the
plain facts of the case forced it upon him, frankly assume
the tone of leadership, as well as discharge the functions
of it ? Once for all he resolved that there should be no

more hinting and beating about the bush, but that he
would fearlessly declare himself; and speak with the
authority of one who felt what he *could do*, if his stern
destiny would but fulfil its seeming promise.

What personal responses to his appeal he received,
upon the issue of the first little book, I do not know ;
but I should imagine they must have been sufficient to
convince him that he was not writing quite in vain : that
practical men were at last listening to him.   At this
time he was already deep in the life of Cromwell. · He
had not yet got himself fairly to work upon the subject,
but had been reading, examining, and diligently collecting facts ; and the character and career of Cromwell had
at last become clear and luminously credible to him.
He had ' seen Balder, the very Balder,'—but could he
bring him back ?   While his mind was wrestling with
this question, he fortunately came upon a small kindred
character, in a still earlier period of English History,
whom he at once saw he *could* bring back, and make
personally visible to all readers.   Here, ready to his
hand, was a practical and living answer to the question
which had often been tauntingly put to him, but sometimes, also, with earnest sincerity :—How find our Able
Man ?   Carlyle had always virtually replied, — By
sincerely and even prayerfully looking for him.   You
will then be ready to recognise and welcome him, should
Providence, in unexpected ways, vouchsafe to send him.
If you have him among you, he *must* show himself to
discerning eyes, in everything he does, or refrains from
doing.   The danger lies not there.   The danger and
tragedy are, that he should stand revealed before you in
living characters which no one has eyes to read !
Samson had shown himself to those poor Monks in

characters which they at least could read : namely, in faithful work, in wise, long-suffering submission to the inevitable, in friendly counsel and ready helpfulness, and in stern inflexibility of character ; in one word, in all manner of trustworthiness : and, when the question was put to them, to answer as before God, the wise among them felt in their deepest hearts that Samson, the servant-of-all-work, the factotum of the whole Monastery, was in very truth the ablest man amongst them. There is always an 'ablest man' in every community, for what-ever work may be in hand ; and, when we are really in earnest about the work, and understand what is wanted, we generally know well enough which amongst us is the man we need. But all depends upon ourselves being sufficiently in earnest.

In order to show us what an Able Man is like, so that we also in this confused generation might learn a little better to understand his value and what really goes to the making of him, and be able to recognise him on every hand wherever we might chance to meet him, Carlyle proposed, if possible,—

"To penetrate a little, by means of certain confused Papers, printed and other, into a somewhat remote Century ; and to look face to face on it, in hope of perhaps illustrating our own poor Century thereby. It seems," he says, " a circuitous way ; but it may prove a way nevertheless. For man has ever been a striving, struggling, and, in spite of widespread calumnies to the contrary, a veracious creature : the Centuries too are all lineal children of one another ; and often, in the portrait of our early grandfathers, this and the other enigmatic feature of the newest grandson shall disclose itself, to mutual elucida-tion. This Editor will venture on such a thing."

This was Carlyle's express purpose in his graphic sketch of Abbot Samson. And he did not doubt that there were many in his own day who would recognise the portrait as that of a brother-soul, whom they might worthily emulate in the new times which had come upon them.

" Yesterday," he says, " a poor mendicant, allowed to possess not above two shillings of money, and without authority to bid a dog run for him, this man to-day finds himself a *Dominus Abbas*, mitred Peer of Parliament, Lord of manor-houses, farms, manors, and wide lands; a man with ' Fifty knights under him,' and dependent, swiftly obedient multitudes of men. It is a change greater than Napoleon's; so sudden withal. As if one of the Chandos day-drudges had, on awakening some morning, found that *he* overnight was become Duke! Let Samson with his clear-beaming eyes see into that, and discern it if he can. We shall now get the measure of him by a new scale of inches, considerably more rigorous than the former was. For if a noble soul is rendered tenfold beautifuller by victory and prosperity, springing now radiant as into his own due element and sun-throne; an ignoble one is rendered tenfold and hundredfold uglier, pitifuller."

How Samson got himself recognised, first by his brother-monks and afterwards by his King; and how he conducted himself as a guide and governor of men, are all shown with a vividness of reality and of practical comment which Carlyle has never surpassed. But the stern summary of all his comments is, that such men are actually living amongst us now; yet that no one even cares to find them; that we prefer a plausible counterfeit, what we call an ' eloquent man,' who will flatter us, rather than a wise man who will honestly tell us what we ought to do, and even compel us to do it if need be. Well, perhaps Carlyle was wrong in all this : the next generation will perhaps be able to tell us with some degree of certainty. Meanwhile, surely even this generation may admit that he was heartily in earnest ; and that what he always strenuously aimed at was the substantial welfare of his country and of the world.

The sketch of Abbot Samson's character and doings is familiar to us all : but of the extraordinary framework of social criticism and prophetic exhortation in which it is placed as the central significant picture, there is still something which must be said as briefly as the matter will allow. The book, like ' Chartism,' opens with a terrible picture of the condition of England previous to the repeal of the Corn-Law; where, " In Rich and Poor," we are told, " instead of noble thrift and plenty, there is idle luxury alternating with mean scarcity and inability ; " where " the Master Worker clamours, in vain hitherto, for a very simple sort of Liberty : the liberty to buy where he finds it cheapest, to sell where he finds it dearest ; " and where—

" The Master Unworker, in a still fataller situation, pauses amid his game-preserves, with awful eye,—as he well may ! Coercing fifty-pound tenants ; coercing, bribing, cajoling ; doing what he likes with his own. His mouth full of loud futilities, and arguments to prove the excellence of his Corn-Law ; and in his heart the blackest misgiving, a desperate half-consciousness that his excellent Corn-Law is *in*defensible, that his loud arguments for it are of a kind to strike men too literally *dumb*."

It would be useless to trouble my readers with a description or criticism of the several chapters of this earnest appeal. Mere criticism is not my object at all. My object is, if possible, once more to show what Carlyle aimed at as a practical worker : for his mere literary fame, we must repeat, he valued as nothing in comparison. In ' Sartor Resartus ' he spoke of that most miraculous of tools, the Pen. "Never since Aaron's Rod went out of practice, or even before it, was there such a wonder-working Tool: greater than all recorded miracles have been performed by Pens." And again in 'Heroes and Hero-Worship' he appealed, as we have seen, directly to the Men of Letters to initiate the new social life of the new times. But he valued the pen simply *as a tool*, a means to a practical end; and he valued literary men simply for the actual social work which could be got out of them. He seems now to have been driven to the conclusion that as yet very little could be got from them of any practical value. In this book, except in the chapter on 'The Gifted,' he hardly mentions them; and even there only to dismiss them with a blessing and a word of warning. He says—

"I conclude that Men of Letters too may become a 'Chivalry,' an actual instead of a virtual Priesthood, with results immeasurable,—so soon as there is nobleness in themselves for that. And, to a certainty, not sooner!"

But although he had evidently signally failed in his expectation of gathering together his two or three literary heroes, he by no means gave up his own personal struggle in the same direction. His thoughts and efforts now assumed a still more practical emphasis. Probably his hopes had already been greatly influenced and encouraged by his study of the character and career of Cromwell, and by his own day-vision of Abbot Samson; and perhaps also by individual responses received to his appeal in 'Chartism.' However that may be, we have to note that his 'desperate hope' was now fixed, not on the Men of Letters, but on some select few among the great Captains of Industry on the one hand, and on some equally select few among the Landed Aristocracy on the other. To these two classes he now strenuously and passionately appealed.

The true Captain of Industry is, he says,—

"A born member of the Ultimate genuine Aristocracy of this Universe, could he have known it! These thousand men that span and toiled around him, they were a regiment whom he had enlisted, man by man; to make war on a very genuine enemy: Bareness of back, and disobedient Cotton-fibre, which will not, unless forced to it, consent to cover bare backs. Here is a most genuine enemy; over which all creatures will wish him victory. He enlisted his thousand men; said to them, 'Come, brothers, let us have a dash at Cotton!' They follow with cheerful shout; they gain such victory over Cotton as the Earth has to admire and clap hands at: but, alas, it is yet only of the Bucanier or Chactaw sort, —as good as no victory! . . . Does he hope to become illustrious by hanging up the scalps in his wigwam, the hundred thousands at his banker's, and saying, Behold my scalps? Why even his own host is all in mutiny: Cotton is conquered; but the bare backs—are worse covered than ever! . . . Plugson, Bucanier-like, says to his men: 'Noble spinners, this is the Hundred Thousand we have gained, wherein I mean to dwell and plant vineyards; the hundred thousand is mine, the three and sixpence daily was yours: adieu, noble spinners; drink my health with this groat each, which I give you over and above!' The entirely unjust Captain of Industry, say I; not Chevalier, but Bucanier!"—"Alas, what a business will this be, which our Continental friends, groping this long while somewhat absurdly about it and about it, call 'Organisation of Labour.'" *

"The vulgarest Plugson of a Master-Worker, who can command Workers, and get work out of them, is already a considerable man. Blessed and thrice-blessed symptoms I discern of Master-Workers who are not vulgar men; who are Nobles, and begin to feel that they must act as such: all speed to these, they are England's hope at present! But in this

* 'Past and Present,' book iii. chap. 10.

Plugson himself, conscious of almost no nobleness whatever, how much is there ! Not without man's faculty, insight, courage, hard energy, is this rugged figure. His words none of the wisest; but his actings cannot be altogether foolish. Think, how were it, stoodst thou suddenly in his shoes !"

"This is not a man I would kill and strangle by Corn-Laws, even if I could ! No, I would fling my Corn-Laws and Shotbelts to the Devil; and try to help this man. I would teach him, by noble precept and law-precept, by noble example most of all, that Mammonism was not the essence of his or of my station in God's Universe. . . . May it please your Serene Highnesses, your Majesties, Lordships and Law-wardships, the proper Epic of this world is not now 'Arms and the Man;' how much less, 'Shirt-frills and the Man:' no, it is now 'Tools and the Man:' that, henceforth to all time is now our Epic;— and you, first of all others, I think, were wise to take note of that !" *

" The Leaders of Industry, if Industry is ever to be led, are virtually the Captains of the world; if there be no nobleness in them, there will never be an Aristocracy more. But let the Captains of Industry consider: once again, are they born of other clay than the old Captains of Slaughter; doomed forever to be no Chivalry, but a mere gold-plated *Doggery*,—what the French well name Canaille ? . . . No Working World, any more than a Fighting World, can be led on without a noble Chivalry of Work, and laws and fixed rules which follow out of that,—far nobler than any Chivalry of Fighting was. As an anarchic multitude on mere Supply-and-demand, it is becoming inevitable that we dwindle in horrid suicidal convulsion, and self-abrasion, frightful to the imagination,—into *Chactaw* Workers. With wigwams and scalps,—with palaces and thousand-pound bills: with savagery, depopulation, chaotic desolation ! Good Heavens, will not one French Revolution and Reign of Terror suffice us, but must there be two ? There will be two if needed; there will be twenty if needed; there will be precisely as many as are needed. The Laws of Nature will have themselves fulfilled. That is a thing certain to me."

"God knows the task will be hard: but no noble task

* 'Past and Present,' book iii. chap. 12.

was ever easy. This task will wear away your lives, and the lives of your sons and grandsons: but for what purpose, if not for tasks like this, were lives given to men?" "The Cliffords, Fitzadelms and Chivalry Fighters 'wished to gain victory,' never doubt it: but victory, unless gained in a certain spirit, was no victory; *defeat, sustained in a certain spirit, was itself victory.* I say again and again, had they counted the scalps alone, they had continued Chactaws, and no Chivalry or lasting victory had been. And in Industrial Fighters and Captains is there no nobleness discoverable? To them, alone of men, there shall forever be no blessedness but in swollen coffers? To see beauty, order, gratitude, loyal human hearts around them, shall be of no moment; to see fuliginous deformity, mutiny, hatred and despair, with the addition of half-a-million guineas, shall be better? . . . If so, I apprise the Mill-owner and Millionaire, that he too must prepare for vanishing; that neither is *he* born to be of the sovereigns of this world." *

"'Men cease to regard money?' cries Bobus of Houndsditch: 'What else do all men strive for? The very Bishop informs me that Christianity cannot get on without a minimum of Four thousand five hundred in its pocket. Cease to regard money? That will be at Doomsday in the afternoon!'—O Bobus, my opinion is somewhat different. My opinion is, that the Upper Powers have not yet determined on destroying this Lower World. A respectable, ever-increasing minority, who do strive for something higher than money, I with confidence anticipate; ever-increasing, till there be a sprinkling of them found in all quarters, as salt of the Earth once more. The Christianity that cannot get on without a minimum of Four thousand five hundred, will give place to something better that can. Thou wilt not join our small minority, thou? Not till Doomsday in the afternoon? Well; *then*, at least, thou wilt join it, thou and the majority in mass!" †

Such is the pith of Carlyle's stern message and appeal to our Captains of Industry: let us now turn

---

* ' Past and Present,' book iv. chap. 4.　　　　† Ibid., iv. chap. 8.

to what he had to say to another class of our Social Leaders.

"To the 'Millo-cracy' so-called, to the Working Aristocracy, steeped too deep in mere ignoble Mammonism, and as yet all unconscious of its noble destinies; as yet but an irrational or semi-rational giant, struggling to awake some soul in itself; —the world will have much to say, reproachfully, reprovingly, admonishingly. But to the Idle Aristocracy, what will the world have to say? Things painful and not pleasant!" *

"It is well said, 'Land is the right basis of an Aristocracy;' whoever possesses the Land, he, more emphatically than any other, is the Governor, Viceking of the people of the Land. It is in these days as it was in those of Henry Plantagenet and Abbot Samson; as it will in all days be. The Land is *Mother* of us all; nourishes, shelters, gladdens, lovingly enriches us all; in how many ways, from our first awakening to our last sleep on her blessed mother-bosom, does she, as with blessed mother-arms, enfold us all! . . . Men talk of 'selling' Land. Land, it is true, like Epic Poems and even higher things, in such a trading world, has to be presented in the market for what it will bring, and as we say be 'sold;' but the notion of selling, for certain bits of metal, the *Iliad* of Homer, how much more the *Land* of the World-Creator, is a ridiculous impossibility! We buy what is saleable of it; nothing more was ever buyable. *Who can, or could, sell it to us?* Properly speaking, the Land belongs to these two: To the Almighty God; and to all His Children of Men that have ever worked well on it, or that shall ever work well on it. No generation of men can or could, with never such solemnity and effect, sell Land on any other principle: it is not the property of any generation, we say, but that of all the past generations that have worked on it, and of all the future ones that shall work on it. . . . From much loud controversy, and Corn-Law debating there rises, loud though inarticulate, once more in these years, this very question among others, Who made the Land of England? Who made it, this respectable English Land, wheat-growing, metalliferous, carboniferous, which will let readily hand over

* 'Past and Present,' book iii. chap. 7.

head for seventy millions or upwards, as it here lies: who did make it?—'We!' answer the much-*consuming* Aristocracy; 'We!' as they ride in, moist with the sweat of Melton Mowbray: it is we that made it; or are the heirs, assigns and representatives of those who did!'—My brothers, You? . . . Infatuated mortals, into what questions are you driving every thinking man in England? I say, you did *not* make the Land of England; and, by the possession of it, you *are* bound to furnish guidance and governance to England! That is the law of your position on this God's-Earth; an everlasting act of Heaven's Parliament, not repealable in St. Stephen's or elsewhere! True government and guidance; not no-government and Laissez-faire; how much less, *mis*-government and Corn-Law! There is not an imprisoned Worker looking out from these Bastilles but appeals, very audibly in Heaven's High Courts, against you, and me, and every one who is not imprisoned, 'Why am I here?' His appeal is audible in Heaven; and will become audible enough on Earth too, if it remain unheeded here. His appeal is against you, foremost of all; you stand in the front-rank of the accused; you, by the very place you hold, have first of all to answer him and Heaven!"

"The Working Aristocracy; Mill-owners, Manufacturers, Commanders of Working Men: alas, against them also much shall be brought in accusation; much,—and the freest Trade in Corn, total abolition of Tariffs, and uttermost 'Increase of Manufactures' and 'Prosperity of Commerce,' will permanently mend no jot of it. The Working Aristocracy must strike into a new path; must understand that money alone is *not* the representative either of man's success in the world, or of man's duties to man; and reform their own selves from top to bottom, if they wish England reformed. England will not be habitable long, unreformed. . . . But the fate of the Idle Aristocracy, as one reads its horoscope hitherto in Corn-Laws and such like, is an abyss that fills one with despair. Yes, my rosy fox-hunting brothers, a terrible *Hippocratic look* reveals itself (God knows, not to my joy) through those fresh buxom countenances of yours. . . . A High Class without duties to do is

like a tree planted on precipices; from the roots of which all
the earth has been crumbling away. . . . What is the meaning
of nobleness, if this be 'noble'? In a valiant suffering for
others, not in a slothful making others suffer for us, did nobleness ever lie. The chief of men is he who stands in the van of
men; fronting the peril which frightens back all others; which,
if it be not vanquished, will devour the others. Every noble
crown is, and on Earth will forever be, a crown of thorns. . . .
Descend, O Donothing Pomp; quit thy down-cushions; expose
thyself to learn what wretches feel, and how to cure it! The
Czar of Russia became a dusty toiling shipwright; worked
with his axe in the Docks of Saardam; and his aim was small
to thine. Descend thou: undertake this horrid 'living chaos
of Ignorance and Hunger' weltering round thy feet; say, 'I
will heal it, or behold I will die foremost in it.' Such is verily
the law. Everywhere and everywhen a man has to '*pay* with
his life;' to do his work, as a soldier does, at the expense of
life. In no Piepowder earthly Court can you sue an Aristocracy to do its work, at this moment: but in the Higher
Court, which even *it* calls 'Court of Honour,' and which is the
Court of Necessity withal, and the eternal Court of the Universe, in which all Fact comes to plead, and every Human
Soul is an apparitor,—the Aristocracy is answerable, and
even now answering, *there*." *

"A man with fifty, with five hundred, with a thousand
pounds a day, given him freely, without condition at all,—
on condition, as it now runs, that he will sit with his hands
in his pockets and do no mischief, pass no Corn-Laws or the
like,—he too, you would say, is or might be a rather strong
Worker! He is a Worker with such tools as no man in this
world ever before had. But in practice, very astonishing, very
ominous to look at, he proves not a strong Worker;—you are
too happy if he will prove but a No-worker, do nothing, and
not be a Wrong-worker. You ask him, at the year's end:
'Where is your three-hundred thousand pound; what have you
realised to us with that?' He answers, in indignant surprise: 'Done with it? Who are you that ask? I have eaten
it; I and my flunkeys, and parasites, and slaves two-footed

* 'Past and Present,' book iii. chap. 8.

and four-footed, in an ornamental manner; and I am here alive by it; *I* am realised by it to you!'—It is, as we have often said, such an answer as was never before given under this Sun. An answer that fills me with boding apprehension, with foreshadows of despair. . . . Ah, how happy were it, if he this Aristocratic Worker would see *his* work and do it! It is frightful seeking another to do it for him. Guillotines, Meudon Tanneries, and half-a-million men shot dead, have already been expended in that business; and it is yet far from done. This man too is something; nay he is a great thing Look on him there: a man of manful aspect; something of the 'cheerfulness of pride' still lingering in him. A free air of graceful stoicism, of easy silent dignity sits well on him; in his heart, could we reach it, lie elements of generosity, self-sacrificing justice, true human valour. Why should he, with such appliances, stand an incumbrance in the Present; perish disastrously out of the Future! From no section of the Future would we lose these noble courtesies, impalpable· yet all-controlling; these dignified reticences, these kingly simplicities;—lose aught of what the fruitful Past still gives us token of, memento of, in this man. Can we not save him:—can he not help us to save him! A brave man he too; had not undivine Ignavia, Hearsay, Speech without meaning,—had not Cant, thousandfold Cant within him and around him, enveloping . him like chokedamp, like thick Egyptian darkness, thrown his soul into asphyxia, as it were extinguished his soul;—so that he sees not, hears not; and Moses and all the Prophets address him in vain."

"A modern Duke of Weimar, not a god he either, but a human duke, levied, as I reckon, in rents and taxes and all incomings whatsoever, less than several of our English Dukes do in rent alone. The Duke of Weimar, with these incomings, had to govern, judge, defend, everyway administer *his* Dukedom. He does all this as few others did: and he improves lands besides all this, makes river-embankments, maintains not soldiers only but Universities and institutions;—and in his Court were these four men: Wieland, Herder, Schiller, Goethe. Not as parasites, which was impossible; not as table-wits and poetic Katerfeltoes; but as noble Spiritual Men working under a noble Practical Man. . . . I reckon that this one Duke of Weimar did more for the Culture of his Nation than all the English Dukes and *Duces* now extant, or that were extant since Henry the Eighth gave them the Church Lands to eat, have done for theirs!—I am ashamed, I am alarmed for my English Dukes: what word have I to say? *If* our Actual Aristocracy, appointed 'Best-and-Bravest,' will be wise, how inexpressibly happy for us! If not,—the voice of God from the whirlwind is very audible to me. Nay, I will thank the Great God, that He has said, in whatever fearful ways, and just wrath against us, 'Idleness shall be no more!' Idleness? The awakened soul of man, all but the asphyxied soul of man, turns from it as from worse than death. It is the life-in-death of Poet Coleridge. That fable of the Dead-Sea Apes ceases to be a fable. The poor Worker starved to death is not the saddest of sights. He lies there" (even as Carlyle in his turn now lies) "dead on his shield; fallen down into the bosom of his old Mother; with haggard pale face, sorrow-worn, but stilled now into divine peace, silently appeals to the Eternal God and all the Universe,—the most silent, the most eloquent of men." *

Let us pause here, if possible for one reverent moment, as if standing beside Carlyle's grave, and read what he says of 'the Gifted':—

"Not a May-game is this man's life; but a battle and a march, a warfare with principalities and powers. No idle promenade through fragrant orange-groves and green flowery spaces, waited on by the choral Muses and the rosy Hours: it is a stern pilgrimage through burning sandy solitudes, through regions of thickribbed ice. He walks among men; loves men, with inexpressible soft pity,—as they *cannot* love him: but his soul dwells in solitude, in the uttermost parts of Creation. In green oases by the palm-tree wells, he rests a space; but anon he has to journey forward, escorted by the Terrors and the Splendours, the Archdemons and Archangels. All Heaven, all Pandemonium are his escort. The stars keen-glancing,

---

* 'Past and Present,' book iv. chap. 6.

from the Immensities, send tidings to him; the graves, silent with their dead, from the Eternities. Deep calls for him unto Deep. . . . Oh, if in this man, whose eyes can flash Heaven's lightning, and make all Calibans into a cramp, there dwelt not, as the essence of his very being, a God's justice, human Nobleness, Veracity and Mercy,—I should tremble for the world. But his *strength*, let us rejoice to understand, is even this: The quantity of Justice, of Valour and Pity that is in him. To hypocrites and tailored quacks in high places, his eyes are lightning; but they melt in dewy pity soft as a mother's to the downpressed, maltreated; in his heart, in his great thought, is a sanctuary for all the wretched." *

"Exceptions," he exclaims, once more speaking of our Actual Aristocracy,—

"Exceptions,—ah yes, thank Heaven, we know there are exceptions. Our case were too hard, were there not exceptions, and partial exceptions not a few, whom we know, and whom we do not know. Honour to the name of Ashley,†— honour to this and the other valiant Abdiel, found faithful still; who would fain, by work and by word, admonish their Order not to rush upon destruction! These are they who will, if not save their Order, postpone the wreck of it;—by whom, under blessing of the Upper Powers, 'a quiet euthanasia spread over generations, instead of a swift torture-death concentrated into years,' may be brought about for many things. All honour and success to these. The noble man can still strive nobly to save and serve his Order;—at lowest, he can remember the precept of the Prophet: 'Come out of her, my people; come out of her.'" ‡

"Some 'Chivalry of Labour,' some noble Humanity and practical Divineness of Labour, will yet be realised on this Earth. Or why *will*; why do we pray to Heaven without setting our own shoulder to the wheel? The Present, if it will have the Future accomplish, shall itself commence. Thou

---

* 'Past and Present,' book iv. chap. 7.
† The late Lord Shaftesbury.
‡ 'Past and Present,' book iv. chap. 6.

who prophesiest, who believest, begin thou to fulfil. Here or nowhere, now equally as at any time! That outcast help-needing thing or person, trampled down under vulgar feet or hoofs, no help 'possible' for it, no prize offered for the saving of it,—canst not thou save it, then, without prize? Put forth thy hand, in God's name; know that 'impossible,' where Truth and Mercy and the everlasting Voice of Nature order, has no place in the brave man's dictionary. That when all men have said 'Impossible,' and tumbled noisily elsewhither, and thou alone art left, then first thy time and possibility have come. It is for thee now; do thou that, and ask no man's counsel, but thy own only and God's. Brother, thou hast possibility in thee for much: the possibility of writing on the eternal skies the record of a heroic life. . . . O, it is great, and there is no other greatness. To make some nook of God's Creation a little fruitfuller, better, more worthy of God; to make some human hearts a little wiser, manfuller, happier,—more blessed, less accursed! . . . God and all men looking on it well pleased." *

"Laissez-faire, Supply-and-demand,—one begins to be weary of all that. Leave all to egoism, to ravenous greed of money, of pleasure, of applause: it is the Gospel of Despair. . . . My unhappy brethren of the Working Mammonism, my unhappier brethren of the Idle Dilettantism, no world was ever held together in that way for long. . . . Supply-and-demand shall do its full part and Free Trade shall be free as air;—thou of the shotbelts, see thou forbid it not. . . . But Trade never so well freed, and all Tariffs settled or abolished, and Supply-and-demand in full operation,—let us all know that we have yet done nothing; that we have merely cleared the ground for doing. . . . The Corn-Laws gone, and Trade made free, it is as good as certain this paralysis of industry will pass away. We shall have another period of commercial enterprise, of victory and prosperity; during which, it is likely, much money will again be made, and all the people may, by the extant methods, still for a space of years, be kept alive and physically fed. The strangling band of Famine will

* 'Past and Present,' book iv. chap. 8.

be loosened from our necks; we shall have room again to breathe; time to bethink ourselves, to repent and consider; A precious and thrice-precious space of years; wherein to struggle as for life in reforming our foul ways; in alleviating, instructing, regulating our people; seeking, as for life, that something like spiritual food be imparted them, some real governance and guidance be provided them! It will be a priceless time. For our new period or paroxysm of commercial prosperity will and can, on the old methods of 'Competition and Devil take the hindmost,' prove but a paroxysm: a new paroxysm,—likely enough, if we do not use it better, to be our *last*." *

The foregoing extracts will abundantly show the intensely vital and wisely conservative aims of 'Past and Present,' and the large-hearted hopes which then animated Carlyle, and carried him on with a strenuous fervour of conviction to speak out his whole soul to his 'brothers' of every class. And surely the concluding paragraph is a sufficiently accurate forecast of our present social condition. The 'paroxysm of commercial prosperity' has already ended; and what have we done with the 'priceless time' accorded to us? We have sown the wind, and are now reaping the whirlwind. Alas, Carlyle's prophet-voice was listened to as little more than a nine-days' wonder. Even Emerson, brilliantly clear and discriminating as he was in its praise, wrote of 'Past and Present' as a singularly successful 'attempt to write a book of wit and imagination on English politics.' † If this is what even Emerson saw in this tempestuous lava-stream, pouring redhot from an aching yet hopeful heart, what could we expect of the 'Mammonism and Dilettantism' of England?

* 'Past and Present,' book iii. chap. 9.
† Criticism of 'Past and Present' in *The Dial*, vol. iv. p. 100.

In this book Carlyle is again most emphatic respecting Education and Emigration, and the almost boundless destiny of the English-speaking race.

"If the whole English People," he says, "during the 'twenty years of respite,' (which were to follow, and which have followed, the abrogation of the Corn-Laws,) be not educated, with at least schoolmaster's education, a tremendous responsibility, before God and men, will rest somewhere!"

His notion of an effective 'Emigration Service' (not for the mere riddance of a troublesome superfluity of population, but for the planting and fostering of future Nations upon the waste spaces of the earth) is certainly very different from anything that would be considered at all practicable even yet. Emigration, in a wholly chaotic helter-skelter fashion, has proceeded rather briskly of late years; with great relief to the labour-market at home, but with what bitter misery of disappointment and destitution to the Emigrants themselves! They leave this country full of hope, but with the vaguest notions of the lands to which they are bound; and when they get there often find themselves almost greater outcasts than they would have been at home. The wide colonial labour-markets are fast becoming practically as glutted as our own. 'Send us Capital, not Labour,' is everywhere more and more the passionate cry. It is the cry of a whole world working with borrowed capital, and tottering under the increasing pressure of irretrievable debt and incipient bankruptcy. All this was far enough from Carlyle's expectation of what the world's future might even yet be, with wisdom to fashion it.

"An effective 'Teaching Service,'" he says, "I do consider that there must be; some Education Secretary, Captain-General of Teachers, who will actually contrive to get us *taught*. Then again, why should there not be an 'Emigration Service,' and Secretary, with adjuncts, with funds, forces, idle Navy-ships, and ever-increasing apparatus; in fine an *effective system* of Emigration ; so that, at length, before our twenty years of respite ended, every honest willing Workman who found England too strait, and the 'Organisation of Labour' not yet sufficiently advanced, might find likewise a bridge built to carry him into new Western Lands, there to 'organise' with more elbow-room some labour for himself ? . . . Is it not scandalous to consider that a Prime Minister could raise within the year, as I have seen it done, a Hundred and Twenty Millions Sterling to shoot the French ; and we are stopt short for want of the hundredth part of that to keep the English living ? The bodies of the English living, and the souls of the English living : these two 'Services,' an Education Service and an Emigration Service, these with others will actually have to be organised !

" A free bridge for Emigrants : why, we should then be on a par with America itself, the most favoured of all lands that have no government ; and we should have, besides, so many traditions and mementos of priceless things which America has cast away. We could proceed deliberately to 'organise Labour,' not doomed to perish unless we effected it within year and day ;—every willing Worker that proved superfluous, finding a bridge ready for him. This verily will have to be done ; the Time is big with this. Our little Isle has grown too narrow for us ; but the world is wide enough yet for another Six Thousand Years. England's sure markets will be among new Colonies of Englishmen in all quarters of the globe. . . . 'Hostile Tariffs' will arise, to shut us out; and then again will fall, to let us in : but the Sons of England, speakers of the English language were it nothing more, will in all times have the ineradicable predisposition to trade with England. Mycale was the *Pan-Ionion*, rendezvous of all the Tribes of Ion, for old Greece : why should not London long continue the *All-Saxon-home*, rendezvous of all the 'Children of the Harz-Rock,' arriving, in select samples, from the Antipodes and elsewhere, by steam and otherwise, to the 'season' here !

—What a Future; wide as the world, if we have the heart and heroism for it,—which by Heaven's blessing, we shall!" *

Such were the practical aims and passionate hopes of which this book was the uncompromising and fearless expression. Can any man, with what he now knows of Carlyle, seriously regard it as a mere literary display? For my own part, I could as easily imagine such a thing of Paul's Epistle to the Ephesians.† If ever book were desperately in earnest this was; earnest in its terrible warnings; in its appeals to the better hopes of all good and wise men; in its solemn assertion of the sacredness of all true work, and of all true human brotherhood; and, above all, in its passionate calls to all true men to live for something better and nobler than mere selfish enjoyment. In all this it is a brother's voice which we hear, appealing to his brothers throughout the land. But when he addresses himself to actual work, and appeals to his great Captains of Industry and his Titled Aristocracy, he proudly warns them there shall be no mistake about himself. Not as a parasite or literary lion, will he hold intercourse with them; but as their indefeasible peer, or, if needs must, even as their Intellectual King. Before a Luther or a Goethe he will bow his head with all reverence; but not before his personal inferiors, however lofty their station or magnificent their equipments. I confess, I admire the tone of royal supremacy which, from this time, he always assumed in his addresses from the intellectual throne. How could he help knowing that he was head and shoulders above the rest of his genera-

* 'Past and Present,' book iv. chap. 3.

† Let me entreat my Christian readers to read once more, in the Revised Version, this wonderful and earnestly faithful Epistle; and then seriously ask themselves whether it does not contain the Christian essence and divine ideal of all that Carlyle ever urged or taught.

tion? God had so made him; and the devil himself should not unmake him, let the world do with him as it would.

There was perversity in all this, I know well. But it was a noble perversity, which even helped to constitute his strength. After all, he was, as he tells us Johnson also claims to have been, essentially one of the politest of men, when other men were polite enough to take him for something like what he was. And it speaks well, both for himself and his high connections, that they were able to associate personally and frankly on such simply human terms. Yet I have often wondered whether there was much, or even any, serious benefit to himself in all that brilliant intercourse. From his own continual confession, the whole thing was evidently to him little better than idle distraction, ending in torturing disappointment and self-accusation. "No man in this fashionable London of yours," he makes Sauerteig exclaim, "speaks a plain word to me." And in self-defence, and to ward off profitless and perhaps sometimes impertinent discussion, he frequently adopted the bantering tone of 'Sartor Resartus,' thus sending away his would-be critics as wise as they came.

"A man," he says, in his lecture on 'Hero as King,' "is always to be himself the judge how much of his mind he will show to other men; even to those he would have work along with him. There are impertinent inquiries made: your rule is, to leave the inquirer *un*informed on that matter; not, if you can help it, *mis*informed, but precisely as dark as he was! This, could one hit the right phrase of response, is what the wise and faithful man would aim to answer in such a case."

Nothing that Carlyle has written more exactly defines

his own attitude to the world ; and even Mr. Froude might do well to make a note of it.

It is very remarkable, this want of simplicity, or, rather, this strange mixture of inborn simplicity, proud shyness and stubborn perversity, in so exceptionably earnest a character. More than anything else, it made him sympathetically inaccessible even to those who sympathised with him most. Sincere he was beyond question, passionately and even awfully sincere ; but his personal aspirations, his self-consciousness, and, above all, his keen sense of the ridiculous, and of the contrast between what he intrinsically was and what he must needs appear, continually overpowered him, and broke out in self-mockery and self-pitying laughter. He never could, like Luther, or like Cromwell, look to the duty and work in hand with perfect simplicity and singleness of eye. He strove desperately to do so, and loaded himself with reproaches at his failure, far bitterer than those he so freely showered upon others. In fact, often in blaming others, he felt that he was blaming a reflex of his own besetting sins, and, strange to say, it gave poignancy to his words. A lurid self-consciousness, half smoke, half flame, clung to him through life ; but the amount of smoke he faithfully converted into clear flame for us, could and can be known only to himself, and to his Maker and ours.

It is clear that, from the time of writing 'Past and Present,' almost to the end of his life, Carlyle earnestly hoped that some select few among our existing aristocracy would listen to his words, and seriously strive to embody them in actual life, and that this feeling constituted the deepest longing of his heart in seeking personal intercourse with them. It is not for me to say how much or how little of that hope was realised.   Perhaps no one could say.   But, apart from this central earnest aim of his, and sometimes perhaps in strange contrast with it, there can be no doubt there was an intense fascination for him in his free intercourse with people of education and position.   He enjoyed his gladiatorial conflicts with the keenest rapiers of the day ; and laughed, as few could laugh, at the shaking of the spear.   Not as a literary lion tamed for the show, with claws neatly trimmed, and voice modulated to all fashionable cadences ; but as a lion of the forest, glorying in his strength, whose spring was final, and whose voice was as the echo of the spheres.   Sometimes also there was the pride of measuring himself with the highest, and drawing parallels and contrasts, not always to his own self-abasement. Thus, writing to his Mother in 1838, he says,—

" My most remarkable party for a great while was at no smaller personage's than—whom think you ?—the Chancellor of the Exchequer.*   I went for the curiosity, for the honour of the thing.   I could not help thinking : ' Here is the man that disposes annually of the whole revenue of England ; and here is another man, who has hardly enough cash to buy potatoes and onions for himself.   Fortune has for the time made these two tenants of one drawing-room.' " †

And doubtless his own grim private reflection was, ' *Why should* this difference be ? '   The fact is, all this fever of excitement and distraction did for Carlyle very much what, with far less reason, he feared it had done for his friend Irving ; and he might well have taken his some- what too-solicitous warnings to his friend more sternly and meekly to his own heart.   Such seductive experiences

* Mr. Spring Rice, afterward Lord Monteagle.
† 'Life in London,' 1834–1881, vol. i. p. 125.

of intellectual supremacy and power only intensified the consciousness of his own isolation, and of his helpless continual disappointment in the one unspoken aim of his life. He often longed to get away from it all, and from London altogether. But it could not be. However disastrous to his peace of mind such a life must have been, it was the element in which he was appointed to work,—could he but have worked on in simple integrity of heart, without once listening to the siren voices which were now singing to him in strains of hope, now taunting him with his palpable defeat. What he longed to get away from was, of course, his own unsatisfied self ; and this he would have carried with him, wherever he went. This his poor Wife knew by bitterest experience ; but no one knew it so bitterly or so self-reproachfully as himself. Three months after he had written to his Mother, as we have seen, he made the following entry in his private Journal :—

"Hardly a day has passed since I returned hither in Autumn last, in which I have not stormfully resolved to myself that I would go out of this dusty hubbub, should I even walk off with the staff in my hand, *and no loadstar whatever.* My wife, herself seemingly sinking into weaker and weaker health, points out to me always that I cannot go ; that I am tied here, seemingly as if to be tortured to death. So in my wild mood I interpret it. Silence on such subjects ! Oh ! how infinitely preferable is silence ! Perhaps, too, my wife is right. Indeed, I myself feel dimly that I have little to look for else than here. Be still, thou wild weak heart, convulsively bursting up against the bars. Silence alone can guide me. Suffer, suffer, if it be necessary so to learn. Last night, weary and worn out with dull blockheadism, chagrin (next to no sleep the night before), I sat down in St. James's Park and thought of these things, looking at the beautiful summer moon, and really quieted myself, became peaceable and submissive for the time,—for the time ; and afterwards, alas ! I was provoked, and in my weak state said foolish words, and went sorrowful to bed. I am a feeble fool. Fool, wilt thou never be wise ? " *

Poor worn-out, patient and impatient, heroic, devoted Wife ; poor stricken, helplessly entangled Prophet of a most high message ; what a fiery torture, striving in vain to quench itself, is here disclosed ! 'Not a May-game was this man's life.' Carlyle could never have denounced the manifold self-tainted sins of the world with his piercing energy of conviction, if he had not first desperately struggled with them in the privacy and self-conviction of his own heart. Perhaps that fiery torture was even a prophetic symbol of what our sins are rapidly bringing upon all earnest hearts amongst us ; for the whole world is even now struggling in pain to bring forth,—it knows not what !

* 'Life in London,' 1834–1881, vol. i. pp. 137, 138. "Consider, ye brutish among the people : and ye fools, when will ye be wise ? . . . He that chastiseth the nations, shall not He correct ? . . . Blessed is the man whom Thou chastenest, O Lord ! " (Psalm xciv. 8–12).

CHAPTER XI.

SURELY Carlyle's exhaustive biography of Cromwell may
be regarded as the most thorough and ' veridical ' of all
our records of English History.   It is almost Biblical
in its intense sincerity, and in the height and depth of
its sympathy and aspiration.   Carlyle does not call it
a biography, nor is it usually so spoken of.   But this is
mainly because the rugged facts have in no case been
tampered with, or chipped and rounded into an ideal
symmetry, according to the bias or fancy of the biographer.   Carlyle's one object was to make Cromwell
known to us, in his actual character, as he lived and
struggled and laboured in those strange Commonwealth
days.   He thought that, in these our own days of
incipient revolution, as he regarded them, it was of vital
importance that Englishmen should be able to distinctly
realise that such an Englishman had actually existed, and
that such a life had been actually lived.   He thought,
if Englishmen could be brought to clearly understand
their own Revolution as they understood and realised

the more recent French Revolution, that both the resemblances and the contrasts might be significant to them.

We are some of us apt to think that revolution in this country, and especially in these enlightened days, would partake of the character of a new social development, and constitutional struggle of bloodless heroisms, rather than that of an actual life-and-death antagonism, and remorseless overthrow of existing institutions. This seems to have been very much what Carlyle thought in the 'Sartor Resartus' days. But the study of actual Revolutionary History,—looking with his own eyes upon two such strangely contrasted revolutions as the English and French,—revealed to him deeper and more terrible springs of action than he had yet taken into his reckoning. He began to see, or at least to imagine that he saw, very clearly, that the overwhelming changes, sooner or later inevitable in this country, were not of a kind to be bloodlessly brought about, unless by an amount of heroic insight and deliberate self-denying courage, such as the world has seldom witnessed. Of course he did not expect his readers generally would accept this warning forecast of his. It would have been almost unparalleled in the history of the world if they had. But he thought, as he so often intimates, that there might be here and there a man who would see what he saw; and he always insisted that England's hope of a successful struggle through her hour of agony would depend first of all on this infinitesimal minority. Thus, in 'Past and Present,' he says,—

"Nor has the Editor forgotten how it fares with your ill-boding Cassandras in Sieges of Troy. Imminent perdition is not usually driven away by words of warning. Didactic

Destiny has other methods in store; or these would fail always. Such words should, nevertheless, be uttered, when they dwell truly in the soul of any man. Words are hard, are importunate; but how much harder the importunate events they foreshadow! Here and there a human soul may listen to the words,—who knows how many human souls? whereby the importunate events, if not diverted and prevented, will be rendered *less* hard. The present Editor's purpose is to himself full of hope. For though fierce travails, though wide seas and roaring gulfs lie before us, is it not something if a Loadstar, in the eternal sky, do once more disclose itself?"

It is not, as I have said, my business to show that Carlyle was either right or wrong in this matter. Let us say he was fanatically wrong, if it will give us any real comfort. All I now insist upon is, that no one will ever understand Carlyle unless he clearly realise that this was the deepest and clearest conviction of his heart.

All Revolutions begin in hope; and Carlyle, as we have seen, was hopeful enough in his grim bantering way when he wrote 'Sartor Resartus.' Even at this later time he had not lost hope. In fact, it was now stronger and deeper than ever; for he felt that in the character and career of Cromwell he had a parable to unfold, which could hardly fail to go straight to many a kindred heart, and do for them, in some measure, what it had already done for him. It had opened his own eyes to facts and terrible responsibilities in human life, which hitherto he had only half discerned. He no longer looked upon the poor 'dunce' as the one entirely fatal person; but saw, as he had never so realised before, that a perverted intellect is infinitely darker and more dangerous than an undeveloped or even stunted intellect;—that intellect without righteousness, or intellect devoting its whole strength to the lowest instead of the Highest ; to evil purposes, or to that which is untrue, or destitute of reality, is not merely futile, but ' poisonous, and forever hateful.' He once thought that all men meant essentially and ulti- mately the same thing ; only that some saw farther and more · clearly than others. Show your thought clearly enough, he would have said to himself, make your meaning practically intelligible to them ; and, if your purpose be a true and wise one, you will have all men virtually on your side. The life-and-death animosities of the Commonwealth struggle taught him a deeper lesson. That fierce conflict of consciences as well as of interests, in which the very hearts of men became audible to him by the intensity of their earnest- ness, or the recklessness of their desperation, taught him that earnestness alone was no security for well- doing ; that earnest men might not merely mean different things, but things utterly and for ever irrecon- cilable ; that what one man may cling to with absorbing love, another man may shrink from with intensest hate. Well might he seriously ask himself, What possible system of education could be devised to reconcile such antagonisms as he there saw in living and deadly struggle, .and which seemed to be again cropping up amongst us in new forms, perhaps for effectual and final settlement !

' It is a futile delusion,' we may almost hear him exclaiming, ' this of universal toleration. It only means that the time is not yet ripe ; that no one cares to risk his skin for nothing. Wait till the day of reckoning arrives, and then tell me what you think of unlimited toleration. The war-cries of the future are already in the air, some day every one of you will either choose practically between them, or else be trodden underfoot as of no account in the settlement. Meantime I will show you what Cromwell thought and did under similar circumstances. When the time comes, perhaps it may have lessons for you, as, even now, it has had for me.' The doubt in Carlyle's mind was not whether such times were actually coming upon us. This he thought ought to be evident to every thinking man. His anxious doubt was, whether or not they would come upon us like a thief in the night, and find us still incredulous and unprepared :—in short, whether our modern Cromwells and Able Men, of whom he always hoped there were many in England, would hold back until compelled at the eleventh hour to come to the front ; or whether they would or could peaceably come forward as practical statesmen, before the worst had arrived, to compel and guide us without bloodshed to a new and a nobler life. Either one or the other, he firmly believed it must inevitably be.

All this new moral discrimination clearly implies a remarkable change in Carlyle's practical convictions, thus to have come upon him at the meridian of his intellectual powers. He frequently refers to it as a kind of crisis, or new starting-point, in his moral growth. And from this time he constantly speaks of Cromwell as his typical hero, the man whom, of all men, it would be well if Englishmen could a little resemble. We might almost say that from this time Cromwell became to him what only Goethe had before been,—his hero-exemplar. Not perhaps that Goethe became less to him, but that Cromwell became more. In 1837 he wrote to John Sterling,—

"As to Goethe, no other man whatever, as I say always,

has yet ascertained what Christianity is to us, and what Paganity is, and all manner of other *anities*, and been alive at all points in his own year of grace with the life appropriate to that. This, in brief, is the definition I have always given of the man since I first knew him. The sight of such a man was to me a Gospel of Gospels, and did literally, I believe save me from destruction outward and inward. We are far' parted now, but the memory of him shall be ever blessed to me as that of a deliverer from death." *

If Goethe was a deliverer from death to Carlyle, then was Cromwell his awakener into a new and far more deeply earnest life. Not all at once did the change come upon him. He was for many years earnestly studying Cromwell and his times, before he realised the full meaning of the lessons they were teaching him. Four years he reckons it cost him in settling to his work, even after he had deliberately taken the subject in hand with a view to writing. "Four years of abstruse toil, obscure speculation, futile wrestling and misery, I used to count it had cost me, before I took to editing the 'Letters and Speeches.'" †
At first he seems to have thought of some kind of History of the Commonwealth Period; but he could not group it into coherence; and the more he studied the subject the more irresistibly his thoughts seem to have gathered around and centred in the person of Cromwell. Thus, in 1842, he wrote to his Wife,—

"Cromwell sometimes rises upon me here, but as a thing lost in the abysses. . . . I never yet was in the right track to do that book. Yet Cromwell is with me a fit subject of a book, could I only say of what book. I must yet hang by *him*. But, indeed, if I live, a new epoch will have to

* 'Life in London,' 1834-1881, vol. i. p. 123.
† 'Reminiscences, vol. ii. p. 226.

unfold itself with me.   There are new things, and as yet no
·new dialect for them." *

The new epoch did at last very sternly unfold itself
in him, and the new dialect, in due course, found full
and manifold utterance.   How greatly they both differed
from any previous epoch or dialect may be sufficiently
seen in the following extracts, which may be regarded
as giving the keynote to the whole working of his mind
while engaged upon the history of Cromwell and his
times.   What both epoch and dialect afterwards grew
to may be seen in the 'Latter-Day Pamphlets.'

"Here, of our own land and lineage, in practical English
shape, were Heroes on the Earth once more.   Who knew in
every fibre, and with heroic daring laid to heart, That an
Almighty Justice does verily rule this world; that it is good
to fight on God's side, and bad to fight on the Devil's side !
The essence of all Heroisms and Veracities that have been,
or that will be." †

"On the whole, say not, good reader, as is often done, ' It
was then all one as now.'   Good reader, it was considerably
different then from now.   Men indolently say, ' The Ages are
all alike; ever the same sorry elements over again, in new
vesture; the issue of it always a melancholy farce-tragedy, in
one Age as in another !'   Wherein lies very obviously a truth ;
but also in secret a very sad error withal.   Sure enough, the
highest Life touches always, by large sections of it, on the
vulgar and universal : he that expects to see a Hero, or a
Heroic Age, step forth into practice in yellow Drury-lane
stage-boots, and speak in blank verse for itself, will look long
in vain.   Sure enough, in the Heroic Century as in the
Unheroic, knaves and cowards, and cunning greedy persons
were not wanting,—were, if you will, extremely abundant.
But the question always remains, Did they lie chained, subordinate in this world's business; coerced by steel-whips, or

* ' Life in London,' 1834–1881, vol. i. p. 250.
† ' Cromwell's Letters and Speeches,' Introduction, chap. i.

in whatever other effectual way, and sent whimpering into
their due subterranean abodes, to beat hemp and repent; a
true never-ending attempt going on to handcuff, to silence and
suppress them ?   Or did they walk openly abroad, the envy of
a general valet-population, and bear sway; professing, without
universal anathema, almost with general assent, that they
were the Orthodox Party, that they, even they, were such
men as you had a right to look for ?—Reader, the Ages differ
greatly, even infinitely, from one another ! " *

"In Oliver's time, as I say, there was still belief in the
Judgments of God; in Oliver's time, there was yet no distracted jargon of 'abolishing Capital Punishments,' of Jean-
Jacques Philanthropy, and universal rose-water in this world
still so full of sin. Men's notion was, not for abolishing
punishments, but for making laws just : God the Maker's
Laws, they considered, had not yet got the Punishment
abolished from them ! Men had a notion, that the difference
between Good and Evil was still considerable ;—equal to the
difference between Heaven and Hell. It was a true notion.
Which all men yet saw, and felt in all fibres of their existence,
to be true. Only in late decadent generations, fast hastening
towards radical change or final perdition, can such indis-
criminate mashing-up of Good and Evil into one universal
patent-treacle, and most unmedical electuary, of Rousseau Sen-
timentalism, universal Pardon and Benevolence, with dinner
and drink and one cheer more, take effect in our earth.
Electuary very poisonous, as sweet as it is, and very nauseous;
of which Oliver, happier than we, had not yet heard the
slightest intimation even in dreams." †

Such was Carlyle's deliberate interpretation of the
spirit of the great Commonwealth Period ; and this
spirit he ever afterwards strove to reawaken in his own
slumbering generation. Need we wonder that he resolutely eschewed all artistic effects in his strenuous effort
to make that great struggle credible and visible to us ?

* 'Cromwell's Letters and Speeches,' Introduction, chap. v.
† Ibid., Introduction to section on the 'Irish War.

Far too anxious was he to enable his readers, each for
himself, to see and understand the actual Cromwell, to
put them off with any mere idealised picture of his
character and career.   Instead of this, he has given
us with scrupulous veracity, and in due biographic
sequence, every fact authentically known of his eventful
life, including every authentic letter and speech that had
come down to us.   That is to say, nearly three hundred
letters and eighteen speeches, some of them of considerable length.   And besides this, with his invariable painstaking industry, he has endeavoured to make each letter
and speech clearly intelligible to us by a graphic expla-
natory setting of all the current historical facts bearing
on the subject in hand that he had been able to gather.
Sometimes his bits of description are really wonderful in
their intense realism.   Of its kind, there is no grander
bit of writing in the English language than his picture
of the Battle of Dunbar.   We see, as if with our own
eyes, not merely the battle-field, and the opposing hosts
gathered for and rushing to the struggle, but as if into
the very faces, and even the very hearts, of the individual men.   No rhetoric, no grandly turned sentences ;
—and yet the memory of that life-picture is like the
memory of a grand and awful experience in which we
ourselves have shared.   No man ever did or could
picture a battle-scene, or the crucial agony of the battle,
like Carlyle.   But then perhaps no man ever had such
eyes for facts as he had.   Nothing that comes within
the range of his vision escapes him.   And nowhere has
he turned this great gift to more faithful account than
in the work in which he was now engaged.   Not only
by picturing the circumstances of Cromwell's battles,
and thus making Cromwell's own despatches read like

records of passing events; but by all manner of incidental explanations, comments, apostrophes, pathetic details, brief touching notes of tenderest sympathy, and sometimes even by bantering expostulation, he gives us such a living panorama of Cromwell's entire career, that we are almost tempted to pronounce it the only authentic chapter of English History that has yet been written.

But we are by no means indebted solely to Carlyle for this vivid and indisputable authenticity; and he doubtless had sufficient reason for not calling his work a biography. It is essentially an autobiography; but edited with a single-hearted thoroughness which I suppose has seldom been equalled or even approached. Carlyle was the first to discern that the letters and speeches of Cromwell, which, by a providence as wonderful as anything in his career, have come down to us, contain a quite exceptionally sincere record of the most important passages of his life; and that, by making them intelligible, everything would be done to elucidate his character that was now possible.

It is very remarkable how Cromwell, little as he was given to express himself in words, was constantly called upon, and even compelled, by the exigencies of his position, to explain almost every step of his unprecedented career. As a soldier he was bound to constantly report himself and his doings to the authorities then existing; and as Lord Protector he was repeatedly no less compelled to explain himself, his aims, his whole career, and his manifold anxieties and hopes, to his several Parliaments, and to those with whom he was practically associated. That by many he was often misunderstood, need not surprise us. How could official men of routine help looking upon him as an able, and sometimes terrible fanatic, needing the most cautious management, and all the packthreads of guidance and restraint their Liliputian ingenuity could fasten upon him? Or, on the other hand, how could the Levellers and other kindred spirits, earnest men who had fought with him in the frenzy of their own impractical faiths; who looked upon all government, however wise and impartial, as a sinful usurpation of authority; and who were eagerly expecting the time when all restraints would be thrown off as tyrannous fetters;—how could they understand Cromwell's awful conviction, that he held authority over them as the called and chosen servant of God? Many people in his own day entirely misunderstood him, in spite of all his earnest efforts to make himself intelligible to them. But, happily for us, the fact remains that he did explain himself; and perhaps we are in a better position to judge him fairly, now that we have his whole career before us, than even they were who listened to his words. He often solemnly declared his conviction that God would yet justify him, and reveal the integrity of his heart; but he could little have thought how thorough the justification, or how full and clear the revelation would be. He was only half understood by his closest friends. His life was an amazement to himself, and a bewilderment to the generation in which he lived. And, in the reaction which followed his death, his character was so execrated and befouled by those who succeeded him in authority, that for two hundred years his name remained a byword in history. But the tree he planted took root in the soil of England, and bears fruit among us to this day. The work he did, not as a soldier only, but much more as a statesman and chief governor; as a practical reformer of morals ; a liberator and protector of all sincere consciences ; a champion of wise freedom, only to be secured by wise restraint and mutual consideration and forbearance ; as a lover of God's truth, and a hater of falsehood and all evil ; as a man who would not palter with iniquity, wherever it showed itself in the light of day ;—in all these things the work he did was work which can never die. And now, after two centuries of almost total eclipse, not one of our great kings or queens, from Alfred to Elizabeth, stands visible and authentic before us like Oliver Cromwell.

One grand characteristic of Carlyle as a writer of history is, that he never tries to foist upon the reader his own views of a character, as if those views were the facts themselves. We are seldom left at a loss to know very clearly what his judgments are ; but his judgments, and the facts upon which they are based, are always kept veridically distinct. The reader's own judgment is thus left perfectly free, either to agree with him or to disagree. ' These are the facts, and this is what I think of them ; but let each man look with his own eyes, and judge for himself.' Perhaps few readers have yet realised the full value of this stern historic authenticity of detail. But one result of it is, that when we are obliged to differ from Carlyle, we are not therefore compelled to close the book, in disgust at the sheer impossibility of getting the truth out of it. The facts recorded remain unshaken. Perhaps they may become even more luminous to us than they otherwise would have been, by the very effort to which we are thus provoked to grasp their truer significance. But what is the poor student of history to do, if the straggling fibres of fact are so dexterously interwoven with what perhaps is no better than supposititious shoddy, that it is practically impossible to distinguish between them ?

Fortunately for the student of history he may differ very materially from Carlyle, and yet trust him implicitly. I am myself in that questionable position. Ever since I first read the 'Letters and Speeches,' now more than thirty years ago, I have felt that, in commenting on some important points in Cromwell's career, instead of over-applauding him, Carlyle had done him but scant justice ; in fact, that he had rather seriously misunderstood him. And yet I know comparatively little of Cromwell beyond what I have learnt from the facts which Carlyle has supplied. I see now, far more clearly than I did then, that Carlyle never practically realised some of the deeper spiritual elements of Cromwell's character. For one thing, in common with all the rest of the world, he never fully realised the really marvellous simplicity and entireness of Cromwell's trust in God ; his daily, hourly, momently, and in all cases looking to Him, for guidance and for His sanction, in all that he did. This simple trust was the source at once of Cromwell's invincible strength, and of his sometimes no less remarkable irresolution and painful hesitancies. So long as he inwardly knew that he was following the clear guidance of God, and was sustained by His sanction revealing itself in his heart, no arrow from the bow could be more direct in its aim, or, if need were, more swift in its course, than was his instant and irresistible resolution. But when, as often befell in his more trying experiences, the purpose of God was not yet as a light to his path, no child was more helpless than he, or more passionately cried from the transparent depths of a childlike heart, for guidance and comfort

through the darkness and agony of that awful suspense.
It was not always in his career that he was free to stand
aside, and trustingly await what he well called the
'births of Providence.' Awful responsibilities were
sometimes laid upon his conscience, when he knew not
what to resolve; when, do what he would, it must be a
thing that his heart shrank from, and an occasion of
stumbling to many whose consciences, he often pathetically declared, were dearer to him than his life. In such
lonely wrestlings of his soul, he cried passionately to
God to spare him, and if possible save him, even by the
release of death, from the terrible alternative. Sometimes the whole army seems to have been quickened by
this searching spirit of overpowering responsibility; and
then we read of prayer-meetings, day after day, in which
the strongest-hearted men in England were assembled
together to pour out the agony of their suspense, with
passionate tears and supplications to the Almighty to
reveal to them what He would in very truth have them
do. This stern, yet contrite spirit of responsibility was
then a very awful fact in England, and no one need
hope to understand Cromwell who does not recognise the
fact. Carlyle recognised it with utter amazement, and
with many self-searching reflections; resulting in what
he clearly felt and spoke of, as a 'new epoch' in his life.
But, although he thus clearly recognised the strange facts
of Cromwell's life and surroundings, they remained
strange. They never came right home to him. He saw
them from the outside, and from afar off. The stern
sense of duty, of responsibility to the Almighty Justice
ruling over all, was his own as well as Cromwell's; and in
this sense they were brothers. But Cromwell's tenderness
of conscience, his childlike and impassioned *waiting* for

God's guidance, and faltering sense of his own inherent helplessness, awoke no equal echoes in Carlyle's heart. He saw this phase of Cromwell's character, and declared it the divinest height a human soul could ever reach; but it remained a thing apart from his own experience. As he himself pathetically confesses, 'He *saw* Balder, the very Balder, with his eyes;—but could not bring him back!' The fact is, the characters of Cromwell and Carlyle were of essentially different types. There was no radical opposition between them; but they lived and thought and worked on different planes of purpose, intelligence, and conscience. Cromwell's was the simpler, higher, more spiritual nature of the two; but Carlyle was broader, more varied, and more distinctly intellectual. We do not first of all think of Cromwell's intellect; but of his simple heartfelt faith in God; his invincible courage and practical insight. With Carlyle, it is always the wonderful grasp of his intellect, his clear ethical discernment, and his iron strength and persistence, which strike us with astonishment. Cromwell could have lived gratefully contented, and not over-solicitous about 'happiness,' as a simple farmer, or, like David, as a keeper of sheep, had God so willed it. 'I would have been glad,' he says, in the last year of his life, 'I would have been glad to have lived under my woodside, to have kept a flock of sheep, rather than have undertaken such a Government as this.'

To this Carlyle makes the following characteristic rejoinder :—

"Yes, your Highness; it had been infinitely quieter, healthier, freer. But it is gone for ever: no woodsides now, and peaceful nibbling sheep, and great still thoughts, and glimpses of God 'in the cool of the evening walking among the trees:' nothing but toil and trouble, double, double, till one's discharge arrive, and the Eternal Portals open! Nay, even there by your woodside, you had not been happy; not you, —with thoughts going down to the Death-kingdoms, and Heaven so near you on this hand, and Hell so near you on that. Nay, who would grudge a little temporary Trouble, when he can do a large spell of eternal Work? Work that is true, and will last through all Eternity! Complain not, your Highness!—His Highness does not complain." *

Carlyle, 'from the shoulders upward' higher than his fellows, could never have been contented with less than the world for his arena. His intellect beat impatiently against the bars of his cramped environment, and tortured him with a constant sense of stifling imprisonment. He longed to find free scope for his irrepressible organising and social energies; and, not finding it, his life was the constant misery to him which we know. Very different was Cromwell's feeling in such matters. He never felt himself to be a man competent to do much good; as he once confessed to his Parliament, when Lord Protector: "I profess I had not that apprehension, when I undertook the Place, that I could so much do good; but I did think I might prevent imminent evil." This evidently was Cromwell's rule through life, and it is worth thinking of. If 'imminent evil' were threatening, and he felt assured that with God's help he could prevent it, then to him the call to action was clear, and imperative on his conscience. He dared not disobey it. If good also came of it, as good sometimes did far beyond his own imaginings, it was to him, not his own doing, but a gracious 'birth of Providence.' He admits that a case *may* occur, in which a man, 'if he deal deliberately with God and his own

* 'Cromwell's Letters and Speeches.' Comment on Speech XVIII.

conscience, may lawfully desire a Place to do good in.'
But this he thinks might savour of self-advancement,
and might prove 'a very tickle case,' of which he himself would evidently be shy.   Not so Carlyle, for he
immediately adds,—

" A tickle case indeed, his Highness candidly allows; yet
a case which does occur,—shame and woe to him, the poor
cowardly Pedant, tied up in cobwebs and tape-thrums, that
neglects it when it does !" *

" Window once more into his Highness !" says
Carlyle.   Yes, and into his Editor too, if we open it a
little way, and look around.   But both views are right,
if rightly followed out ; and one is but the complement
of the other.   At the same time, they mark very clearly
the different tempers of two such really kindred minds.
Carlyle was constitutionally, and sometimes almost
mercilessly impatient of mere spiritual perplexities and
struggles, and of all 'dubitations,' whether his own or
another's, which could not speedily end themselves in
decisive action of some sort.   Cromwell was a very great
contrast in this respect.   He not only had a very deep
layer of such painful experiences, but he tenderly sympathised with all consciences similarly oppressed, and no
less tenderly craved their sympathy with himself.   All
this was a weariness to Carlyle ; and we continually
find his impatient feelings irrepressibly breaking out in
his comments on Cromwell's Speeches to his Parliaments,
when in his sore difficulties he appeals to them for their
confidence and sympathy, and tries to lay his very heart
bare before them.

During what we may consider the first half of Crom-

* ' Cromwell's Letters and Speeches.'   Comment on Speech XI.

well's career, when he was leading on his terrible Iron-sides conquering and to conquer, advancing steadily step by step, through danger after danger, with clear eye and firm tread, as a man who knew his appointed work and did it fearlessly and thoroughly, at whatever risk to himself; and again, when he summarily turned out a Parliament grown faithless to its high trust before God and man, and tried to build up a better government in its place;—in all this, and all similarly decisive work, Carlyle's sympathy with him was perfect, and continued so to the end. Nothing can be keener or more appreciative than his eye for all Cromwell's administrative ability. He dwells upon his genius for guiding, organising, and governing, as if it was a revelation even to himself. In all such practical matters he looked upon Cromwell as his ideal King,—the man that *could*, and *did*. But he never could quite understand why Cromwell, thus placed at the head of affairs, not by his own seeking, but by the clear call of necessity, did not more frankly assert himself, and more resolutely seize the clear duties and responsibilities of his position. At this point, it must be evident to every careful reader, Carlyle and Cromwell distinctly part company. Cromwell never desired to be a King, or to be anything other than a faithful servant of God.

"Truly," he says, "I have, as before God, often thought that I could not tell what my business was, nor what I was in the place I stood in, save comparing myself to a good constable set to keep the peace of the Parish."

But we shall have to consider the matter of 'the Kingship' more in detail presently.

Let us now try to realise the essential characteristics of Cromwell's speeches to his several Parliaments. The first characteristic we may note in them is, the total absence of what Carlyle calls 'attorneyism;' that is to say, they never attempt to express anything but the speaker's own intense convictions. The second is, there is no artifice in them, either to arrest attention, or to give a pleasant flavour to unpalatable truths. The third, that they are not the words of a Dictator announcing his policy and giving not-to-be-questioned instructions from the throne; but the words of a plain man, speaking to his fellow-men directly from his heart; often in tenderest appeal, but sometimes in scathing expostulation; yet always anxious only to convince, and make himself understood. All these sterling characteristics, when directed to the despatch of business, were entirely after Carlyle's own heart. But sometimes Cromwell's very sincerity seemed to block the way of business. Cromwell, always bent upon convincing and not dictating, found himself again and again in a stress of responsibilities which his Parliaments could not realise, and which with all his efforts he could not make them understand. He exhorts, expostulates, reasons with them, appeals to all they know of his life, and God's marvellous dealings with him and with the nation; until his tender brooding patience seems to have known no limit. And then Carlyle's patience begins to totter; and he is ready to exclaim, as some one once wrote to him,* 'Leave off holding forth, and lay on!' Cases of conscience, as matters of speech, were not much in Carlyle's line; and certainly, if a man cannot realise a scruple of conscience when clearly

---

* Or, rather, appealed to Carlyle and his readers, in a brief practical letter to one of the weekly magazines, while the 'Latter-Day Pamphlets' were in the course of publication: a letter calling attention to the project of 'Queen's Members' put forward in 'The New Downing Street.'

laid before him, no urgency of endeavour will drive it into him ; as Cromwell often found to his sorrow, and as we also must try to recollect. And yet, however he may have failed with the majority of his listeners, there surely can be no doubt that he met with a deep enough response from the few whose hearts were earnest enough to follow him ; and it was to them, perhaps, that he more consciously addressed himself. My ' advanced ' readers must pardon me an occasional indulgence in such old-fashioned moralising ; for they must bear in mind that Cromwell's piety was altogether of the old-fashioned sort ; and there is really no other way of taking accurate account of him : he had not yet ' advanced ' beyond the tenderest aspirations of the psalms of David, the stern righteousness of the prophets, and his own old-fashioned yet heartfelt trust in the promise, ' He that endureth to the end shall be saved.' The day foretold, when ' many should run to and fro, and knowledge should abound,' and piety be laid up in lavender or trodden underfoot as of no account, had not yet dawned.

But there is another matter relating to Cromwell's speeches to which I must now solicit attention. Carlyle frequently refers to the imperfect and ' very accidental condition ' of reporting in those days. Some of the speeches are said to have been ' reported by one knows not whom.' Of one speech there are two independent reports, with ' considerable discrepancies in one important paragraph, which, however, with faithful insight prove mutually elucidative.' In another speech a paragraph is said to be ' irretrievably misreported ;' and on one occasion Carlyle exclaims, ' Never was such a Reporter since the Tower of Babel fell !' At the end of Speech XVII. we are introduced behind the scene, and shown how the report in that instance was actually concocted. As soon as the speech was done, Rushworth, Smythe, and the Writer of 'Burton's Diary' went to York House, and sat together till late, "comparing Notes of his Highness's Speech. Could not finish the business that night, our Notes being a little cramp. It was grown quite dark before his Highness had done; so that we could hardly see our pencils go, at the time." Cromwell himself seems to have taken no thought whatever about the reports; and on one occasion, when formally requested by the Commons to furnish them with a copy of a Speech, answered that "he did not remember four lines of it in a piece, and that he could not furnish a Copy."

Such, by Carlyle's own clear showing, was the very crude condition of reporting in Cromwell's time. And yet, strange to say, in commenting on the Speeches so reported, as he unfolds them before us, he almost invariably treats them as if they had been reported *verbatim*, as we should expect to find important speeches reported in our own day. Thus in Speech III., where there are some broken sentences, instead of concluding that the reporter had failed to follow, he says, "His Highness, bursting with meaning, completes neither of these sentences; but pours himself, like an irregular torrent, through other orifices and openings." On another occasion, in Speech IV., when, for anything that appears, it may have been the reporter who was staggered at what he was listening to, Carlyle says, " An embarrassed sentence; characteristic of his Highness." Again, in Speech V., "'Do themselves partly approve my plan,' he means to say; but starting off into broken sentences, as he is liable to do, never says it." Again, in the same Speech,

Cromwell says, 'The State is hugely in debt; I believe it comes to—— ' Upon this Carlyle adds, " Reporter cannot hear; on his Paper is mere Blank;—nay I think his Highness stutters, does not clearly articulate any sum." Perhaps, rather, the reporter knew better than to put on record the actual condition of the treasury; but surely the notion of Cromwell stuttering or mumbling over a plain statement of fact, which he was trying to make his listeners very clearly and solemnly understand, is not a likely one. And so, throughout the Speeches, there is a continual sprinkling of notes like the following :— " Sentence breaks down,"—" Sentence catches fire abruptly, and explodes here,"—" Sentence broken; try it another way :" and in one paragraph, of Speech XII., evidently consisting of mere reporter's jottings, we have the whole of the following interpolations to account for breaks in the sense :—" The sentence falls prostrate, and we must start again,"—" Sentence pauses, never gets started again,"—" This sentence also finds that it will come to nothing, and so calls halt,"—" Halt again. In what bottomless imbroglios . . . is his poor Highness plunging !" I am quite at a loss to understand how Carlyle, knowing what he did of the condition of reporting at that time, could have credited Cromwell with any such disjointed and sometimes meaningless utterances. I suppose that, while writing, his vivid imagination so intensely realised Cromwell as personally before him, that he could only think of his speeches as if he were actually listening to them; but what may well surprise us is, that he should have allowed his pictorial imagination to have made him so forgetful of his own unpictorial and corrective facts.

That this was the attitude of Carlyle's mind must be

evident to every one; and it is astonishing with what vividness he has kindled a similarly realistic conception in his readers. But unfortunately, in thus picturing Cromwell to us, he too often unconsciously overloads, and even warps, the essential simplicity of his character. It is not always the very Cromwell that is pictured to us, but too often Cromwell arrayed in mere Carlylean trappings, or else in Carlylean splendours. To me it is impossible to think of Cromwell as a man floundering before his Parliaments in a chaos of helplessly broken sentences, and bursting with meanings too big and varied for utterance, when he was really speaking to them on subjects, and in a cause, as familiar to him as his daily bread. He was not a man of many imaginations, in which he might haply chance to lose himself; but a man of the clearest and swiftest insight. He had no need to select his words, or to balance his sentences, either in writing or in speaking. He was essentially, and to his heart's core, an extemporaneous man, swiftly ready, both in speech and action, whenever there was peril to be averted. But it was one thing to express his meaning clearly, and quite another to make those who had no eyes for such meaning, see it. This was Cromwell's real difficulty; and, with all Carlyle's splendour and incisiveness of utterance, it was no less his own. I do not call Cromwell a great 'inarticulate' man, so much as a great unimagining man. He was foreseeing and farseeing, with hopes, not only unutterable, but unimaginable, —which no 'chamber of imagery' could localise or arrest. If he was inarticulate, it was not at all in the immediate duties of life, but in his inability to express his awful sense of God's dealings with His people. Sufficient for him, as his rule in life, were the responsibilities and possibilities of the day ; and for this no man was ever readier than he, whether in speech or in action : what the morrow would bring forth, was for him implicitly in the hands of God.   Thus he says, in Speech III., when dismissing his first Protectorate Parliament, " I have always been of this mind, since I first entered upon my office, If God will not bear it up, let it sink. . . . I called not myself to this place.   I say again, I called not myself to this place.   Of that God is witness. And I have many witnesses who, I do believe, could lay down their lives bearing testimony to the truth of that. But, being in it, . . . if my calling be from God, and my testimony from the people, God and the people shall take it from me ; else I will not part with it."   And again he says, in Speech IV., " I bless God I have been inured to difficulties ; and I never found God failing when I trusted in Him."

In strange contrast with such confiding singleness of purpose, Carlyle's far-reaching, hope-fed imaginations were at once the splendour and the terror of his life.   He did try most passionately to forecast the very shape and presence of the future, and to keep it as a 'Loadstar' before him ; and he never could quite bring himself to understand how Cromwell could have done otherwise. He saw with reverent appreciation the earnest entireness of his submission to the Divine Will, and his heartfelt shrinking from all attempts to forecast plans for the future, especially with reference to his own career ; but he never could quite appropriate the lesson to himself, and frequently credited Cromwell with aspirations and purposes utterly foreign to the almost plodding simplicity of his character.   Thus, in seeming to defend him from the customary charges of personal ambition, etc., he practically admits the charge, and eloquently justifies what he evidently could not doubt must have been a ruling passion in a man of such practical eminence.

"The love of 'power,' if thou understand what to the manful heart 'power' signifies, is a very noble and indispensable love. And here and there, in the outer world too, there is a due throne for the noble man;—which let him see well that he seize, and valiantly defend against all men and things. God gives it him; let no Devil take it away. Thou also art called by the God's message. This, if thou canst read the Heavenly omens and dare do them, this work is *thine.* Voiceless, or with no articulate voice, Occasion, god-sent, rushes storming on, amid the world's events; swift, perilous; like a whirlwind, like a fleet lightning-steed: manfully thou shalt clutch it by the mane, and vault into thy seat on it, and ride and guide there, thou! Wreck and ignominious overthrow, if thou have dared when the Occasion was *not* thine: everlasting scorn to thee if thou dare not when it is." *

Nothing can be grander than this picture of the fleet lightning-steed, with its firm-handed and dauntless rider compelling it to his will; and surely nothing could well be more eloquently said in behalf of what is fairly understood as an honourable, and even noble, personal ambition. But this is no elucidation of the character of Cromwell; it is simply unmitigated Carlyle. It is, however, of the first importance that this passionate outburst should be clearly apprehended; for it affords a key, not only to Carlyle's own character, but also to what I cannot but regard as his fundamental misconception of Cromwell's.

Let me here most emphatically say, or repeat, that I am by no means trying to throw any disparagement upon Carlyle, in thus frankly pointing out what I

* ' Cromwell's Letters and Speeches,' end of Part VII.

believe to be a serious misconception on his part. I honour Carlyle as, next to Shakspeare, the greatest, truest, and richest intellect in English Literature; and, if he had little of Shakspeare's sympathetic and almost omniscient insight into the workings of the merely human heart, or of his sunny exuberance of soul, and perfect balance of intuitive judgment, yet he had a kingly and sacred earnestness of purpose and effort to do the Good Will on earth of ' the Most High God,' of which Shakspeare gives but little indication. Of course it is not yet the fashion to say so, for Carlyle also must bide his time. But this is distinctly my own grateful conviction, and has been for many years. And not the least of my obligations to him, and, as I believe, of England's obligations, is, that he has given us this wonderfully conscientious and painstaking record of Cromwell, which will assuredly last as long as English History has any interest for England. It is easy for us now,—reading the book with fresh eyes, and profiting by all the labour Carlyle expended on it,—to see many points which he, in the characteristic concentration of his mind, overlooked; and even to discern elements of character which he failed to penetrate. But this is no disparagement of the book; it is the best certificate of its perennial value. Without further apology, I now beg the serious attention of any reader really anxious to understand both Carlyle and Cromwell, while I try to make clear two rather serious instances of the kind of misapprehension I have ventured to indicate. And I hope to make it clear that in these instances at least Cromwell really and simply said what he meant, and meant what he said.

CHAPTER XII.

THE first 'Protectorate Parliament,' being the Second Parliament summoned by Cromwell, was, as Carlyle says, not successful. The fact is, no sooner did the Parliament meet for deliberation, than Honourable Members took upon themselves to practically ignore the Authority which had called them together ; and, instead of looking to the practical condition of the country, and to the despatch of imperative business, they immediately set themselves to discuss the entire framework of the Government, as if nothing had yet been settled ; as if they were the only constituted Authority, and the actually existing Executive which had summoned them was holding office only on their sufferance. This was a piece of pedantic impertinence, and of gross trifling with the urgent requirements of the country, which neither Cromwell, nor his Council of State, nor his Council of Ironsides, were disposed to submit to. Accordingly, after three days of such bottomless discussions, the astonished Parliament was suddenly summoned to meet his Highness in the 'Painted Chamber;' when, in order to prevent any mistake for the future as to the mutual relations of Executive and Parliament, each member was required to sign a Declaration of adherence to the existing Government, whose call he had obeyed, before being again admitted to the exercise of his functions. It was a bitter disappointment to Cromwell, to be thus unexpectedly compelled to intervene by an exertion of his personal authority; and his address on the occasion (Speech III.) shows how deeply and how keenly he felt it.

This Speech was no Royal State-Manifesto, from the lips of one who 'loved power,' and having seized it was determined to keep it. It was just the passionate outpouring of a disappointed and overburdened heart; and marks the conscious beginning of Cromwell's sorest troubles and heaviest responsibilities. It is impossible to imagine a speech,—making all needful allowance for the incoherences of imperfect reporting,—more transparently, earnestly, and unaffectedly truthful. And it should be recollected that it was not merely spoken by Cromwell to the general Parliament, some of whom may have been comparative strangers to him and his doings, but also before men who knew him and implicitly trusted him, and whose confidence he was bound to keep: some of whom had been with him almost from the beginning, and could check off the truth of every word he uttered; and whom, he says afterwards (Speech IV.), ' I think truly would scorn to own me in a lie.' These were not men who loved ' power; ' but men who feared God, and loved their poor bleeding country. If they had loved power, by far their easiest course would have been to have kept it firmly in their own hands when they had once got it. Whenever they were driven to assume it, as they again and again were, through the impossibility of getting a working Parliament, their own course in carrying on the Government was clear and straightforward and effective enough. But both Cromwell and they felt that this was no lasting settlement for England; neither was it what they all longed for, and had been ready to spend their blood for. What they wanted was to see England governed in freedom and in righteousness; and, upon such terms, if they could only ensure them, the more voluntary and self-governed they could make it, the more deeply would they have felt that God had blessed their efforts.

In this Speech III., an extract from which has been already given, Cromwell tries to make them all clearly understand his position; and not only solemnly declares that he 'called not himself' to the post he held, but, after briefly recapitulating his dealings with the Long Parliament, he says,—

"I hoped to have had leave to retire to private life. I begged to be dismissed of my charge. I begged it again and again; and God be Judge between me and all men, if I lie in this matter. The *fact* is known to very many: but whether I tell a lie in my heart, as labouring to represent to you what was not upon my heart, I say the Lord be Judge."

He then gives a swift account of his earnest efforts to induce the Long Parliament to bring the Government to some just settlement, but which they would not listen to. And 'when they were dissolved,' he says, 'so far as I could discern, there was not so much as the barking of a dog, or any general and visible repining at it.'

He then carries his story a stage further; and, referring to the calling of the 'Assembly of Puritan Notables,' he says with solemn emphasis,—

"It is a tender thing to make appeals to God, yet in such exigencies as these I trust it will not offend His Majesty; especially to make them before Persons that know God, and know what it is to 'lie before the Lord;'" and then protests that, "as a principal end in calling that Assembly was the settlement of the Nation, so a chief end to myself was, to lay down the Power which was in my hands. I say to you again, in the Presence of that God who hath blessed, and been with me in all my adversities and successes,—that was, as to myself, my greatest end." At that time, "the Authority I had in my hand was boundless; for, by Act of Parliament, I was General of all the Forces in the three Nations of England, Scotland and Ireland; in which unlimited condition I did not desire to live a day."

His hope, however, of being able to lay down his power, or any portion of it, proved vain; for this First Parliament (known as the Little Parliament), after five months' earnest endeavour, choosing a Council of State and passing various good Acts, being finally unable to agree, —the Opposition to the extreme Gospel Party (an Opposition *not* consisting of Cromwell's special friends, be it noted) contrived unexpectedly to pass a resolution to 'resign unto his Excellency their said Powers. And Mr. Speaker, attended by the Members, did present the same to his Excellency accordingly.'

Cromwell now declares to his new Parliament, "I did not know one tittle of that Resignation, till they all came and brought it, and delivered it into my hands. Of this also there are in this presence many witnesses." With reference to this Resignation Carlyle tells us,—

"The Lord General Cromwell testified much emotion and surprise at this result. . . . From Monday (the day of resignation) onwards, the excitement of the public mind in old London and whithersoever the news went, in those winter days, must have been great. The 'Lord General called a Council of Officers and other Persons of Interest in the Nation;' and there was 'much seeking of God by prayer,' and abstruse advising of this matter,—the matter being really great, and to some of us even awful! The dialogues, conferences, and abstruse advisings are all lost; the result we know for certain. Monday was 12th of December; on Friday 16th, the result became manifest to all the world: That the ablest of Englishmen, Oliver Cromwell, was henceforth to be recognised as Supremely Able; and that the Title of him was to be 'Lord Protector of the Commonwealth of England, Scotland and Ireland,' with 'Instrument of Government', 'Council of Fifteen or of Twenty-one,' and other necessary, less important circumstances, of the like conceivable nature."

Let us now hear what Cromwell has to say in explanation of this matter; still, in the same Speech, addressing his new Parliament:—

"The Gentlemen that undertook to frame this Government did consult divers days together (men of known integrity and ability) how to frame somewhat that might give us settlement. They did consult; and that I was not privy to their councils, they know it. When they had finished their model in some measure, or made a good preparation of it, they became communicative. They told me that, except I would undertake the Government, they thought things would hardly come to a composure or settlement, but blood and confusion would break in upon us. I refused it again and again; not complimentingly, as they know, and as God knows. I confess,—after many arguments, they urging me, 'that I did not hereby receive anything which put me in a *higher* capacity than before; but that it *limited* me; that it bound my hands to act nothing without the consent of a Council, until the Parliament, and then limited me by Parliament, as the Act of Government expresseth,'—I did accept it."

We need not pursue the story further. This I humbly presume to say is Cromwell's case. Now, I ask any unprejudiced clear-hearted man or woman whether, upon the face of it, there is any shadow of equivocation in Cromwell's statement of the facts? The men of known integrity and ability, to whom he refers as having drawn up the Articles of Government, were there before him; and he appeals to them as witnesses to the absolute sincerity of every word he spoke. And yet this is what Carlyle strangely says about it:—

"'Divers persons who do know whether I lie in that,' says the Lord Protector. What a position for a hero, to be reduced continually to say He does not lie!—Consider well, nevertheless, What else could Oliver do? To get on with this new Parliament was clearly his one chance of governing peaceably."

But Cromwell's words are, "I have many witnesses who, I do believe, could lay down their lives bearing testimony to the truth of that. . . . And God be Judge between me and all men, if I lie in this matter." And as to 'governing peaceably,'—Cromwell's only notion of governing peaceably, or of governing at all, was governing in simple veracity of word, deed, and heart, by the grace and power of God. "I have been always," he says, " of this mind, since I first entered upon my office, —if God will not bear it up, let it sink." But Carlyle continues :—

"Again, with regard to the scheme of the Protectorship, which his Highness says was done by 'the Gentlemen that undertook to frame this Government,' after divers days' con-

sulting, and without the least privity of his: You never
guessed what they were doing, your Highness?   Alas, his
Highness guessed it,—and yet must not say, or think, he
guessed it."

And when he comes to the passage in the speech itself,
Carlyle sorrowfully droops his gaze, and cries " Alas ! "
Surely this is the most gratuitous slur ever unintention-
ally cast by one hero upon another whom he loved and
reverenced with his whole heart.   There is really no
foundation for it whatever.   Cromwell does not say it
was 'without the least privity of his.'   He merely says,
'That he was not privy to their councils,' they well
knew, and would be ready to testify; but that, when
they had roughly drawn up their plan, 'they became
communicative.'   This *can* only mean, and could, at
the time, only have been understood as meaning, that
he left them entirely to their own deliberations, and did
not interfere in any way; but conscientiously, and even
in pious awe, waited aloof until they voluntarily communicated with him, and laid their proposals before him ;
and even then he paused before the heavy responsibility,
and tried to dissuade them.   In other words, he reverently
waited, as in all cases, to see what God would really have
him do.   But always, when this was once clear to him,
his obedience was implicit, and his resolution immovable
as the foundations of the earth.

Let us now call to mind what Carlyle says about
a noble 'love of power;' and the difference between
valiantly seizing the due throne, and valiantly accepting
an awful responsibility, will be sufficiently apparent.

We have now to consider an even more serious, and
far more elaborate misconception on Carlyle's part,

arising almost entirely from this difference of moral or spiritual standpoint. I refer to his impatient comments on the spirit and manner of Cromwell's refusal of the Title of King.

"Readers," he says, "know what choking dust-whirlwinds in certain portions of 'the Page of History' this last business has given rise to! Dust-History, true to its nature, has treated this as one of the most important businesses in Oliver's Protectorate; though intrinsically it was to Oliver, and is to us, a mere 'feather in a man's cap,' throwing no new light on Oliver."

I agree with Carlyle in thinking that the question of Kingship was intrinsically one of very little importance in the actual business of the Protectorate; but, to the parties urging it, it was felt to be a very serious matter indeed; and certainly the spirit and manner of Cromwell's refusal of the Title throws a flood of light, not merely upon his character, but on his entire career.

It must be understood that the First Protectorate Parliament, already referred to, has been gone three years: an altogether unsuccessful Parliament: and that for some two years after, Cromwell governed the country by a system of 'Major-Generals.' All England was divided into Districts: Ten Districts, with a Major-General for each. This system seems to have worked fairly well, and the more dangerous spirits of insubordination had become sufficiently curbed. But the time had arrived for a renewed attempt at some approximate form of Parliamentary Government; and a Second Protectorate Parliament, from which the extreme Levelling elements had been rigorously eliminated, was now earnestly at work. But the limits of the respective functions of the Protector and the Parliament had not yet been defined with sufficient exactness, and difficulties arose.   One instance,—and perhaps the turning-point of such practical difficulties,—was the case of James Nayler, a mad fanatic, " fancying," says Carlyle, " or seeming to fancy himself, what is not uncommon since, a new Incarnation of Christ."   His case was solemnly brought before Parliament.

" Four-hundred Gentlemen of England, and I think a sprinkling of Lords among them, assembled from all Counties and Boroughs of the Three Nations, sat in solemn debate, for three long months and odd, on this terrific Phenomenon." And, as the result of their strenuous debates,—" the honourable Gentlemen set Nayler to ride, with his face to the tail, through various streets and cities; to be whipt (poor Nayler), to be branded, to be bored through the tongue, and then to do oakum *ad libitum* upon bread-and-water; after which he repented and confessed himself mad."

All this was done by them without any communication with Cromwell, the Head of the Government; and without even asking for his sanction to so severe a sentence. This naturally led Cromwell to ponder very seriously, what such high-handed proceedings, if unchecked, might ultimately grow to.   If such a case were allowed to pass into a precedent, any man's life might come to hang on the mere majority-vote of an excited Parliament.   Accordingly he addressed to the Speaker an official request for an explanation, ending as follows:—

" We, being entrusted in the present Government, on behalf of the People of these Nations; and not knowing how far such Proceeding, entered into wholly without Us, may extend in the consequence of it,—Do desire that the House will let Us know the grounds and reasons whereupon they have proceeded."

" A pertinent inquiry," Carlyle says; " which will lead us

into new wildernesses of Debate, into ever deeper wildernesses;—and in fact into our far notablest achievement. . . .
That of reconstructing the Instrument of Government upon a
more liberal footing, explaining better the boundaries of Parliament's and Single Person's jurisdiction; and offering his
Highness the Title of King."

It was necessary to recapitulate the initial points of
this great business, in order that we might have the
whole question before us, and might see how naturally
it grew to its subsequent dimensions. The Speeches and
Colloquies which followed, " reported by one knows not
whom," extended " from March to May of the year
1657, and were very private at the time." The original
movers, and most strenuous urgers in the matter were,
what we may call the Constitutional Party of the House,
by no means especially the friends of Cromwell. " The
Lawyer-party is all zealous for it ; certain of the Soldier-
party have their jealousies." The notion clearly was to
return as closely as possible to the old accustomed form
of Government. But it took much discussion before
the several suggestions grew into definite shape, or
before the title of King was definitely proposed. Meantime a " Deputation of a Hundred Officers " waited upon
Cromwell, " to signify that they have heard with real
dismay of some project now on foot to make his Highness King." Cromwell replied, that " he now specifically
heard of this project for the first time ; that he had not
been caballing about it, for it or against it : " and that,
as to the Title, " some of them well knew it had been
already offered to him, and pressed upon him, by themselves, when this Government was undertaken ; and
that the Title of King, a feather in a hat, was as little
valuable to him as to them." It is evident Cromwell

cared really nothing about any mere Title, either of one kind or another. But he did not think it wise, in the circumstances, to distinctly pledge himself to either side. He certainly was not prepared to accept the Title, as we shall hereafter clearly enough see; but to have summarily refused it at this stage of the proceedings, and even before it had been definitely offered, would have seriously disheartened the Constitutional Party, who were strenuously labouring for a settlement of the Government, and who looked upon a Constitutional King as an indispensable condition of any permanent settlement.

Probably at this time it was not quite clear to Cromwell what his duty might ultimately prove to be. If he could have been convinced that the peace and settlement of the country could not have been permanently secured without his acceptance of the title, I suppose there can be no doubt that he would have accepted it. Even his enemies would admit this, although they would have given a very different interpretation to his motives. There were many weighty arguments, and many important interests in the country, distinctly in its favour; and, for a time, it may well have been to him a very serious and somewhat inscrutable problem. He would wait, and listen patiently and warily to all that could be said on both sides. Meantime, I imagine that from the first his own private feelings, for reasons of his own, were distinctly repugnant; as I hope presently to be able to show. This is where I again join issue with Carlyle. Carlyle thought otherwise: he seems to have taken it for granted that Cromwell would have really liked to be King, if he could have accepted the title without giving serious offence to the more staunch

Republicans. He seems to have thought, How could such a man have a Kingship distinctly within his reach, and not desire to seize it ? But to Carlyle the Title of King was, and had always been, the express and highest symbol of Supreme Ability : his Able Man was always a King of men : and here was a man clearly recognised by the devoutest hearts in England, as the one Supremely Able Man amongst them ;—why, then, should he not receive the Title which clearly belonged to him ?

Let us now read Carlyle's own words on the subject :—

"Since the First constitutioning Parliament went its ways, here is a great change among us : three years of successful experiment have thrown some light on Oliver, and his mode of ruling, to all Englishmen. What can a wise Puritan Englishman do but decide on complying with Oliver, on strengthening the hands of Oliver ? Is he not verily doing the thing we all wanted to see done ? The old Parchments of the case may have been a little hustled, as indeed in a Ten-years Civil War, ending in the Execution of a King, they could hardly fail to be ;—but the divine Fact of the case, meseems, is well cared for ! Here is a Governing Man, unde-niably the most English of Englishmen, the most Puritan of Puritans, the Pattern Man, I must say, according to the model of the Seventeenth Century in England ; and a Great Man, denizen of all the Centuries, or he could never have been the Pattern one in that. Truly, my friends, I think, you may go farther and fare worse !" *

So the Parliament thought : and now they were about to solemnly recognise his greatness, by offering him the Title, as well as establishing him in the fact, of the King-ship of the country. Why should he not accept it ? To Carlyle, no sequence could be clearer or more reasonably

* 'Cromwell's Letters and Speeches,' Introduction to Speech VII.

inevitable.   There is your throne ; and, if you be the
man I take you for, you will seize it without scruple, for
it is verily yours !   But Cromwell had scruples.   He
knew that it was not his.   He knew and felt in every
fibre of his heart, that all thrones belonged to the King
of kings ; and that He would give them to whom He
would, and cast down whom He would ; and he dared
not take it, until assured of His sanction, as well as
man's.   That he was the actual Head of the Government he well knew ; and he sternly declared, against all
gainsayers, that he held his appointed post by as clear
and indefeasible a sanction as any King that ever
reigned.   But when he was asked to take up a Title and
return to an Order of things, against which in his eyes
God's judgments had gone forth, he hesitated.

" On Tuesday, 31st March, 1657, ' the House rose at eleven
o'clock, and Speaker Widdrington, attended by the whole
House, repaired to his Highness at Whitehall,' to present
their Petition and Advice, ' engrossed on vellum,' and with
the Title of King recommended to him in it."

The whole subject was thus at length definitely and
legitimately brought before him.   But he required time
to consider it, and replied accordingly.   Referring, with
a heavy feeling of responsibility, to the whole Frame of
Government thus submitted to him, he, cautiously, yet
with perfect frankness, says,—

" The thing is of weight ; the greatest weight of anything
that ever was laid upon a man.   And therefore, it being of
that weight, and consisting of so many parts, in each of which
much more than my life is concerned,—truly I think I have
no more to desire of you at present, but that you would give
me time to deliberate and consider what particular answer I
may return to so great a business.   I have lived the latter

part of my age in, if I may say so, the fire; in the midst of troubles. . . . And truly my comfort in all my life hath been, that the burdens which have lain heavy upon me, were laid upon me by the hand of God. I have been many times at a loss which way to stand under them, except by looking to the conduct and pleasure of God in it. . . . I have therefore but this one word to say to you,—That seeing you have made progress in this business, and completed the work on your part, I may have some short time to ask counsel of God and of my own heart. And I hope that neither the humour of weak unwise people, nor yet the desires of any who may be lusting after things that are not good, shall steer me to give other than such answer as may be ingenuous and thankful" (Speech VII.).

Three days afterwards a Committee of the House was invited to attend his Highness, and receive his deliberate answer as to their entire Frame of Government. It was already well known to them that Cromwell had scruples about assuming the proposed Title; but his reluctance was regarded more as a scruple of prudence on his part, than as a serious matter of conscience; and accordingly they tried to smoothe the way for him, and to give him a reasonable excuse for acceptance, by making it a condition that he should accept 'the whole Petition and Advice, or reject the whole of it.' He could not therefore in courtesy to them do otherwise. He speaks in the highest terms of some of the Articles, and especially of those providing for Civil and Religious Liberty; but then adds, to the utter disconcertion of their schemes and hopes,—

"Meanwhile give me leave to say, and to say it seriously, for the issue will prove it serious, that you have one or two considerations which do stick with me. One is, you have named me by another Title than I now bear. You necessitate my answer to be categorical; and have left me without a liberty of choice, save as to all. I question not your wisdom in doing so; and think myself obliged to acquiesce in your determination; knowing you to be men of wisdom, and considering the trust you are under. . . . But I must needs say, That may be fit for you to offer, which it may not be fit for me to undertake. . . . So you will not take it unkindly if I beg of you this addition to the Parliament's favour, love and indulgence to me,—That it be taken in tender part, if I give such an answer as I find in my heart to give in this business . . . namely, that I am not able for such a trust and charge. And, if the answer of the tongue as well as the preparation of the heart, be from God, I must say my heart and thoughts, ever since I heard the Parliament were upon this business (for, though I could not take notice of your proceeding without breach of your privileges, yet as a common person I confess I heard of it in common with others);—I must say, I have been able to attain no farther than this, That, seeing the way is hedged up as it is to me, and that I cannot accept the things offered unless I accept all, I have not been able to find it my duty to God and you, to undertake this charge under that Title. . . . Nothing must make a man's conscience a servant; and really and sincerely it is my conscience which guides me to this answer" (Speech VIII.).

What words could be more explicit, or more tenderly final, than these of Cromwell's, in which he distinctly declines the proffered dignity? Surely by any man with a conscience like his own, they would have been regarded as hopelessly final; for Cromwell believed, as earnestly and as entirely as Luther did, 'it is not *safe* for a man to do aught against conscience.' To me it is so like looking into Cromwell's very heart, that I would gladly forbear calling special attention to Carlyle's comments; for to quote them seems almost an impiety against himself. But the whole passage is too significant to be suppressed in our present inquiry; and it must even stand as it was written.

"Refuses," Carlyle says, "yet not so very peremptorily!"—

" His Highness would not in all circumstances be inexorable, one would think !—No ; he is groping his way through a very intricate business, which grows as he gropes ; the final shape of which is not yet disclosed to any soul. The actual shape of it on this Friday afternoon, 3rd April, 1657, I suppose he has, in his own manner, pretty faithfully, and not without sufficient skill and dignity, contrived to express. Many considerations weigh upon his Highness ; and in itself it is a most unexampled matter, this of negociating about being made a King ! Need of wise speech ; of wise reticence no less. Nay, it is of the nature of a Courtship withal ; the young lady cannot answer on the first blush of the business ; if you insist on her answering, why then she must answer, No ! "

Again I say, This is not Cromwell, or anything like him. It is the picture of a man, letting ' I dare not ' wait upon ' I would.' But, in saying this, it is only fair to Carlyle again to call to mind what a work he successfully accomplished in rescuing Cromwell's character out of what he well calls the very smoke of the Pit, and showing him to us in the light of day. Small wonder is it if he should have left a little of the sooty deposit still clinging. The wonder is that, coming thus unexpectedly upon a character distinctly aloof from his own personal experiences, he yet saw Cromwell as clearly as he did.

Carlyle continues,—

" Wednesday, 8th April, 1657. The Parliament, justly interpreting," or altogether misinterpreting, " this *No* of his Highness, has decided that it will adhere to its Petition and Advice, and that it will ' present reasons to his Highness ; ' has got, thanks to our learned Bulstrode and others, its reasons ready ;—and, this day, ' at three in the afternoon,' walks over in a body to the Banqueting-House ; Speaker Widdrington carrying in his hand the Engrossed Vellum, and a Written Paper of ' Reasons,' to present the same. . . . They are in the form of a Vote or Resolution, of date yesterday, 7th April, 1657:

"'*Resolved*, That the Parliament, having lately presented their Humble Petition and Advice to your Highness, whereunto they have not as yet received satisfaction; and the matters contained in that Petition and Advice being agreed upon by the Great Council and Representative of the Three Nations; which matters, in their judgment, are most conducing to the good of the People thereof both in Spiritual and Civil concernments: They have therefore thought fit

" 'To adhere to this Advice; and to put your Highness in mind of the great obligation which rests upon you in respect of this Advice; and again to desire you to give your Assent thereunto.'

"Which brief Paper of Reasons, Speaker Widdrington having read, and then delivered to his Highness, . . . his Highness, with a look I think of more than usual seriousness, thus answers the Assembled Parliament and him."

Before giving the necessary extracts from the short Speech which follows, I may mention that it is evidently far more imperfectly reported than most of them. Under the circumstances there may well have been some little delicacy about making a formal report of it. The Parliament could hardly have expected a final answer then and there. The utmost they could have aimed at, was to reopen the negotiation, and get Cromwell to reconsider the whole subject. In this they perfectly succeeded, although not with the result they hoped. Cromwell, as I have said, was as anxious as they were to come to a satisfactory agreement and settlement; but they had bound him down, either to accept 'the whole Petition and Advice,' including the Title, or to reject the whole. To this his answer had been as explicit and final as words kindly spoken could easily have made it. In again urging the matter upon him, and presenting

what they called 'reasons to his Highness,' without
again specially insisting on his acceptance of the whole
or none, they practically waived the point, and invited
him to a discussion of details from which they had previously debarred him. This was precisely what Cromwell desired. There were many other matters in the
Petition and Advice, besides that of the Kingship, of
vital importance to the country ; and he was most
anxious to find out, in a friendly spirit, upon what fundamental Articles they could really agree. It would
then be for them to consider whether they could accept
such Articles as the basis of settlement. Accordingly,
in replying to this second appeal to him, he is very
careful to avoid any further express decision upon the
one subject on which he felt that it could hardly be
possible for him to comply with their wishes, and to
which he had already given a sufficiently distinct negative. If any of them still hoped that he would eventu-
ally be induced to change that negative into an affirma-
tive, he at least gave no encouragement to the hope,
beyond assuring them that in this, as in all cases, he
would obey the clear monitions of God, if any of them
could show him his duty more clearly than he yet saw it.

" No man," he says, " can put a greater value than I hope
I do, and shall do, upon the desires and advices of the Parliament . . . and especially at such a time as this, when truly
I may think the Nation is big with expectation. . . . What
I have expressed, hath been, if I flatter not myself, from a
very honest heart towards you ; for we are all past complimenting, and all considerations of that kind : we must all be
very real now, if ever we will be so." You urge me to accept
your Advice, " but I would not lay a burden on my beast, but
I would consider his strength to bear it. . . . And if you lay a
burden upon a man who is conscious of his own infirmity and

disabilities, . . . I hope it will be no evil in me to measure your advice with my own infirmities. . . . And therefore, when I had an opportunity to make an answer to you, I made that answer which you know. And I have been, before then and since, a person lifting up my heart to God, to know what might be my duty, at such a time as this, and upon such an occasion and trial as this was to me. . . . And, to speak very clearly and plainly to you, I had, and I have, my hesitations as to that individual thing. If I undertake anything not in faith, I shall serve you in my own unbelief; and then I shall be the most unprofitable servant that any People or Nation ever had.

"Give me leave, therefore, to ask counsel. I am ready to render a reason of my apprehensions; which haply may be overcome by better apprehensions. I think, so far, I have deserved no blame; nor do I take it you will lay any upon me. Only you mind me of the duty that is incumbent upon me. . . . There are many things in the Instrument of Government, besides that one of the name and title, which deserve much to be elucidated by you. It is you that can capacitate me to receive satisfaction in them. Otherwise I must say truly, I am not persuaded of them as my trust and duty. . . . Truly I hope that, when I understand the ground of those things,—the whole being neither for your good nor for mine, but for the good of the Nation,—we may find out what may answer our duty: mine, and all our duties, to those whom we serve. And this is what I do, with a great deal of affection and honour and respect, now offer to you " (Speech IX.).

Carlyle now adds,—

" Thus has the Honourable House gone a second time in a body, and not yet prevailed. We gather that his Highness has doubts, has scruples; on which, however, he is willing to be dealt with, ' to receive satisfaction,'—has intimated, in fact, that though the answer is still No, the Courtship may continue."

Certainly that is one way of putting the case. But it hardly indicates the temper of a man who declares in solemn earnestness, "We are all past complimenting, and all considerations of that kind : we must all be very real now, if ever we will be so." The fact is, Cromwell was painfully, almost desperately anxious to carry the Parliament with him. He believed he saw his own duty in the matter of the Kingship, and possibly in the other 'many things' to which he refers ; but he wanted, if possible, that all should see it. If they could have convinced him he was wrong, he was 'a person who lifted up his heart to God, to know what might be his duty ;' and he would have done it. On the other hand, if he could have convinced them that he was right, his peace of mind would have been complete. 'Come let us reason together,' he said in the spirit of a brother, anxious only to do right ; and not at all in the spirit of 'I would, but dare not.' He was willing to listen with openness of mind to all they could urge in support of their views ; but he claimed the right of reply, and, above all, of freely deciding in the end according to his own conscience, on a matter in which he was personally responsible.

Accordingly, 'a Committee to give satisfaction is straightway nominated ; ninety-nine of them in all ; and is ready to confer with his Highness.' We need not now trouble ourselves with the somewhat wearying details of the interviews which immediately followed. But it is curious to note the evident reluctance on both sides to open the discussion. The Committee wished Cromwell to begin by stating his objections to what the Parliament had proposed to him ; they undertaking to do their best to reply to his difficulties. But this was not the view Cromwell took of the situation. This would have been practically to make them the final judges of the issue.　If they could have replied to all his objections to their own satisfaction, logically they would have expected him to have yielded, whatever his own scruples of conscience might still have been.　Cromwell virtually said,—but in cautiously respectful tones and words,—Not so; you found, when you came here, a Government already established, the authority of which you acknowledged by coming.　You now propose certain changes, some of which, and especially this of the change of Title, do not seem to me advisable.　It is for you to explain why you propose them.

This was the position which Cromwell took from the beginning of the conference.　And I look upon his scrupulously careful, preliminary marking-out of the ground, as in itself conclusive evidence that he was thoroughly in earnest.　If he had been looking for a reasonable excuse for accepting the Kingship, he would have allowed himself to be caught in the net which the Committee so warily laid for him.　It is strange that Carlyle did not realise the crucial significance of this preliminary skirmish.　He had got the ' Young Lady ' theory into his head; and he made it do duty to the end of the chapter.　Thus he says, " All men are very uncertain how to act.　Who shall begin?　His Highness wishes much *they* would begin; and in a delicate way urges and again urges them to do so; and not till after great labour and repeated failures, succeeds."　And again, ,"What curious pickeering, floundering, and fencing backwards and forwards, before the parties will come to close action !　As in other affairs of courtship."　Then he puts such interpretive words into Cromwell's mouth as these : " I had counted on being drawn out, not on COMING out : I understood I was the young lady, and YOU the wooer!" Surely all this is quite unworthy both of Carlyle and of Cromwell; and I should much like, for Carlyle's sake, even more than Cromwell's, to see an edition of the 'Letters and Speeches' in which all these mere flippancies of an impatient temperament were charitably expunged.

CHAPTER XIII.

Arguments for the Kingship—Cromwell's Reply—How he enlisted the 'Ironsides'—God's dealings with the Nation—'I will not seek to set up that which His Providence hath laid in the dust'—Cromwell's painful isolation—Carlyle with the Philistines—Further arguings, and end of the discussion—'I cannot undertake this Government with the Title of King'—Carlyle's impatient yet almost boundless admiration—Indications of the 'new epoch' in himself, and of his unspeakable hope for England.

THE question of the Kingship was to Cromwell one of the most solemn and trying questions he had ever been personally called upon to answer ; and, if we would really understand his conduct in the matter, we must try to look at it in something like the same earnest spirit. We have seen that, by patient persistence, he at last succeeded in compelling the Parliamentary Committee to state their reasons for urging him to consent to the change of title, notwithstanding his having so distinctly expressed his utter repugnance to it. Let us now consider what those Reasons were ; and it will soon be evident that the Constitutional Party knew very clearly what it was they really wanted. It was no obsequious or courtly compliment they were paying to Cromwell, and neither they nor he so understood it ; although some of them would not, perhaps, have been displeased if they could have induced him to accept it as such. What they wanted—and especially the legal part of them who were the chief movers in the matter—was to return, as nearly as possible, to the old-established constitutional form of Government, which they understood, and which, only, they could look upon as a final settlement of the country. The really weighty Reasons which they now urged for consideration were as follow:—

1. "If we keep the title of Protector, our Instrument of Government will only have its own footing to rest upon ; but with that of King, it will ground itself in all the ancient foundations of the Laws of England."

2. "The whole body of the Law is based upon the Chief Magistrate being called King. The title of Protector is not limited by any known rule of Law ; the title of King is."—"It is the voice of the Three Nations that offers your Highness this Title."

3. Then comes a very practical consideration, which could hardly have failed to carry great weight with every one of them. None could know how long this new order of things might last. If it broke down,—as it actually did at Cromwell's death,—what would become of them all !—".By an Act already existing (the 11th of Henry VII.), all persons that obey a 'King *de facto*' are to be held guiltless ; not so, if they serve a Protector *de facto*."

It cannot be denied that these are all very serious and very practical considerations: and we need not wonder that the Constitutional Party should have strained every nerve, and every argument they could think of, to get them practically recognised by Cromwell ; or, on the other hand, that Cromwell should have felt himself placed in a most difficult, and seemingly most ungracious position, in being compelled by his own personal scruples

o

to reject them. This is precisely what Cromwell did feel ; but he also felt in his inmost soul, like Luther, that there could be no real safety in doing aught against conscience. We may call him a fanatic if we like. He certainly was not a mere truster in Constitutions. He did not believe in the power of any Constitution to uphold a nation : he believed only in the power of God. 'If God will not hold it up, let it fall.' This had been his rule of life from the beginning ; and he had 'never known God fail him, when he trusted in Him.' He believed that he was upholding the Cause of God in the country ; and that so long as God sustained it, it would stand ; but not a day longer, let who would try to avert the inevitable by constitutional props and kingly prestige.

With such feelings,—and in this heartfelt and contrite Trust in God, which is ' the key of David ' we read of,—Cromwell tried, very seriously and very tenderly, to show the Parliamentary Committee that, though there was great weight and cogency in the reasons which they had offered, yet their arguments were not conclusive as to the actual necessity of the change proposed. He tells them they admit that the Kingship is not a mere Title, but a practical Office. And, he argues, if this be so, then it is the *Office*, and not the mere Name, which is so interwoven with the fundamental Laws of this Nation, that they could not well be executed without it. But I must now simply and faithfully condense his own words. He says,—

"The title King, is simply a Name of Office plainly implying the Supreme Authority. But if that Supreme Authority actually exists, I should suppose that whatever name hath been, or shall be, the Name under which that Supreme Authority acts, would carry with it a like significance, and could equally run through the whole of the Laws. If this be so, why then I should say, there is nothing of *necessity* in your argument; and all turns on a consideration of the expedience of it. Truly, if I had to choose, and if it had not been already settled, I had rather have any name from this Parliament, than any other name without it: so much do I value the authority of this Parliament. And, undoubtedly, what the Parliament settles, is what will 'run through the Laws.' It is in your power to dispose and settle; and, beforehand, we can have confidence that what you do settle will be as authentic as the things that were of old, and especially as to this thing of the name or title. In proof of this, let us look to our own experience. It is a short one; but a true one, and is known to you all in the fact of it. The Supreme Authority, going by another name and under another title than that of King, hath been already twice complied with. (In the case of the Long Parliament, and now in that of his own Protectorate.) And truly I may say, that almost universal obedience hath been given by all ranks and sorts of men to both. And, as for my own part (my own Protectorate), I profess I think I may say,— since the beginning of that change to this day, there hath not been a freer procedure of the Laws in this country. I do not think, under favour, that the Laws have had a freer exercise, more uninterrupted by the hand of Power; or that the Judges have been less solicited by letters or private interpositions, either of my own or other men's. And, if more of my Lords the Judges were here than now are, they could tell us, perhaps, somewhat farther. And therefore I say, under favour, these two experiences do manifestly show that it is not a *Title*, though never so interwoven with the Laws, that makes the Law to have its free passage, and to do its office without interruption, as we venture to think it is even now doing.

"I hope it will be understood, that I am not contending for the present name, or for any name; but that I am truly and plainly speaking, as in the Lord's presence. For truly I have, as before God, often thought that I could not tell what my business was, nor what I myself was, in the place I stood in, save comparing myself to a good Constable set to keep the peace of the Parish. I say therefore, I do judge, for myself, there is no such necessity for this name of King; for other names may do as well.

"But I must now say a little,—for I think I have somewhat of conscience to answer as to the matter,—why I cannot undertake this name.

"I am a person who, from my first employment, was suddenly preferred and lifted up from lesser trusts to greater, from being a Captain of a Troop of Horse; and did labour as well as I could to discharge my trust: and God blessed me as it pleased Him. I had a very worthy friend at that time; and he was a very noble person; and I know his memory is very grateful to you all,—Mr. John Hampden. Upon first going into this business, I saw that our men were beaten on every hand; and I urged him to make some additions to my Lord Essex's Army of some new regiments; and told him I would be serviceable to him in bringing such men in as I thought had a spirit that would do something in the work. I did so: and truly I must needs say this to you,—impute it as you please,—I raised such men as had the fear of God before them, as made some conscience of what they did. And, from that day forward, I must say to you, they were never beaten; and, wherever they were engaged against the enemy, they beat continually. And truly this is a matter of praise to God; and hath some instruction in it to the religious and godly. I will be bold to apply this to our present purpose, because it is my all.

"I tell you there are such men in this Nation; godly men, of the same spirit. And, to deal plainly and faithfully with you, I cannot think God would bless an undertaking of anything which would, justly and with cause, grieve them. True, they may be troubled without cause; and I must be a slave if I should comply with any such humour as that. But I say, there are honest men and faithful men, true to the great things of the Government, who in their consciences cannot swallow this Title. And I must say, it is my duty and my conscience to beg of you, that there may be no hard things put upon me, or upon them. If the Nation may be as well provided for, without these things we have been speaking of,—as, according to my apprehension, it may,—then truly I think it will be to you, as it was to David in another case, 'no grief of heart in time coming' that you had a tenderness even for what may seem weakness, in those who have integrity and faithfulness, and are not despisers of authority.

"I will now say something for myself. As for my own mind, I do profess I am not a man scrupulous about words, or names, or such things. But I must needs say, I have had a great deal of experience of Providence. And truly the Providence of God hath laid aside this Title of King providentially *de facto:* and that not by sudden humour or passion; but it hath been by issue of as great deliberation as ever was in a Nation. I will not defend the justice of what was done; nor will I tell you what my opinion is, in the case were it *de novo* to be done. But it was not done by me, nor by them that tendered me the Government I now act in. It was done by the Long Parliament. And, to me, God hath seemed Providential, not only in striking at the Family; but to the very eradication of the Name and Title. It is blotted out: it is a thing cast out by an Act of Parliament; and it hath been kept out to this day. And, as Jude saith, speaking of abominable sins that should be in the Latter Days, we should 'hate even the garments spotted with the flesh.' God hath seemed so to deal with the Persons and the Family, that He blasted the very Title! And, when we come, *a parte post,* to reflect; and have seen this actually done, this Title laid in the dust, I confess I can come to no other conclusion. The like of this may make a strong impression upon such weak men as I am; and perhaps upon weaker men, if there be such, it may make even a stronger. I will not seek to set up that which Providence hath destroyed, and laid in the dust. I would not build Jericho again! This, in truth it is this, that hath an awe upon my spirit.

" I would not that you should lose any servant or friend who might help in this work; or that any such should be offended by a thing of no more practical importance than this. I do not think the thing necessary : I do not. I would not that you should lose a friend for it. I may say, that I cannot with conveniency to myself, nor with good to this service which I wish so well to, speak out all my arguments as to the safety of your proposal, and its tendency to the effectual carrying on of this Work ; but I shall pray to God Almighty, that He would direct you to do what is according to His will. And this is that poor account I am able to give of myself in this thing " (Speech XI.).

This, in condensed form, but in his own words, is Cromwell's emphatic reply to all arguments of statecraft and worldly prudence ; showing very frankly and very tenderly why he cannot, and even dare not, accept the Kingship. To me it is amazing that any one of average intelligence, knowing anything of Cromwell's character, of the earnestness of his convictions and the clear decisiveness of his judgment, could have regarded it as anything else than his final word on the subject. And yet the Parliamentary Committee seem to have listened to this earnest appeal to their consciences and charitable forbearance, and what to Cromwell were the manifest Judgments of God, as if to mere evasive words spoken to gain time. Ears had they, but they heard not. It is almost pathetic to see with what easy persistence these really able statesmen and skilful debaters return to the charge, repeating the old arguments in new phrases, as if all this sensitive outpouring of Cromwell's inmost heart were the merest moonshine which he was only waiting to be enticed out of. Nothing shows more touchingly, and even tragically, the painful isolation of his position, than this blank unconsciousness on their part that he had as yet said anything at all conclusive on the subject. What *could* he say, or what could now be said, to convince such minds ? He felt that the task was hopeless, as it always must be when there is no common ground of perception ; and yet he persisted to the end, praying that God might do for him and them what he himself was powerless to accomplish. Through-

out these speeches he appeals to them again and again
to believe that he gives, as he says, 'such answers as are
not feigned in my thoughts, but such wherein I express
the truth and honesty of my heart;' and the very
earnestness and repeated emphasis of his asseverations
have been looked upon as a 'ground of suspicion' against
him.   Cromwell was not testifying to himself, but to
the presence and power of God.   God verily did all this
before your own eyes, as I well know to my heart's
core; and yet you will not trust in Him.   Well might
he say to them, 'This is very true that I tell you; God
knows I lie not.'—All this, I should say, is a ground for
something very different from suspicion; and it may
well be believed that some of his listeners thought so
too.*

But the strangest thing to me is, that Carlyle in this
matter should have gone over so frankly to the Philistines.   He believed absolutely in Cromwell's sincerity,
and yet he could not see that Cromwell had clearly
spoken his final decisive words on the matter of the
Kingship.   I feel bound to lay some stress on this point,
because it marks so sharply the special deficiency in
Carlyle's own mind.   Few could see, or picture with
more accurate precision than he did, the outward characteristics of a man's life and personality; but for all
the struggles and misgivings of conscience which might

---

* To show that Cromwell was not alone in such passionate and reiterated asseverations of his integrity before God, when speaking of God's
dealings with him, I will content myself with calling attention to the two
following instances from Paul's Epistles :—'The God and Father of the
Lord Jesus, He who is blessed for evermore, knoweth that I lie not'
(2 Cor. xi. 31).   And again : 'Now touching the things which I write
unto you, behold, before God, I lie not' (Gal. i. 20).   Paul, in each of
these instances, had been recounting very parallel experiences, of comfort
amid disaster, to those of Cromwell.

be going on within, he had little or no intuitive sympathy. Cromwell as a man of decisive action was distinctly intelligible to him; but Cromwell, helpless and weighed down with tender scruples of conscience, was disappointingly unheroic: he was sorry for him, but was glad to get away from it all. Not the motive of a man's conduct, but the conduct itself, so that it was sincere and manful, was the essential thing to Carlyle. 'How can we judge of a man's motives?' people continually say; and yet it is the one thing of everlasting interest about him. Until we know something of the character of a man's motives, we cannot be said to know him at all. Cromwell, in these speeches, not only shows us his outward conduct, but also the very springs of action as they well up from his wearied heart. All this Carlyle was constitutionally unable to picture to himself, and he impatiently hurries on to more congenial topics. Upon this remarkable Speech we still have such comments as this: "The Young Lady will, and she will not;" and he concludes by saying, "And so enough for Monday, which is now far spent: 'till to-morrow at three o'clock' let us adjourn; and diligently consider in the interim."—"His Highness is evidently very far yet from having made up his mind as to this thing; the undeveloped Yes still balancing itself against the undeveloped No, in a huge dark intricate manner with him."

On the morrow, Tuesday, the Committee attending at Whitehall finds his Highness unwell, which we need hardly wonder at; are to come again on Wednesday. Wednesday they come again; but his Highness is still too unwell to see them, and appoints Thursday.

"Thursday, 10th April, 1657," Carlyle continues, "Committee attending for the third time, the Interview does take

effect.   Six of the Grandees . . . take up in their order
the various objections of his Highness's former Speech, of
Monday last, and learnedly rebut the same, in a learned and
to us insupportably wearisome manner; fit only to be entirely
omitted.   Whitlocke urges on his Highness,—That, in refusing
this Kingship, he will do what never any that were actual
Kings of England did, reject the advice of his Parliament.
Another says,—'It is his duty; let him by no means shrink
from his duty.' . . . His Highness said, These were weighty
arguments; give him till to-morrow to think of them."

Accordingly on the morrow they are once more in
attendance, full of hope in the persuasive power of their
own eloquence.   Let us now, with them, listen as we
can to Cromwell's somewhat curt reply; and candidly
ask ourselves whether or not it is sufficiently explicit.
He thus addresses them :—

"I have, as well as I could, considered the arguments used
by you the other day, to enforce your conclusion as to that
Name and Title.   I will not now spend your time nor my
own much, in recapitulating those arguments, or giving
answers to them; for I think they were but the same we
formerly had, only with some additional inforcements by new
instances.   And truly, at this rate of debate, I might spend
your time, which I know is very precious, very unprofitably.
I will therefore say a word or two to that only which I think
was new.

"Your arguments founded upon the Law do all make for
the Kingship.   Because, say you, it doth agree with the Law:
the Law knows it; and the People know it, and are likelier to
receive satisfaction that way.   But those are arguments that
have been used already; and truly I know nothing that I
have to add in reply to them.   And therefore I say, those
arguments may stand as we found them and have left them
already.   Except, truly, this,—It hath been said to me, that I
am a person who meditate to do what never any that were
actual Kings of England did: Refuse the Advice of Parliament.   I confess that runs deeply enough: that may be

accounted a very great fault in me; and may even rise up in judgment against me another time, if my case be not different from any man's that ever was in the Chief Command and Government of these Nations before. But truly I think all that have been in this Office before, were inheritors coming to it by birthright; or, if owned by the authority of Parliament, they yet had some previous pretence of title or claim to it. But I have no such Title to the Government of these Nations: but only what was taken up in a case of necessity, and as a temporary means to meet the actual emergency without which the country must needs have been thrown into utter confusion. That was visible to me as the day, unless I undertook it: and so it was put upon me, I being then General by Act of Parliament. And now I say,—speaking in the plainness and simplicity of my heart, as before Almighty God,—when I did, out of necessity, undertake that which I think no man but myself would have undertaken, it hath since pleased God that I have been instrumental in keeping the peace of the Nation to this day. And this I may further say: I have not desired the continuance of my power or place, either under one title or another. If the wisdom of this Parliament,—and I speak not this vainly or as a fool, but as to God,—if the wisdom of this Parliament had found a way to settle the interests of this Nation, upon the foundations of justice and truth and liberty, to the people of God and the concernments of men as Englishmen, I would have lain at their feet, or at anybody else's feet, that things might have run in such a current. I say I have no pretensions to things for myself; to ask this or that, or to avoid this or that. I know the censures of the world may quickly pass upon me; but I thank God, I know where to lay the weight that is laid upon me; I mean the weight of reproach and contempt and scorn that hath been cast upon me.

"I have not offered you any Name in competition with Kingship. I know the evil spirits of men may easily cast it upon a man, that he would have a Name which the Laws know not, and which is boundless, and one under which he may exercise more arbitrariness. But I know there is nothing in that argument; for, whatever the Name, you would bound

it and limit it sufficiently. And I wish it were come to this:
that no favour should be shown me; but that the good of
these Nations should be consulted, as I am confident it will
be by you in whatever you do. But I may say a word to
one thing which doth a little pinch upon me :—'That it is
my duty to accept this Title.' I think it can be no man's
duty but between God and himself, if he be conscious of his
own infirmities, disabilities and weakness; and I say, I do
not know what way it can be imputed to me for a fault, or
laid upon me as a duty.

"You will pardon me that I speak these things in such a
way as this. I may be borne withal, for I have not truly well
stood the exercise that hath been upon me these three or four
days. I have told you my thoughts, and have laid them
before you. You have been pleased to give me your grounds;
and I have given you mine, speaking to you out of the abundance of difficulty and trouble that lies upon me. Any man
may give me leave to die; every one may give me leave to be
as a dead man, when God takes away the spirit and life and
activity that are necessary for the carrying on of such a
work " (Speech XII.).

And so ends this discussion on the question of the
Kingship. Cromwell does not say peremptorily that
he will not accept it : he only tells them, with the passionate emphasis of his whole moral and spiritual convictions, that he cannot and dare not accept it; evidently
hoping they would be considerate enough to spare him
the pain and seeming ungraciousness of a positive
refusal. And all this gracious weakness, and tenderness
for others, was exhibited, at the very moment of his
highest exaltation, by the strongest and most courageous
heart that ever ruled the destinies of England. 'Blessed
are the poor in spirit : for theirs is the kingdom of
Heaven.' 'Poor-spirited,' indeed, some of his would-be
tempters must have thought him ; and he was quite
willing to be so estimated. Without any further posi-

tive Yes or No, he, with quiet dignity, but with a
bruised and wearied heart, invited them to meet him
the next day, to discuss the other more practical points
of their proposed Instrument of Government ; and, not
till every other point had been mutually settled, did he
again refer to the Kingship, which he has been supposed,
all through the discussion, so much to have coveted.
Finding, at the last, that they still persisted in urging
it upon him, he tells them plainly, but still as delicately
as he can contrive to say it,—

"Truly this is my answer, That, although I think the Act
of Government doth consist of very excellent parts, in all but
that one thing, of the Title as to me, yet I should not be an
honest man, if I did not tell you I cannot accept of the
Government, nor undertake the trouble and charge of it,—as
to which I have a little more experimented than everybody,
what troubles and difficulties do befall men under such trusts,
and in such undertakings,—I say, and I am compelled * to
return this answer to you, That I cannot undertake this
Government with the Title of King. And that is mine
answer to this great and weighty business " (Speech XIV.).

To this Carlyle adds,—

"And so *exeunt* Widdrington and Parliament. . . . 'The
Protector,' says Bulstrode, ' was satisfied in his private judgment that it was fit for him to accept this Title of King,' and
matters were prepared in order thereunto. But afterwards,
' by solicitation of the Commonwealth's men,' by solicitation,
representation and even denunciation from the ' Commonwealth's men ' and ' many Officers of the Army,' he decided
' to attend some better season and opportunity in the business,
and refused at this time.' With which summary account let
us rest satisfied.".

* ' Persuaded ' is the word Cromwell uses ; but he means ' persuaded
in his own conscience,' which compels him to give this undesired answer.

Let us rather pause in wonder at so significant an instance of clear daylight being mistaken for thick fog; and when we have sufficiently read the solemn lesson it ought to convey to us, let us consign all needless criticism to charitable oblivion. Oh for a little earth, in which to bury from human memory all such spiritual ineptitudes!

Of all the troubles of Cromwell's life, his troubles with his Parliaments were the greatest and sorest. The rest of the Petition and Advice, Carlyle says, was accepted; "a much improved Frame of Government; with a Second House of Parliament; with a Chief Magistrate, who was to 'nominate his successor,' and be King in all points except the name;" and this First Session of the Parliament with which we have been more specially concerned seemed to close auspiciously enough. But the very next Session "proved entirely unsuccessful; perhaps the unsuccessfullest of all Sessions or Parliaments hitherto," whatever the future may yet have in store for us. Under the New Constitution a number of refractory spirits got in, upon taking the prescribed Oath accepting the 'Frame of Government' thus guaranteed; and then at once proceeded, by methods not unknown in our own days, to make Parliamentary government impossible. Cromwell bore with it, with an aching and disappointed heart: expostulated with them in one of the most solemnly earnest of his speeches that have come down to us (Speech XVII.); and finding, after sore strugglings both with them and with his own conscience, that all he could do or say was of no avail to bring them to a wiser sense of their duty to their country, and that their reckless contumacy and practical violation of the oath they had taken was on the very eve of precipitating the

whole country into a scene of renewed bloodshed, finally
dismissed them,—concluding his last speech to them,
greatly to their astonishment (and as Carlyle says, 'sentence now all beautifully blazing !') in these decisive
words : " If this be the end of your sitting, and this be
your carriage, I think it high time that *an end be put to
your sittings.* I DO DISSOLVE THIS PARLIAMENT ! And
let God be Judge between you and me" (Speech XVIII.).

It was Cromwell's last attempt at Parliamentary
government. In seven months from the date of this
speech he was released from his heavy responsibilities,
and no Parliamentary strife and confusion could trouble
him more.

Seven months after Cromwell's death, John Maidston,
who had been an Officer of his Household and a Member
of his Parliaments, wrote a somewhat lengthy account
of the Commonwealth proceedings to John Winthrope,
Governor of Connecticut ; and, referring to the " great
burden " laid upon Cromwell by these his last Parliamentary difficulties, thus testifies,—

" I doubt not to say, it drank up his spirits, (of which his
natural constitution yielded a vast stock,) and brought him to
his grave : his interment being the seedtime of his glory, and
of England's calamity. Before I pass further pardon me in
troubling you with the character of his person, which, by
reason of my nearness to him, I had opportunity well to
observe.

" His body was well compact and strong, his stature under
six feet (I believe about two inches) ; his head so shaped, as
you might see it a storehouse and shop, both, of a vast treasure of natural parts. His temper exceeding fiery, as I have
known (!) ; but the flame of it kept down, for the most part,
or soon allayed with those moral endowments he had. He
was naturally compassionate towards objects in distress, even

to an effeminate measure; though God had made him a heart, wherein was little room for any fear but what was due to Himself, of which there was a large proportion; yet did he exceed in tenderness towards sufferers. A larger soul, I think, hath seldom dwelt in a house of clay." *

In the summaries I have given from Cromwell's Speeches, I have done little more than omit repetitions, amplifications, and digressive reflections; which, without the looks and tones which belonged to them, and especially in their imperfect condition, rather obscure his direct line of thought. Cromwell had other solemn matters to impress upon his listeners besides his mere argument against the Kingship. All which matter, in any way extraneous, I have endeavoured to omit. I have also slightly condensed a few of his sentences; and have here and there slightly altered Carlyle's punctuation, where it was evident to me that he had not quite caught Cromwell's meaning. I venture to submit these summaries as a faithful and complete abstract of Cromwell's actual utterances on the proposed change of Title, so far as they can now be gathered from his reported speeches. Any reader can easily check off their accuracy by comparing them with the reported versions as given in Carlyle's volumes. I need offer no further apology for venturing to differ from Carlyle in his estimate of Cromwell. My immediate purpose has been, the faithful elucidation of his own character and genius; and what he saw, or failed to see in Cromwell, or fancied he saw when not there, is, to use his own phrase, 'like a window' into himself. If I have also succeeded in throwing any clearer light upon Cromwell's character, surely Carlyle would not be one to blame me.

* Thurloe's State Papers, vol. i. p. 766.

Thirty-five years ago, when I first read the 'Letters and Speeches,' and wrote him what must have been a very crude statement of my impressions, he replied, "It is a real satisfaction to me to be chidden from that side of the Cromwell Controversy; and I am well pleased to read your letter." Perhaps, if I could have written my convictions as fully then as I have written now, he might have seen that there was more in it than he then supposed; and perhaps, with even deeper reason, have concluded his letter to me, as he did then when I was an entire stranger to him,—

"With many thanks for your good-will to me, and much fellow-feeling with you in your reverence for Oliver, whom I only wish both of us, and all men, could a little resemble in their life pilgrimage,

"I remain, yours very sincerely,
"T. CARLYLE."

I prized these words very highly when I first read them, and they have lost none of their value and significance to me even now.

I must now turn to the more gracious and grateful task of showing how very high Carlyle's actual estimate of Cromwell was. We have already seen that Cromwell's influence upon him formed what he well called 'a new epoch' in his life. Not only did it deepen his moral convictions of the essential antagonism between Good and Evil, 'between the righteous and the wicked, between him that serveth God and him that serveth Him not;' but it also gave him loftier hopes of the Possibilities which, with God's blessing, lie in mankind, and awakened in him a deeper religious and God-fearing spirit than he had ever before manifested in any of his writings. From this time forth, ' the Most High God ' was to him also a very real and awful Presence, before Whom his whole soul bowed in devoutest reverence. If he still failed to realise Cromwell's loving, entire, and contrite trust in the All-Righteous Loving Father, yet in that Father's House are many mansions ; and it would be strange indeed if, among them all, so grandly faithful a soul as Carlyle's could not find an eternal Home. His faith was, that God expected Work from him ; not words or mere emotions of the heart : and noble godlike work was what he longed for with the whole strength of his soul. Not only was his conscience quickened and deepened by his faithful study of Cromwell, but his hopes for himself and for England, and through England for the world, became literally unspeakable. I will give a few remarkable instances.

Cromwell, in his opening Speech to his First Protectorate Parliament (Speech II.), tried to make them realise the many ' spiritual evils ' and other serious dangers by which they were surrounded. Among the ' spiritual evils ' he showed them how ' the grace of God is sometimes turned into wantonness, and Christ and the Spirit of God made a cloak for all villany and spurious apprehensions.' He then says,—

"There is another error of more refined sort, which many honest people, whose hearts are sincere to God, have fallen into : the mistaken notion of the Fifth Monarchy ; a thing professing more spirituality than anything else. A notion I hope we all honour, and wait for, and hope for :—That Jesus Christ will have a time to set up His Reign in all our Hearts ; by subduing those corruptions and lusts and evils which are there ; and which now reign more in the world than, I hope, in His time they will do. And, when more fulness of the Spirit is poured forth to subdue iniquity, and bring in everlasting righteousness, *then* will the approach of that glory be."

To this Carlyle characteristically adds, "Most true; and not till then !" But he also gives, in the assumed words of " our latest impatient Commentator," the following account of the hopes of the ' Fifth Monarchy Men,' to whom Cromwell refers, supplementing it with an irrepressible utterance of his own high hopes in the same direction :—

"The common mode of treating Universal History, not yet entirely fallen obsolete in this country, though it has been abandoned with much ridicule everywhere else for half a century now, was to group the Aggregate Transactions of the Human Species into Four Monarchies; the Assyrian Monarchy of Nebuchadnezzar and Company; the Persian of Cyrus and ditto; the Greek of Alexander; and lastly the Roman. These I think were they, but am no great authority on the subject. Under the dregs of this last, or Roman Empire, which is maintained yet by express name in Germany, *Das heilige Römische Reich*, we poor moderns still live. But now, say Major-General Harrison and a number of men, founding on Bible Prophecies, Now shall be a Fifth Monarchy, by far the blessedest and the only real one,—the Monarchy of Jesus Christ, His Saints reigning for Him on Earth; if not He Himself, which is probable or possible; for a thousand years, etc., etc. . . . . O Heavens, there are tears for human destiny; and immortal Hope itself is beautiful because it is steeped in Sorrow, and foolish Desire lies vanquished under its feet ! They who merely laugh at Harrison take but a small portion of his meaning with them. Thou, with some tear for the valiant Harrison, if with any thought of him at all, tend thou also valiantly in thy day and generation, whither he was tending; and know that, in far wider and diviner figure than that of Harrison, the Prophecy is sure,—that it *shall* be sure while one brave man survives among the dim bewildered populations of this world. Good shall reign on this Earth : has *not* the Most High said it ?"

This was no mere flourish of rhetoric on Carlyle's part; it had grown to be his deepest and most practical conviction. Again, on one occasion (Speech V.) Cromwell, while yet sanguine of heart as to carrying his hearers with him, actually quoted the Eighty-fifth Psalm to his astonished Parliament; appealing to, and trying to encourage them, with the Prophecy—

‘Mercy and Truth are met together; Righteousness and Peace have kissed each other. Truth shall spring out of the Earth, and Righteousness shall look down from Heaven. Yea, the Lord shall give that which is good, and our Land shall yield her increase. Righteousness shall go before Him, and shall set us in the way of His steps.’

What would Honourable Members now say, if any Prime Minister, in the passionate fervour of his heart, were to venture to hold up such an Ideal to them, for their practical acceptance? Perhaps—‘Hear, hear;’ or ‘Question, question;’ or even ‘Peace we know, and Increase we know; but what have we to do with Righteousness?’—Well, this is what Carlyle says:—

“What a vision of celestial hope is this: vista into Lands of Light, God's Will done on Earth, this poor English Earth an Emblem of Heaven; where God's Blessing reigns supreme; where ghastly Falsity and brutal Greed and Baseness, and Cruelty and Cowardice, and Sin and Fear, and all the Helldogs of Gehenna shall lie chained under our feet; and Man, august in divine manhood, shall step victorious over them, heavenward, like a god! O Oliver, I could weep,—and yet it steads not. Do not I too look into ‘Psalms,’ into a kind of Eternal Psalm, unalterable as adamant,—which the whole world yet will look into? Courage, my brave one!”

It is generally considered that Cromwell's work died with him, and that it proved for England little better than an entire failure.   Not so thought Carlyle.   Puritanism, as a social organism, undoubtedly fell ignominiously enough, but not until Cromwell and it had given a moral impulse to England which is alive to this day.

"Puritanism, the King of it once away, fell loose very naturally in every fibre,—fell into *Kinglessness*, what we call Anarchy ; crumbled down, ever faster, for Sixteen Months, in mad suicide, and universal clashing and collision ; proved, by trial after trial, that there lay not in it either Government or so much as Self-government any more; that a Government of England by *it* was henceforth an impossibility. Amid the general wreck of things, all Government threatening now to be impossible, the Reminiscence of Royalty rose again ; 'Let us take refuge in the Past, the Future is not possible !'—and Major-General Monk crossed the Tweed at Coldstream, with results which are well known.

"Results which we will not quarrel with, very mournful as they have been ! If it please Heaven, these Two-hundred Years of universal Cant in Speech, with so much of Cotton-spinning, Coal-boring, Commercing, and other valuable Sincerity of Work going on the while, shall not be quite lost to us !   Our Cant will vanish, our whole baleful cunningly-compacted Universe of Cant, as does a heavy Nightmare Dream. We shall awaken ; and find ourselves in a world greatly *widened.*—Why Puritanism could not continue ? My friend Puritanism was *not* the Complete Theory of this immense Universe ; no, only a part thereof ! To me it seems, in my hours of hope, as if the Destinies meant something grander with England than even Oliver Protector did ! We will not quarrel with the Destinies; *we will work as we can towards fulfilment of them.*"

" 'Blessed are the dead that die in the Lord ;' blessed are the valiant that have lived in the Lord. 'Amen, saith the Spirit,'—Amen. 'They do rest from their labours, and their works follow them.'

"Their works follow them. As, I think, this Oliver Cromwell's works have done and are still doing ! We have had our

' Revolutions of Eighty-eight,' officially called ' glorious ; ' and other Revolutions not yet called glorious ; and somewhat has been gained for poor mankind. Men's ears are not now slit off by rash Officiality ; Officiality will, for long henceforth, be more cautious about men's ears. The tyrannous Star-chambers, branding-irons, chimerical Kings and Surplices at All-hallowtide, they are gone, or with immense velocity going. Oliver's works do follow him !—The works of a man, bury them under what guano-mountains and obscene owl-droppings you will, do not perish, cannot perish. What of Heroism, what of Eternal Light was in a Man and his Life, *is with very great exactness added to the Eternities ;* remains forever a new divine portion of the Sum of Things ; and no owl's voice, this way or that, in the least avails in the matter."

" The Genius of England no longer soars Sunward, world-defiant, like an Eagle through the storms, ' mewing her mighty youth,' as John Milton saw her do : the Genius of England, much liker a greedy Ostrich intent on provender and a whole skin mainly, stands with its *other* extremity Sunward ; with its Ostrich-head stuck into the readiest bush, of old Church-tippets, King-cloaks, or what other ' sheltering Fallacy ' there may be, and *so* awaits the issue. The issue has been slow ; but it is now seen to have been inevitable. No Ostrich, intent on gross terrene provender, and sticking its head into Fal-lacies, but will be awakened one day,—in a terrible *a-pos-teriori* manner, if not otherwise ! . . . Awake before it come to that ; gods and men bid us awake ! The Voices of our Fathers, with thousandfold stern monition to one and all, bid us awake."

So closes Carlyle's loving and faithful record of the doings and utterances of Oliver Cromwell ; and so opens the strange ' new epoch ' of his own struggling, unspeak-ably aspiring life.

CHAPTER XIV.

Carlyle's renewed efforts—' Latter-Day Pamphlets '—Every British man can now elect himself into Parliament—Veracity of thought and purpose—Births of Providence—No man has a right to think as he pleases—All original men intrinsically self-elected—Government by Popular Clamour—Sir Robert Peel—England once more called to ' show the Nations how to live '—Carlyle's faith in true men—Will Sir Robert Peel undertake Reform of Downing Street ?—His sudden death—Carlyle's bitter disappointment—His notions of Administrative Reform.

I HAVE dwelt somewhat fully upon Carlyle's intense sympathy with Cromwell, and upon his strange obtuseness as to some of the deeper spiritual elements of Cromwell's character, not only because of the self-revealing light which is thus thrown upon his own character, both in its strength and in its insufficiency, but also because the example of Cromwell, and what he learnt from Cromwell's hitherto unparalleled career, gave the final shape and impetus to his whole future social efforts, which can only be truly read in the light thus afforded. Here was a Heroism and an Example worth following, could he but interpret truly the essential spirit of it, so as to bring it home to the widely different circumstances and needs of our modern English life ! This thought now burned in his secret soul with an awful and deathless hope, as a message of encouragement and duty to him from the same Almighty God Who had upheld

Cromwell, in Whom we live and move and have our being, and Who holds the destinies of all Nations in the hollow of His Hand. But, alas, he lacked Cromwell's directness and simplicity of heart. He believed in God with his whole soul; but he could not implicitly wait upon His ceaseless and inscrutable Providences, content to be a servant of servants, or even as a little child, while faithfully striving to serve and trust in Him. He longed to assert himself; to be an actual *doer* of God's Will. He instinctively believed that whatever true thing he faithfully did was, by God's bounty, his own spiritual possession; and, under God, would, in some very real way, be his kingly charge for ever, and become for ever 'a new divine portion of the Sum of Things.' And, in the darkness of his despair, he too often felt that the world and the devil were defrauding him,—as if such a thing were possible,—of his just heritage in God's infinite possibilities. He knew, in his calmer moments, that all this brooding and self-asserting impatience was folly and madness; but he could not shake it off. It was the 'Nessus' Shirt' which clung to him in spite of all his efforts to tear it from him; scorching his soul with purgatorial fires; at times making his life almost unendurable to himself and to those about him; and sometimes giving to his denunciations of evil and poltroonery a tone of fierceness, which, if not more intense than they deserved, was at least far more so than a clearer and more trusting heart would have deemed wisely effective.

But Carlyle, as he deeply felt, was not constituted or commissioned to baptize the world with 'rose-water,' nor yet with the 'gentle dew of Heaven;' but, rather, with a Niagara-flood, more befitting the commencement of what he calls the 'Scavenger Age,'—the Age, appointed and prepared from afar off, for inexorably sweeping and washing away, as with a great deluge, all social hypocrisies and impious unclean monstrosities. Neither was he to be rewarded with personal success in his magnificent aspirations and hopes for his country.

'For,' to slightly extend the application of his own wise words, 'the Destinies are opulent; and send here and there a man into the world to do work, for which they do not mean to pay him in' personal success. 'And they smite him beneficently with sore afflictions, and blight his world all into grim frozen ruins round him,—and can make a wandering Exile of their Dante, and not a soft-bedded Podestà of Florence, if they wish to get a *Divine Comedy* out of him. Nay that rather is their way, when they have worthy work for such a man; they scourge him manifoldly to the due pitch, sometimes nearly of despair, that he may search desperately for his work, and find it; they urge him on still with beneficent stripes when needful, as is constantly the case between whiles; and, in fact, have privately decided to reward him with beneficent death by-and-by,' and not with personal success in this life at all.

So was it with Carlyle himself, throughout his whole life, even to the lingering end: under the name of 'Howard,' he was giving a picture of his own tragic experience. But, perhaps, at no time of his life was he driven to search so desperately for his work, or was he so tragically overwhelmed with unspeakable thoughts, hopes, and passionate despairings, and with all the burden and responsibility thus laid upon him, as in the years immediately following his study of Cromwell, until the inward tempestuous misery at last culminated in the issue of his 'Latter-Day Pamphlets.'

In his Reminiscences of his Wife, referring sorrowfully to her sore trouble with him, he says—

" Latter-Day Pamphlet time, and especially the time that preceded it (1848, etc.), must have been very sore and heavy. My heart was long overloaded with the meanings at length uttered there."

Thus he wrote in his private Journal of that time,—

" Words cannot express the love and sorrow of my old memories, chiefly out of boyhood, as they occasionally rise upon me, and I have now no voice for them at all. One's heart becomes a grim Hades, peopled only with silent preternaturalism. No more of this ! God help me ! God soften me again,—so far as now softness can be suitable for such a soul ; or rather let me pray for *wisdom*, for silent capability to manage this huge haggard world,—at once a Hades and an Elysium, a celestial and an infernal as I see, which has been given me to inhabit for a time and to rule over as I can. No lonelier soul, I do believe, lies under the sky at this moment than myself. Masses of written stuff, which I grudge a little to burn, and try to sort something out of for magazine articles, series of pamphlets, or whatever they will promise to turn to,—does not yet succeed with me at all : am not yet in the 'paroxysm of clairvoyance' which is indispensable. Is it ? . . . In dissent from all the world; in black contradiction, deep as the bases of my life, to all the philanthropic, emancipatory, constitutional, and other anarchic revolutionary jargon, with which the world, so far as I can conceive, is now full. . . . The worst is, however, I am not yet true to myself; I cannot yet call in my wandering truant being, and bid it wholly set to the work fit for *it* in this hour. Oh, let me persist, persist,—may the heavens grant me power to persist in that till I do succeed in it!"

" It is a sad feature in employments like mine, that you cannot carry them on continuously. My work needs all to be done with my nerves in a kind of blaze; such a state of soul and body would soon *kill* me, if not intermitted." *

Can we wonder that a set of writings, thus begotten in the very fire and whirlwind of his soul, to him 'awful

* ' Life in London,' 1834–1881, vol. ii. p. 22.

as Sinai and the thunders of the Lord,' were of a character to fill the hearts of many of his former admirers
with wonder and dismay ? Not often has a series of
pamphlets from one held in honour, who so strove to
speak the truth, so jarred upon the 'finer sensibilities'
of those to whom the 'God's Message' was addressed.
Significant also is that 'paroxysm of clairvoyance,'
which he felt to be so indispensable for the clearest and
fullest utterance of his deepest convictions ; for it ex-
plains and vitally accounts for the occasional inconsis-
tencies and even contradictions, between some of his
deepest written utterances, and casual conversations
which have been perhaps imperfectly reported to us, and
even some of his privately written scepticisms, evidently
the reaction of his own constitutional and moody de-
spondency. For, as he once wrote, quoting from Goethe,
'The instant we begin to speak we are more or less
wrong ; the first word we utter there is error in it :'
how much more, then, must this be the case, when the
truer sentinels of the soul are off guard, and, as it were,
standing at ease. I think it only fair to a man, so
moody, yet desperately sincere as Carlyle undoubtedly
was, to take his own deliberately published words as
expressing, so far as any words of his could express them,
his actual convictions.

Certainly the 'Latter-Day Pamphlets' were very far
from being a literary success. But that he never
expected them to be. They were written with intensely
practical aims, and were intended almost as much to
warn off the wrong people, as, if possible, to open the
eyes and awaken the souls of the right people,—of
people who could feel in their own hearts that, in spite
of all shortcomings and discrepancies, his aims and

admonitions, however unpalatable for the moment, were essentially true and just.

" If we will consider it," he says, " the essential truth of the matter is, every British man can now elect *himself* to Parliament without consulting the hustings at all. If there be any vote, idea or notion in him, or any earthly or heavenly thing, cannot he take a pen, and therewith autocratically pour forth the same into the ears and hearts of all people, so far as it will go ? Precisely so far; and, what is a great advantage too, no farther."

The 'Latter-Day Pamphlets' are Carlyle's strenuously faithful diagnosis of the social maladies of England; with practical suggestions for the beginning of cure, and for the final return to social health. Whatever we, individually, may think of his diagnosis and remedies, I suppose no man with a conscience of his own to guide him can at this day doubt that Carlyle himself believed in them. After more than thirty years' faithful study of his writings, such as few of his most devoted readers can have given them, I have no hesitation in declaring my opinion that, in the 'Latter-Day Pamphlets,' pre-eminently among all his works, Carlyle may be seen in the full vigour and maturity of his moral and intellectual development. Whoever would know Carlyle,—his personal aspirations, and sometimes uncontrollable despair; his wonderful insight and strange ethical shortcomings; his ideal of a social organism; his far-reaching aims as a social reformer; and his true place in English social history,—will find it all in what he calls ' this offensive and alarming set of Pamphlets,' or nowhere. Whatever else this portentous outpouring of his soul may have been, it was at least the truest and sincerest utterance of his deepest convictions that, in the full maturity of his powers and of his influence, he knew how to make.

Let me once more candidly confess, as explicitly as I am able, that, with all my admiration and even reverence for his teaching, I never was entirely at one with Carlyle in spiritual sympathy, or in my deepest hopes for the final triumph of good over evil in this checkered world. I have always sorrowfully felt that his insight stopped short where the highest spiritual life really begins, even as Goethe ethically stopped short where Carlyle's ethical work began. But why do we quarrel with these ethical preparers of the ground? They both strove by veracity of thought and effort, each according to his gifts and commission from the Almighty Providence, to make straight for themselves and for us, through all the illusions and self-deceptions of the age, a Path to the Highest. If 'we Christians' had been faithfully living a Christ-like life one with another, instead of so generally making Christianity a mere lubricant to our consciences, and a socially presentable varnish for our selfishness and sins, there would have been no need for either a Goethe or a Carlyle, in the nineteenth century, to call us back into the straight path of veracity, any more than there would have been for a Luther in the fifteenth. 'But the Lord is ever mindful of His own,' in Europe and through the recent centuries, no less than on the road to Damascus; and 'chosen vessels' of the Almighty ever-renewing Spirit of Truth, recognised or unrecognised, have never failed. From generation to generation the mighty Births of Providence have visited us in their splendours and their terrors; seal after seal has been opened, trumpet after trumpet has been sounded, the seven thunders have uttered their voices:

first the great awakening of individual consciences at the call of Luther, then the judgments and terrors and triumphant march of the great French Revolution, and then the greater, because deeper and truer, transcendental and ethical Revolution, which had its centre in Germany and Goethe, but perhaps its most heartfelt manifestation in the spiritually impassioned poetry, the lofty hopes and the generous aspirations, which kindled our own country into a glow of spiritually chaotic enthusiasm altogether unprecedented. All this Carlyle had long felt himself destined to gather together into organic intelligibility, and to interpret for the guidance of himself and of his generation. Many were the efforts he made in this direction, as we have already seen; but his crowning and almost expiring effort was these same 'Latter-Day Pamphlets,' which have given such scandal and offence to nearly all his readers, and which really seemed to aim at 'ruling all Nations with a rod of iron.'

When Carlyle is called a mere destructive and puller-down, I suppose it is chiefly the Pamphlets which are thought of. And certainly the besom of destruction has seldom been more vigorously handled than in these sweeping condemnations of what he believed to be poisonous and infectious delusions. Into this branch of the subject I do not now propose to enter. I merely ask any thoughtful reader who wishes to judge Carlyle fairly, to try to estimate for himself how many of the seemingly ruthless utterances, which gave most offence when first put forth, have now become practically absorbed into our modes of thinking and acting, little conscious of their own origin. It is the way with unpalatable truths. First there is a loud burst of universal indignation, or of derisive execration; then

a few more candid minds begin to think that after all
there may really be something in them, although somewhat too pungently spoken ; then the leavening influence
extends and deepens, until at last we become hardly
aware that we ever thought otherwise. The believers
in Carlyle can afford to wait. The seed he scattered
has taken root, and will yet grow to harvest. We are
not obliged to see with his eyes ; in fact he has done
little for us, unless he has really helped and encouraged
us to use our own. We will leave the admonitions and
condemnations for a time to the consciences of his
readers. Our more immediate purpose is to gather
together what traces we can find, tending to elucidate
his own personality and to show what it was that he
practically strove to accomplish.

But first I must frankly admit that Carlyle had no
scheme of easy-going government to propose, which,
once well adopted, would convert the whole community
into a kind of fool's paradise of universal toleration and
indulgence. He believed in the awful obligations and
sovereign authority of the individual conscience. In
this, Luther and he are entirely at one. It is the secret
of his almost worship of Luther. But his belief, and
Luther's belief, were very different from the loose popular
notion that every man has a right to think as he pleases.
He would have said, and Luther would have said with
his whole heart and soul, ' No man has any such right,
or anything like it. Only the Father of Lies could have
put such a notion into men's hearts.' And surely any
man or woman, to whom conscience is as the urgency of
God upon their own souls, would shudder at such a
notion. Not to think as we like ; but to strive with our
whole moral strength that our poor thought should be

a true and just thought, such as the Maker of us all could sanction and approve, is what the voice of conscience would dictate to us, if we have any real conscience at all. It was to men's God-fearing consciences that Carlyle appealed; not to their self-sufficiency, their love of novelties, or their sense of enjoyment. 'No Paradise for anybody. He that cannot do without Paradise, go his ways. Suppose we tried that for a while! I reckon that the safer version.' This was his stern invitation to the kind of men he longed to rally round him; and he knew only too well that such men were few and very far between.

But, although he had no clever scheme to propose, for securing prosperity out of the unbridled activities of folly and selfishness in the affairs of a Nation, he had a very clear notion of what he considered the one thing needful for practical success in any human enterprise whatsoever. If we are really in earnest about any given enterprise, we strive to secure the services and co-operation of the fittest-men anywhere obtainable. 'Indisputably true,' all the Voices exclaim, 'but in the enterprise of Governing a Nation, how do you propose to find your fittest men?' To this Carlyle's constant reply was, 'Essentially in the same way that we find them in every other enterprise of difficulty and importance.' The fact is, that we outsiders do not, by any insight of our own, find them at all. How could we, who confessedly do not practically understand the requirements of the business in question, discern the fittest man to undertake it, until he had proved his fitness by actual work already done? One who is competent to do the work himself, could by many sympathetic indications judge of the competence of another, without that final and conclusive test; but to the incompetent man it is for ever impossible. In all cases of extremest difficulty, essentially the competent man elects himself to his work ; or, better still, feels himself called and urged to it by a higher power than his own will. Who elected Watt to invent the steam-engine ? Columbus to find America ? Shakspeare to write his Plays ? Luther to liberate all consciences ? or Cromwell to enrol his invincible Ironsides ?

All this is the veriest truism in our daily practical lives ; and no sensible man attempts to interfere with what he knows he does not understand : still less does he ask for the advice or vote of other people, whom he knows are no better informed on the matter than himself ; for he is perfectly aware that adding ignorance to ignorance is not the way to pile up wisdom. What master-manufacturer could act upon the authoritative advice or votes of any mere majority of his work-people, as to the intellectual competence of an untried manager, the choice of as yet unopened markets, the kind of new goods it would be profitable to make, or the new methods or machinery it would be advisable to devise and attempt under altering circumstances ? In many respects his majority may all be as intelligent as himself ; but in such matters he well knows, and they know, that he must depend on his own judgment, if he would keep clear of the bankruptcy courts. What should we expect, if all the navvies engaged on a projected railway line elected and authoritatively directed their own contractors, instead of the contractors electing and directing them ? Or, if the working builders of a St. Paul's claimed to elect their own Architect, out of a number of untried, plausible, and eloquent competitors for their suffrages ? The whole thing is absurd. The perfect competence of men to dig barrow-loads of clay, or to lay bricks and timber and stone with the most skilful accuracy, is no measure whatever of their competence to discern beforehand the worth of an original intellect. And yet, strange to say, we are all considered competent to select with sufficient wisdom our Social Architects and Administrators; and to decide authoritatively what they shall do, and how they shall do it, even in the most complex and unprecedented emergencies, the practical difficulties of which we know nothing about! What must, sooner or later, be the inevitable consequences of thus yielding up the destinies of a great Nation to the authoritative control of mere aggregated incompetence? One consequence will be, Government by Popular Clamour; and, instead of the Chief Offices in the Administration being filled by the ablest practical men in the country, they will be fought after, and distributed among themselves, by the men who have been ablest to tell a plausible story about their own doings, and especially by men ablest to make black appear white, and folly look like wisdom. Carlyle saw with painful and prophetic distinctness whither all this was tending; and the problem which pressed upon him for solution was,—How to open a way, gradually and unobtrusively, for the selection of the practically able, by the able and experienced; for this he well knew was verily the only possible way of ever even approximately realising his prophetic dream of practical government and guidance by the Wisest and Best. It is hardly too much to say, that thorough Administrative Reform, with all that might ultimately grow out of it, was the one 'motive' of his 'Latter-Day Pamphlets.'

The first number of the Pamphlets, called 'The

Present Time,' was published on the 1st of February, 1850, exactly two years after the outbreak of the French Revolution of February, 1848 ; and nearly four years after the resignation of Sir Robert Peel, in consequence of his abolition of the Corn-Laws ; which measure was carried by him,—probably with a good deal of the old-fashioned feeling of ' repentance ' for his own misdeeds in the matter ; but certainly at great personal sacrifice, and in the teeth of a most envenomed personal persecution, in June, 1846.   Since that time Peel had been in almost total eclipse.   Denounced as a ' traitor,' and cut off with something very like execration from his old party ties,—the ablest Conservative Statesman of our times had to accept as he could the consequences of not having persisted in turning a deaf ear to the distress of his country.   But the party hatred which encompassed, and mercilessly hustled him, within the walls of the House, by no means extended to the nation generally.   Thoughtful men of all parties felt that they owed him a deep debt of gratitude ; and many were the speculations as to when he would once more come to the front, and what shape his future career would probably take.   About this time, also, Carlyle and he became personally acquainted, to their mutual interest and satisfaction.   Naturally Carlyle, with his veracious photographing eyes, took, as we shall see he did, very careful and thorough measure of so important a man, thus effectually freed from all party obligations ; and by whom a new career, if undertaken at all, must of necessity have been undertaken on altogether new lines.   Need we wonder if the personal appreciation of such a man, and the thought of all the possibilities which might lie in him, came as a new dawn of practical hope to Carlyle in the morbid darkness of his isolation and despair?

To many readers it might seem strangely wide of the mark to talk of hope in connection with the 'Latter-Day Pamphlets,' for they seem to have been generally regarded as little better than a reckless outburst of universal condemnation, defiance, and hopeless execration. Nevertheless I venture to affirm that in every page there is evidence, if we will open our eyes to it, of the inspiring urgency and almost bursting-pressure of that intense 'desperate hope,' which he so often speaks of as characteristic of himself. He had been brooding over the 'Condition-of-England Question,' in an agony of effort to give clear utterance to his thoughts, ever since he had finished with Cromwell. He had already said, years before in 'Past and Present,' as we have seen,—

"Trade never so well freed, and all Tariffs settled or abolished, and Supply-and-demand in full operation,—let us all know that we have yet done nothing; that we have merely cleared the ground for doing. Yes, were the Corn-Laws ended to-morrow, there is nothing yet ended; there is only room made for all manner of things beginning. . . . We shall have another period of commercial enterprise, of victory and prosperity; during which, it is likely, much money will again be made, and all the people may, by the extant methods, still for a space of years, be kept alive and physically fed. . . . A precious and thrice-precious space of years; wherein to struggle as for life in reforming our foul ways; in alleviating, instructing, regulating our people; seeking, as for life, that something like spiritual food be imparted them, some real governance and guidance be provided them! It will be a priceless time."

And now to him that priceless time had actually come; and what was he himself yet doing that the poor country might profit by it ? His self-reproachful thoughts burned in him like a smothered volcano, leaving him no rest through sleepless nights and lingering days. Then came the general collapse of European Governments of 1848, with all the wild blaze of triumphant enthusiasms exulting over their downfall ; and he believed ' the hour of crisis had verily come :' that whatever there was of manfulness in England must verily bestir itself, before all faith in an Organised National Existence was lost among us.

"England," he passionately exclaims, "as I read the omens, is now called a second time to 'show the Nations how to live.' . . . England still contains in it many *kings;* possesses, as old Rome did, many men not needing 'election' to command, but eternally elected for it by the Maker Himself. England's one hope is in these just now."

And again,—

"In England heroic wisdom is not yet dead, and quite replaced by attorneyism ; the honest beaver faculty yet abounds with us, the heroic manful faculty shows itself also to the observant eye, not dead but dangerously sleeping. I said there were many *kings* in England : if these can be rallied into strenuous activity, and set to govern England in Downing Street and elsewhere, which their function always is,—then England can be saved . . . England with the largest mass of real living interests ever entrusted to a Nation."

And again he says,—

"What the *New* Downing Street can grow to, and will and must, if England is to have a Downing Street beyond a few years longer, it is not for me, in my remote watch-tower, to say with precision. A Downing Street inhabited by the gifted of the intellects of England ; directing all its energies upon the real and living interests of England, and silently but incessantly, in the alembics of the place, burning up the extinct imaginary interests of England, that we may see God's sky a little plainer overhead, and have *all of us* a great accession of ' heroic wisdom ' to dispose of: such a Downing Street —to draw the plan of it, will require architects; many successive architects and builders will be needed there. Let not editors, and remote unprofessional persons, interfere too much ! —Change in the present edifice, however, radical change, all men can discern to be inevitable, and even, if there shall not worse swiftly follow, to be imminent. Outlines of the future edifice paint themselves against the sky (to men that still have a *sky*, and are above the miserable London fogs of the hour); noble elements of new State Architecture, foreshadows of a New Downing Street for the New Era that is come. These with pious hope all men can see; and it is good that *all men*, with whatever faculty they have, were earnestly looking thitherward !" *

Surely these are not the words of a ' hopeless ' man ; but the words of a man whose whole soul is alive with a hope, too big, and even too sacredly awful, for articulate utterance. The work he aimed at was a thing, not to be talked of, but to be done ; which he could only passionately indicate as if from afar off, that haply, here and there, some kindred soul might catch a glimpse of it, and help to realise it, without express articulation. Anyhow, it is at least sufficiently clear that intrinsically he was by no means so hopeless as he sometimes looked and even felt. Neither was heartfelt faith in his country a minus quantity with him. He believed in the great destiny of England, and in the moral strength of the English character, as profoundly as Cromwell did. But, like Cromwell, he believed only in men who had the fear of God in their hearts, and who had no other fear ; men who would act from con-

* ' The New Downing Street.'

science, and not from the lowest motives of self-interest ; men who would hold together, through good report or through evil report, for their country's sake ; and who would be 'very glad to spend all their blood,' rather than stand by and see the best interests of their country sacrificed by imbecility, unfaithfulness, or any form of baseness, either in high places or in low. Carlyle believed that such men still lived amongst us ; that the spirit of the Ironsides was not extinct, but was waiting in silent and perhaps unconscious preparation for nobler and grander developments, could the right modern Cromwell be found with the eye to discern them, and the faith to hold and bind them together. He is often charged with having had no faith in humanity. But what people mean, when they attach any meaning to such words, is that he had no faith in the temporary delusions of his own age. Yet he had something better than this. He had both implicit and explicit faith, that all such delusions would pass away, and that humanity would yet rise above them ; and he showed his faith by doing his utmost to extinguish the delusions, and to raise humanity to a higher level. He had boundless faith in humanity,—in the might of wisdom, and in the impregnable security of righteousness and faithful obedience to the manifested Will of God. He had devoutest faith in all that he could recognise as noble and wise in humanity, but no faith at all in what he clearly discerned to be ignoble and foolish. He not only believed in 'humanity,' but he believed in *men*, when he could see that they were men ; and this is precisely where he and his critics are on opposition benches. He believed that an honest man would act honestly, and that we should do well to trust him ;

they believe that no man will act honestly for long, unless you carefully keep both eyes on him. And this is our boasted 'faith in humanity !'

The practical effort of our present social arrangements is becoming, more and more avowedly, to try, by checks and counterchecks, to do without honesty; clever roguery, well watched and counterchecked, being found so much handier for many purposes. The question, even as to a young man seeking employment in business, is not now, 'Is he trustworthy ?'—only a trustworthy employer could be much interested in such a question as that,—but, 'Has he got devil enough ? Is he sufficiently self-seeking and self-asserting ? If so, we shall understand one another.' So is it through life ; and, in spite of Carlyle's life-long wrestle with him, the 'Prince of this World' seems for the present to be having it all his own way. We do not expect to get 'Servants' whom we can trust, and we still less expect to get 'Governors' whom we can trust. Our 'faith in humanity' means little more than faith that no one *can* be trusted ; that is to say, faith in our own acuteness, and in the universal despicability of mankind ; faith that clever sin and clever folly will lead to social well-being, by much shorter cuts than mere humdrum honesty ; faith that, do what we will, it will all come right in the end, and that if we freely 'swarm' together, each following the bent of his own will, we shall thus attain the perfection of all social relations, and of individual felicity ! If this be 'faith in humanity,' Carlyle had none of it. And, what is more, he had no manner of faith in any kind of men who held such a faith. It was not to such men that he addressed himself.

I trust I have now made it sufficiently clear that Carlyle had hope enough and faith enough, of a kind. Not the kind now most fashionable, or likely to be during our present enthusiasm of universal disintegration ; but the kind, in the moral strength of which all great and fruitful work has taken root. He had faith that there were many Able Men in England,—men of priceless practical sagacity, but with no qualifications whatever for appealing to popular suffrage,—who if frankly recognised, and called upon to assist in the Administration of Government, would serve their country with a soldier's faithfulness, at whatever cost or sacrifice to themselves. If he was mistaken in this faith ; if in very truth we have no such priceless men wasting their lives amongst us,—then of course the 'Latter-Day Pamphlets,' on that point, were reckoning without their host. But the time will yet come when readers will begin to ask, if only as a matter of literary curiosity, what it was that Carlyle really meant by these strange Pamphlets. Whenever this question comes to be seriously discussed, there will probably be as many answers as there have been to similar questions as to Goethe. In what I have written, I must again and again repeat, I have tried to indicate little more than one line of thought, namely, that which will more especially help to elucidate Carlyle's personal character ; and to this line of thought I must still confine my efforts. Show us what a man is trying to do, and the man himself becomes intelligible to us. Two things, mutually tending to one result, may be noted which Carlyle clearly aimed at. The first was to awaken the attention, and if possible kindle a new hope in the hearts, of those scattered workers, wherever they might be, to whom he looked as a possible future Executive of England.   The second was, to get such hitherto 'foiled potentialities' gradually recognised, and at length set to the several tasks for which they were individually fit. These are two things which Carlyle clearly aimed at, in the full conviction that, if they could be only approximately realised, Cromwell's enrolment of his Ironsides would be a very small matter in comparison.   We have seen how many tentative yet strenuous efforts he had already made in a similar direction,—efforts continually baffled, but never relinquished ; and always shaping themselves anew to more practical issues, as new opportunities seemed to open before him.   But now, for the first time, he practically grappled with the very problem itself.   Very warily, and as an almost extraneous suggestion, which might perhaps be worth thinking of in default of anything better ; but a suggestion which, if it could have been adequately realised, would have remodelled the British Constitution, ·and perhaps have given us a firmly coherent Social Edifice, instead of a crumbling ruin with just social cohesion enough to hold one stone tottering upon another.

I have already alluded to the very peculiar position and personal qualifications of Sir Robert Peel : also to his personal acquaintance with Carlyle at the time, which will be seen more in detail in another chapter : I have also sufficiently called attention to the fact, that Carlyle really believed 'the hour of crisis for England' had verily come.   With these three facts to help us, it is easy to understand how, in the desperateness of his hope, he had come to look upon Sir Robert Peel as the man fated to inaugurate the new order of things for which he had himself been so long and so strenuously working.

He had already evidently exerted no slight influence on Peel's essentially practical mind. Indeed, I have always considered that 'Past and Present' had much to do in converting him into a resolute Corn-Law Repealer. And, when we look at the contrast between the 'Sir Jabesh Windbag' of that work, and what Carlyle now had to say of him, I think it speaks well for the magnanimity of them both. In every way, without too much seeming to do so, Carlyle now tried to strengthen Peel's position, and to point to him as the one man 'strong enough for the place.' There are two express references to him in the Pamphlets : one in 'Downing Street,' the other in 'The New Downing Street.' We must content ourselves with an extract from the latter, which will sufficiently indicate the eager yet restrained intensity of Carlyle's hopes.

"Whether Sir Robert Peel will undertake the Reform of Downing Street for us, or any Ministry or Reform farther, is not known. He, they say, is getting old, does himself recoil from it, and shudder at it ; which is possible enough. The clubs and coteries appear to have settled that he surely will not ; that this melancholy wriggling seesaw of redtape Trojans and Protectionist Greeks must continue its course till— what *can* happen, my friends, if this go on continuing ?

"And yet, perhaps, England has by no means so settled it. Quit the clubs and coteries, you do not hear two rational men speak long together upon politics, without pointing their inquiries towards this man. A Minister that will attack the Augias Stable of Downing Street, and begin producing a real Management, no longer an imaginary one, of our affairs ; *he*, or else *in a few years Chartist Parliament and the Deluge come :* that seems the alternative. As I read the omens, there was no man in my time more authentically called to a post of difficulty, of danger, and of honour than this man. The enterprise is ready for him, if he is ready for it. He has but to lift his finger in this enterprise, and whatsoever is wise and manful in England will rally round him. If faculty and heart for it be in him, he, strangely and almost tragically if we look upon his history, is to have leave to try it; he now, at the eleventh hour, has the opportunity for such a feat in reform as has not, in these late generations, been attempted by all our reformers put together."

By an awfully chastening fatality which seems almost to have lain in wait for Carlyle at some of the most momentous crises of his life,—three short months after these solemnly hopeful words had gone forth to his country, and while thoughtful men were beginning to ponder seriously their significance, Sir Robert Peel was thrown from his horse and killed. What Carlyle's feelings were at such a sudden smiting to the ground of his personal hopes and his generous sympathy, I suppose he has nowhere expressly recorded. The bitterness, disappointment, and humiliation of the rebuff must have sunk too deep into his soul for him to have found relief in any words, although he has left conclusive evidence how cruelly inexorable he felt it to be. He bowed in silence before the sternly awful fact, with wrestlings and self-searchings unspeakable; and once more strove to gird himself together, for what might in mercy yet be possible for him under the now tragically changed conditions. But, up to this time, he had undoubtedly looked to Sir Robert Peel as the man providentially prepared and equipped,—by natural endowment, long experience, bitter chastenings, and the silent admonitions of his own conscience,—for inaugurating the great work of root and branch Administrative Reform which he believed to be at hand. Such a work he well knew could only be effectually accomplished by fit men, wisely selected by a Chief Man having real insight into the characters and capabilities of men, and practical experience of the kind and quality of the manifold work needing to be done. As a wise General selects his Officers, not by the mere suffrages of the rank and file, but by what he himself knows or can learn of them, so he contended a wise Chief Statesman must attract, select, and appoint the leading Officers of his Administration. Such a wise Chief Statesman he believed we had actually got in Sir Robert Peel; and he believed the country instinctively believed so too. How, then, should we best strengthen the hands of such a man,—could we but induce him to accept the terrible responsibility? First of all, Carlyle thought, by ourselves frankly recognising him for what he was, namely, our wisest and strongest available man. Next that,—very gradually, but no less surely,—the whole length and breadth and depth of the country should be thrown open to him to select from :— 'many kings in England,' and a wise 'Statesman-King' to recognise and foster kingly worth wheresoever it could contrive to practically show itself. Let us confess the notion does sound somewhat utopian; perhaps as utopian as Cromwell's proposed enlistment of his Ironsides sounded to his cousin Hampden. But again I say, I am not called upon to defend Carlyle's views. They need no defence. I am simply trying to explain them. Perhaps a vote for every one, and a practical and honourable career for no one, may not be found too utopian.

CHAPTER XV.

One wise Statesman with practical experience indispensable—How to strengthen his hands—Carlyle's ' Project of Reform '—Cromwell's ' Self-denying Ordinance '—Carlyle not to be a ' Queen's Member '—Ceases in despair as a Social Reformer—His sensitive aloofness—Not ' common clay after all '—Self-revealing Letters to Emerson—' Eighteen Million *bores* '—A personal tiff—Mutual magnanimity, and the inexorable laws of spiritual life.

LET us now consider how Carlyle proposed to practically initiate the grandly utopian revolution in the administration of Government, the essential purpose of which we have already briefly indicated. In this instance, if in no other, his suggestion had the merit of perfect simplicity, and of suitability to the end in view. And the extremely wary, and as it were casual way, in which it is introduced, is in itself almost sufficient to show the vital importance he attached to it. But it should be distinctly remembered, that when Carlyle made the suggestion, we had in Sir Robert Peel a Chief Statesman who, in all human probability, would have been well able to have taken it up, and fairly started it in one form or another. The man who had won the thanks of the Crown and the profound gratitude of the country,—who by sheer strength of character had compelled the abolition of the Corn-Laws upon a reluctant Ministry, and had set the trade of the country free,—was a man

whom Carlyle might well have deemed equal to a clear
all-round stroke administrative reform.   Accordingly he
assumes it as possible that we might get, "at the very
lowest, one real Statesman, to shape the dim tendencies
of Parliament, and guide them wisely to the goal."

"One such," he says, "perhaps might be attained ; one such
might prove discoverable among our Parliamentary populations?   That one, in such an enterprise as this of Downing
Street, might be invaluable !   One noble man, at once of natural
wisdom and practical experience ; one Intellect still really
human, and not redtapish, owlish and pedantical, appearing
there in that dim chaos, with word of command ; to brandish
Hercules-like the divine broom and shovel, and turn running
water in upon the place, and say as with a fiat, 'Here shall be
truth and real work, and talent to do it henceforth ; I will
seek for able men to work here, as for the elixir of life to this
poor place and me :'—what might not one such man effect
there !"

"'By what method, then ; by what method?' ask many.
—Method alas ! To secure an increased supply of Human
Intellect to Downing Street, there will evidently be no quite
effectual 'method' but that of increasing the supply of Human
Intellect, otherwise definable as Human Worth, *in Society
generally ;* increasing the supply of sacred reverence for it, of
loyalty to it, and of life-and-death desire and pursuit of it,
among all classes,—if we but knew such a method !"

"Meanwhile, that our one reforming Statesman may have
free command of what Intellect there is among us, and room
to try all means for awakening and inviting ever more of it,
there has one small Project of Improvement been suggested ;
which finds a certain degree of favour wherever I hear it talked
of, and which seems to merit much more consideration than it
has yet received.   Practical men themselves approve of it
hitherto, so far as it goes ; the one objection being that the
world is not yet prepared to insist on it,—which of course the
world can never be, till once the world consider it, and in
the first place hear tell of it !   I have, for my own part, a good
opinion of this project. The old unreformed Parliament of

rotten boroughs *had* one advantage ; but that is hereby, in a far more fruitful and effective manner, secured to the new.

"The Proposal is, That Secretaries under and upper, that all manner of changeable or permanent servants in the Government Offices shall be selected *without* reference to their power of getting into Parliament :—that, in short, the Queen shall have power of nominating the half-dozen or half-score Officers of the Administration, whose presence is thought necessary in Parliament, to official seats there, without reference to any constituency but her own only, which of course will mean her Prime Minister's. A very small encroachment on the present constitution of Parliament ; offering the minimum of change in present methods, and I almost think a maximum in results to be derived therefrom.—The Queen nominates John Thomas (the fittest man she, much-inquiring, can hear tell of in her three kingdoms) President of the Poor-Law Board, Under Secretary of the Colonies, Under, or perhaps even Upper Secretary of what she and her Premier find suitablest for a working head so eminent, a talent so precious ; and grants him, by her direct authority, seat and vote in Parliament so long as he holds that office. Upper Secretaries, having more to do in Parliament, and being so bound to be in favour there, would, I suppose, at least till new times and habits come, be expected to be chosen from among the *People's* Members as at present. But whether the Prime Minister himself is, in all times, bound to be first a People's Member ; and which, or how many, of his Secretaries and subordinates he might be allowed to take as *Queen's* Members, my authority does not say,— perhaps has not himself settled ; the project being yet in mere outline or foreshadow, the practical embodiment in all details to be fixed by authorities much more competent than he. The soul of his project is, That the Crown also have power to elect a few members to Parliament.

"From which project, however wisely it were embodied, there could probably, at first or all at once, no great 'accession of intellect' to the Government Offices ensue ; though a little might, even at first, and a little is always precious : but in its ulterior operation, were that faithfully developed, and wisely presided over, I fancy an immense accession of intellect might ensue ;—nay a natural ingress might thereby be opened to all manner of accessions, and the actual flower of whatever intellect the British Nation had might be attracted towards Downing Street, and continue flowing steadily thither ! For let us see a little what effects this simple change carries in it the possibilities of. Here are beneficent germs, which the presence of one truly wise man as Chief Minister, steadily fostering them for even a few years, with the sacred fidelity and vigilance that would beseem him, might ripen into living practices, and habitual facts, invaluable to us all."

Such was Carlyle's Project for gradually infusing a new practical life into our Administrative Services. It was necessary to give so important a suggestion in his own full and carefully considered words, not only because of the intrinsic value of the suggestion, but also because it reveals to us so clearly his own tentative method and practical aims. Perhaps in future years, when we have had a little further experience of the inevitable inefficacy of a mere Parliamentary or Debating-Club Executive, the Project itself, with whatever necessary modifications, may even come to be deemed worthy of serious consideration. The crucial objection to any such scheme of course is, that it would take away from Honourable Members the exclusive right to the highest Prizes of their own personal ambition, and throw them open to the country at large, wherever the fittest men could be found. Whether such a change would bring a benefit to the country at all commensurate with the damper it would certainly inflict upon the 'Parliamentary scramble for Office,' is a question on which there would probably be differences of opinion. The question is—Should the Practical Intellects of the country have an equal chance with the Eloquent Talkers ? One advantage of the change would be, that it would tend to make more distinct the functions of Parliament as an advising and controlling body, and the functions of the Executive as an acting and organising body. For, as Carlyle points out, Parliament has in these days usurped a function, which the more popular it becomes the more impossible it will be for it to efficiently discharge. It now practically assumes to be itself the Executive; and in actual fact the Executive and the Parliament have got so hopelessly mingled and muddled together into one inextricable tangle, that the Gordian Knot was a trifle to it. Carlyle tried desperately to loosen the knot, but was mocked at for his pains; and possibly it now waits the sword of an Alexander or a Cromwell to give the effective stroke. Or, when the National Debating-Club has shown a little more clearly what its true and only possible function really is, perhaps Honourable Members themselves may find sufficient heart of grace to pass a 'Self-denying Ordinance,' and so untie the knot effectually and for ever; adjuring each other, perhaps in the words of Cromwell on a similar occasion,—

"I hope we have such true English hearts, and zealous affections towards the general weal of our Mother Country, as no Members of either House will scruple to *deny* themselves, and their own private interests, for the public good; nor account it to be a dishonour done to them, whatever the Parliament shall resolve upon this weighty matter."

But 'much water must run by' before such a day can dawn upon us. Nevertheless,—perhaps long after our deluge of oratory has spent itself and subsided,—in our future Ideal Commonwealth, our Working Executive, and our Popular Tribune, or representative Voice of the Nation, will, in one good way or another, very certainly become two sufficiently distinct, yet mutually co-operative entities. This is not a prophecy; it is only an expression of utopian confidence in the practical sagacity of the country, when sufficiently taught by bitter experience.

Mr. Froude tells us that he once asked Carlyle whether he had ever thought of going into Parliament, and that his reply was, " Well, I did think of it at the time of the 'Latter-Day Pamphlets.' " Surely we may safely say, it could only have been at this time, and as a 'Queen's Member,' that Carlyle ever had any serious thought or possibility of obtaining a seat in Parliament. What 'might have happened' if Sir Robert Peel had lived ; what Carlyle himself might have grown to be as the years rolled on ; and what England and the Anglo-Saxon Race,—are for us, now, all matters of idle speculation. But to Carlyle, in the days which then were, they were questions all kindling and swelling with unborn life, filling him with suppressed hopes, unspeakable and almost unthinkable. Such was the spirit in which the ' Latter-Day Pamphlets ' were conceived and commenced. Not a spirit of hopelessness by any means, but of hope grown desperate ; standing as it were at bay, and grimly resolved to speak the truth or die. Carlyle always hoped that a small minority of influential men would yet stand by him. " On the whole," he says, " honour to small minorities,—when they are genuine ones. Severe is their battle sometimes, but it is victorious always, like that of gods." What Sir Robert Peel thought of these passionate and sometimes scathing utterances, will probably never be known. But we have positive evidence that he was really interested both in Carlyle and in his writings. Carlyle had not spared him in ' Past and Present,' while he was as yet the responsible leader of the Corn-Law Party ; and I should fancy that the man who had not scorned to profit by the parable of 'Sir Jabesh Windbag,' could hardly have read the early numbers of the 'Latter-Day Pamphlets' without a very clear sense of the intensely practical aims which inspired, even if they did not always justify, all their seeming extravagance. They were Carlyle's last great social effort to make himself a power in his country. The death of Sir Robert Peel, to whom 'Downing Street' and 'The New Downing Street' were almost specially addressed, must have been death to his own hopes of attaining to any practical influence in the administration of government. Indeed, from every indication it would seem that from this time,—with one passing exception which we shall see,—he had given up all thought of being able to do anything effectual to avert that universal and remorseless disintegration which he now felt must be our doom as a Nation. He withdrew utterly from the position of Social Reformer which he had so long and so zealously occupied, and from all Condition-of-England questions; and, as it were, with one parting word,—his 'Life of Sterling,' written almost in tears,—he sought relief from the restless gnawing ennui of his heart in a foreign subject, and in a multiplicity of details which gave little scope for the higher emotions which had made such a havoc of his life.

It was at this period of his career, while he was engaged on his 'Life of Frederick,' that I ventured to offer him my poor services ; which offer was thankfully accepted by him, and led to some ten years of constant and intimate intercourse, the story of which I have elsewhere fully told. I may as well frankly confess that I went to him with much of the feeling of a young

Cadet vowing fealty to his feudal Sovereign. I had
already seen into his 'secret,' pretty much as I see it
now; but far less vividly, less circumstantially, and
certainly with no adequate appreciation of his intense
loneliness, or of the disappointment and despair which
had settled upon his heart. I saw the inspiration of his
influence in the literature of the time; and I never
doubted his being the friend and counsellor of the best
and most practical intellects amongst us. Yet I can
honestly say that I was urged by no weak ambition to
be patronised and personally noticed, either by him or
by them. It was the one thing I shrank from, as he
soon well knew. My one qualification I felt to be, that
I understood Carlyle, and his Works and Work; and,
having heard that he was really in need of help, my one
wish was, if possible, to help him. I can understand
now, better than I could then, the feeling of sensitive
aloofness between us, of which we were both often
uncomfortably conscious. He knew, and Mrs. Carlyle
knew, that I looked to him to do more, and to be more,
than was now humanly possible. Our highest ideals of
life were certainly not the same, and he knew it, for I
never made the least secret of it; but besides this, he
must also have been painfully conscious that I had some
sort of feeling of his baffled aspirations. If they had
not been so sorely baffled, he might have been grateful
for the recognition; but the wound was too sore to be
looked upon by any eyes, even his own; and he tried
hard to forget it. I never heard him speak of the
'Latter-Day Pamphlets' in any but a kind of proud
slighting way; and yet I knew they had been to him
like drops of his heart's blood. They had not drawn to
him the kind of people he had looked for, but chiefly a

few impractical enthusiasts with whom he could do nothing; and his main hope, as we have seen, had been suddenly stricken down, as if visibly by the Hand of God. For the first time he must have experienced in his own heart the bitter humiliation of Cromwell's helplessness, in his despairing efforts to open the eyes of his unsympathising Parliaments. What could even his adamantine endurance and iron will do, in the face of such a rebuke as he had received? Surely it says something for his intrinsic humility and true loftiness of heart, that he bowed his head in silence to the chastisement, and still trusted that he might continue to live some kind of manful life in obedience to his deepest convictions. But was it in the power of flesh and blood for him to have been a genial companion while thus inwardly writhing under a more than Promethean torture? Mr. Froude, in his first instalment of Carlyle's biography, referring to his own abundant revelations of Carlyle's ' faults,' says,—

"It is the nature of men to dwell on the faults of those who stand above them. They are comforted by perceiving that the person whom they have heard so much admired was but of common clay after all." *

I venture to say,—in the name of that God whose image is latent in us all, however darkly it may sometimes be eclipsed by our own self-conceit,—that such a sentiment is a libel on human nature. Only what Carlyle calls a ' valet soul ' could feel comforted by such a discovery, or could deliberately pander to such a feeling. No reader of Carlyle, who ever became the better for his teaching,

* ' History of the First Forty Years,' vol. ii. p. 470.

has been in the least degree comforted, but every one of them has been cruelly pained and disheartened, by the unstinted petty scandals and hardly decent private exposures which have been authoritatively given to the world as a biography of one of the grandest and most sorely baffled souls that ever strove to do God's Will in our earth. I have known Carlyle in the maturity of his manhood, almost as intimately as any one now living; I have seen him in his moral and intellectual strength, and in his manifold irritable infirmities; and have reverenced the one while I sorely grieved over the other: and I unhesitatingly declare, there was no such despicable inconsistency between the man and his teaching as, for our puny comfort, we have been given to suppose. Carlyle never posed himself before the world as a Marcus Aurelius of spotless perfection, 'clear-starched into consciousness of his own moral sublime.' He knew the passionate infirmities of his heart as well as any one ; and that his very zeal for what he believed to be God's Truth often carried him into excesses of utterance, even with his dearest friends, which he could not always control. 'As if I could have *helped*,' he wrote in these very years to Emerson, 'growing to be, by aid of time and destiny, the grim Ishmaelite I am.' He flattered no man's prejudices, but slashed his way sheer through all foolish opposition and conventional hypocrisies. He longed to save his country in its own despite. He tried to reach men's convictions, not to win their applause. 'God help us,'—he said to Emerson, in the same letter, of 1852,— 'this is growing a very lonely place, this distracted dog-kennel of a world ! And it is no joy to me to see it about to have its throat cut for its immeasurable devilries.' All this sensitive misery and boundless aspiration and disappointment he had to shut down within his own solitary consciousness as with an iron lid. People are much mistaken about his great doctrine of Silence. Witty persons talked about his preaching for hours on the 'blessedness of silence ;' but they knew nothing of the silent passionate longings brooding unspeakable in the chastened depths of his soul.

In Carlyle's Letters to Emerson we find some of the frankest and simplest utterances of his heart anywhere recorded. The whole Correspondence, on both sides,—which has been most faithfully arranged and edited by Mr. Charles Eliot Norton,*—is especially remarkable for intense unswerving veracity both of thought and word, like the free intercourse of men between whom nothing vital could be hidden. It is almost unnecessary, then, to say that Carlyle's Letters, written at the time of his great trouble, afford very clear and pathetic evidence of the subdued anguish of soul from which he was vainly struggling to get free. In writing to Emerson, he felt that he was writing to the one man whom he could honestly regard as his intellectual peer ; a man, also, who had earnestly and courteously befriended him at a time of his greatest need, and whom no antagonism of conviction could make him cease to esteem and love from the depths of his heart. A wide spiritual gulf had yawned between them ; but this only seemed to increase his passionate longing to reach across all differences, that he might yet feel the unaccustomed touch of human sympathy. Sir Robert Peel died on the second of July, 1850 ; and with his death Carlyle's practical interest in English social life died too. On the

* 'The Correspondence of Thomas Carlyle and Ralph Waldo Emerson' 1834–1872. 2 vols.

nineteenth of the same month he thus laid bare to his friend the exceeding sorrow of his heart :—

"My dear Emerson, my Friend, my Friend,—You behold before you a remorseful man ! It is well-nigh a year now since I despatched some hurried rag of paper to you out of Scotland, indicating doubtless that I would speedily follow it with a longer letter ; and here, when gray Autumn is at hand again, I have still written nothing to you, heard nothing from you ! . . . The fact is, my life has been black with care and toil,—labour above board and far worse labour below ;—I have hardly had a heavier year (overloaded too with a kind of 'health' which may be called frightful) : to 'burn my own smoke' in some measure, has really been all I was up to ; and except on sheer immediate compulsion I have not written a word to any creature.—Yesternight I finished the last of these extraordinary Pamphlets ; am about running off somewhither into the deserts, of Wales or Scotland, Scandinavia or still remoter deserts ;—and my first signal of revived reminiscence is to you.

"Nay I have not at any time forgotten you, be that justice done the unfortunate : and though I see well enough what a deep cleft divides us, in our ways of practically looking at this world,—I see also (as probably you do yourself) where the rock-strata, miles deep, unite again ; and the two poor souls are at one. Poor devils !—Nay, if there were no point of agreement at all, and I were more intolerant 'of ways of thinking' than even I am,—yet has not the man Emerson, from old years, been a Human Friend to me ? Can I ever forget, or think otherwise than lovingly of the man Emerson ? . . . No more of this. Write to me in your first good hour, and say there is still a brother-soul left to me alive in this world, and a kind thought surviving far over the sea !"

To this letter, charged throughout as it is with the burden of unshed tears, Carlyle received a reply from Emerson while in Scotland, but the letter is reported as missing. But Emerson also wrote to him, then or previously, another letter which had rather a curious fate. He sent it by the hand of a friend whom he wished to introduce to Carlyle ; and the letter was never delivered. The fact is, Carlyle had in his first Pamphlet given great offence to all American visitors, by Smelfungus's impatient growl at the 'Eighteen Millions of the greatest *bores* ever seen in this world before ;' and, not quite unnaturally, the gentleman in question preferred not to be received as one of them. Accordingly, at the moment of his departure he wrote to Carlyle, politely informing him of the letter he had brought as an introduction ; and, also, that he was taking it back with him, unused, to America. Emerson too was evidently deeply hurt by this and other sweeping expressions,—some of which he may have felt to be almost personal to himself,—to which Carlyle in that Pamphlet had given utterance ; and this feeling could hardly have been lessened by Carlyle's sorrowful allusion to the 'deep cleft' which divided them. Upon learning how Emerson's letter had been kept from him, he at once wrote him the following eager and emphatic protest :—

"The fact in that is very far different indeed from the superficial semblance ; and I appeal to all the *gentlemen* that are in America for a candid interpretation of the same. 'Eighteen Million bores,'—good Heavens don't I know how many of that species we also have ; and how with us, as with you, the difference between *them* and the Eighteen thousand noble-men and *non*-bores is immeasurable and inconceivable?"

That Carlyle had personally nothing but the kindest and most loving feelings towards Emerson is abundantly evident in all his letters to him ; but the letter first quoted from is finally and pathetically conclusive. In the midst of his own personal misery he could not help

brooding upon the thought that probably he had also
estranged his friend ; and with a heart craving for sympathy and overflowing with remorse, yet entirely intolerant of even friendly hypocrisy, he tried to restore
their brotherly intercourse on the only terms now
honestly possible : he must either convince his brother,
or they must in sheer personal lovingkindness agree to
differ with their eyes open. Accordingly, in replying
to the letter he got in Scotland, he tried with generous
and urgent solicitude to indicate what he conceived to
be the essential Nothingness of Emerson's moral standpoint. For the Pamphlets, in their uncompromising
sincerity, and their stern insistence on the intrinsic
antagonism between good and evil, and between good
men and evil men, had brought them to a clear recognition of the fact,—which there was no longer any possibility of ignoring,—of the actual moral gulf which
divided them, and even threatened to separate them for
ever. Emerson strenuously taught that there was no
such intrinsic antagonism ; that evil was properly the
raw material and imperfect incipiency of good ; that the
possibility of 'sin against God' was a fiction of the childhood of the world ; and that, do what we will, all
would finally be well with us. An all-compensating and
self-sufficing gospel, truly. Poppies in the brain, and
iron in the blood, are but poor exoteric symbols of its
inward potency. 'I am an endless seeker, with No Past
at my back,' exclaims Emerson with serenest self-con-
tentment.

"You are bountiful abundantly," Carlyle wrote to him,
" in your reception of those Latter-Day Pamphlets ; and right
in all you say of them ;—and yet withal you are not right,
my Friend, but I am ! Truly it does behove a man to know

the inmost resources of this universe : and, for the sake both of his peace and of his dignity, to possess his soul in patience, and look nothing doubting (nothing wincing even, if that be his humour) upon all things. For it is most indubitable there is good in all ;—and, if you even see an Oliver Cromwell assassinated, it is certain you may get a cartload of turnips from his carcase. Ah me, and I suppose we had too much forgotten all this, or there had not been a man like you sent to show it us so emphatically ! Let us well remember it ; and yet remember too that it is *not* good always, or ever, to be ' at ease in Zion ; ' good often to be in fierce rage in Zion ; and that the vile Pythons of this Mud-World do verily require to have sun-arrows shot into them, and red-hot pokers struck through them, according to occasion : woe to the man that carries either of these weapons, and does not use them in their presence ! Here, at this moment, a miserable Italian organ-grinder has struck up the *Marseillaise* under my window, for example : was the *Marseillaise* fought out on a bed of down, or is it worth nothing when fought ? On those wretched Pamphlets I set no value at all, or even less than none : to me their one benefit is, my own heart is clear of them (a benefit *not* to be despised, I assure you !)—and in the Public, athwart this storm of curses, and emptyings of vessels of dis-honour, I can already perceive that it is all well enough there too in reference to them ; and the controversy of the Eighteen millions *versus* the Eighteen thousand, or Eighteen units, is going on very handsomely in that quarter of it, for aught I can see ! . . . Oh my Friend, have tolerance for me, have sympathy with me ; you know not quite (I imagine) what a burden mine is, or perhaps you would find this duty, which you always do, a little easier done ! "

To the letter, dated 14th November, 1850, from which the foregoing extract is taken, there seems to have been no reponse, for on the 8th of July following Carlyle again wrote as follows :—

" DEAR EMERSON,—Don't you still remember very well that there is such a man ? I know you do, and will do. But it is a ruinously long while since we have heard a word from each other;—a state of matters that ought immediately to *cease*. It was your turn, I think, to write? It certainly was somebody's turn! Nay I heard lately you complained of bad eyes; and were grown abstinent of writing. Pray contradict this. I cannot do without some regard from you while we are both here. Spite of your many sins, you are among the most human of all the beings I now know in the world;—who are a very select set, and are growing ever more so, I can inform you! In late months, feeling greatly broken and without heart for anything weighty, I have been upon a 'Life of John Sterling;' which will not be good for much, but will as usual gratify me by taking itself off my hands: it was one of the things I felt a kind of obligation to do, and so am thankful to have done."

He then asks a little favour of his friend, about introducing the forthcoming book to America; and, after the usual items of information and comment on various matters, thus concludes :—

"Adieu, dear Emerson; I expect to get a great deal brisker by and by,—and, in the first place, to have a Missive from Boston again. My Wife sends you many regards."

This letter called forth an immediate reply (28th July), informing Carlyle that the little service he had asked for had been promptly attended to. Yet in the opening words of the reply we cannot but note a tone of wounded feeling and proud humility, as of a man who felt that he had been disparagingly dealt with by his friend, and who painfully recognised the rupture of true spiritual sympathy between them as final.

"You must always," he says, "thank me for silence, be it never so long, and must put on it the most generous interpretations. For I am too sure of your genius and goodness, and too glad that they shine steadily for all, to importune you to make assurance sure by a private beam very often. There is very little in this village to be said to you; and, with all my love of your letters, I think it the kind part to defend you from our imbecilities,—my own, and other men's. Besides, my eyes are bad, and prone to mutiny at any hint of white paper."

To this gently pungent and grieved rebuke, Carlyle lost little time in replying. And we may as well follow this little spurt of incipient antagonism to its conclusion,—not because it comfortably convinces us that they were made of 'common clay' like the rest of us, but because it shows they were both animated by a spirit of magnanimity which we should all do well to emulate. On the 25th of August following Carlyle wrote,—

"Many thanks for your letter, which found me about a week ago, and gave a full solution to my bibliopolic difficulties. However sore your eyes, or however taciturn your mood, there is no delay of writing when any service is to be done by it! In fact you are very good to me, and always were, in all manner of ways."

Nearly eight months after, on the 14th of April, 1852, Emerson again wrote, saying,—

"I have not grown so callous by my sulky habit, but that I know where my friends are; and who can help me, in time of need. And I have to crave your good offices to-day, and in a matter relating once more to Margaret Fuller, etc., etc., etc."

So each had at length cemented his friendly reconciliation with the other, by a favour asked and a favour granted. The personal tiff was now frankly ended, and they both found there was nothing for them but to agree to differ. The commencement of Carlyle's reply, dated 7th of May, from which an extract has already been given, must now close this unique epistolary dialogue.

"Dear Emerson,—I was delighted at the sight of your hand again. My manifold sins against you, involuntary all of them I may well say, are often enough present to my sad thoughts; and a kind of remorse is mixed with the sorrow,— as if I could have *helped* growing to be, by aid of time and destiny, the grim Ishmaelite I am, and so shocking your serenity by my ferocities! I admit you were like an angel to me, and absorbed in the beautifullest manner all thunder-clouds into the depths of your immeasurable æther;—and it is indubitable I love you very well, and have long done, and mean to do. And on the whole you will have to rally yourself into some kind of correspondence with me again: I believe you will find that also to be a commanded duty by and by! To me at any rate, I can say, it is a great want, and adds perceptibly to the sternness of these years. Deep as is my dissent from your Gymnosophist view of Heaven and Earth, I find an agreement that swallows up all conceivable dissents: in the whole world I hardly get, to my spoken human word any other word of response which is authentically human."

Alas! the laws of deepest spiritual life are inexorable; and two more intrinsically incompatible Ideals were never formulated than that of Emerson, and that to which Carlyle now clung, in the full maturity of his intellect, with such passionate and uncompromising devotion. ' O thou sword of the Lord, how long will it be ere thou be quiet? Put up thyself into thy scabbard; rest, and be still. How canst thou be quiet, seeing the Lord hath given thee this charge ? '

CHAPTER XVI.

Stormy noontide of Carlyle's life—His Irish Tour—Slavery and true freedom—Not an enemy of the Negro—Anti-servitude masking itself in the cry of Anti-slavery—Carlyle's lifelong compassion for the deserving poor—What we are even now doing to 'seek and to save '—National Sin of Pauperism—All idleness contributes its share —Industrial Regiments—Help to the helpless—Our wide Colonial Empire—England unequal to her destiny—As if we were not men, but a kind of apes.

WE have now followed Carlyle through the more distinctly marked periods of his spiritual growth ; from the golden dawn of ' Sartor Resartus,' when Emerson and he found so much common ground for sympathy, up to the stormy noontide and wonderful social and ethical insight of the ' Latter-Day Pamphlets,' where they sorrowfully parted. If we, of the ' Eighteen thousands or Eighteen units,' who feel and know that we have had much folly washed clean out of us by the purifying rush of their Niagara-baptism, also feel that we cannot altogether acquit him from the charge of a wilful perversity which sometimes defeated the very objects he had most at heart,—let us frankly ask ourselves whether any mere man could possibly have initiated the convictions, and made the mark he did, in such days as ours, without even such an endowment of wide-sweeping impetuosity and of rocklike stubbornness. 'Stubbornly perverse in the utterance of his thoughts, Carlyle undoubtedly was ; and if we wish to understand his true meaning, it is often indispensable to bear this besetting sin of his distinctly in mind.   He scorned to palter with the truth to gain any man's suffrage.   But, more than this, he often when at white heat realised a grim Berserker satisfaction in pitting himself single-handed against the folly and fro-wardness of ' the united posterity of Adam.'   God's Truth, against a World all bristling with lies, was the war-cry of his heart ; and, stripping himself of every rag of conventional self-defence, he threw himself into the hottest of the fray, and swept all before him by the sheer fervour of his convictions.   Far more of a grim Berserk was he, than the Ishmaelite he called himself. His uncompromising exaggerative humour too was of the true old Norse type : well might he say, ' runs in the blood of us, I fancy ! '   ' Brutal,' it has been called, when it seemed to shake the very life out of some of our most petted convictions.   But Pity itself has been known, before now, to express itself somewhat fiercely ; and if we have not life and strength of conviction enough in us to withstand the shock of his terrible on-slaught, and even to gather ourselves together and look him frankly in the face, we shall never discern the still foundations of sad unspeakable earnestness which under-lie, and so often give a touching pathos even to his grimmest humour.   For instance, writing to Emerson, 19th of April, 1849, some few months before the ' Latter-Day Pamphlets,' and while they were yet fermenting within him, he says,—

"It seems likely Lord John Russell will shortly walk out (forever, it is hoped), and Sir R. Peel come in ; to make what effort is in him towards delivering us from the *pedant* method of treating Ireland. The beginning, as I think, of salvation (if he can prosper a little) to England, and to all Europe as well. For they will have to learn that man does need government; and that an able-bodied starving beggar is and remains (whatever Exeter Hall may say to it) a *Slave* destitute of a *Master;* of which facts England, and convulsed Europe, are fallen profoundly ignorant in these bad ages, and will plunge ever deeper till they rediscover the same. Alas, alas, the Future for us is not to be made of *butter*, as the Platforms prophecy; I think it will be harder than steel for some ages! No noble age was ever a soft one, nor ever will or can be."

And again, what can be grimmer than the following account of the results to himself of his ' Tour in Ireland,' written also to Emerson in the August of the same year?—

" I have been terribly knocked about too : jolted in Irish Cars, bothered almost to madness with Irish balderdash, above all kept on dreadfully short allowance of sleep ;—so that now first, when fairly down to rest, all aches and bruises begin to be fairly sensible and my clearest feeling at this present is the uncomfortable one, that ' I am not a Caliban, but a Cramp :' terribly cramped indeed, if I could tell you everything !

" What the other results of this Irish Tour are to be for me I cannot in the least specify. For one thing, I seem to be farther from *speech* on any subject than ever : such masses of chaotic ruin everywhere fronted me, the general fruit of long-continued universal falsity and folly ; and such mountains of delusion yet possessing all hearts and tongues. . . . Alas, alas ! The Gospels of Political Economy, of *Laissez-faire*, No-Government, Paradise to all comers, and so many fatal Gospels,—generally, one may say, all the Gospels of this blessed ' New Era,'—will first have to be tried, and found wanting. With a quantity of written and uttered nonsense, and of suffered and inflicted misery, which one sinks fairly dumb to estimate ! . . . What is to be done ? asks every one ; incapable of *hearing* any answer, were there even one ready to be imparted to him. ' *Blacklead* these two million idle beggars,' I sometimes advised ; . . . perhaps Parliament, on sweet constraint, will allow you to—advance them to be Niggers !"

Atrocious! cry all philanthropists with a shudder; as if Carlyle had seriously proposed this as his remedy, when in truth he was, with poignant intensity of emphasis, trying to express his heart-breaking conviction that the very Negroes might well be envied in comparison;—in short, that no amount of bodily hardship and physical ill-treatment could compare in horror with the moral putrefaction and slavery of soul which everywhere revealed itself to him.

Beyond question Carlyle did not think the sin of Negro Slavery the blackest of all the sins for which we had to answer. And this brings us to a consideration of the gravest offence against the moral sensibilities of his age with which he stands charged,—namely, what is called 'his advocacy of slavery.' What, then, were his actual convictions on this extremely sensitive subject? I have no intention of shirking the question, for I believe it to be fundamental and crucial, both for those who agree with him, and for those who utterly reject and even execrate his teaching. But first let us clearly understand what we mean by slavery. Do we mean irksome and compulsory servitude of all kinds? or, do we mean hopeless servitude under an absolute ownership, from which there is no possibility of honourably rising by any amount or quality of faithful effort? If by slavery we mean the former, then we must all be slaves, if we would be men at all and not mere lotus-eaters; and some of us have to slave very hard, seemingly for very little. This form of circumstantial 'slavery,' if we choose to so name it, Carlyle teaches is not merely perfectly compatible with the highest inward freedom, but is the only manful training for it. Not to do as we like, without let or hindrance,—which he held to be the broad way to destruction, however pleasant it might look,—but to do, voluntarily and even 'gladly,' what we know we must and ought, is Carlyle's definition of the highest freedom. And whether the stern discipline come to us by the compulsory guidance of a wise master, or by the compulsory buffeting of adverse circumstances,—in one form or the other, it is the one preliminary condition of all true manhood.

In Carlyle's terminology, the only real slave is he who has never thus gained the inward masterhood of his own soul. We are all more or less slaves to begin with : slaves to our own inclinations, to the opinions of others, to our hopes, anxieties and terrors. Who will help us to guide and govern ourselves, that we may indeed be free ? He, whosoever he may be, or however hard his discipline, is our truest benefactor. The man who does not wish to believe this, need not trouble himself to read Carlyle, for he will find nothing in his teaching that will at all please him. If the Negro, or any other human fellow-creature with imperfect ability for self-guidance, is in a condition of wholesome servitude,—call it 'slavery,' or what we will,—which is gradually but surely training him for a higher level of humanity ; then, in Carlyle's opinion, he is already in the condition of his truest blessedness, and if there be any incipiency of real wisdom in him, he will one day be himself wise enough to know it. If he be not in such a condition ; if his condition (as was too often the case with the Negro slave) be frightfully and flagrantly the reverse of this ; then his truest friends would be those who strove most earnestly to secure it for him. Not cutting recklessly asunder the fixed and recognised relation of master and servant, and leaving the poor Negro in his darkness and folly to guide and shift for himself; but sternly insisting on a just relation between them,—a relation of mutual benefit; and, for the Negro, a relation which would make clearly possible for him the highest level of humanity his own self-conquest might gradually qualify him to attain. This, in brief, was Carlyle's whole position in relation to the much-exasperated question of slavery, either black or white; and I beg to add, it was St. Paul's position too, whatever we may think of it.

That Carlyle was scornfully impatient with the 'Negro Philanthropists,' and overwhelming in his caustic mockery of what he irreverently called their 'mournful twaddle,' is of course a very grave charge against him which cannot be gainsaid. But that he seriously held that any strong man should be permitted to make a mere chattel of even the most helpless of his fellow-men for his own selfish gain, is too absurdly inconsistent with every word he has written to be gravely discussed with any one who has taken the least trouble to understand him. "Alas, my friends, I understand well," he tells us, "your rage against the poor Negro's slavery; what said rage proceeds from; and have a perfect sympathy with it, and even know it by experience." But what kindled his own rage far more deeply was, the cheap sensibilities so copiously poured forth about the 'forced labour' of the Negro,—as if that were in itself such a hardship,— by men and women who were almost entirely oblivious of the 'enforced idleness,' with all its consequent sin and misery, which was rotting the souls out of themselves, and out of their own sisters and brothers, in their own homes and at their own doors. "My friends, my friends," he exclaims, "I fear we are a stupid people;

and stuffed with such delusions, above all, with such immense hypocrisies and self-delusions, from our birth upwards, as no people were before!"

I repeat, Carlyle's undoubted contempt for the anti-slavery cries which were so self-exultant at the time, did not spring from any feeling of toleration for any of the righteously denounced and oppressive cruelties perpetrated against the Negro; and surely every thoughtful reader of his much-execrated pamphlet, 'The Nigger Question,' ought to have candour enough to see this. What moved him to such energy of scorn was the really alarming fact, that under the hated name of 'slavery' impassioned orators and frenzied writers were undermining every feeling of reverence for honourable servitude. A changed condition of things since the title 'Servant of the servants of God' was chosen, perhaps with a proud humility, for the Highest in Christendom! So far have we now progressed on the broad road of emancipation and social disintegration, that the once honoured name of Servant is fast becoming with us almost as opprobrious a social stigma as that of Slave; as it has long been in emancipated America. In fact, 'domestic servant' and 'domestic slavey' have colloquially become for us convertible terms. And yet we wonder that so few good servants are now to be got for either love or money. Little room can there be for love, with such feelings in our hearts; and as for money,—I suppose money will just buy money's worth. 'It is good for a man that he bear the yoke in his youth.' Time was when the highest in the land went through an apprenticeship of faithful service; and from highest to lowest all were, or had been, veritable Servants in their several degrees. All this modern vanity and vainglory of 'anti-servitude,' masking itself behind the philanthropic cry of 'anti-slavery,' was very despicable in Carlyle's eyes; and assuredly he gave it no quarter. We might almost say his one ethical aim was to restore our reverence for faithful work, and for well-organised faithful service. What is, or can be, that 'Organisation of Labour,' which he so constantly speaks of as the great problem of the future, but a wisely regulated organisation of faithful and Honourable Servitude? Let us not palter with facts. It either means that, or it does not mean organisation at all. The hands *must* serve the head, the feet *must* carry the body, if any work is to be done, or any progress made. Wise guidance, just mastership, faithful service,—we are now trying very hopefully to do without them; and, by universal substitution of selfish rights for social duties, to attain the perfect blessedness of perfect individual liberty, and perfect social equality; wherein each individual shall do as he likes, and all, of course, will like what they have to do. But what will be the meaning of fraternity in the struggle to attain it, we shall know better when the grip of the struggle really comes.

The Organisation of Labour! What might it not grow to! Where and how shall we begin? These were thoughts constantly working in Carlyle's mind; and they were thoughts which went deepest into his heart. He well knew what mountains of obstruction would need to be removed before a step could be taken; but he also felt that he had the faith which can move mountains, and cast them into the sea. I suppose few writers have dwelt with such earnest and reiterated compassion upon the miseries and helplessness of the deserving but down-trodden poor as Carlyle has done. Who does not at once call to mind his compassionate sympathy with the struggling operatives of Glasgow in his younger days, as recorded in his 'Reminiscences'? or his stern description of the 'Poor Drudges' in 'Sartor Resartus'? or the touching picture,—evidently a picture of his own loved Father,—of 'the toilworn Craftsman, that with earth-made Implement laboriously conquers the Earth, and makes her man's'? In 'Chartism,' he pitifully tells us of the 'Half-a-million handloom weavers, working fifteen hours a-day, in perpetual inability to procure thereby enough of the coarsest food; English farm-labourers at nine shillings and at seven shillings a week; Scotch farm-labourers who, in districts the half of whose husbandry is that of cows, taste no milk, can procure no milk.' In 'Past and Present,' he says with heartfelt indignation,—

"Some two million workers, it is counted (1842), sit in Workhouses, Poor-Law Prisons; or have 'out-door relief' flung over the wall to them,—the workhouse Bastille being filled to bursting, and the strong Poor-Law broken asunder by a stronger. They sit there, these many months now; their hope of deliverance as yet small. In workhouses, pleasantly so-named, because work cannot be done in them. Twelve hundred thousand in England alone; their cunning right-hand lamed, lying idle in their sorrowful bosom; their hopes, outlooks, share of this fair world, shut in by narrow walls. They sit there, pent up, as in a kind of horrid enchantment. . . . Passing by the Workhouse of St. Ives in Huntingdonshire, on a bright day last Autumn, I saw sitting on wooden benches, in front of their Bastille and within their ring-wall and its railings, some half-hundred or more of these men. Tall robust figures, young mostly or of middle age; of honest countenance, many of them thoughtful and even intelligent-looking men. They sat there, near by one another; but in a kind of torpor, especially in a silence which was very striking. In silence: for, alas, what word was to be said ?   An Earth all lying round, crying, Come and till me, come and reap me;—yet we here sit enchanted! In the eyes and brows of these men hung the gloomiest expression, not of anger, but of grief and shame and manifold inarticulate distress and weariness; they returned my glance with a glance which seemed to say, ' Do not look at us. We sit enchanted here and know not why. The Sun shines and the Earth calls; and, by the governing Powers and Impotences of this England, we are forbidden to obey. It is impossible, they tell us!' There was something that reminded me of Dante's Hell in the look of all this; and I rode swiftly away."

Once more, what a picture is that of the poor Irish Widow! "A poor Irish Widow, her husband having died in one of the Lanes of Edinburgh, went forth with her three children, bare of all resource, to solicit help from the Charitable Establishments of that City. At this Charitable Establishment and then at that she was refused; referred from one to the other, helped by none; —till she had exhausted them all; till her strength and her heart failed her : she sank down in typhus-fever; died, and infected her Lane with fever, so that ' seventeen other persons' died of fever in consequence. . . . She applied to her fellow-creatures, as if saying, ' Behold I am sinking, bare of help : ye must help me ! I am your sister, bone of your bone; one God made us : ye must help me !' "—But, he adds, she had ' to prove her sisterhood,' by dying of typhus-fever and killing seventeen of them. ' Had human creature ever to go lower for proof?'

It would be easy to multiply instances, page after page, of Carlyle's heart-aching compassion for the helpless hopeless misery of the deserving poor, struggling under burdens too heavy for them, without a soul to look to for human sympathy and kindly aid. All this widespread, hourly agony of breaking hearts and 'foiled potentialities,' which most of us contrive very comfortably to ignore as no business of ours, was constantly and vividly present before him. His own childhood and early manhood had been darkened by the shadow of it. He had seen it with his eyes, and had felt it aching in his own heart. "Words cannot express," he wrote, in words already quoted, "the love and sorrow of my old memories, chiefly out of boyhood, as they occasionally rise upon me." How could he forget such things,—with those searching photographing eyes of his, and that retentive panoramic memory which seemed to make everything he had once seen a part of his very existence? Unhappy? —Yes, he was bound to be unhappy; and to sternly make up his mind to 'do without Paradise,' until some beginning of a remedy could be manfully initiated. It was the God's burden laid upon him at his birth, and which he carried with him through life; only to be released with, 'Well done, good and faithful Servant,' beyond the grave.

Perhaps the most hopeful sign of God's working presence amongst us, in the days which have now come upon us, is the wide and growing compassion,—growing in wisdom as well as in stature and in strength,—of the well-to-do for their less fortunate sisters and brothers, showing us once more how even 'they that have riches' may enter the kingdom of Heaven. Of course there is the inevitable leaven of idle vanity and craving for the last new excitement; playing at ministering angels in what are now the fashionable slums, while treating the servants in their own homes as soulless 'menials' beneath

their human sympathy : all which the true workers
sorrowfully confess, and shrink from as from the touch
of leprosy ; and which Carlyle would have known very
well how to deal with.   But, in spite of all fashionable
folly and kid-glove sentimentalisms, the amount of true
earnest work which is now being silently and unosten-
tatiously carried through to help the helpless to help one
another, is a thing for which Carlyle would have been
unspeakably thankful, if he could have lived to practically realise its worth.   I allude more especially to such
Organised Beneficences as the Industrial Schools for both
boys and girls ; the Emigration Services for those who
as they grow up can find no steady occupation at home ;
the efforts to improve the homes of the poor ; the loving
consideration for their children, in sending thousands of
them annually for a real holiday in the pleasant country,
and so gladdening their young lives, and making their
parents feel how many motherly, fatherly, sisterly, and
brotherly hearts sympathise with them in their priva-
tions ; and, lastly, to the efforts of such institutions as
the Metropolitan Association for befriending young
servants, by which 4491 situations were found for
otherwise helpless girls in 1884.   Out of this number
the Whitechapel Branch alone found 409 situations, in
response to 504 applications ; Wandsworth, 438 to 760
applications ; and Poplar, 448 to 918 applications.
These numbers are the highest in the published list ;
and although they show how much still needs to be
done, they also show that the largest amount of actual
work is being done where it is most needed.   Out of
the total number of girls for whom situations were
found, 1031 were provided with clothing ; and out of
that number, no less than 861 had, up to the time of

making up the Report, since repaid, either wholly or in part, the money thus advanced to them. Surely this fact alone speaks highly both for the honourable feelings of the girls, and for the kindly interest taken in them.

Truly there is much earnest work being done in our country which is not tending to social disintegration : less noisy than the disintegrating sort, and making no pretension to remodel our entire social relations. And yet, if one only knew, one might be inclined to prophesy a little. This, at least, we may all know; that it is precisely such work as this which will bind class and class together in bonds of mutual helpfulness, and of heartfelt devotion to a Common-Weal; which will awaken all that is best and strongest within us and without us, and will grow with our growth and strengthen with our strength : it is twice blessed, blessing him that gives and him that receives; and, if faithfully carried through,—for there lies the only doubt,—will at last make God's Will done on Earth, even as it is done in Heaven. Founded on the rock of Everlasting Faithfulness, it would rise high above all social deluges, and be a rallying cry and pillar of light through the darkest storms. It is a consummation devoutly to be wished.

I have often wondered how many of our really earnest workers have ever realised how much we owe to Carlyle for initiating all this deep sympathising compassion for deserving helplessness. I have tried to show that his whole life was one passionate effort to awaken us to the need of it. But since the time of the 'Latter-Day Pamphlets' we have heard so much about his deep abhorrence of determined idleness and sinful folly; and even professing Christians have been so shocked that he

should pretend to 'discern between him that serveth
God, and him that serveth Him not,' that he has almost
come to be looked upon by many as our one entirely
uncompassionate man.   Well, there are people, who
would not like to consider themselves faithless before
God, who seem to look upon 'lost sheep' and 'prowling
wolves' pretty much alike, or even prefer the latter, if
only in sheep's clothing, as objects of interest and compassion ; and I suppose to such people the 'Latter-Day
Pamphlets' must needs seem utterly merciless in their
righteous discrimination.   But, however that may be, the
fact remains, that we owe Carlyle an incalculable debt
of gratitude for all that he did to awaken the country
from its sleep of death.   'He that believeth in Me,' said
the Light of the World, 'the works that I do he shall do
also.'   If Carlyle did not quite touch the highest mark
of Christian self-devotion, let all those who aim at a
more simply Christ-like life, take both encouragement
and warning from him, and do better in proportion to
the higher light which points their way.   Let us be as
wise and simply Christian as we may, it will be long
before we reach, as a Nation, the height and depth and
breadth of individual devotion to the common good to
which he would fain have led us.

But not by any amount of temporary benevolences,
however warm-hearted, and still less by any mere
ministering of amusements, however kindly meant or
gratefully accepted, did Carlyle believe that human
justice would ever be secured for the helpless amongst
us, or the National Sin of Pauperism ever be condoned.
Work, organised faithful work, and the fruit of it
honestly secured to the Worker, was his one notion of
social salvation, for himself and for all men.   "Some

Chivalry of Labour," he insisted in 'Past and Present' with prophetic earnestness, "will yet be realised on this Earth. Or why *will*; why do we pray to Heaven, without setting our own shoulder to the wheel? The Present, if it will have the Future accomplish, shall itself commence. Thou who prophesiest, who believest, begin thou to fulfil. Here or nowhere, now equally as at any time! That outcast help-needing thing or person, trampled down under vulgar feet or hoofs, no help 'possible' for it, no prize offered for the saving of it,—canst not thou save it, then, without prize? Put forth thy hand, in God's name; know that 'impossibility,' where Truth and Mercy and the everlasting Voice of Nature order, has no place in the brave man's dictionary. That when all men have said 'Impossible,' and tumbled noisily elsewhither, and thou alone art left, then first *thy* time and possibility have come." Surely these are not the words of him that hath a devil.

Let us now turn once more to the 'Latter-Day Pamphlets,' in which unwise readers imagine he had grown unfaithful to his earlier teaching. Let us, for instance, try to understand what he there says of Pauperism; and candidly ask ourselves whether it is not the same compassionate heart striving with us, only with yet deeper earnestness and with a clearer and even more steadfast aim.

"Pauperism," he says, "though it now absorbs its high figure of millions annually, is by no means a question of money only, but of infinitely higher and greater than all conceivable money. If our Chancellor of the Exchequer had a Fortunatus' purse, and miraculous sacks of Indian meal that would stand scooping from forever,—I say even on these terms Pauperism could not be endured : and it would vitally concern all British Citizens to abate Pauperism, and never rest till they had ended it again. Pauperism is the general leakage through every joint of the ship that is rotten. Were all men doing their duty, or even seriously trying to do it, there would be no Pauper. . . . Not an idle Sham lounging about Creation upon false pretences, *upon means which he has not earned, upon theories which he does not practise*, but yields his share of Pauperism somewhere or other. His sham-work oozes down; finds its last issue as human Pauperism,—in a human being who by those false pretences cannot live. The Idle Workhouse, now about to burst of overfilling, what is it but the scandalous poison-tank of drainage from the universal Stygian quagmire of our affairs ? Workhouse Paupers ; immortal sons of Adam rotted into that scandalous condition, *subter-slavish*,—demanding that you would make slaves of them as an unattainable blessing ! My friends, I perceive the quagmire must be drained, or we cannot live. And farther, I perceive this of Pauperism is the corner where we must *begin*,—the levels all pointing thitherward, the possibilities lying all clearly there. On that Problem we shall find that innumerable things, that all things whatsoever hang. By courageous steadfast persistence in that, I can foresee Society itself regenerated. In the course of long strenuous centuries, I can see the State become what it is actually bound to be, the keystone of a most real ' Organisation of Labour,'—and on this Earth a world of some veracity, and some heroism, once more worth living in ! "

Of course all this will be at once stigmatised as ' mere Socialism ; ' and, if every effort for mutual helpfulness and individual devotion to the common good is what we are to understand as being ' socialistic,' let the stigma remain, for this is the one indispensable condition of social existence and of all social greatness. But the Organisation of Labour here spoken of, means national unity, not national disintegration : it means social discipline, and the due subordination of the less wise to the wiser, and of the wiser to the wisest, for the maximum good of all ; not a mere aggregation of individuals acknowledging no higher or more imperative obligation than their own personal sympathies, and what they may consider their own rights of enjoyment. It is no more socialistic, in the ordinary acceptance of the word, than a National Army is socialistic, or the National Post Office, or the National Mint, or the Board of Works, or any other organised State Administration for the common good of the nation. Carlyle's notion was, that, as we gather idle men from all parts of the country, and, by due discipline and experienced guidance and control, convert them from a desultory mob into a united Regiment of loyal and mutually sustaining men, bound together by strong ties of comradeship, and ready to risk their lives at the word of command,—so might we, in spite of Political Economy, if we had but wisdom and manhood enough for the work, enlist all our idle hands and outcast population into Industrial Regiments ; and, instead of spending our ' high figure of millions annually ' in barely keeping them alive in degrading idleness and corroding misery, guide and organise them into countless forms of noble manhood and noble womanhood, and thus convert them into a priceless blessing to themselves and to all of us. This he believed, if honestly and wisely carried through would inevitably lead to the regeneration of Society itself.

"Suppose," he says, " the State to have fairly started its 'Industrial Regiments of the New Era,' which, alas, are yet only beginning to be talked of,—what continents of new real work opened out for the Home and all other Public Offices among us ! Suppose the Home Office looking out, as for life and salvation, for proper men to command these ' Regiments.'

Suppose the announcement were practically made to all British souls that the want of wants, more indispensable than any jewel in the crown, was that of men *able to command men in ways of industrial and moral welldoing;* that the State would give its very life for such men; that such men *were* the State; that the quantity of them to be found in England, lamentably small at present, was the exact measure of England's worth,—what a new dawn of everlasting day for all British souls! . . . Wise obedience and wise command, I foresee that the regimenting of Pauper Banditti into Soldiers of Industry is but the beginning of this blessed process, which will extend to the topmost heights of our Society; and, in the course of generations, make us all once more a Governed Commonwealth, and *Civitas Dei,* if it please God!"

In like manner, Jethro the priest of Midian advised Moses, saying, " ' Provide out of all the people able men, such as fear God, men of truth, hating unjust gain ; and place such over them, to be rulers of thousands, rulers of hundreds, rulers of fifties, and rulers of tens ; and let them judge the people at all seasons: and it shall be, that every great matter they shall bring to thee, but every small matter they shall judge themselves.' And Moses hearkened to the voice of his father-in-law, and did all that he had said."

' What a door to open to corruption !' exclaim the Political Economists. ' We have no such men ; or, if we have, how are *we* to distinguish the one from the other ? It would never do, in these advanced ages of the world, to trust the State with any such functions. We must learn to do without all this antiquated "fear of God" and "hatred of unjust gain ;" and look to our own alert political machinery, and the system of universal check which we have now brought almost to perfection !' These are what Carlyle calls ' Professors of the Dismal

Science ;' and, for a long while yet, they seem in this matter to be destined to have their dismal way.

Meanwhile, if all such things are as yet 'impossible' for the State, there is no little comfort for us in the fact that many of them have already become distinctly possible to men and women with human hearts, with both the fear and love of God stirring within them. If we cannot as yet even attempt to drain the rotting quagmire of Pauperism, and compel the recklessly idle to a life of industry, let us thank God it is at least possible to snatch by thousands those who would gladly work if they only knew how, from the foul welter in which they are helplessly engulfed, and start them on some poor beginning of a human career. We can save young girls from a life of degradation, and train them to all manner of womanly and honourable service. We can establish and foster Industrial Schools and Work-shops for the young, and even for adults if we have humanity enough for it ; and even help them to prosper in the open markets of the world, which 'Political Economy'—the noble science of taking care of oneself —would so fain hold sacred from the touch and contami-nation of Christian compassion.

It is not to be expected that every good work and industrial enterprise should pay its own way and be perfectly satisfactory from the beginning. It is enough that it should be faithfully and earnestly tending, and daily and hourly growing, to its own ideal of practical success. Give it time and patient nurture, that every limb may grow and strengthen, and the new life become a second nature, before you expect from it the indepen-dence and fulness and aptitude of maturity. Above all, do not teach the helpless that they are degraded in

T

frankly accepting help from those who gladly afford it, for it is the divinest tie that can knit two human souls together.　All honour to the genuine helper, and to the really helped.　But the all-searching, all-momentous question always is, What kind of help,—and for what? Are we really helping, and thus co-operating with, honest industry; or are we sinfully pandering to, and thus participating in, dishonest idleness?　The problem is not an easy one; but it involves the whole difference between honour and dishonour, between renewed life and accelerated death, to the recipient of our intended benevolence.　If Carlyle execrated the latter spirit as a mother of abominations, who shall say he did not reverence and strive to initiate and encourage the other, with an earnestness of effort, and prophetic conviction of its eventual triumph, altogether without parallel in our day?

I must now call attention very briefly to one more subject,—not of a higher nature, yet literally boundless in its all-embracing beneficence,—in order to illustrate once more the grandly realistic character of Carlyle's aims.　We hear much talk in these days of what is called our Colonial Empire,—that wider, if not yet greater Britain, upon which the Sun never sets; which embraces the globe, and is gradually filling vast continents, innumerable islands, and other fertile portions of the Earth's surface, with, to adopt Carlyle's glowing symbol, 'Children of the Hartz Rock.'　Are there no divine or human means by which this world-wide Brotherhood of Nations, children of one family and speaking the same Mother-tongue, can become more intimately knit to the 'Old House at Home,' by ties of mutual helpfulness and practical good will?　Many

earnest hearts, both at home and in the Colonies, are now pondering this great question; for the problem is pressing for solution, however hopeless our prospects in that direction, as in so many others, may yet for a long while be. The heartfelt desire is here; but the practical wisdom to foster and embody such a spirit, and the consistency and continuity of effort, needed to carry through any great far-reaching and generous policy, are not here, nor, as Carlyle would say, soon likely to be. A political seesaw, with its dismal alternation of mutually destructive Administrations, calling itself 'Party Government' (which means simply a House divided against itself), must necessarily leave all such problems to individual patriotism, and to the changes and chances of the hour. For a long while little or nothing will be done to any practical effect, which does not promise an immediate material return.

I do not call attention to the following extract with any thought of indicating what might now be done, either for the Colonies or by them; for I suppose they too, like the rest of the world, will have to learn 'what a game that of trying for cure in the Medea's-cauldron of Revolution is,' before any real beginning of knitting together can be hopefully looked for. I merely give the passage as one more illustration of Carlyle's vivid conception of the mighty empire of industry and co-operative beneficence, to which the Anglo-Saxon Race might one day grow, if wisely organised, and justly cared for, by 'The New Downing Street' which he once hoped to assist in establishing.

"An instinct," he says, "deeper than the Gospel of M'Crowdy teaches all men that Colonies are worth something to a country! That if, under the present Colonial Office, they

are a vexation to us and themselves, some other Colonial
Office can and must be contrived which shall render them a
blessing; and that the remedy will be to contrive such a
Colonial Office or method of administration, and by no means
to cut the Colonies loose. Colonies are not to be picked off
the street every day; not a Colony of them but has been
bought dear, well purchased by toil and blood of those we
have the honour to be sons of; and we cannot just afford to
cut them away because M'Crowdy finds the present management of them cost money. The present management will
indeed require to be cut away;—but as for the Colonies, we
purpose through Heaven's blessing to retain them a while
yet! Shame on us for unworthy sons of brave fathers if we
do not. Brave fathers, by valiant blood and sweat, purchased
for us, from the bounty of Heaven, rich possessions in all
zones;—and we, wretched imbeciles, cannot do the function
of administering them?"

"Britain, whether it be known or not, has other tasks
appointed her in God's Universe than the making of money;
and woe will betide her if she forget those other withal.
Tasks, colonial and domestic, which are of an eternally *divine*
nature, and compared with which all money, and all that is
procurable by money, are in strict arithmetic an imponderable
quantity, have been assigned this Nation; and they also at
last are coming upon her again, clamorous, abstruse, inevitable,
much to her bewilderment just now!

"This poor Nation, painfully dark about said tasks and
the way of doing them, means to keep its Colonies nevertheless, as things which somehow or other must have a value,
were it better seen into. They are portions of the general
Earth, where the children of Britain now dwell; where the
gods have so far sanctioned their endeavour, as to say that
they have a right to dwell. England will not readily admit
that her own children are worth nothing but to be flung out
of doors! England looking on her Colonies can say: 'Here
are lands and seas, spice-lands, corn-lands, timber-lands, over-
arched by zodiacs and stars, clasped by many-sounding seas;
wide spaces of the Maker's building, fit for the cradle yet of
mighty Nations and their Sciences and Heroisms. Fertile

continents still inhabited by wild beasts are mine, into which all the distressed populations of Europe might pour themselves, and make at once an Old World and a New World human. By the eternal fiat of the gods, this must yet one day be; this, by all the Divine Silences that rule this Universe, silent to fools, eloquent and awful to the hearts of the wise, is incessantly at this moment, and at all moments, commanded to begin to be. Unspeakable deliverance, and new destiny of thousandfold expanded manfulness for all men, dawns out of the Future here. To me has fallen the godlike task of initiating all that: of me and my Colonies, the abstruse Future asks, Are you wise enough for so sublime a Destiny? Are you too foolish?'"

So far, England's reply seems to be: 'Too foolish; far too foolish. The thing is impossible. No such Empire of Beneficence can ever be founded. It is true that now, with all our modern facilities and equipments physical and moral, such a world-wide Empire might conceivably be far more efficiently administered than England itself could have been a few generations back; but we lack wisdom, and largeness of heart, and heroic devotion to the common-weal; and must even scramble on as we can, with such paltry aims as are clearly visible to us, and safely within the limits of our feeble grasp.' Well might Carlyle exclaim in passionate despair, "You unfortunates, what is the use of your money-bags, of your territories, funded properties, your mountains of possessions, equipments and mechanic inventions, which the flunkey pauses over, awestruck, and almost rises into epos and prophecy at sight of? No use, or less than none. Your skin is covered, and your digestive and other bodily apparatus is supplied; and you have but to wish in these respects, and more is ready; and—the Devils, I think, are quizzing you.

You ask for 'happiness,' 'O give me happiness!'—and they hand you ever new varieties of covering for the skin, ever new kinds of supply for the digestive apparatus, new and ever new, worse or not a whit better than the old; and—and—this is your 'happiness?' As if you were sick children; as if you were not men, but a kind of apes!"

And so we leave the 'Latter-Day Pamphlets:' the sincerest utterances of a compassionate, stormful, and courageous heart, since Luther stood before the Diet of Worms. As the days roll on, and our troubles increase, they will become more and more credible. They will work their own appointed work, in spite of all gainsaying. They will carry their God's Message as far as it will go,—'and, what is a great advantage too, no farther.'

CHAPTER XVII.

No practical career now possible for Carlyle—His frustrated hope in Sir
Robert Peel—Sending him copy of ' Cromwell ' : Letter and Reply—
Mutual esteem—Meeting by arrangement at Lady Ashburton's—
Wary advances on Carlyle's part—Invitation to dine with Sir Robert
—Second meeting at Bath House—' Except him, there was nobody
I had the smallest hope in '—Deep concern at the news of his death.

WE have now seen the leading points of Carlyle's magnificent forecast of the possible future of England ; and
we have also seen sufficient indications of the intense
personal hope of participating in its realisation which
had fully taken possession of him when he commenced
writing the ' Latter-Day Pamphlets.' His hopes at that
time clearly centred themselves in Sir Robert Peel, as
the one Statesman fitted, by position, experience, and
original endowment, for taking the lead in such an
arduous work of Administrative Reform as he strove to
show was both practicable and necessary. But Sir
Robert Peel, as we have seen, died suddenly before the
Pamphlets were completed ; and Carlyle thus found the
ground suddenly cut from under him. What difference
this occasioned in his original intention as to his manner
of concluding them, I suppose we shall never know. He
originally contemplated a series of twelve, and there are
only eight. " Some twelve pamphlets, if I can but get
them written at all," he says. Did he intend some

further graphic illustrations of what England might become, by wise government and guidance, and a worthy career opened for every honest and practical intellect amongst us ?   We do not know what he intended in this matter, if his destiny had been propitious, and his own especial 'loadstar' had not been so sternly blotted out. We can only note that the seventh pamphlet, 'Hudson's Statue,'—published the day before Sir Robert Peel's death, and treating of the 'New Aristocracy' which he discerned in the future,—is all bristling with a strenuous spirit of reform, with desperate hope, and with his own pronounced individuality and personal aspirations, like all those which had preceded it; but in the last of the pamphlets, 'Jesuitism,'—published a month afterwards,— all that fervour of effort, distinctness of purpose, and forecasting of events, had entirely passed away : there are no more prophetic intimations or outlines either of a New Downing Street, an efficient Parliament, or a genuine Aristocracy yet to come; his loadstars seem all to have sunk below the horizon, and he mournfully restricts himself to a doom-like apocalypse of our moral rottenness and social life-in-death.   Again I say, it was the turning-point at which hope left him, and despair took possession of his soul.

But Carlyle's earnest hope that Sir Robert Peel might some day be induced to return to Office, and there make possible some beginning of a New Downing Street; and the tragic extinction of that hope; together constituted so momentous a crisis in his life, that it will be of more than ordinary interest to trace all that is known of their personal intercourse; for, however tentative it may have been, the details are not wanting in special significance.

In 'Past and Present' Carlyle had condemned in no

stinted terms the folly, cruelty, and general iniquity of
the Corn-Laws. He gave no special chapter on them,
declaring them utterly beneath all honest argument.
But he did give a chapter, which was very evidently and
very emphatically addressed to Sir Robert Peel, which
he entitled 'Sir Jabesh Windbag.' In this chapter he
points to and pictures Cromwell as our Pattern Governor,
and solemnly contrasts his earnest faith in God, with
our poor modern 'faith that Paragraphs and Plausibilities bring votes.' It is the most solemnly personal
appeal in the whole book. As I have already intimated,
there can be little doubt, taking all the facts into consideration, that 'Past and Present' had much to do in
convincing Sir Robert Peel of the utter indefensibility of
his position ; and Carlyle may therefore reasonably have
regarded him with something of the interest of a highly
encouraging and indeed invaluable disciple ; and he may
well have speculated on the possibility of influencing
him still further. But, whatever we may think about
the hope of further influencing him, it is at least evident
that, by his repeal of the Corn-Laws, and by his frankly-
generous and courageous manner of doing it, he clearly
convinced Carlyle that he was no mere 'Windbag ;' and,
accordingly, Carlyle took the earliest opportunity of
assuring him of his heartfelt sympathy and respect.

Mr. Froude says,—speaking of the second edition
of the 'Letters and Speeches,'—" 'Cromwell,' thus
enlarged, was now in its final form ; and as soon as it
was done, he took a step in connection with it which,
I believe, he never took before or after with any of his
writings ; he presented a copy of it to the Prime
Minister." This unusual step for Carlyle was taken
immediately after Peel had carried his great measure

through Parliament, and in the very midst of the fierce Parliamentary storm he had thus raised around him. The letter he wrote on the occasion, and the answer he punctually received, are too significantly important, and bear too expressly on the matter in hand, to be passed over with a mere reference. Both letters are well worth the very thoughtful perusal of any reader who wishes to realise for himself the solid ground of hope on which Carlyle afterwards laboured so earnestly to build. His own letter was as follows :—

" Chelsea : June 18, 1846.

"Sir,—Will you be pleased to accept from a very private citizen of the community this copy of a book which he has been occupied in putting together, while you, our most conspicuous citizen, were victoriously labouring in quite other work ? Labour, so far as it is true, and sanctionable by the Supreme Worker and World Founder, may claim brotherhood with labour. The great work and the little are alike definable as an extricating of the true from its imprisonment among the false; a victorious evoking of order and fact from disorder and semblance of fact. In any case, citizens who feel grateful to a citizen are permitted and enjoined to testify that feeling, each in such manner as he can. Let this poor labour of mine be a small testimony of that sort to a late great and valiant labour of yours, and claim reception as such.

"The book, should you find leisure to read and master it, may perhaps have interest for you—may perhaps—who knows ?—have admonition, exhortation, in various ways instruction and encouragement for yet other labours which England, in a voiceless but most impressive manner, still expects and demands of you. The authentic words and actings of the noblest governor England ever had may well have interest for all governors of England; may well be, as all Scripture is, as all genuine words and writings are, ' profitable,' —profitable for reproof, for correction, and for edifying and strengthening withal. Hansard's Debates are not a kind of literature I have been familiar with; nor indeed is the arena they proceed from much more than a distress to me in these days. Loud-sounding clamour and rhetorical vocables grounded not on fact, nor even on belief of fact, one knows from of old whither all that and what depends on it is bound. But by-and-by, as I believe, all England will say what already many a one begins to feel, that whatever were the spoken unveracities of Parliament, and they are many on all hands, lamentable to gods and men, here has a great veracity been *done* in Parliament, considerably our greatest for many years past,—a strenuous, courageous, and needful thing, to which all of us that so see it are bound to give our loyal recognition and furtherance as we can.

"I have the honour to be, Sir,
"Your obliged fellow-citizen and obedient servant,
"T. CARLYLE." *

Evidently such a letter as the foregoing could neither have been written by Carlyle, nor have been received by Sir Robert Peel, as a mere personal compliment. It must have been written by Carlyle with a full consciousness of the chapter on 'Sir Jabesh Windbag' in his mind, and without any intention of ignoring the solemn condemnation he had then felt himself bound to pronounce : for he again laments the many 'spoken unveracities of Parliament,' in which Peel had had his inevitable share ; but this time only to contrast it with the 'great veracity' which had now been *done*. He had before referred to Cromwell only to point to the unspeakable contrast between the methods of the two men ; but he now spoke of Cromwell as a man whose example might be 'profitable for reproof, for correction, and for edifying and strengthening withal.' He evidently felt that Peel had really listened to the warning, and he wished to put himself frankly square with a man so open to honest conviction, and so resolute to carry his convictions into

* 'Life in London, 1834–1881,' vol. i. p. 375.

effect. Nor was Peel behindhand in this interesting passage of courteous acknowledgment; for he admits his familiarity with Carlyle's exertions as a writer, and therefore, by implication, with what he had written in 'Past and Present,' and expresses himself both able to appreciate, and grateful for, his 'favourable opinion.' The following is what he wrote in reply:—

"Whitehall: June 22, 1846.

"Sir,—Whatever may have been the pressure of my public engagements, it has not been so overwhelming as to prevent me from being familiar with your exertions in another department of labour, as incessant and severe as that which I have undergone.

"I am the better enabled, therefore, to appreciate the value of your favourable opinion; and to thank you, not out of mere courtesy, but very sincerely, for the volumes which you have sent for my acceptance; most interesting as throwing a new light upon a very important chapter of our history; and gratifying to me as a token of your personal esteem.

"I have the honour to be, Sir,

"Your obedient servant,

"Robert Peel."

Surely if anything were wanting to show Sir Robert Peel's intrinsic veracity of heart, this letter might well be put in as conclusive evidence. A week after it was written, he resigned his post as Prime Minister; having been defeated by his enemies in Parliament, in a half-frantic spirit of revenge for his great service done to the country, but to the damage, as they thought, of their own personal interests. For nearly two years after this interchange of courtesies, there does not appear to have been any further intercourse between them; and clearly there was no further personal advance on Carlyle's part. Mr. Froude says, "Peel had known him by sight since the present of 'Cromwell,' and had given him looks of recognition when they met in the street." But Carlyle was not a man to obtrude himself upon any one, and least of all upon so distinguished a personage in whom he felt so deeply interested. But in 1848 he seems to have come to the conclusion that it might be good for them to be brought personally together; and, accordingly, a meeting of the great practical man and the great seeing man was arranged to take place at a dinner at Bath House: a meeting evidently brought about by the friendly management of Lady Ashburton. The following is Carlyle's account of the interview, as noted at the time in his private Journal :—

"*March* 27.—Went to the Peel enterprise; sate next Sir Robert,—an evening not unpleasant to remember. Peel is a finely-made man of strong, not heavy, rather of elegant, stature; stands straight, head slightly thrown back, and eyelids modestly drooping; every way mild and gentle, yet with less of that fixed smile than his portraits give him. He is towards sixty, and, though not broken at all, carries, especially in his complexion, when you are *near* him, marks of that age : clear, strong blue eyes which kindle on occasion, voice extremely good, low-toned, something of *cooing* in it, rustic, affectionate, honest, mildly persuasive. Spoke about French Revolutions new and old ; well read in all that; had seen General Dumouriez. Reserved seemingly by nature, obtrudes nothing of *diplomatic* reserve, on the contrary, a vein of mild *fun* in him, real sensibility to the ludicrous, which feature I liked best of all. Nothing in that slight inspection seemed to promise better in him than his laugh. . . . Shall I see the Premier again ? I consider him by far our first public man—which indeed is saying little —and hope that England in these frightful times may still get some good of him.

"N.B.—This night with Peel was the night in which Berlin city executed its last terrible battle (19th of March to Sunday morning the 20th, five o'clock). While we sat there the streets of Berlin city were all blazing with grapeshot and the war of enraged men. What is to become of all that? I have a book to write about it. Alas!

"We hear of a great Chartist petition to be presented by 200,000 men. People here keep up their old foolish levity in speaking of these things; but considerate persons find them to be very grave; and indeed all, even the laughers, are in considerable secret alarm." *

So passed the first interview with Sir Robert Peel; and such was the man, in his eyes, whom he was already dubiously looking to for some kind of deliverance. But he was still groping in the dark, and borne down with all manner of wretched misgivings.—'Shall I see the Premier again?'—'While we sat there the streets of Berlin city were all blazing with grapeshot and the war of enraged men. What is to become of all that? I have a book to write about it. Alas!' The burden of the 'Latter-Day Pamphlets' already weighed heavily upon him, but the way before him was pathless, dismal, and inscrutable as chaos. Thirteen months later, there is the following entry in his Journal :—

"*April* 26, 1849.—Little done hitherto,—nothing definite done at all. What other book will follow? That is ever the question, and hitherto the unanswered one. Silent hitherto, not from having nothing to say, but from having *all*,—a whole world to say at once. I am weak too,—forlorn, bewildered, and nigh *lost*,—too weak for my place, I too. Article in the 'Spectator' about *Peel and Ireland;* very cruel upon Russell, commanding him to get about his business for ever. Was written very ill, but really to satisfy my conscience in some measure. . . . My voice sounds to me like a One Voice in the world, too frightful to me, with a heart so sick and a head growing grey! I say often *Was thut's? Be silent then!* all which I know is very weak." †

---

* 'Life in London, 1834–1881,' vol. i. p. 433.   † Ibid., p. 452.

Then, in 1850, came the 'Latter-Day Pamphlets.' While they were yet appearing in monthly numbers,—in fact very shortly after 'The New Downing Street,' and 'Stump Orator,'—Mr. Froude tells us that, "in the midst of the storm which he had raised, he was surprised agreeably by an invitation to dine with Sir Robert Peel. . . . The dinner was in the second week of May. The ostensible object was to bring about a meeting between Carlyle and Prescott." The account of the gathering is noted at some length in his Journal, and throughout all its graphic details shows very clearly how completely Carlyle's interest had been centred in Peel himself. I omit all that is not essential to our immediate purpose, and for the full details must refer the reader to Mr. Froude's volumes.

"There was a great party, Prescott, Milman, Barry (architect), Lord Mahon, Sheil, Gibson (sculptor), Cubitt (builder), etc., etc. About Prescott I cared little, and indeed, there or elsewhere, did not speak with him at all; but what I noted of Peel I will now put down. I was the second that entered the big drawing-room, a picture gallery as well, which looks out over the Thames (Whitehall Gardens, second house to the eastward of Montague House), commands Westminster Bridge too, with its wrecked parapets [old Westminster Bridge], and the new Parliament Houses, being, I fancy, of *semicircular* figure in that part and projecting into the shore of the river. Old Cubitt, a hoary, modest, sensible-looking man, was alone with Peel when I entered. My reception was abundantly cordial. Talk went on about the new Houses of Parliament, and the impossibility or difficulty of hearing in them,—others entering, Milman, etc., joined in it as I had done. Sir Robert, in his mild kindly voice, talked of the difficulties architects had in making out that part of their problem. Nobody then knew how it was to be done. . . . People now came in thick and rapid. I went about the gallery with those already come, and saw little more of Sir Robert then. I remember, in presenting Barry to

Prescott, he said with kindly emphasis, 'I have wished to show you some of our most distinguished men: allow me to introduce,' etc.   Barry had been getting rebuked in the House of Commons in those very days and hours, and had been defended there by Sir Robert. . . . Panizzi, even *Scribe*, came to the dinner, no ladies there; nothing but two sons of Peel, one at each end, he himself in the middle about opposite to where I sate; Mahon on his left hand, on his right Van de Weyer (Belgian ambassador); not a creature there for whom I cared one penny, except Peel himself.   Dinner sumptuous and excellently served, but I should think rather wearisome to everybody, as it certainly was for me.   After all the servants but the butler were gone, we began to hear a little of Peel's quiet talk across the table, unimportant, distinguished by its sense of the ludicrous shining through a strong official *rationality* and even seriousness of temper. . . . All which was very pretty and human as Peel gave it us.   In rising we had some question about the pictures in his dining-room. . . . Doubts rising about who some lady portrait was, I went to the window and asked Sir Robert himself, who turned with alacrity and talked to us about that and the rest.   The *hand* in Johnson's portrait brought an anecdote from him about Wilkie and it at Drayton.   Peel spread his hand over it, an inch or two off, to illustrate or enforce,—as fine a man's hand as I remember to have seen, strong, delicate, and scrupulously clean.   Upstairs, most of the people having soon gone, he showed us his volume of autographs,—Mirabeau, Johnson, Byron, Scott, and many English kings and officialities: excellent cheerful talk and description; human, but official in all things.   Then, with cordial shake of the hand, dismissal; and the Bishop of Oxford, insisting on it, took me home in his carriage." *

A few days later Carlyle and Peel again met at a dinner at Bath House.   Of this interview he afterwards wrote :—

"He was fresh and hearty, with delicate, gentle, yet frank manners; a kindly man.   His reserve as to all great or public

* 'Life in London, 1834–1881,' vol. ii. p. 42.

matters sits him quite naturally and enhances your respect,
—a warm sense of fun, really of genuine broad drollery, looks
through him; the hopefullest feature I could clearly see in
this last interview or any other. At tea he talked to us
readily, on slight hint from me, about Byron (Birron he called
him) and their old school-days; kindly reminiscences, agree-
able to hear at first hand, though nothing new in them to us." [*]

Again in a few days, and very shortly before his
sudden death, Peel met Carlyle very cordially in the
street.

"The only time," Carlyle said, "we had ever saluted,
owing to mutual bashfulness and pride of humility, I do
believe. Sir Robert, with smiling look, extended his left hand
and cordially grasped mine in it, with a 'How are you?' pleasant to think of. It struck me that there might certainly be
some valuable reform work still in Peel, though the look of all
things, his own strict conservatism and even officiality of view,
and still more the *cohue* of objects and persons his life was
cast amidst, did not increase my hopes of a great result.
But he seemed happy and humane and hopeful, still strong
and fresh to look upon. Except him, there was nobody I had
the smallest hope in; and what he *would* do, which seemed
now soon to be tried, was always an interesting feature of the
coming time for me. I had an authentic regard for this man,
and a wish to know more of him,—nearly the one man alive
of whom I could say so much." [†]

How deeply Carlyle was concerned at the terrible
news which was so soon to break upon him, is sufficiently
shown in the following extract from his Journal. No
date is given with the extract; but from the almost
doubtful phrase, '29th of June it must have been,' the
entry seems evidently to have been written some time
after the event.

"On a Saturday evening, bright sunny weather, Jane being

<hr>

[*] 'Life in London, 1834–1881,' vol. ii. p. 44.   [†] Ibid., p. 47.

out at Addiscombe, and I to go next day, 29th of June it must have been, I had gone up Piccadilly between four and five p.m., and was returning; half-past six when I got to Hyde Park Corner. Old Marquis of Anglesey was riding a brisk skittish horse, a good way down Piccadilly, just ahead of me; he entered the park as I passed, his horse capering among the carriages, somewhat to my alarm, not to his. It must have been some five or ten minutes before this, that Sir Robert had been thrown on Constitution Hill and got his death-hurt. I did not hear of it at all till next day at Addiscombe, when the anxiety, which I had hoped was exaggerated, was considerable about him. To this hour, it is impossible to know how the fall took place. . . . It turned out after death that a rib had been broken (as well as the collar-bone), driven in upon the region of the lungs or heart. It had been *enough*. On Monday I walked up to some club to get the bulletin, which pretended to be favourable. We went then to the house itself, saw carriages, a scattered crowd simmering about, learnt nothing further, but came home in hope. Tuesday morning, 2nd of July, Postman reported 'a bad night;' uncertain rumours of good and evil through the day. (Ruskin, etc., here in the evening; good report from Aubrey de Vere, about 11 p.m.) I had still an obstinate hope. Wednesday morning 'Postman' reported Sir Robert Peel died last night, I think about nine. *Eheu! eheu!* Great expressions of national sorrow, really a serious expression of regret in the public; an affectionate appreciation of this man which he himself was far from being sure of, or aware of, while he lived. I myself have said nothing: hardly know what to think,—feel only in general that I have now no definite hope of peaceable improvement for this country; that the one statesman we had, or the least similitude of a statesman so far as I can guess, is suddenly snatched away from us. What will become of it? God knows. A *peaceable* result I now hardly expect for this huge wen of corruptions and diseases and miseries; and in the meanwhile the wrigglings and strugglings in Parliament, how they now do, or what they now do there, have become mere zero to me, tedious as a tale that has been told." *

* 'Life in London, 1834–1881,' vol. ii. p. 47.

Mr. Froude says, "Up to this time Carlyle had perhaps some hope or purpose of being employed actively in public life. All idea of this kind, if he ever seriously entertained it, had now vanished." How very seriously and even solemnly he had through life actually entertained such a hope, and how tragically his whole soul was now crushed within him, will I think no longer be doubtful to any thoughtful reader.

CHAPTER XVIII.

UNFORTUNATELY the gloom and misery which had now settled on Carlyle's life,—the gloom and misery of a great and grandly passionate soul that had lost its way, and was utterly without hope for itself and the country, —was not confined to his own experience of it. To live in mere outward contact with such deep unspoken wretchedness was a trial to the strongest nerves. He had always been, as his poor Mother confessed, ' gey ill to deal wi' ; ' but now, to any one with a heart unhardened against the contagion of a settled despair, it had become almost a stark impossibility. And the worst of all was, he could not speak of it. He had shut down all the lids with such shrinking sensitiveness, that, even to his own clear-hearted and clear-sighted Wife,—clear and vividly truthful in all ways, even if too sceptical of the highest and deepest longings of his soul,—he had become an inexplicable mystery. He refused to be comforted on any lower ground than that from which he had fallen.   He had passed into a darkness whither she could not follow him,—into which no sympathy could reach him, and from which almost no practical sympathy could come ; and their lives, beyond the power of their control, for a long time after became lamed, broken, and desperate.   He did plead with her by letter ; although, from constitutional thin-skinned irritability, now grown almost skinless, and from what he calls 'bashfulness and the pride of humility,' he was,—alas for them both !— little able to do so in daily life and by spoken words.

In the August following, he was away from home, seeking the rest he could nowhere find ; and, only a few short weeks after his crushing defeat, he wrote to her,— "Thanks to thee !   Oh ! know that I have thanked thee sometimes in my silent hours as no words could.   For indeed I am sometimes terribly driven into corners in this my life pilgrimage, of late especially ; and the thing that is in my heart is known, or can be known, to the Almighty Maker alone." *   No one can doubt that Carlyle meant kindly ; but, touching as these words are now to us as we read them, it could hardly have been comforting to his poor devoted, equally lonely Wife, to be thus solemnly told, however tenderly in tone, that the sorrow, which now more than ever was eating away his life, could never be known to her.   What could this sorrow mean ?   Had she not been a solace and comfort and ever-present help to him, in all his struggles with adversity, poverty, and neglect ?   Had she not studied his every whim, and devoted her whole existence to his comfort, and to the furtherance of his aims, as few Wives have ever done ?   And was he not continually assuring her how deeply he felt that she had been all this

* 'Life in London, 1834–1881,' vol. ii. p. 53.

to him ? What, then, was this terrible shadow which had now come between them, making her comfort of no avail, and her very presence seemingly a burden to him ? Can we wonder that she looked upon the facts which alone were plainly visible to her, and put her own interpretation on the cause of the estrangement ?

Surely Carlyle ought, even in his own misery, to have realised a Wife's feelings better than he did. He did realise them when it was too late, either for her peace of mind or his own ; and would have given his life for only one hour to have poured out his sorrow to her, in chastened humility and trustfulness of heart. As it was,—little thinking, what he was not the less deliberately doing,—he only made her heart as sore and as solitary as his own. Her letters to him at this time were written with all her customary lightness of stoical humour, and crisp, piquant, and picturesque gossip,— perhaps with even more than her usual vividness,—as if she were resolved to prove herself equal to all calls upon her resources ; but her heart refused to follow such high-strung efforts ; and she sometimes fairly broke down with a cry of bitter anguish, as her friend Mazzini might have said, ' significant of much.'

Carlyle had written to her from Dumfries, even of his own family, " The kindness of these friends, their very kindness, works me misery of which they have no idea. . . . Alas ! alas ! I ought to be wrapped in cotton wool, and laid in a locked drawer at present. I can stand nothing. I am really ashamed of the figure I cut among creatures in the ordinary human situation. One couldn't do without human creatures altogether. [Not even without one's Wife, she must wearily have thought.] Oh ! no. But at present, in such moods as I am now

in, it were such an inexpressible saving of fret and
botheration and futile distress, if they would but let
me alone.   Woe's me !   Woe *is* me !"*—And now, with
such feelings in his heart, he was about to return once
more to his own sorrowful home ; and, for the first time
in their married lives, she would not be there to receive
him.

In compliance with his expressed wish, she was preparing to spend some days at 'The Grange,' to visit
Lady Ashburton,—the one person whom she believed
could comfort him ; and, on the 23rd of September,
1850, in her bitter misery, she thus wrote to him :—

"Alas, dear ! I am very sorry for you.   You, as well as
I, are too 'vivid;' to you, as well as to me, has a skin been
given much too thin for the rough purposes of human life.
They could not make ball-gloves of our skins, dear, never to
dream of breeches.†   But it is to be hoped you will feel some
benefit from all this knocking about, when it is over and you
are settled at home, such as it is.   It does not help to raise
my spirits, for my own adventure [the visit she shrank from],
that you are likely to arrive here in my absence.   You may
be better without me, so far as my company goes.   I make
myself no illusions on that head; my company, I know, is
generally worse than none ; and you cannot suffer more from
the fact than I do from the consciousness of it.   God knows
how gladly I would be sweet-tempered and cheerful-hearted,
and all that sort of thing, for your single sake, if my temper
were not soured and my heart saddened beyond my own
power to mend them." ‡

'For your single sake,' she says, with an almost
bursting heart trying stoically to hold itself together as

* 'Life in London, 1834–1881,' vol. ii. p. 57.
† A bitter allusion to the Tannery of Meudon, described by Carlyle
in his ' French Revolution.'
‡ 'Letters and Memorials,' vol. ii. p. 133.

if with clasps of steel. To this heartaching appeal to him
for sympathy, Carlyle replied,—not even dreaming how
much of the fault was on his own side,—"Oh ! if you
could but cease being conscious of what your company
is to me ! The consciousness is *all* the malady in that.
Ah me ! Ah me ! But that, too, will mend if it please
God." *   'The consciousness is *all !*'   Alas, yes ; and it
was no less so, as he well knew, with his own sick
misery ; and yet, so conscious was he of his own rectitude, that he almost stubbornly withheld any real
explanation. He insisted on regarding the whole misunderstanding as mere morbid folly on her part, quite
unworthy of her. How could the most loyal-hearted of
wives have kept herself in easy unconsciousness before
such affectionate perversity of sensitiveness ? How
could she help being bitterly conscious that all was
not well between them? On the 3rd of October, writing
from 'The Grange,' whither she had then gone, she
said,—

"I have put a lucifer to my bedroom fire, dear, and sat
down to write, but I feel more disposed to lay my head on the
table and cry. By this time I suppose you are at home;
returned after a two months' absence, arrived off a long journey
—and I not there ! nobody there but a stranger servant, who
will need to be told everything you want of her, and a mercy
if she can do it even then. The comfort which offers itself
under this last innovation in our life together (for it is the
first time in all the twenty years I have lived beside you that
you ever arrived at home and I away) is the greatest part of
the grievance for my irrational mind. I am not consoled, but
'aggravated' by reflecting that in point of fact you will prefer
finding 'perfect solitude' in your own house, and that if I
were to do as nature prompts me to do, and start off home by
the next train, I should take more from your comfort on one

* 'Life in London, 1834–1881,' vol. ii. p. 59.

side than I should add to it on another, besides being considered here as beyond measure ridiculous. Certainly, this is the best school that the like of me was ever put to for getting cured of every particle of 'the finer sensibilities.' . . . And so I will now go and try to walk off the headache I have got by —by what do you think ?—crying, actually. Prosaic as this letter looks, I have not, somehow, been able to 'dry myself up' while writing it. I suppose it is the 'compress' put on me in the drawing-room that makes me bubble up at no allowance when I am alone." *

With such feelings struggling beneath all her stoical resolution, and with such despairing self-absorption on her husband's part, small comfort could it have given her at any time, that he should, in the very earnestness and crude simplicity of his heart, write to her, " O Jeannie, you know nothing about me just now. With all the clearness of vision you have, your lynx-eyes do not reach into the inner region of me, and know not what is in my heart, what, on the whole, was always, and will always be there. I wish you did ; I wish you did." † Never was there a misunderstanding between two faithfully loving hearts more simply tragic, or more sacredly appealing to our heartfelt reverence and human pity. And yet this long bleeding agony of truest affection, which might well draw tears such as angels weep, has been mercilessly laid bare, and piquantly or sorrowfully discussed in all drawing-rooms, as the last new scandal of our ' common clay.' O the pity of it,—the pity of it !

It surely cannot be unintelligible to any loyal Wife, in any English home, to whom her Husband's confi-

---

* ' Letters and Memorials,' vol. ii. p. 136.
† ' Life in London, 1834–1881,' vol. ii. p. 130.

dence and trusting affection are as the very jewel of her life, that Mrs. Carlyle should at last have grown desperate under this deepening sense of estrangement and gloom.   Neither can it be surprising to any one that she should have connected in her thoughts Carlyle's growing and sometimes uncontrollable moroseness at home with the influence of a lady of commanding genius and influence, whom he avowedly regarded as his confidential friend and social patroness.   So far as I can weigh the evidence, I should judge that Lady Ashburton, perhaps partly from sympathy of ambition, had really penetrated the secret of Carlyle's life, so far as his personal aims were concerned ; and that, with womanly tact, she had made him feel that whatever she divined was perfectly safe in her keeping.   It was at Bath House that his personal acquaintance with Sir Robert Peel began.   The meeting evidently had been carefully prearranged in his behalf ; for he notes in his Journal, as we have seen, ' Went to the Peel enterprise ; sate next Sir Robert,' etc.   And at Bath House they were invited to meet a second time.   He was at Addiscombe when he heard of the fatal accident, ' when the anxiety, which he had hoped was exaggerated, was considerable about him.'   This was in 1850.   Four years afterwards, it was through Lady Ashburton's influence that he obtained his only introduction to Prince Albert.   Of this interview he says briefly, "November 8, 1854, I had run out to Windsor (introduced by Lady Ashburton and her high people) in quest of Prussian prints and portraits,— saw some,—saw Prince Albert, my one interview, for about an hour, till Majesty summoned him out to walk. The Prince was very good and human." *   It would

* 'Letters and Memorials,' vol. ii. p. 249.

almost seem from these words, that he was even more interested in the Prince than in the prints and portraits which were the ostensible objects of his visit. But, whatever his real purpose may have been in thus gaining a personal interview with the Prince,—on which subject more remains to be said,—these facts are sufficient to show that his intimacy with Lady Ashburton, and her friendly interest in him, was not exactly the 'lingering in the primrose path of dalliance,' the questionable 'leisure for Bath House,' or the sentimental 'Gloriana worship,' which Miss Jewsbury and Mr. Froude supposed it to have been. The fact was, that through Lady Ashburton and her influence, especially in her gatherings of the social and intellectual notabilities of the day, he found almost his only means of gaining personal intercourse, on anything like an equal footing, with the leading minds and Ruling Powers of the country ; and it is sufficiently evident she was by no means ignorant of the kind of help she was affording him.

Carlyle's interview with Prince Albert,—which Lady Ashburton had obtained for him,—had beyond question some other and deeper object besides that of examining Prussian prints and portraits. He wanted to see him with his own eyes, and if possible take his own measure of him. In the course of his German reading, he had come upon an interesting and rather touching event in the life of one of the Prince's ancestors ; and the question had evidently arisen in his mind,—Should he avail himself of this little scrap of history, to make, without intrusion, some sort of personal appeal to his Highness ; and thus try to deepen whatever sense he already had of the very serious and peculiar responsibility of his position, in the new times which were fast coming upon us? The result of his interview was, evidently, not to discourage him altogether from making the attempt; for, within two months from the date of his visit, namely, on the first of the following January, there appeared in the *Westminster Review* a very carefully written and singularly didactic article, entitled 'The Prinzenraub: A Glimpse of Saxon History.' In this article we have a graphic sketch of a small romantic incident which in the year 1455 occasioned considerable excitement in Germany: namely, the stealing and recovery of two young Princes, brothers, then boys of twelve and fourteen. The elder of the boys was a direct ancestor of Prince Albert, and of the Duchess of Kent, the Queen's Mother. But it was Prince Albert whom Carlyle more especially sought to interest; and the entire article was evidently as expressly written for his special reading, as anything in the 'Latter-Day Pamphlets' was written for Sir Robert Peel. He traces the two lines of descent from the two brothers; giving with a few masterly touches the essential characteristics of the leading notabilities in each line, and contrasting the seeming success, but intrinsic failure, of the younger branch, with what he thinks might possibly yet prove to be the supreme triumph of the elder. All this is given with careful brevity in Carlyle's most perfect style of delineation, with a lightness of touch intended rather to provoke inquiry, and to suggest practical applications, than to afford an exhaustive statement of the matter. But Carlyle was no courtly flatterer, and we may well wonder what Prince Albert could have thought of such practical ancestral parables with modern applications as the following :—

"Noble Johann Frederick, who lost the Electorate, and retired to Weimar, nobler for his losses, is not to be particularly blamed for splitting his territory into pieces, and founding that imbroglio of little dukedoms, which run about, ever shifting, like a mass of quicksilver cut into little separate pools and drops; distractive to the human mind, in a geographical and in far deeper senses. The case was not peculiar to Johann Frederick of the Ernestine Line; but was common to all German dukes and lines. The pious German mind grudges to lop anything away; holds by the palpably superfluous; and in general 'cannot annihilate rubbish.' . . . It would be too cruel to say of these Ernestine little Dukes that they have no history; though it must be owned, in the modern state of the world, they are ever more, and have long been, almost in the impossibility of having any. To build big bassoons, and play on them from trap-ladders; to do hunting, build opera-houses, give court-shows: what else, if they do not care to serve in foreign armies, is possible for them? It is a fatal position; and they really ought to be delivered from it. Perhaps then they might do better. Nay, perhaps already here and there they have more history than we are all aware of. The late Duke of Weimar (also of the Ernestine Line) was beneficent to men-of-letters; had the altogether essential merit, too, which is a very singular one, of finding out for that object the real men-of-letters instead of the counterfeit. . . . On the whole, I rather think they would still gladly have histories if they could; and am willing to regret that brave men and princes, descended presumably from Witekind and the gods, certainly from John the Steadfast and John Frederick the Magnanimous, should be reduced to stand inert in the whirling arena of the world in that manner, swathed in old wrappages and packthread meshes, into inability to move; watching sadly the Centuries with their stormful opulences rush past you. Century after Century in vain!

"But it is better we should close. Of the Ernestine Line in its disintegrated state, let us mention only two names, in the briefest manner, who are not quite without significance to men and Englishmen; and therewith really end. The first is Bernhard of Weimar; champion of Elizabeth Stuart, Ex-queen of Bohemia, famed captain in the Thirty-Years' War; a really notable man. Whose *Life* Goethe once thought of writing. . . . Another individual of the Ernestine Line, surely notable to Englishmen, and much to be distinguished amid that imbroglio of little Dukes, is the '*Prinz Albrecht Franz August Karl Emanuel von Sachsen-Coburg-Gotha;*' whom we call, in briefer English, Prince Albert of Saxe-Coburg; actual Prince Consort of these happy realms. He also is a late, very late, grandson of that little stolen Ernst. Concerning whom both English History and English Prophecy might say something,—but not conveniently in this place. By the generality of thinking Englishmen he is regarded as a man of solid sense and worth, seemingly of superior talent, placed in circumstances beyond measure singular. Very complicated circumstances; and which do not promise to grow less so, but the contrary. For the Horologe of Time goes inexorably on; and the Sick Ages ripen (with terrible rapidity at present) towards—Who can tell us what? The human wisdom of this Prince, whatever share of it he has, may one day be unspeakably important to mankind!—But enough, enough. We will here subjoin his Pedigree at least; which is a very innocent Document, riddled from the big Historical cinderheaps, and may be comfortable to some persons." *

So ends, with solemn admonition and encouragement, the story of 'The Prinzenraub' and this passing glimpse of Saxon history. We have no right to suppose that Carlyle fancied there could be the slightest hope, or even possibility, of himself ever standing in the most distant relation towards Prince Albert, in any way similar to that of Goethe with the Duke of Weimar, to which he as it were incidentally alludes; and yet, if transcendent conventionalism had not so thrown its icy mantle over the mountain-tops, and all the higher levels of our social existence, why should the very thought of such a relation seem to us in the low-lying

* See 'Miscellaneous Essays,' vol. iv.

valleys so inconceivably presumptuous and impracticable ?
Alas, we may at least say this : that Carlyle, with his
usual keen insight into the practical bearings of a difficult
position, saw that, since the death of Peel, Prince Albert,
by the perilous height of his position, and by the terrible
responsibilities which were accumulating and growing
around him (and from which he also only escaped by
death), was called upon to face wisely and valorously
the coming troubles of the country, as no other living
man then was or could be. 'The human wisdom of
this Prince,' said Carlyle, 'whatever share of it he has,
may one day be unspeakably important to mankind.'
And, having thus faithfully delivered his message to the
whole People, to the Premier, and to the Prince, he once
more turned wearily to his own more immediate work.
He had no second interview with Prince Albert; and
five years from this time the Prince was taken from us
as unexpectedly and almost as suddenly as Sir Robert
Peel had been. Who shall say that the 'burden' of
Carlyle's life was the mere physical misery of dyspepsia ?
Surely not those who are at last beginning to see that
all is not quite so well with our country as had been
fondly and foolishly hoped. We may accept Carlyle's
warnings, or we may utterly reject them; but no one
who thoughtfully realises the stern significance of his
consistent and unceasing efforts ought to be able to
doubt that his forebodings of perplexity and disaster,
and his earnest desire to save his country from itself,
were not only very real feelings in his heart, but were
literally the secret burden of his life.

Two and a half years after Carlyle's interview with
Prince Albert, Lady Ashburton died, and her generous
patronage was thus ended. " Monday, May 4, at

Paris," he notes in his Journal, "died Lady Ashburton, a great and irreparable sorrow to me, yet with some beautiful consolations in it too; a thing that fills all my mind since yesterday afternoon that Milnes came to me with the sad news, which I had never once anticipated, though warned sometimes vaguely to do so. 'God sanctify my sorrow,' as the old pious phrase went. To her I believe it is a great gain; and the exit has in it much of noble beauty as well as pure sadness worthy of such a woman. Adieu! adieu! Her work,—call it her grand and noble endurance of want of work,—is all done!" And again, many years later, after hearing some one describe her, he wrote, "A sketch true in every feature, I perceived, as painted on the mind of Mrs. L——; nor was that a character quite simple to read. On the contrary, since Lady Harriet died I have never heard another that so read it. Very strange to me. A *tragic* Lady Harriet, deeply though she veiled herself in smiles, in light, gay humour and drawing-room wit, which she had much at command. Essentially a most veracious soul too. Noble and gifted by nature, had Fortune but granted any real career. She was the greatest lady of rank I ever saw, with the soul of a princess and captainess had there been any career possible to her but that fashionable one." *

Such was the actual relation between Carlyle and Lady Ashburton; a relation, in itself, surely greatly to the credit of them both. It is perfectly intelligible, and coherent with the rest of Carlyle's life; and, if there had been no other human heart to be taken into consideration, there would be no need to add another word

* 'Life in London, 1834–1881,' vol. ii. pp. 186, 187.

on the subject.   But if Carlyle could not be expected to
be peacefully turned aside from what he deeply believed
to be his appointed work, neither could we expect his
Wife to forget that she had a woman's heart, and such
wifely claims on his consideration as perhaps few Wives
in these superlative days of universal independence and
self-assertion could have any pretension to.   Busy as the
old serpent still is with the best amongst us, it is hardly
wonderful that misunderstandings and irritations should
have come between them.   But the irritations did not
last to the ' bitter end,' and a clearer and more trustful
day did kindly dawn for them both, as with two such
faithful hearts it well might.   Why, then, did not Carlyle,
when the records of their mutual fallibility passed
through his hands,—why did he not, when his eyes
were at last fairly opened, in his tender reverence for his
Wife's memory, himself piously and pitifully destroy
them ?   Alas, at that time he was a broken-hearted,
utterly baffled, worn out, feeble, and remorseful man ;
the granite-like persistence which had been almost a besetting sin through life, had become as clay in the hands
of the potter ; he felt that he had not been blameless
through all that bitter misery, and he dared not sit in
judgment on his own case.   The once resolute man had
become helpless and wavering ; like a fractious child
worn out with suffering, and longing to rest its tortured
head upon some friendly bosom.   His one wish till death
was, that his poor Wife's memory should be held for ever
sacred by all who heard of her ; and he thought he had
found a friend in whose faithful discretion he could implicitly trust.

x

CHAPTER XIX.

Mr. Froude's sacred trust—What were Carlyle's real wishes?—Carlyle's
honourable gratitude to Lady Ashburton, but unfortunate reticence
with his Wife—Her utter loneliness—Constitutional differences—
Hardly the elements of a happy home—'Her part, brighter and
braver than my own'—Mr. Froude's two opposite judgments—Few
men knowingly did less wrong than Carlyle.

Mr. Froude has made such an extraordinary use of the
generous and unbounded trust which Carlyle placed in
him, that it is absolutely necessary, in trying to understand Carlyle, to examine somewhat closely into the real
nature of that trust ; for Carlyle's character is at stake
in the matter, equally with Mr. Froude's. Beyond all
question the essential and most solemn injunction laid
upon Mr. Froude by Carlyle was, to render justice and
honour to his Wife's memory, but above all to be very
tenderly careful as to what he published of her letters.
He himself confesses,—

"Carlyle warned me that, before they were published, they
would require anxious revision. Written with the unreserve
of confidential communications, they contained anecdotes,
allusions, reflections, expressions of opinion and feeling, which
were intended, obviously, for no eye save that of the person to
whom they were addressed. He believed at the time I speak
of, that his own life was near its end; and seeing the difficulty
in which I might be placed, he left me at last with discretion

to destroy the whole of them, should I find the task of dis-criminating too intricate a problem."

This very clear and entirely credible statement of the case was given by Mr. Froude in his Preface to Carlyle's 'Reminiscences,' published immediately after Carlyle's death. It was therefore his own frank conception of the trust he had distinctly undertaken, before any adverse criticisms had been expressed as to his manner of fulfil-ling it. We need not trouble ourselves with the many after-recollections, and modified versious of this original statement, with which we have from time to time been favoured, as occasion seemed to call for them, because no after-explanations can in the least unsay these per-fectly intelligible and sufficient words. This clearly was Carlyle's real feeling in the matter; and it is in perfect agreement with the solemn warning with which he concluded the account of his Wife contained in his 'Reminiscences:' which solemn warning and emphatic expression of his wishes Mr. Froude considered it consistent with his duty both to disregard and to sup-press; or, perhaps, not so much consistent with his duty as with his own good pleasure; for he distinctly claims that "all these"—namely, letters, journals, and ' the records of their most secret thoughts'—"Mr. Carlyle, scarcely remembering what they contained, but with characteristic fearlessness, gave me leave to use as I might please." Which seems to be exactly what Mr. Froude has done. The following are Carlyle's words :—

" I still mainly mean to burn this book before my depar-ture, but feel that I shall always have a kind of grudge to do it, an indolent excuse; 'not yet; wait; any day that can be done;' and that it is possible the thing may be left behind me, legible to interested survivors—*friends only, I will hope;*

and with worthy curiosity, not unworthy. In which event, I solemnly forbid them, each and all; and warn them that without fit editing, no part of it should be printed (nor, so far as I can order, shall ever be); and that fit editing of perhaps nine-tenths of it will, after I am gone, become impossible. Saturday, 28th July, 1866.—T. C."

He seems, however, to have at last comforted himself with the conviction that he had found the fit editor which he had once thought impossible. Mr. Froude might well say, " Higher confidence was never placed by any man in another." But why, then, was the above statement, written with such sacred emphasis at the time when the whole subject was fresh before him, and showing so clearly that the ' Reminiscences ' were not written by Carlyle with any purpose of publication, but simply as a relief to the overwhelming pressure of his thoughts,—why was such a statement, giving as it does the much-needed keynote to the whole of the ' Reminiscences,' and really excusing so much which would otherwise be inexcusable, deliberately and entirely suppressed, without so much as an allusion to it ? The statement was afterwards published by Mrs. Alexander Carlyle in a letter to the *Times;* and Mr. Froude justified the suppression of it upon the plea, that many years afterwards, when he had almost forgotten what he had written, Carlyle in private conversations with himself had revoked all that, and had given him permission to use the whole of the materials ' as he might please ;' in short, that Carlyle had ' made him a present of them.' A more extraordinary justification it would be difficult to imagine.

We need not wish for clearer evidence than even that which Mr. Froude himself gives of Carlyle's real feelings in connection with this painful subject, both of the reminiscences and the private letters. Practically, Carlyle said to him, 'I am a broken-hearted, old and worn-out man. I would gladly give all my reputation, and all that I can call my own, if I could only do justice to my poor Wife's memory. Shortsighted that I was, I never did her justice while she was spending her fragile life to serve me and shield me from annoyance; and now it is too late! O my friend! for the love of God, and in pity to an old man to whom you say you owe something, can you and will you help me, that I may depart in peace? I confide every secret of our lives to your keeping, and trust implicitly to your faithful discretion. If you find " the task of discriminating too intricate a problem," then in mercy destroy the poor unintended records of her misery, and let reverent silence be her only monument.' Mr. Froude accepted the trust, and we all know what has come of it. He tells us, with a tone of authority as if to silence once and for ever all gainsayers, " Mr. Carlyle requested in his will that my judgment in the matter should be accepted as his own." How, then, is it that Mr. Froude's 'judgment,' however coincident it may have been with Carlyle's while Carlyle lived, has ended, since he died, in exactly reversing itself? But it is useless questioning: all we can now do is to accept the facts which have been thus freely laid before us, and try whether they cannot even yet be resolved into coherence and human credibility.

We have seen what it really was that honourably bound Carlyle to Lady Ashburton with feelings of respectful esteem and heartfelt gratitude. She was trying unobtrusively to aid him in the one great unspoken ambition of his life. And she did aid him most efficiently ; for the prize at one time seemed almost ready for his grasp, had not his destiny been otherwise so tragically decreed. Never was there a more trying slip between the cup and the lip. Can we wonder at his gratitude ? Can we blame him, through all that fevered hope, even for submitting to her caprices, attending her gatherings, and making such practical acknowledgment of his heartfelt thanks as was within his power ? All this by itself calls for something the reverse of apology. But why was not his true-hearted Wife frankly taken into his confidence ? Why did he content himself with telling her, perhaps not always in the gentlest tones, that she did not and could not understand it ? Why did he, in letter after letter, when he saw that her life had grown desperate with the thought that he had ceased to care for her ; and while telling her how indispensable she was to him,—as if that went for much,—and imploring her to believe in his unaltered affection,—why did he persist in emphasizing the unspeakable, 'just and laudable' somewhat, which bound him to Lady Ashburton, of which she knew and could know nothing ? Poor comfort that for a devoted and wounded heart ! Who was Lady Ashburton, that she should thus decoy from her her husband's hitherto unbroken confidence, and share with him unutterable secrets which his 'poor little Jeannie' was unworthy even to meddle with ? And yet, in the stubborn consciousness of his own rectitude, he not only insisted that she should not interfere with him, but that she should try to be gracious to the very woman in whom he avowedly confided, and whom she believed was practically supplanting her in his esteem. What she deeply felt was, that this mysteriously cherished secret,—whether she penetrated it or not,—seemed to possess his very soul, to absorb all his thoughts, and to shut her out from all sympathy with his life. That he spent his evenings in brilliant company; entertaining them with the varied abundance of his passionate discoursing; and, upon his return home, hung up his fiddle at his own door, and gave way to the dregs of that humiliating and crushed sense of defeat which inevitably followed such wasted evenings of excitement. What sort of a Wife could she have been, if she could have hardened herself to the point of placidly accepting the situation, and dismissing all feverish anxiety from her heart ? Certainly anything but the passionately affectionate and devoted Wife she had always hitherto been to him. And to think that a few tenderly confiding words from her husband might have dispelled all that bitter misery,—and yet those words never to have been spoken ! What a piercing meaning such a thought gives to his cry of anguish after she had been snatched from him : ‘ Oh that I had you yet for but five minutes, to tell you all !’ It was a sad muddle, and Carlyle might well remorsefully feel that he had not been blameless in the matter. But why did he not frankly confide in her ? Mr. Froude perhaps would tell us, “ The only answer is, that Carlyle was Carlyle.” Yes, and if he had made that all-including summary the sum-total of his biography, even Carlyle could have had no cause to complain of his lack of reticence and discretion.

The truth is, Carlyle could not for the life of him have put into spoken words the fevered hopes which even to himself must have seemed to be almost bordering on insanity; and which events proved were to be for ever denied him. It was easy for Lady Ashburton, in her exalted position, to see how he longed to get into practical relation with the governing powers; and, sympathising with his ambition and believing in his abilities, it was only generous on her part to aid and encourage him. From any evidence we have, this would seem to have been the full extent of their mutual confidences. With his Wife it was widely different. She had seen him successful only as a writer and talker. She had recognised his genius from the first, with the subtle sympathy of kindred genius. She had frankly cast her lot with his, in the face of present poverty, warnings of friends, and all discouragements; in the full conviction that he would yet make a position, and win a name, and gain an influence for good by his writings, which she might well be proud to share. She had seen him wretchedly dissatisfied with his career as a writer, and striving vainly again and again to get into some practical employment. But, in spite of all his dissatisfaction, Literature had been his one success; and in this he had succeeded beyond her wildest dreams. Even if she had penetrated into his secret aims,—and with her quick intelligence she surely must have had many a shrewd glimpse of what was in the wind,—she would probably have shrunk from all such thoughts, as from an infatuation doomed from the beginning to disastrous disappointment: in which case she must necessarily have shrunk from the Bath House influences as from siren flatteries tempting him to destruction. She knew how difficult he was to work with, how impatient he was of all practical contradiction, how instant and unmeasured his scorn for all futile stupidities and make-believing palaver; and, knowing all this,—whatever else she knew or was ignorant of,—she certainly could have been in no condition of mind to make tender confidences on such a subject at all easy. Indeed, I have often wondered whether in her own heart she must not have had, long before, a far deeper sympathy than Carlyle would have meekly tolerated, with Lord Jeffrey's persistent avoidance of all help in any but a literary career. And who can now say she was not practically right? No one can say with any finality of assurance. The whole problem of what Carlyle 'might have been' must for ever remain one of the unverified possibilities or impossibilities of history. But, —judging from the passionate intensity of his remorse, and his almost worship of her, after her death,—it is not at all improbable, when all illusive hopes had become by her loss finally quenched in blackest night, and he longed only to forget them, he then began to see for the first time in his life that, through all that impatient misery, she had been practically more clear-sighted and more self-devoted than himself.

And yet it is no less true that there was in him, through all his stormful exuberance of passionate aspiration, a sacredness of piety, and solemn consecration of his whole soul to what he believed to be the appointments of the Most High, of which she had but an imperfect and far-off appreciation. Invincible stoicism, devoted affection, and sympathetic kindness of heart, she always had, far above the common measure of humanity. And, during her later days, a feeling of resignation to the Infinite Unfathomable Wisdom and pious recognition of the fruitful discipline of sorrow gradually crept over her, very touching and comforting to think of for those who loved her, and not least so for Carlyle himself. But her soul was not formed, like his, to dwell alone, under a burden of unappreciated thoughts and aspirations, for ever striving for a companionship in well-doing, which seemed to be for ever unattainable; and she fretted and chafed at his admonitions and exceeding earnestness, and retaliated with sparkling raillery, and sometimes with sharpest sarcasms. With the struggles, disappointments, and opulent beneficences of 'genius' she had the kindest and heartiest sympathy; but the 'prophet's burden' was little more to her than another form of the 'gift of tongues.'

The following extract from a letter to one of her cousins in Liverpool (January 20, 1847) will be interesting, as a frankly characteristic utterance of that unpretentious and spontaneous kind-heartedness of which her whole life was a loving and practical illustration :—

"The fact is, happiness is but a low thing, and there is a confusion of ideas in running after it on stilts. When Sir Philip Sidney took the water from his own parched lips to give it to the dying soldier, I could take my Bible oath that it was not happiness he felt; and that he would never have done that much-admired action if his only compensation had been the 'pleasure' resulting to him from seeing the dying soldier drink the water: he did it because he could not help himself: because the sense of duty, of self-denial, was stronger in him at that moment than low human appetite; because the soul in him said,—do it; not because utilitarian philosophy suggested that he would find his advantage in doing it, nor because Socinian dilettantism required of him a beautiful action!" *

Let us at least judge with kindly judgment. She had been 'an only child,' the pet and pride of the fondest parents; and she missed and craved the atmosphere of

* 'Letters and Memorials,' vol. i. p. 387.

thoughtful loving-kindliness to which she had been accustomed, and which her husband's grim and solitary training had little qualified him to afford. He wished to be the kindest and truest of husbands ; but he had no tact for the little amenities of domestic life, which go so far to make the atmosphere and sunshine of home. He was as quick-tempered as herself; with a 'pride,' as he tells us, 'fierce and sore,' which almost courted the un-broken blast from every side, and even hugged its own agony. Then, again, he was constitutionally and rigidly frugal ; frugal in the manifestations of personal affection ; frugal in praise ; and especially frugal in his own personal comforts, and in what he deemed wisely need-ful for others. Add to this his almost total absorption in the work and struggles of his life, his gnawing misery of chronic dyspepsia, and, what he himself exaggera-tively calls, an 'obstinacy as *of ten mules*,'* and it will be evident that here were hardly the elements of what we could call a happy home. Yet neither could we call it a home deliberately divided against itself. No two hearts ever yearned more faithfully for the loving con-fidence of each other than did these two, even in the darkest hour of their mutual misunderstanding. Alas, they were not two souls united utterly in one earnest ideal of life, but two loving souls gazing strangely, sorrowfully, and wistfully at each other. Yet, when the ' hard battle against fate,—hard, but not quite unvic-torious,'—was all over with them, these are the words in which Carlyle refers to it : " I say deliberately, her part in the stern battle, and except myself none knows how stern, was brighter and braver than my own." Could any words be more conclusive, or any authority more

* ' Reminiscences,' vol. i. p. 242.

absolutely final, save that of the All-seeing Maker, who made their hearts, and led them through light and through darkness to a better and tenderer victory than either had looked for ? Small kindness, to a man like Carlyle, could it be to try to justify him at his poor Wife's expense, and few things could have so awakened his utter scorn and indignation. Faults they both had ; but they were honest faults, and in no way destructive of the most heartfelt mutual esteem. And whenever the truth as to himself becomes clearly recognised, it will also be gratefully seen and tenderly confessed, that whatever we owe to his writings, next to himself we owe to the persistent encouragement, loving helpfulness, and lifelong self-devotion of his sorely tried, if sometimes far too sensitive, Wife.

Mr. Froude says, " It was hard on Carlyle that, while engaged with work into which he was throwing his entire heart and soul, he should be disturbed and perplexed with domestic confusions." * And again, " Such letters as this throw strange lights into Carlyle's domestic life, sad and infinitely touching. When he complains so often of the burdens that were laid upon him, one begins to understand what he meant." † What he meant, Mr. Froude would have us imagine, was even this : that the Wife to whom he appeals in the very letter referred to, as his ' poor little Protectress,' and whom throughout their entire married life he gratefully regarded, and invariably spoke of, as the loving and indispensable *sharer* of his burden, was herself, ' when one begins to understand,' that very burden. Carlyle's burden ought to be plain to every one, even without any saying : it was the

* ' Life in London, 1834–1881,' vol. i. p. 379.   † Ibid., vol. ii. p. 179.

burden of his own heart, of his own unrealised ideal, of his own manifold infirmities, spiritual and bodily; it was the burden of feeling a heavy work laid upon him which he could not get accomplished. And it was his Wife's share in all that weary burden which broke down her own strength, and wore her life away in one long-continued death.

Mr. Froude seems to have found himself in a somewhat difficult position; and if it were not for the scandal he has raised, and his cynical disregard of it, we might really be sorry for him. He knew Carlyle's deliberate estimation of his Wife and of all she had been to him, and he knew the solemn charge which Carlyle had laid upon him in her behalf; and, accordingly, in his first two volumes, and in the three volumes of her 'Letters and Memorials,' he appears before us, with the serenest conviction that he is carrying out Carlyle's express meaning, as Counsel for Mrs. Carlyle, and as what he well calls 'Devil's Advocate' for Carlyle himself. She is the perfect ministering angel, and her life 'a sad fate for a person so bright and gifted;' while he is the 'negligent, inconsiderate, and selfish' husband, a sad mixture of 'common clay,' like the rest of us. Such an easy forensic solution of all biographical difficulties naturally awoke a very general cry of indignant protest from those who knew Carlyle; and unfortunately, in the reaction of feelings, Mrs. Carlyle's credit rather fell in the gossip market. All this seems to have suggested a new view of the subject. Mr. Froude had already discharged his obligation to Carlyle with respect to his Wife; and in fact, as he tells us, had written all that he considered necessary on that subject. But why should he not now take the matter up from the opposite point of view, and so please all parties ? So he burnt the first brief, as no longer binding upon him ; and accepted a new one : not from Carlyle this time, but from,—perhaps from public opinion, and a laudable desire to be impartial, even at the expense of his own consistency. In accordance with this new inspiration, we were favoured with two extra volumes ; *not* written from Carlyle's point of view, but written in a spirit of judicial disparagement of his Wife, and glorification of Carlyle in spite of Carlyle. We were no longer to look upon Carlyle's passionate remorse as springing from a righteous and repentant discernment of his own shortcomings, and of his Wife's almost unparalleled devotion to him ; but rather as almost conclusive evidence that his heart was far too tender ever to have done anything really unkind, if he had not at times been provoked to it beyond all power of endurance.

But is it not really too bad that two such characters should be used as make-weights for a rhetorical see-saw ? If Mr. Froude felt, as he well might after the earnest protests he had been compelled to listen to, that in his first five volumes he had rendered very scant justice to his friend and master, could he not have rectified his halting judgment, and made his tardy amends to the one, without trying to increase the effect by disparaging the other ? Was it necessary to drag down the Wife to the dust, in order to exalt the Husband to the empyrean ? Mr. Froude, seemingly in a moment of playful confidence, lets us into the following little secret :—" An experienced publisher," he tells us, " once said to me : ' Sir, if you wish to write a book which will sell, consider the ladies'-maids.' " Considering the sentimental, three-volume style, in which he dwells upon blighted first-loves and ineffaceable scars ; how he treats his readers to all piquant circumstances of courtship and wedding, and other exquisitely private gossip; and how he first sets off the victim Wife against the blue-beard Husband, and then the meekly forgiving Husband against the shrewish Wife,—it would hardly seem that the hint had fallen unfruitful upon stony ground. I venture to say that, to more than one poor judgment, we are honouring Carlyle almost infinitely more, in believing that he had grievously sinned in the moody stubbornness of his heart, as so many of us constantly do, but also, and what is far more exceptional, that he lived to see clearly that he had done so, and to make what little amends was then despairingly possible,—than we should be, in regarding his heart-breaking remorse as a mere sentimental delusion of overcharged and self-indulging sorrow.

Carlyle's life would have had no spiritual completeness or wholeness without that last heartfelt act of repentant sacrifice. He *was* hard—there is no denying it; hard to himself, and hard as chilled iron to those who thwarted him. He was hard to his Wife, little dreaming how hard, and only conscious of his hardness as his most impregnable virtue. He knew that he meant no wrong, and he had been quite unconscious that he was inflicting any; but when the fact was revealed to him by a lightning-stroke which pierced his very heart, like David, he at once, in bitterest remorse, confessed his error; his hardness dropped like a poor bursting egg-shell in fragments around him, and his intrinsic goodness and lovingkindness tremblingly and passionately declared itself. If we are not to give Carlyle credit for the sternest veracity and clearest self-judgment in all this, what are we to think of his sanity? Or what noble meaning could his life have for any of us ? And yet all this truest and most deeply tragic nobility of soul, as of the 'High and Lofty One' dwelling and working in a broken and contrite heart, Mr. Froude, in his revised version of his character, tries to explain away by continual suggestions that it was mainly his Wife's fault she could not get on with him !

Few men ever knowingly did less wrong than Carlyle ; but, also, few men with his earnest sincerity of purpose have been so heavily weighted with constitutional infirmities. To understand such a man rightly, we must understand both his far-reachings and his short-comings ; both his strength and his weakness ; both what he had to give, and what he had not to give. His was not one of those simple natures whose characteristics can be summed in a few balanced phrases and generalising epithets. No ethical averages or conventional standards will in the least define him. He was pre-eminently what he himself calls an ' original man ; ' with an individuality as intensely pronounced as it was unprecedented in structure. To understand him we must see him in his total personality. Not a theory of him, but the man himself, is what we have to look at. And, if we wish to know what his Wife in very truth was to him, we must know frankly what the trials were to which she was put. It was with this intent he so earnestly enjoined that his own faults, wherever they illustrated her worth, should by no means be extenuated. His own life, even in its darkest conflicts with difficulty, temptation, and despair, was one faithful, ever-renewed struggle to do right, and to right wrong wheresoever he discerned it ; and we all know, and really ought to believe, what he deliberately tells us of her share in the same stern battle.

CHAPTER XX.

No disloyalty to Carlyle in speaking of published facts with perfect frankness—His Wife's grief at her Mother's death—Carlyle, as sole executor, takes possession of the property—No interchange of confidences —'She has never once in the most distant way seemed to know it to be hers '—His impatient thriftiness—Threatening bankruptcy of the household exchequer — *Budget of a Femme Incomprise* — 'Great laughter,' even with money down, not quite the response which might have been looked for—Mrs. Carlyle's character no less heroically exceptional than his own.

WE have already seen one instance, namely, his obligations to Lady Ashburton, in which Carlyle's sensitive and even tragic incommunicableness wrought bitter misery, where he longed only to find trusting affection. But we must now turn to another very striking example of a similar character, for which it is difficult to find any justification whatever. The facts have been laid before the world, and are patent to every one having eyes to see them ; there can, then, be no necessary disloyalty on my part towards Carlyle in speaking of them with perfect frankness. Indeed, I sincerely believe I am only carrying out his dying wishes in trying to elucidate their sad significance. I feel that I should be faithless to the worthiest and most heartfelt purpose he ever formed, and faithless to my own sincere friendship for Mrs. Carlyle, if I shrank from the painful details which

Y

we have now impartially to consider. I have known both Carlyle and Mrs. Carlyle, perhaps, as I have already said, with as practical an intimacy as any one now living; and all that I knew of them, and all that I have since gathered from Mr. Froude's copious revelations, only serves, the more I think of it, to deepen my reverence for the faithful sincerity of their lives.

Those who have read Mr. Froude's first volume of 'Carlyle's Life in London, 1834–1881,' will hardly fail to recollect the account there given of Mrs. Carlyle's inconsolable grief at the sudden loss of her Mother. Altogether unexpectedly the painful news came from Templand that her Mother had been stricken by apoplexy, and was dangerously ill. Unfit as she then was for travelling, she immediately started by train for Liverpool, on her way to her. But, on arriving at her uncle's house in Liverpool, she learned that she was already too late; that her mother had had another stroke which had ended her life. The shock was too great for Mrs. Carlyle's feeble strength; she was carried to bed unconscious, and was unable to leave it for many days. Of course Carlyle also was greatly distressed and shocked. He followed his Wife at once to Liverpool; and, after briefly consulting with her, proceeded to Templand with one of her cousins to make such arrangements as might now be necessary. He was sole executor, and all that had belonged to Mrs. Welsh now became his Wife's.

Carlyle remained at Templand over six weeks. A few relics and things portable were packed and sent to London. But the lease of Templand was disposed of, and everything else was sold by auction. There was also a sum of 189*l.* lying in the bank. We are not told how much the whole amounted to; but, whatever it was, he, as sole executor, took legal possession of. Besides this, Craigenputtock had now fallen to them, the income of which would for the future be theirs. Mr. Froude loosely calls it 'from 200*l.* to 300*l.* a year,' which, he adds, was to them, " with such habits as hers and her husband's, independence, and even wealth." Carlyle, as we shall see, reckoned it 150*l.* a year, but he himself afterwards spoke of it, in his ' Reminiscences,' as " 200*l.* yearly or so." But however moderate may have been the total addition to his means which thus fell to him through his Wife, it was certainly, added to his own already improving resources, amply sufficient to place him above the fear of want, and to have enabled him to relax a little the sternness of his thrifty grip upon their outlay so far as his Wife was concerned. Indeed, with the unbounded confidence he really placed in her, one would naturally suppose he would have taken the first quiet opportunity of delicately ascertaining what her feelings were on the matter; whether she had any little cherished wishes, either of kindliness to others or of comfort to herself, which might now be safely listened to; whether she had any wish as to the final disposal of Craigenputtock; whether, in short, she had anything to suggest in consequence of their now improved position. Strange to say, such thoughts never seem to have occurred to him. It was from no positive unkindness; he had no thought of spending the money on his own gratifications: he considered they were doing very well as they were, and he saw no necessity whatever for spending the money at all, merely because they were fortunate enough to have got it. This was long before the time of the 'Latter-Day Pamphlets,' and no one could tell what need they might yet find for it. So he added the money to his little safety-hoard in the bank ; and, so far as the evidence goes, seems never once to have mentioned the subject to her,—certainly never with any serious idea of frankly advising with her about it. As to the final disposal of Craigenputtock, even after her death, when he was so earnestly desirous to make amends for his obliviousness, and when this special instance seems to have come dismally and reproachfully enough before him, he had to consider most anxiously what her wishes would probably have been, if he had only been able to consult her. And for the rest, we have his own words to show how total and impassable the silence between them, for whatever reason, actually was.

February 9, 1848, six years after Mrs. Welsh's death, and two years previous to the 'Latter-Day Pamphlets' time, Carlyle made an entry in his Journal of an estimate of his average income, which, however, he frugally put low enough ; and this is what he wrote :—

"My poor books of late have yielded me a certain fluctuating annual income ; at all events, I am quite at my ease as to money, and that on such low terms. I often wonder at the luxurious ways of the age. Some 1,500*l.*, I think, is what has accumulated in the bank. Of fixed income (from Craigenputtock) 150*l.* a year. Perhaps as much from my books may lie fixed amid the huge fluctuation (last year, for instance, it was 800*l.* ; the year before that, about 700*l.* ; this year again it is like to be 100*l.* ; the next perhaps nothing—very fluctuating indeed)—some 300*l.* in all ; and that amply suffices me. For my wife is the best of housewives ; noble, too, in reference to the property which is *hers* (the italics are his own), which she has never once in the most distant way seemed to know to be hers. Be this noted and remembered ; my thrifty little lady— every inch a lady." *

* 'Life in London, 1834–1881,' vol. i. p. 420.

I confess I can hardly read these words without a pang almost of despair at such calmly unsympathetic obtuseness; for nothing can be clearer than Carlyle's utter unconsciousness that he had been in any way unsympathising or unkind. He evidently believed that his 'thrifty little lady' appreciated what he regarded as only his own thrift, as highly as he did himself, and that her silence implied rather admiration of his prudent reserve. But, if Mrs. Carlyle thought differently, why did she keep her thoughts sealed so hermetically within her own heart? Why did she not tell him plainly that his conduct was both ungenerous and unfair? Well, if she had had a little more of our common clay in her composition, perhaps she would have done so, and at once have demanded and insisted on her rights. But the Lady Ashburton misunderstanding was all this while going on, which made confidences difficult. And, apart from all that, there was something Mrs. Carlyle valued more than money, or all that money could buy. She valued her husband's sympathy and thoughtful loving-kindness; and, if he could not freely give her that, all the money or money's worth he could have given her would be worthless. Sincerely and emphatically, she would rather not have it, and would try to think no more about it. 'She never once, in the most distant way, seemed to know it to be hers.' And, after all his recognition and admiration of her self-denial, what did her husband do in recognition of his indebtedness to her? He gave her 3*l.* yearly, to continue a pension which her Mother had allowed to an old servant; and he made her some little present out of her own money each Christmas and birthday, until she refused to receive any more; and then he gave her 5*l.* yearly on New-Year's Day instead.

The whole thing would be painfully incredible, if the facts were not beyond the possibility of doubt. This sore state of things actually continued for seven years after the foregoing entry in the Journal. But the matter did not end here. As time went on, and troubles thickened,—troubles of mutual irritability, troubles connected with Carlyle's visits to the Ashburtons, and troubles with her own persistently stinted allowance for household expenses,—she was at last compelled to speak plainly. And when she did speak, it was as if with the intense veracity and heart-searching sadness of his own accusing angel: could he have listened to the voice, as he did in after years, it might have been the beginning of happier days for them both.

We have seen how completely Carlyle appreciated the perfect thrift and wise discretion of her household management; calling her, as he always did and well might, 'the best of housewives.' But, unfortunately, this theoretical appreciation made little difference in his practical conduct upon any question of increased outlay. Their style of living, and the expenses of supporting it, had been gradually rising, mainly through his own increasing notoriety and extending circle of acquaintances; provisions, etc., also had risen in price, and many other little demands had to be met from the household purse, until Mrs. Carlyle was driven to her wits'-end to keep free from debt. Again and again she tried to induce him to realise for himself their altered position, and the harassing difficulties which were accumulating and increasing upon her. But he would hear nothing of it; would not see 'why the allowance, which had sufficed in former years, no longer sufficed.' At length she was driven desperate, and it must be confessed her pent-up sense of wrong found very effectual and emphatic utterance. She wrote a statement of her pecuniary difficulties, and laid it upon Carlyle's writing-table, for him to find when he came in from the garden fresh from his soothing pipe. If she knew how to tell him plainly and incisively the saddest truths, she knew equally well how to administer the reproof with wisest discretion. She not only chose the most propitious moment, but, knowing well how intimately laughter and tears were mingled together in the constitution of his mind, she aimed straight at his keen sense of humour, with a very clever and pungent imitation of his own grim style of irony,—which, it is pleasant to add, he was magnanimous enough at once to appreciate, although it was directed so unflinchingly against himself.

The result showed that she had not missed her aim, even if she had not penetrated as deeply as she may well have hoped. She had given keenest utterance to all the bitter sense of wrong which had been so long smoulder-ing in her heart ; and yet she managed it so skilfully, and with such perfect womanly self-command, that he could not take offence at it, but actually laughed heartily at his own discomfiture, and gave her what she asked for. But the matchless wit and incisiveness of her protest, perfect as they are of their kind, are of far less interest to us now, than is the sadly authentic light which the whole protest, if well read, throws upon herself and her actual feelings and position ; for it must be borne in mind that every word was addressed solely to Carlyle for his own private behoof, and he would know as well as she whether or not they constituted a true bill. The protest, which she entitled '*Budget of a Femme Incom-prise,*' is too long and far too interestingly important to be transferred to these pages without special permission. I must therefore entreat my readers to refer to Mr. Froude's volumes, and judge for themselves whether I have in any degree over-estimated its sorrowful significance. Mr. Froude, of course, can call it 'a shrewing,' since it so pleases him; but surely he can hardly claim that 'his judgment in the matter is to be accepted as Carlyle's.'

Let us now once more hear Carlyle. After reading this very remarkable communication from a Wife to her Husband,—which, possibly, touched his conscience far more deeply than he cared to confess, even to himself, for he surely must have seen the essential drift of it,— he at once wrote at the foot of the last page: " Excellent, my dear clever Goody, thriftiest, wittiest, and cleverest of women. I will set thee up again to a certainty, and thy 30*l.* more shall be granted, thy bits of debts paid, and thy will be done.—T. C., Feb. 12, 1855." * He afterwards folded it up and put it carefully away, first endorsing it, " Jane's Missive on the Budget," and adding, " The enclosed was read with great laughter ; had been found lying on my table as I returned out of the frosty garden from smoking. Debt is already paid off. Quarterly income to be 58*l.* henceforth ; and all is settled to poor Goody's heart's content. The piece is so clever that I cannot just yet find in my heart to burn it, as perhaps I ought to do.—T. C." †

Certainly we must admit that, if Carlyle was constitutionally hard and inconsiderate, he was by no means impervious to an appeal for justice when fairly brought home to him ; and yet surely 'great laughter,'

* 'Life in London, 1834–1881,' vol. ii. p. 162.   † Ibid., p. 170.

unmingled with tears, was not quite the response which might have been looked for. It ought to have opened his eyes to many things besides money troubles. "Stony-hearted; shame on me!" he afterwards exclaimed, in the bitterness of his terrible remorse. He gave her what she asked, but left his 'poor Goody's heart' as sore and as lonely as ever. All this deep-felt sorrow on her part is revealed but too clearly in a fragment of diary which she commenced only a few months later, of which fragment Carlyle afterwards wrote,—" Of that year (1855–6) there is a bit of private diary, by chance left unburnt; found by me since her death, and not to be destroyed, however tragical and sternly sad are parts of it. . . . Certain enough, she wrote various bits of diary and private record, unknown to me: but never anything so sore, down-hearted, harshly distressed and sad as certain pages (right sure am I!) which alone remain as specimen! The rest all burnt; no trace of them seek where I may." *

Nothing can be more certain, from a total view of the facts, than Mrs. Carlyle's painful and crushed sense of helplessness at the grim way in which, without once thinking he was acting inconsiderately and unkindly, he had summarily disposed of her poor Mother's effects,—all now enshrined in loving memories,—while she herself lay ill in bed, with no power to compose her thoughts, or to speak a word as to what she would like done with them; and

* 'Reminiscences,' vol. ii. p. 244. For fragment of diary referred to, see 'Letters and Memorials,' vol. ii. pp. 257–261. See also her confession, in a letter to her husband, of the tumult of intense emotion with which she opened a packet which had been despatched from Templand at the time of her Mother's death (p. 200); and her touching narrative of a visit to her old home after long years of absence (p. 53); all showing the exceeding sensitiveness of her heart as to everything connected with her early memories.

then, as the merest matter of course, had himself taken possession of her property, without 'in the most distant way seeming to know it to be *hers.*' The extraordinary fact is that Carlyle should have been unable to see her side of the question or realise her feelings ; or see that, what he praised as heroic self-renunciation in her, was really nothing less than unheroic stolidity on his part. He evidently thought he was doing rather a handsome thing, in giving her 5*l.* a year out of her own money as a present from himself. Well might she say to him, 'I know the meaning of that 5*l.* quite well ;' and it was the only protest she ever deigned to make on the whole painful subject.

How ill at ease Carlyle's conscience was on the matter, when the flinty scales at last fell from his eyes, and yet how utterly and strangely unable he still was to realise his Wife's feelings, is sufficiently shown in the uneasy and gently tentative account of the transaction which he jotted down in his private 'Reminiscences' for the comfort and deliverance of his own mind, but which private memoranda have since been given to the world with as little compunction as if they had been avowedly written for general perusal. He saw and felt remorsefully enough how hard he had been, and how 'queenlike' his Wife had acted in comparison ; but he tried to pacify his accusing conscience with dim recollections of words which, however kindly meant, had evidently been spoken wide of the mark, and had not restored a feeling of sympathy between them. Let us now read his own sorrowful words on the subject, recollecting that they were not addressed to us in his own justification, but that we are really listening to a secret and sacred struggle between self-reproach and self-pity in his own heart.

"How well I remember," he writes, " the dismal evening, when we got word of her mother's dangerous crisis of illness (a stroke, in fact, which ended it); and her wildly impressive look, laden as if with resolution, affection, and prophetic woe, while she sate in the railway carriage and rolled away from me in the dark. 'Poor, poor Jeannie!' thought I; and yet my sympathy how paltry and imperfect was it to what hers would have been for me! Stony-hearted; shame on me! She was stopped at Liverpool by news of the worst; I found her sharply wretched, on my following; and had a strange two or three months' slowly settling everything at Templand.* . . . Her grief, at my return and for months afterwards, was still poignant, constant; and oh how inferior my sympathy with her to what hers would have been with me; woe on my dull hard ways in comparison ! "

"I find it was in 1842 (February 20) that my poor mother-in-law died. . . . Craigenputtock lapsed to her in 1842, therefore. . . . To my kindred it has no relation, nor shall it go to them; it is much a problem with me how I shall leave it settled ('Bursaries for Edinburgh College,' or what were best ?) after my poor interest in it is over. Considerably a problem; and what her wish in it would have actually been ? 'Bursaries' had come into my own head, when we heard that poor final young Welsh was in consumption, but to her I never mentioned it. ('Wait till the young man's decease do suggest it ?'), and now I have only hypothesis and guess. She never liked to speak of the thing, even on question, which hardly once or twice ever rose; and except on question, a stone was not more silent. Beautiful queenlike woman, I did admire her complete perfection on this head of the actual 'dowry' she had brought, 200*l.* yearly or so, which to us was a highly considerable sum, and how she absolutely ignored it, and as it were had not done it at all. Once or so I can dimly remember telling her as much (thank God I did so), to which she answered scarcely by a look, and certainly without word." †

* It seems to have been really from the beginning of March to the 15th of April.

† 'Reminiscences,' vol. ii. p. 194–197.

Alas, the heart knoweth its own burden, but when shall we learn to see and bear one another's!

But it may be asked,—How would Mrs. Carlyle have acted, had she stood in her Husband's position, and he in hers? Well, Carlyle himself admiringly tells us how she once acted with money which was not merely hers, but in her own hands. She once had a legacy all to herself, of, I suppose, a hundred pounds, less legacy duty. The exact date is not given, but is indicated as probably 1851, and therefore several years after her Mother's death, and previous to the writing of the 'Budget.' Carlyle is giving an account of the arrival into the house of her little pet dog Nero.

"A little Cuban (Maltese? and otherwise mongrel)," he says, "shock, mostly white—a most affectionate, lively little dog, otherwise of small merit, and little or no training. Much innocent sport there rose out of him. . . . Once, perhaps in his third year here, he came pattering upstairs to my garret; scratched duly, was let in, and brought me (literally) the *Gift of a Horse* (which I had talked of needing)! Brought me, to wit, a letter hung to his neck, inclosing on a saddler's card the picture of a horse, and adjoined to it her cheque for 50*l.*—full half of some poor legacy which had fallen to her! Can I ever forget such a thing? I was not slave enough to take the money; and got a horse next year, on the common terms—but all Potosi, and the diggings new and old, had not in them, as I now feel, so rich a gift." *

What further evidence can we need to convince us, not only of the tragic reality, but also of the spiritual sanity and imperativeness, of Carlyle's passionate remorse? Again I say, his life could have had no deep spiritual foundation of veracity and of manhood with-

* 'Letters and Memorials,' vol. ii. p. 91.

out it.   Happily for his heart's comfort, he never even
at the last clearly realised how very hard he had actually
been.   But he did, sanely enough, realise tragic shortcomings in himself, and how ' peerless ' she had been in
comparison.

We have thus far been led almost inevitably, from
a consideration of the social and more public aims of
Carlyle's life, to a review of his strictly private character,
as exemplified in two painful and singularly dramatic
instances of misunderstanding between himself and his
Wife,—misunderstandings which, in the absolute sincerity and mutual faithfulness of their hearts, seem to
reveal their very souls before us.   Well might we pause
even in awe before such a revelation.   For who are we,
that we should thus look into the inmost secrets of a
man's, or still more of a woman's, heart ?   It is a strange
supplement to a most untoward destiny, that the most
private details of two such sensitive lives should now
have become, in direct consequence of Carlyle's own act,
as much public property as are the books which he has
published.   Every seal has been broken, every secret
has been unlocked, there was nothing hidden which has
not been revealed ; and henceforth no attempt to understand the growth and total significance of Carlyle's
extraordinary character can be anything but a mere
summary of outside facts, which does not include the
frankest consideration of his Wife's share in the burden
of his life.

Let us, then, if there be any real spirit of chivalry
left among us, look well to it that her memory is
not left to suffer the injustice of flippant misrepresen-
tation, in addition to the desecration, which she would

have shrunk from with more sensitive horror than any
other woman I ever met, of having the tenderest secrets
of her life canvassed and commented on by unfeeling
strangers. Happily her character was no less heroically
exceptional and self-devoted to what she believed to be
her duty than was that of Carlyle himself, although
cast in a singularly different mould; and perhaps few
women so tried would have had less to be wholesomely
ashamed of. Her intellect was as clear and incisive as
his, yet altogether womanly in character; her heart was
as truthful, and her courage as unswerving. She was a
Wife in the noblest sense of that sacred name. She had
a gift of literary expression as unique as his; as tender
a sympathy with human sorrow and need; as clear an
eye for all conventional hypocrisies and folly; as vivid
powers of description and illustration; and also, it must
be confessed, when the spirit of mockery was strong
upon her, as keen an edge to her flashing wit and
humour, and as scornful a disregard of the conventional
proprieties. But she was no literary hermaphrodite.
She never intellectually strode forth before the world
upon masculine stilts; nor, in private life, did she fro-
wardly push to the front, in the vanity of showing she
was as clever and considerable as her husband. She
longed, with a true woman's longing heart, to be appreciated by him, and by those she loved; and, for her,
all extraneous applause might whistle with the wind.
But if her husband was a king in literature, so might
she have been a queen. Her influence with him for
good cannot be questioned by any one having eyes to
discern. And if she sacrificed her own vanity for personal distinction, in order to make his work possible
for him, who shall say she did not choose the nobler

and better part?—for she came to him, 'not to be ministered unto, but to minister.' Carlyle never wrote truer words, or words more worthy of him, than when he wrote, " I say deliberately, her part in the stern battle was brighter and braver than my own."

CHAPTER XXI.

'Life of Sterling'—Carlyle's Herculean labours on the 'History of
   Frederick'—Almost the only books of his written without ulterior
   practical aims—The great Kaiser Barbarossa—Carlyle's great task
   concluded—Public sympathy and homage, followed by his Wife's
   sudden death—Remorse, and heartfelt loyalty to her memory—
   'God pity and forgive me!'—Blessings in disguise—Long years of
   helpless craving for work—Heard are the Voices—Carlyle's heartfelt
   trust in God.

WE have seen how Carlyle's long-continued effort to
become a leader of social reform in England culminated
in the 'Latter-Day Pamphlets,' and ended in the death of
Sir Robert Peel. But Carlyle was not a man to throw
aside a task, once seriously taken in hand, until he had
wrung from it its full practical possibility. Tragic and
total as his disappointment was, he not only completed
the Pamphlets, but soon after wrote his 'Life of Sterling;'
a book essentially begotten of the same impulse. Such
a task must have been peculiarly soothing to him in his
then state of mind. Here was a beautiful brother-soul,
whom he had really loved and admired ; whose aspirations had been even more sorrowfully baffled than his
own, and yet who had continued his brief life-struggle
faithfully to the end : and now his lost friend, from the
silence of Eternity, seemed wistfully to appeal to him
for a word of kindly recognition. There were none of

the usual agonies of gestation over the production of
this kindliest of his books. He wrote it with the ease
of a letter to a friend ; and his sorely chastened heart
seemed to draw comfort from the thoughts and sympathies which it stirred within him. The whole book is
saturated with convictions, admonitions, and solemn
exhortations, in strictest unison with the teaching of
the 'Latter-Day Pamphlets.' But it is no longer as
the trumpet of the archangel, summoning the hosts of
heaven to battle ; it is rather as if he had mournfully
said,—' My friends, we will not quarrel about the practically unattainable. The captain I looked for has been
stricken from his post, and the battle for the present is
lost. But my own convictions and hopes remain ; and,
sooner or later, the awful battle, of sincerity against
make-believe in every form whatever, will yet be fought.
Be ye also ready ! '—But when his tribute to his friend's
memory was completed, and he had no longer any wholesome occupation to draw him from himself, his lonely
sense of helplessness was as terrible as ever. Writing
to his poor old Mother, to tell her the book was in the
hands of the printers, he says, " I am weak, very irritable, too, under my bits of burdens, and bad company
for anybody ; and shall need a long spell in the country
somewhere, if I can get it. In general, I feel as if it
would be very good for me to be *covered under a tub*
wherever I go ; or, at least, set to work, like James
Aitkin's half-mad friend, ' ay maistly in a place by
himsel.' " *

It was long before he could get fairly settled to his
Herculean labour on the 'History of Frederick.' He felt
that he must have something to work at which would

* 'Life in London, 1834–1881,' vol. ii. p. 76.

tax his utmost energy, or he should really go mad; but he could not as yet compel his thoughts to any steady occupation. Thus he notes in his Journal, January, 1852,—

"I make slow progress, and am sensible how *lame* I now am in such things. *Hope* is what I want. Hope is as if dead within me for most part; which makes me affect solitude, and wish much, if wishing were worth aught, that I had even one serious intelligent man to take counsel with, and communicate my thoughts to. But this is weak, so no more of this: know what the inevitable years have brought thee, and reconcile thyself to it. An unspeakable grandeur withal sometimes shines out of all this, like eternal light across the scandalous London fogs of time. Patience! courage! steady, steady!" *

It is very touching and significant, that wish of his, —that he had even one serious intelligent man to take counsel with, and communicate his thoughts to. But he could not have uttered them; they were too nearly on the verge of frenzy to be spoken of, even to himself. Alas, if he could only have gained the 'patience' he cried for, how different all would have been, both for himself and for his Wife! But patience, or utter contrite trust, was to him as yet an unattainable blessing.

April 13, 1853, a year later, he wrote :—

"Still struggling and haggling about Frederick. Ditto ditto, alas! about many things! No words can express the forlorn, heart-broken, silent, utterly *enchanted* kind of humour I am kept in; the worthless, empty, and painfully contemptible way in which, with no company but my own, with my *eyes* open, but as with my hands bound, I pass these days and months, and even years. Good Heavens! Shall I never more rally in this world then; but lie buried under mud

* 'Life in London, 1834–1881,' vol. ii. p. 90.

and imbecility, till the *end* itself (which cannot be distant, and is coming on as with seven-league boots) overtake me ?" *

Again, after another year had fled, in April, 1854, he made the following entry :—

"No way made with my book, nor like to be made. I am in a heavy, stupefying state of health, too ; and have no capacity of grasping the big chaos that lies around me, and reducing it to order. Order! Reducing! It is like compelling the grave to give up its dead, were it rightly done ; and I am in no capacity for working such a miracle. Yet all things point to work,—tell me sternly enough that, except in work, there is simply no hope for me at all, no good that *can* now come to me." †

Nevertheless, he had been desperately working at his self-imposed task ever since January, 1852 : reading assiduously innumerable books about Germany and Frederick ; and, with his friend Neuberg's indefatigable assistance, visiting Germany to collect materials, and ransacking the State Paper Office in London, " in hopes of getting some illumination for his dim, dreary, impossible course through the desert of Brandenburg sand." But he could not get his materials into shape ; and again, September 16, 1854, he mournfully wrote :—

" 'The harvest is past, the summer is ended, and we are not saved.' What a fearful word ! I cannot find how to take up that miserable ' Frederick,' or what on earth to do with it. ' Hohenzollerns,' ' Sketches of German History,'—something of all that I have tried, but everything breaks down from innumerable outward impediments,—alas ! alas ! from the defect of inward fire. I am getting old, yet would grudge to depart without trying to tell a little more of my mind. . . . I am as if beaten, disgracefully vanquished, in this ' last of my fields.' I am weak,—a poor angry-hearted mortal, sick, soli-

---

* ' Life in London, 1834–1881,' vol. ii. p. 128.   † Ibid., p. 154.

tary, and altogether foiled. . . . Nothing but *remorse*, the sharp sting of conscience for time wasted, carries me along. Alas ! I am not yet *into* the thing. Generally, it seems as if I never should or could get into it. What will become of me ? Am I absolutely beaten by this, and the thousand other paltry things that have gone wrong with me in these late times ? " *

Shall we mournfully shake our wiser heads, and say, ' Of course all this is extremely morbid,' and so pass on in our own unruffled equanimity ? If that be all we can see in it, by all means let us do so. But are we not too apt to call all deep misery 'morbid' which transcends the limit of our own experience ? Really morbid it may have been in some of its constitutional excess ; but intrinsically it was the inevitable outcome of the central facts of his life. It was the painful cry of an 'imprisoned heroism,' which seemed as if it would burst the very walls of its prison to get out. However, he did at last get his heavy labour fairly in hand, and continued to work at it till completed ; year after year, with stubborn perseverance, and with no less stubborn determination to crush down the baffled romance of his life. His Herculean labour on the ' History of Frederick,' and of Frederick's surroundings, and of the European events and doings which led up to them, are, in fact, his own practical life-version of the ' Sorrows of Teufelsdröckh.' Surely Hercules himself might have shuddered at such a task under such conditions.

Of course, with all this 'stern pilgrimage through burning sandy solitudes,' Carlyle had also what he might well call his ' green oases by the palm-tree wells,' at which times he was the most affectionate, genial, and

* 'Life in London, 1834–1881,' vol. ii. p. 172.

gracious of companions. The feeble thread of his poor
Wife's life would have snapped asunder long before it
did, if it had not been so. When, about this time, he
accepted my proffered help, I little dreamt what a
house of weary sorrow I was about to become familiar
with, or what a mingled experience of grateful acknowledgment and disheartening exigency was before me.
There was a deep satisfaction in it, undoubtedly ; but it
was the satisfaction of self-discipline, of learning and
practising stoical endurance ; of helping one who was
worthy of help, and in his heart deeply grateful for it ;
and, perhaps above all, the satisfaction of doing faithful
work which was really worth doing. But it was 'no
May-game,' 'no idle promenade,' either for his Wife, or
for his friend Neuberg, or for myself, or, least of all, for
him. Through all that struggle with his hard destiny,
Carlyle's only real happiness was 'the happiness of
getting his work done,' and there was no other certain
happiness for those who were with him. But assuredly
he was never intentionally unkind. I also know that
his was 'the kindest of hearts,' when the stress of his
own misery relaxed and allowed his better feelings a free
activity. One more extract,—this time from a letter to
his brother from Chelsea, dated June 11, 1857,—will
show him very favourably in the more peaceful and
considerate mood.

"Probably I am rather better in health; the industrious
riding on this excellent horse sometimes seems to myself to be
slowly telling on me; but I am habitually in sombre, mournful mood, conscious of great weakness, a defeated kind of
creature, with a right good load of sorrow hanging on me;
*and no goal, that looks very glorious to aim towards, now
within sight.* All my days and hours go to that sad task of
mine. At it I keep, weakly grubbing and puddling, weakly

but steadily; try to make daily some little way, as now almost the one thing useful. . . . In fact, I do make a little way, and shall perhaps live to see the thing honestly done after all. Jane is decidedly better; gets out daily, etc., but is still as weak as possible; and though we have the perfection of weather, warm yet never sultry, the poor mistress does not yet get even into her old strength for walking or the like. She went out to East Hampstead, Marquis of Downshire's people, beyond Windsor; and got so much good of her three days there, I have been desirous she could get to Scotland or somewhither for a couple of months; and she did seem to have some such intention. Sunny Bank the place; but that has misgone, I fear. [She did go, in July, and stayed till September.] Meanwhile, she is busy ornamenting the garden, poor little soul; has two China seats, speculates even upon an awning, or quasi-tent, against the blazes of July that are coming, which, you see, are good signs." *

Mrs. Carlyle went to Sunny Bank, on a visit to her very dear old friends, the Donaldsons, 'friends of Dr. Welsh's family in early days;' and on the 5th of August Carlyle wrote to her, giving her the following tender little picture of a summer daybreak: "Sunday I started broad awake at 3 a.m., went downstairs, out, smoked a cigar on the stool: have not seen so lovely, sad, and grand a summer weather scene for twenty years back. Trees stood all as if cast in bronze, not an aspen leaf stirring; sky was a silver mirror, getting yellowish to the north-east; and only one big star, star of the morning, visible in the increasing light." †

Sad to him was all that beauty of the opening day, for he had nothing answering to it in his own dim life. 'No goal, that looks very glorious to aim towards, now within sight. All my days and hours go to that sad task of mine.' These few words tell the whole sad story

---

* 'Life in London, 1834–1881,' vol. ii. p. 188.   † Ibid., p. 193.

of the years during which I was working with him. His 'History of Frederick called the Great' is universally acknowledged to be the ablest and most successful of all his literary efforts. But this is sufficiently accounted for by the fact that it was the only thing he ever wrote since the Essays,—with the exception of his Life of Sterling, and the Kings of Norway,—which was not, essentially, an earnest striving towards a goal which seemed to him far nobler and worthier than any conceivable literary success. Every other book of his, as he continually asserts, was written with 'far other than literary aims.' His heart's desire was to *make* History, not merely to write about what others had made. And when he at last settled down to 'Frederick,' he seems to have said to himself in grimmest earnest—'Clearly no other goal is now possible to me. But since literature is destined to be my whole vocation in this world, I will at least show the world what is still honestly possible even in that secondary department of human labour.' And thus he threw his whole strength into the work, with such triumphant success, and such clear illumination of the hard facts and practical details of every business taken in hand, as we all now recognise, but which no one with any certainty could have anticipated. Who can say whether, with the responsibilities of power to have awakened him to the full activities and duties of his life, he would, or would not, have amazed us with a far greater, if to some of us far grimmer, Social Success, if he had only had leave to try? It forms no part of my present plan to attempt any criticism of this his one great literary effort. The practical lessons on governmental administration and social well-being which he constantly emphasises, speak plainly enough upon every page of it.　But I may specially note, as one further illustration of his own personal feelings, how .the old longing for action pulses through his veins, whenever he comes across a bit of real kingly heroism.　I must content myself with one instance, which may be taken as a type of all.　Few of his readers probably will have forgotten his grandly sympathetic account of the great Barbarossa ; yet, well as it may be recollected, it is so pregnant with significance of himself, that it will well repay a fresh perusal from our present point of view.

"It was now the flower-time of the Romish Kaisership of Germany ; about the middle or noon of Barbarossa himself, second of the Hohenstaufens, and greatest of all the kaisers of that or of any other House.　Kaiser fallen unintelligible to most modern readers, and wholly unknown ; which is a pity. No king so furnished out with apparatus and arena, with personal faculty to rule and scene to do it in, has appeared elsewhere.　A magnificent magnanimous man ; holding the reins of the world, not quite in an imaginary sense ; scourging anarchy down, and urging noble effort up, really on a grand scale.　A terror to evildoers and a praise to welldoers in this world, probably beyond what was ever seen since.　Whom also we salute across the centuries, as a choice Beneficence of Heaven.　'Encamped on the Plain of Roncaglia' (when he entered Italy, as he too often had occasion to do), 'his shield was hung out on a high mast over his tent :' and it meant in those old days, 'Ho, every one that has suffered wrong ; here is a Kaiser come to judge you, as he shall answer it to *his* Master.'　And men gathered round him ; and actually found some justice,—if they could discern it when found.　Which they could not always do ; neither was the justice capable of being perfect always.　A fearfully difficult function, that of Friedrich Redbeard.　But an inexorably indispensable one in this world ;—though sometimes dispensed with (to the huge joy of Anarchy, which sings Hallelujah through all its Newspapers)—for a season.

"Kaiser Friedrich had immense difficulties with his Popes, with his Milanese, and the like;—besieged Milan six times over, among other anarchies;—had indeed a heavy-laden hard time of it, his task being great and the greatest. He made Gebhardus, the anarchic Governor of Milan, 'lie chained under his table, like a dog, for three days.' For the man was in earnest, in that earnest time:—and let us say, they are but paltry sham-men who are not so, in any time; paltry, and far worse than paltry, however high their plumes may be. Of whom the sick world (Anarchy, both vocal and silent, having now swollen rather high) is everywhere getting weary.—Gebhardus, the anarchic Governor, lay three days under the Kaiser's table; as it would be well if every anarchic Governor, of the soft type and of the hard, were made to do on occasion; asking himself, in terrible earnest, 'Am I a dog, then; alas, am not I a dog?' Those were serious old times.

"On the other hand, Kaiser Friedrich had his Tourneys, his gleams of bright joyances now and then; one great gathering of all chivalries at Maintz, which lasted for three weeks long, the grandest Tourney ever seen in this world. Glenhausen, in the Wetterau (ruin still worth seeing, on its Island in the Kinzig river), is understood to have been one of his Houses; Kaiserslauten (Kaiser's *Limpid*, from its clear spring-water) in the Platz (what we call *Palatinate*), another. He went on the Crusade in his seventieth year (A.D. 1189; Saladin having, to the universal sorrow, taken Jerusalem); thinking to himself, 'Let us end with one clear act of piety:'—he cut his way through the 'dangerous Greek attorneyisms, through the hungry mountain passes, furious Turk fanaticisms, like a gray old hero. 'Woe is me, my son has perished, then?' said he once, tears wetting the beard now white enough: 'My son is slain!—But Christ still lives; let us on, my men!' And gained great victories, and even found his son; but never returned home;—died, some unknown sudden death, 'in the river Cydnus,' say the most. Nay, German Tradition thinks he is not yet dead; but only sleeping, till the bad world reach its worst, when he will reappear. He sits within the Hill near Salzburg yonder,—says German Tradition, its fancy kindled by the strange noises in that Hill (limestone Hill) from hidden waters, and by the grand rocky look of the place:—A peasant once, stumbling into the interior, saw the Kaiser in his stone cavern; Kaiser sat at a marble table, leaning on his elbow; winking, only half asleep; beard had grown through the table, and streamed out on the floor; he looked at the peasant one moment; asked him something about the time it was; then drooped his eyelids again: Not yet time, but will be soon! He is winking as if to awake. To awake, and set his shield aloft by the Roncalic Fields again, with: Ho, every one that is suffering wrong;—or that has strayed guideless, devil-ward, and done wrong, which is far fataller."

Here, thought Carlyle, was something like a Kaiser! One that would be worth waking up, could we know where to find him!—But, before quitting the 'History of Frederick,' I may just mention that Carlyle, while writing it, always contemplated finishing it with an emphatic and fairly complete account of Frederick's wonderful administrative and crowning victory, in restoring his shattered and almost ruined kingdom to prosperity, after the seven-years' frightful devastation had swept over it. This Carlyle regarded as the most important and instructive lesson of his career; and he may even have thought it would, some day, 'when the bad world had reached its worst,' become of very special significance to ourselves. But, by the time he had arrived at this concluding portion of his subject, his energies were utterly spent: his own health, and his Wife's, had painfully broken down under the long-continued strain; the History had already extended far beyond any limit he had originally anticipated; and he felt there was really nothing for him but to wind the whole thing up as summarily as was consistently possible. And, in addition to his own private impediments and loss of energy, he found the records of the whole important affair so strictly official, that, after all, anything he could make of it would be little more than a massing together of dry details and statistics, in which probably his readers would feel little interest. He therefore contented himself with picking out, with his usual clear insight, such personal sayings and doings, and sufferings and successes, as were most significant of Frederick's methods of procedure, and thankfully shook off from himself any further responsibility in the matter.

Thus was Carlyle's great task concluded; and he felt that he had now neither goal, nor work, nor hope of any kind, left him in the world. He longed only to be at rest. But rest, equally with free activity of life, was an unpermitted boon which he longed for in vain. Within one short year after the completion of 'Frederick,' he received in Edinburgh the warmest expression of public sympathy and homage that any literary man ever received in our country;—to be almost immediately followed by the news of his poor Wife's sudden death. "The stroke," he said, writing to his friend Mr. Erskine, "that has fallen on me is immeasurable, and has shattered in pieces my whole existence, which now suddenly lies all in ruins round me." This was literally true. All other disappointments were now as nothing to him. For the rest of his life on earth,—nearly fifteen years of protracted misery, —he was a broken-down and broken-hearted man; his 'fierce pride' crushed, his iron resolution all gone, and his impatient exigency of temper all melted into tears and the sick irritability of a tender and passionate remorse. And yet, so unquenchable was his deep sense of the obligation laid upon each of us to 'work while it is day,' that even in the bitterest agony of his affliction it never left him.   In the same letter to Mr. Erskine in which he spoke of his life 'now all in ruins,' he added, "In her name, whom I have lost, I must try to repair it, rebuild it into something of order for the few years or days that now remain to me, try not to waste them further, but to do something useful with them, under the stern monition I have had."

More than a year afterwards, November 30, 1867, calling up many old memories, he wrote in his Journal:—

"Have been remembering vividly all morning, with inexpressible emotion, how my loved one, at Craigenputtock, six or seven-and-thirty years ago, on summer mornings after breakfast, used very often to come up to the little dressing-room where I was shaving, and seat herself on a chair behind me, for the privilege of a little further talk while this went on.   Instantly on finishing I took to my work, and probably we did not meet much again till dinner.   How loving this of her, the dear one!   I never saw fully till now what a trust, a kindness, love, and perfect unity of heart this indicated in her. The figure of her bright, cheery, beautiful face mirrored in the glass beside my own rugged, soapy one, answering curtly to keep up her cheerful, pretty talk, is as lively before me as if I saw it with eyes. . . . Of late, in my total lameness and impotency for work (which is a chief evil for me), I have sometimes thought, 'One thing you could do,—write some record of her; make some selection of her letters, which you think justly among the cleverest ever written, and none but yourself can quite understand.'   But no! but no!   How speak of her to such an audience?   What can it do for her or for me?"*

Again, December 22nd, still restlessly longing for worthy occupation, he wrote :—

* 'Life in London, 1834–1881,' vol. ii. p. 358.

" Some mornings ago I said to myself, ' Is there no book of piety you could still write ? Forget the basenesses, miseries, and abominations of this fast-sinking world,—its punishments, come, or at hand ; and dwell among the poor struggling elements of pity, of love, of awe and worship, you can still discern in it !' Better so. Right, surely, far better. I wish, I wish I· could. Was my great grief sent to me perhaps for that end ? In rare better moments I sometimes strive to entertain an imagination of that kind ; but as to doing any-thing in consequence, alas ! alas !" *

" One evening," he afterwards adds, " I think in the spring of 1866 [only a few weeks before her death], we two had come up from dinner and were sitting in this room, very weak and weary creatures ; perhaps even I the wearier, though she far the weaker ; I at least far more inclined to sleep, which directly after dinner was not good for me. ' Lie on the sofa there,' said she,—the ever kind and graceful, herself refusing to do so,—' there, but don't sleep ; ' and I, after some super-ficial objecting, did. In old years I used to lie that way, and she would play the piano to me : a long series of Scotch tunes, which set my mind finely wandering through the realms of memory and romance, and effectually prevented sleep. That evening I had lain but a few minutes, when she turned round to her piano, got out the Thomson Burns book ; and, to my surprise and joy, broke out again into her bright little stream of harmony and poesy, silent for at least ten years before ; and gave me, in soft tinkling beauty, pathos and melody, all my old favourites : ' Banks and Braes,' Flowers of the Forest,' ' Gilderoy,' not forgetting ' Duncan Gray,' ' Cauld Kail,' ' Irish Coolin,' or any of my favourites, tragic or comic ; all which she did with modest neatness and completeness. . . . Foolish soul ! I fancied this was to be the beginning of old days ; that her health was now so much improved, and her spirits espe-cially, that she would often do me this favour ; and part of my thanks and glad speech to her went in that sense ; to which, I remember, she merely finished shutting her piano, and answered nothing. That piano has never again sounded, nor in my time will or shall. In late months it has grown

* ' Life in London, 1834-1881,' vol. ii. p. 361.

clearer to me than ever that she had said to herself that night, 'I will play him his tunes all yet once;' and had thought it would be but once." *

Surely the two little pictures he here gives, one from the beginning, and the other from the close of his married life, are sufficient in their touching simplicity to show what that married life essentially had been or might have been. I may now give an extract from his 'Reminiscences,' which ought no longer be in the least incredible to any one with a human heart. He is speaking of his Wife's early days, and of her great grief at the loss of her Father; and he tells us :—

" In effect it was her first sorrow, and her greatest of all. It broke her health for the next two or three years, and in a sense almost broke her heart. A father so mourned and loved, I have never seen; to the end of her life his title even to me was 'he' and 'him;' not above twice or thrice, quite in late years, did she ever mention (and then in quiet slow tone), 'my father.' Nay, I have a kind of notion (beautiful to me and sad exceedingly), she never was as happy again, after that sunniest youth of hers, as in the last eighteen months, and especially the last two weeks of her life ; when, after the wild rain deluges and black tempests many, the sun shone forth again for another's sake with full mild brightness, taking sweet farewell. Oh, it is beautiful to me, and oh, it is humbling and it is sad ! Where was my Jeannie's peer in this world ? And she fell to me, and I could not screen her from the bitterest distresses ! God pity and forgive me. My own burden, too, might have broken a stronger back, had not she been so loyal and loving." †

" Sometimes the image of her, gone in her car of victory, and as if nodding to me with a smile,—' I am gone, loved one ; work a little longer if thou carest; if not, follow. There is no baseness, and no misery here. Courage, courage to the last ! '

* 'Life in London, 1834–1881,' p. 362.
† 'Reminiscences,' vol. ii. p. 94.

—that, sometimes, as in this moment, is inexpressibly· beautiful to me, and comes nearer to bringing. tears than it once did." *

Few things can be clearer than that Carlyle's long stern life of sorrow, suffering, and crushing defeat, had at last opened in his heart, no less than in his Wife's, a depth of tender sympathy, and of pious trust and submissiveness, which came to him, as practically it had already come to her, as a new-birth of God's sanctifying Spirit in his soul.   Not only was his own faithful work now almost finished in the world, but the merciful work of the 'Eternal Father' was almost accomplished in him, as he himself most deeply and gratefully felt.   While engaged in collecting and arranging the memorials of his Wife, he made the following very remarkable entry in his Journal, showing very clearly and pathetically whither his most earnest thoughts were now tending; and showing, also, how far he was, in the still depths of his struggling heart,—and notwithstanding his occasional contradictions of his own deepest intuitions,— from the shallow scepticism with which he is so often credited :—

"*April* 29, 1869.—Perhaps this mournful, but pious, and ever interesting task, escorted by such miseries, night after night, and month after month,—perhaps all this may be wholesome punishment, purification, and monition, and again *a blessing in disguise.* I have had many such in my life. Some strange belief in an actual particular Providence rises always in me at intervals,—faint but indestructible belief, in spite of logic and arithmetic, which does me good. If it be true and a fact,—as Kant and the clearest scientific people keep asserting,—that there is no Time and no Space; then, I say to myself, sometimes, all minor 'Logic,' and counting by

* ' Reminiscences,' vol. ii. p. 231.

the fingers, becomes in such provinces an incompetent thing. Believe what thou must; that is a rule that needs no enforcing." *

Yet once more : on the 4th of the following December, he writes, "This is my seventy-fourth birthday. For seventy-four years have I lived in this world. That is a fact awakening cause enough for reflection in the dullest man. . . . If this be my last birthday, as is often not improbable to me, may the Eternal Father grant that I be ready for it, frail worm that I am." † Alas, it was far from being his last birthday. He had yet full ten years of lingering probation to pass through before he could hear the welcoming words—Well done, good and faithful servant: thou hast been faithful over a few things; enter into the joy of thy Lord, and into the fruition of thy life! But from this time he grew feebler and feebler in body, until he at last lost the use of his right hand; and even literature, which he had once looked upon as so poor a thing, was now forbidden him. His last entry in his Journal (December 6, 1873), almost illegible, we are told, from the trembling of his pencil,—for he had given up attempting to write with a pen,—is wonderfully characteristic in its undying craving for work, and deeply and solemnly suggestive of many thoughts to us all: "Thy seventy-eighth year is finished then. . . . A life without work in it, as mine now is, has less and less worth to me. The poor soul still vividly enough alive, but struggling in vain under the strong imprisonment of the dying or half-dead body. For many months past, except for idle *reading*, I am pitifully idle. Shame, shame! I say to myself, but cannot help it. Great and strange glimpses of thought come to me

* 'Life in London, 1834–1881,' vol. ii. p. 381. 　　　　† Ibid., p. 387.

at intervals, but to prosecute and fix them down is denied me. Weak, too weak, the flesh; though the spirit is willing." *

Yet eight years of helpless and isolated misery he lingered on, when the strong bands of imprisonment gave way, and the poor soul, still vividly enough alive, was at length set free. The last words reported of him are, " I am very ill. Is it not strange those people should have chosen the very oldest man in all Britain to make suffer in this way?" Mr. Froude, supposing him to be wandering, answered, humouring him, " ' They may have reasons that we cannot guess at.' ' Yes,' he said, with a flash of the old intellect, ' it would be rash to say they have no reasons.' " But by what wisdom do we call this dim perception of perhaps hitherto unseen realities, this new flash of the old intellect, the mere wandering of delirium? Was Carlyle also wandering, while reverently listening to the still voices of the ' cloud of witnesses and brothers ' to whom he so often appealed for encouragement, and whom in later years, with even more practical emphasis, he called the ' immortal gods '? Or was he following a delusion, when he so often repeated Goethe's psalm-like interpretation of their ' Voices ' with such earnestness of conviction? They both reverently avoided any detailed theory on the subject; but, also, they were both content, either with or without logic, to ' believe what they must.' Thus, in a letter to Sir Walter Scott, in which he refers to Byron's early death as a loss to himself and to all the world, Goethe takes comfort in the conviction, that he had " joined the noble spiritual company of high-hearted men, capable of love, friendship and confidence, that

* ' Life in London, 1834–1881,' vol. ii. p. 424.

2 A

had left this sphere before him;" as we also have kindred spirits, still on earth, yet not more visible to us than those of past ages, "with whom we have a right to feel a brother-like connection, which is indeed our richest inheritance." * Neither could the loving and much-loved Sterling articulate his convictions with any certainty of demonstrative utterance; yet in his last letter to Carlyle, written shortly before his own death, he said, "Towards me it is still more true than towards England, that no man has been and done like you. Heaven bless you! If I can lend you a hand when THERE, that will not be wanting. It is all very strange, but not one hundredth part so sad as it seems to the standers-by." †

No one can read Carlyle's works with any real sympathy of understanding, and yet doubt his absolute belief in God's universal, eternal, and ever-working Providence, however he may sometimes have baffled himself with half-hearted doubts, in his own particular applications of a conception so vast and all-including. This great belief with him,—from the time of his mature manhood, when it became vitally and intuitively his own, even if it had ever for a moment been otherwise,—was no mere speculative conception of a universal congruity of Eternal Forces, playing together, now in clear harmony and now in seeming discord, on the bosom of Immensity to the still music of the spheres:—it was a working belief; earnest as his very life. He believed in a God of Justice and of Judgment; Creator and Upholder of the Universe; the Eternal and continual Giver of life and of every good thing; a 'terror to the evil-doer,' and a succour and ever-present refuge to those who serve Him. Nature was not God, but a 'God-written Apoca-

* Lockhart's 'Life of Scott.'   † 'Life of Sterling.'

lypse,' the 'Living Garment of God.' Neither, with Emerson, did he, 'the imperfect, worship his own Perfect.' He had no Theory of Divinity, and he wanted none. But he had an inarticulate belief in the infinitely just 'Most High God,'—the 'Eternal Father,' to whom he cried, not in vain, for pity and pardon from the depths of his affliction,—and in an Individual Immortality, the merciful fruition of all faithful efforts on God's earth, as profound, as intuitive, and as unassailable, as his belief in his own personal existence. This faith, the summary of all the Divine Silences which filled his heart with awe and wonder, was the working faith of his richly fruitful and faithful life; and, if it does not reach to the clear heaven of Christian love and self-devotion, it is at least their everlasting basis, the measured outline of the Holy City, the straight path to the Highest through the wilderness of life.

So have we heard the message of Eternal Righteousness, 'the song of Moses the servant of God,' even in our own poor days of spiritual darkness and confusion; and the inspiring tones have sunk deep into many hearts. Surely we have not now long to wait before 'the song of the Lamb,' sung by all the sons of God, shall join in one awakening chorus; when the sad wail of despairing and mistaken love, 'They have taken away my Lord, and I know not where they have laid Him,' will be changed for the passionate conviction,— 'I have seen the Lord,' and He has shown me what He would have me do!

CHAPTER XXII.

WE have still Carlyle's 'last words' to his country to
consider, and as I believe them to be well-nigh the
most solemnly practical words he ever wrote, and as
they undoubtedly express his own final and deepest
convictions as to the future troubles and possibilities of
England, I have reserved them until we had faithfully
followed our Latter-day Seer to the close of his earthly
career. They were written within twelve months after
his Wife's death, with no thought or care of ambition for
himself, but simply for the deliverance of his own soul.
He notes in his Journal at the time—

"There is no spirit in me to write, though I try it sometimes; no topic and no audience that is in the least dear or
great to me. Reform Bill going its fated road, *i.e.* England
getting into the *Niagara rapids* far sooner than I expected;
even this no longer irritates me, much affects me. I say
rather, Well! why not? Is not national death, with new-
birth or without, perhaps preferable to such utter rottenness
of national life, so called, as there has long hopelessly been?

. . . Indeed, all England, heavily though languidly *averse* to this embarking on the Niagara rapids, is strangely indifferent to whatever may follow it. 'Niagara, or what you like, we shall at least have a villa on the Mediterranean, when Church and State have gone,' said a certain shining Countess to me, yesterday. Newspaper editors, in private, I am told, and discerning people of every rank, as is partly apparent to myself, talk of approaching 'revolution,' 'Common-wealth,' '*Common-illth,*' or whatever it may be, with a singular composure." *

At length he could bear, what seemed to him his own sinful inertness, no longer; and, exactly seventeen years after the last Latter-Day Pamphlet was published, he once more took up his old 'Condition-of-England Question,' and added one more pamphlet to the number. Short as it is, he confesses that it 'took up a good deal of time' in writing; and that, although he was as usual greatly dissatisfied with it, he was nevertheless 'secretly rather glad than otherwise' that it was out of him. We may therefore conclude, even if its own internal evidence were not sufficient to show it, that this, which he himself calls his 'last word' on the subject, was one of the most deliberate, if not *the* most deliberate and sacredly earnest, of any he ever uttered. It is remarkable, considering the long interval between them, how exactly the new pamphlet took up the burden of the old. We have seen how essentially Carlyle's ethical principles had become modified, from the time of 'Sartor Resartus' to that of the 'Latter-Day Pamphlets;' but from that time there was no further change; only a deepening and chastening of his own purposes and hopes. And yet there is this noteworthy difference between the two later epochs. The 'Latter-day Pamphlets' were written in the ripe vigour of his manhood, and with a strenuous

* 'Life in London, 1834–1881,' vol. ii. p. 349.

effort to avert the utter social disintegration with which he believed England was threatened. That effort, as we have seen, so far as he was personally concerned, signally failed. Disintegration was in the very air we breathed ; it was sweeping through the world like a moral epidemic ; it was increasing in strength as the years rolled on, with 'all men singing *Gloria in excelsis* to it ;' until, aided by his own personal disappointment, it became clear to him that nothing could arrest its course ; but that it would now rage on, year after year, till not one stone was left standing in its place upon another of all our social edifice. 'For who can change the opinion of these people ?'—He turned away from the hopeless effort ; and, upon foreign ground and with a foreign theme, tried to show what sheer administrative ability, indomitable persistence, and a keen eye for the practical business in hand could do, even upon the poorest level of human activity. And now, when he had become stricken in years, bowed down with weariness and many sorrows, and 'the light of his life gone out,' the old distressing problem at home confronted him once more, but with the new difficulties of the rapidly advancing time : What *can* become of England, when all these things shall have come to pass ?

I know well what utter foolishness all this must seem to those who are still elate with auroral forecastings of unbridled freedom, spontaneous utopias, and every evil working its own good cure. But it was not to such minds that Carlyle with any hope addressed himself : 'for who can change the opinion of these people ?' He knew that nothing he could say would open their eyes, and he cared not how quickly they closed his books. But, in order that 'the infinitesimally small minority of wise men and good citizens,' who in any degree saw what he saw, might know that his latter-day convictions had only deepened with his deeper insight into the essential facts, he commenced his new pamphlet with a swift, pungent, and stern denunciation of the primary social delusions which he had previously assailed. Into that portion of the subject it would be futile now to enter. Indeed, its chief interest to us now lies in the conclusive evidence it affords that the 'Latter-Day Pamphlets' were no mere " discharge of acrid humours and bilious indignation with which his whole soul was loaded," but were the deep, abiding, and passionately earnest convictions of his heart and conscience. Whether we accept them as the truest and most prophetic utterances of our time, or execrate them as summaries of all uncharitableness, it really ought not to be doubtful that they expressed his deliberate, kindly meant, and final diagnosis of our present social maladies and self-deluding sins.

What is really new in the pamphlet which he quaintly entitled 'Shooting Niagara : and After ? ' is the practical suggestions it offers towards some actual beginning of, what in Sartorial language he called ' the Palingenesia or Newbirth of Society ; ' and, for this reason, the ' and After ? ' was to him by far the more important half of the problem.   For it must be further noted that it was an actual Newbirth he was now looking for ; no " blessed transition period, without solution of continuity," as he once hoped. The time for that was passed. We were already in the rapids, and no power on earth could now arrest our vaunted ' progress.' Power ? he might have asked,—where is there any longer any power left among us, for repressing anarchy however turbulent ? Already, he says, it has become "safer to humour the mob than repress them. . . . Everybody sees this official slinking-off, has a secret fellow-feeling with it ; nobody admires it ; but the spoken disapproval is languid, and generally from the teeth outwards. . . . So that, if loud mobs, supported by one or two Eloquences in the House, choose to proclaim, some day, with vociferation, as some day they will, ' Enough of Kingship, and its grimacings and futilities ! Is it not a Hypocrisy and Humbug, as you yourselves well know ? We demand to become *Commonwealth of England;* that will perhaps be better, worse it cannot be ! '—in such case, how much of available resistance does the reader think would ensue ? From official persons, with the rope round their necks, should you expect a great amount ? I do not ; or that resistance to the death would anywhere, ' within these walls ' or without, be the prevailing phenomenon."

This is the sort of thing to which, Carlyle clearly saw, we were enthusiastically progressing. Is it wonderful that he had no manner of respect for such sheer infatuated Gadarene Progress? Or, is such a state of things less threatening at the present day than it was eighteen years ago? Every one knows that the political progress we have since made has been avowedly and triumphantly in the same fatal direction, and that such a consummation as Carlyle indicates, or something equivalent to it, is very widely looked upon as a mere question of time. Every one is now to be 'governed' as he likes: 'All who are for the disintegration of the Empire, hold up your hands !' Really, as Carlyle says, most people seem to talk of approaching revolution with singular composure. But the fact is, few people have honestly tried to realise in their own minds what 'revolution' must inevitably mean, in a country like ours.

Let us imagine the Commonwealth established, either with or without a nominal King, based upon universal suffrage, eloquent plausibilities, vote by ballot, *and every one seeking his own personal advantage;* and this in a country where the few have much to lose, and where the great majority of the people can find no worthy career either for themselves or for their children. Surely this is a condition of things which might give rise to reflections. Are we simple enough to expect, now that the power has been taken from the hands of the fortunate and placed in the hands of the unfortunate, that there will be no reprisals? The gospel of disintegration,—Every one for himself, let who will fall to the ground,—has long been everywhere preached amongst us as the only common-sense rule of life. Apply such a gospel to our new social condition, and can any one seriously doubt the result? It is easy to shriek at 'confiscation,' as an impossible and almost inconceivable atrocity. But it is as idle as it is easy. Social revolution, carried through upon the lines of selfishness, means confiscation, wherever there is great need or great greed on the one hand, and anything to confiscate on the other. Let our landed and industrial aristocracies look to this, if it be not already too late; for not only are many eloquently tempting cries already eagerly listened to on every hand, but they themselves are at last compelled to notice them, if only to show how pungently they feel their force. Carlyle was the best and truest friend they ever had, or perhaps are now likely to have, if they could but have heeded him in time. His whole writings, from 'Sartor Resartus' to the end, were a continual warning and appeal to them to prove themselves worthy of their high positions. And what has it all profited ? Never was any Nation, not even the Children of Israel in the day of their coming desolation, more distinctly or more earnestly forewarned ; and never did any nation more flippantly turn away from the message which might have saved them. Here and there a man, like the late Lord Shaftesbury, or like Charles Kingsley among the clergy, or like Ruskin among independent thinkers, noble in heart as well as high in position, has shown what a Real Aristocracy might do,—if they only had the hearts to go and do likewise, each in his own way, and according to his own conscience of what would be best for his country. Who can doubt that, if they had really done so, with any unity and persistence of effort, they would not only have saved their own households, but have rallied round them all that was noblest, best, and strongest amongst us, in one common effort for the Common Weal ? But we need not indulge in any virtuous indignation on the subject ; they were not worse than the rest of us. Nearly all the world was going the same heedless road. Their misfortune was that, by their very position, they were called upon to be so much wiser and better. How could they be Dukes or Leaders, in any manful sense of the word, if they could not lead us to something nobler and wiser than we already knew ?

   "For ever impossible, say you ? " asked Carlyle,— "contrary to all our notions, regulations and ways of proceeding or of thinking !—Well, I dare say." Meantime, eighteen years ago, this is what he ventured to suggest to the Landed Aristocracy as to what might have been :—

"In their own Domains and land territories," he then said, "it is evident each of them can still, for certain years and decades, be a complete king; and may, if he strenuously try, mould and manage everything, till both his people and his dominion correspond gradually to the ideal he has formed. Refractory subjects he has the means of *banishing;* the relations between all classes, from the biggest farmer to the poorest orphan ploughboy, are under his control; nothing ugly or unjust or improper, but he could by degrees undertake steady war against, and manfully subdue or extirpate. Till all his Domain were, through every field and homestead of it, and were maintained in continuing and being, manlike, decorous, fit; comely to the eye and to the soul of whoever wisely looked on it. This is a beautiful ideal; which might be carried out on all sides to indefinite lengths,—not in management of land only, but in thousandfold countenancing, protecting and encouraging of human worth, and *discountenancing* and sternly repressing the want of ditto, wherever met with among surrounding mankind. Till the whole surroundings of a nobleman were made noble like himself: and all men should recognise that here verily was a bit of knighthood ruling 'by the Grace of God,' in difficult circumstances, but *not* in vain.

"This were a way, if this were commonly adopted, of by degrees reinstating Aristocracy in all the privileges, authorities, reverences and honours it ever had, in its palmiest days. . . . But, alas, this is an ideal, and I have practically little faith in it. Discerning well how *few* would seriously adopt this as a trade in life, I can only say, 'Blessed is everyone that does!'" —Readers can observe that only zealous aspirants to *be* 'noble' and worthy of their title (who are not a numerous class) could adopt this trade; and that of these few, only the fewest, or the actually *noble*, could to much effect do it when adopted. 'Management of one's land on this principle,' yes, in some degree this might be possible: but as to 'fostering merit' or human worth——!"

Nevertheless Carlyle would not despair: for he always well knew, and earnestly insisted, that, if only 'two or three Living Men' were gathered together in such a spirit,—there would a living Society be, or the sacred beginning of it.   Accordingly he continues,—

"How many of our Titular Aristocracy will prove real gold when thrown into the crucible?   That is always a highly interesting question to me; and my answer, or guess, has still something considerable of hope lurking in it.   But the question as to our Aristocracy by Patent from God the Maker, is infinitely interesting.   How many of these, amid the ever-increasing bewilderments and welter of impediments, will be able to develop themselves into something of Heroic Welldoing by act and by word . . . in their various wisest ways; and never ceasing or slackening till they die ?   This is the question of questions, on which all turns; in the answer to this, could we give it clearly, as no man can, lies the oracle-response, 'Life for you,' 'Death for you!'   Looking into this, there are fearful dubitations many.   But considering what of Piety, the devoutest and bravest yet known, there once was in England, one is inclined timidly to hope the best!

"The *best* : for if this small Aristocratic nucleus can hold out and work, it is in the sure case to increase and increase; to become (as Oliver once termed them) 'a company of poor men, who will spend all their blood rather' . . . I see well it must at length come to battle; actual fighting, bloody wrestling, and a great deal of it : but were it unit against thousand, or against thousand-thousand, on the above terms, I know the issue, and have no fear about it.   That also is an issue which has been often tried in Human History; and, 'while God lives '—(I hope the phrase is not yet obsolete, for the fact is eternal, though so many have forgotten it !)—said issue can or will fall only one way."

Assuredly Carlyle does not teach us to hope for an easy solution of our social difficulties.   But, whatever we may think of his notions, the foregoing extracts will at least serve to show his own Ideal of the true functions of a Landed Aristocracy.   Of course he may have been altogether mistaken in the men he appealed to.   Perhaps our Aristocracies of Title and of Wealth have not the slightest intention of fighting to the death, either for their homes or for their convictions. Their only thought may be, how to make the best terms, each for himself, when at last it comes to the crucial pinch. If so, there may well be no bloodshed upon that count. Nothing more than a selfish scramble, more despicable than any earnest fighting. Or they may still be thinking, ' O it's been lang o' coming; let us hope it may never come:' and so slumber on, until their very beds are suddenly snatched from under them! It was so in 1789; and do they think the Nemesis of Human History has forgotten them? From men who deliberately shut their eyes to it, no danger can be averted. And yet it is hard to believe that Carlyle's lifelong effort is destined to bear no good fruit for his country; or, as he says, that England, after so many generations of heroic effort, has now no rallying power left in any of her sons. Surely we cannot believe it. There must be, and we know there is, everywhere becoming visible, a wiser and nobler spirit, such as Carlyle struggled to evoke, working irresistible amongst us, which will yet put to shame the vulgar self-seeking and self-assertion which for the present, both in high life and in low life, seems to be sweeping everything before it. A spirit of human brotherhood, quixotic enough in some of its manifestations, but altogether hopeful in tendency, is on every hand struggling into active life; not in one class alone, but in every class, from the highest to the lowest. A spirit of pity for the unfortunate, of help to the helpless, and of passionate effort to rescue the thousands upon thousands of miserable lives trodden underfoot by the remorseless and selfish march of modern civilisation.

Who will join this chosen army of martyrs ?　The secret of the future is in their hearts, and the hope of the world is in their keeping.　If our aristocracies of wealth, with their boundless resources and unprecedented facility of position, will not unite together and take the lead which Providence has placed in their hands, they must even go their ways.　The future is not for them, and God's heritage will be passed over to those who fear Him, and dare to do His Will upon the earth.

Alas, how much might even yet be done, if the right men and women were but ready and earnest to do it ! It is needless, and perhaps would be futile, to attempt any summary of Carlyle's pregnant and friendly counsel to those whom he calls the Three Aristocracies of England, —the 'Landed,' the 'Industrial,' and the 'Vocal or Teaching one.'　All this, and much else, I must hopefully leave to the private intuitions and reflections of my readers, in the earnest faith that some few,—'Noble by Patent of God their Maker,'—may be induced to look once more into this last of the 'Latter-Day Pamphlets,' and ask, each for himself, with the seriousness of a life-or-death question, whether it contains no special message of any kind to his own heart and conscience.　Carlyle knew, better than any of us, what a tragically intricate problem their work in life must necessarily be, if taken seriously in hand, and how impossible it would be to give any detailed advice which would be practically available in the new circumstances.　He accordingly contented himself with offering a few typical suggestions, by way of indicating the kind of work pressingly needed to be begun.　The 'right men,' if they exist anywhere, will alone be able to judge what is possible for them, and what is not.　We will therefore conclude with a few tender words of saddest encouragement, which show very clearly with what mingled feelings of hope and despair the whole of these his 'last words' to his country were written by Carlyle; and so leave his many-sided character and earnest life-work to point their own moral; to admonish the slack-hearted, and strengthen the hearts of the wise; until England, the Mother of Nations, the World's Old Home and Fortress of unfettered consciences, the rallying-ground of true independence, of Christian zeal and of national and family faithfulness, shall, with God's blessing, be in a position 'once more to show the Nations how to live.'

Referring to what he sadly regarded as his own poor suggestions, he thus commits them, with an old Prophet's farewell benison, to all whom they may vitally concern :—

"These are a kind of enterprises, hypothetical as yet, but possible evidently more or less; and, in all degrees of them, tending towards noble benefit to oneself and to all one's fellow-creatures; which a man born noble by title and by nature, with ample territories and revenues, and a life to dispose of as he pleased, might go into, and win honour by, even in the England that now is. To my fancy, they are bright little potential breaks, and *upturnings*, of that disastrous cloud which now overshadows his best capabilities and him;—as every blackest cloud in this world has withal a 'silver lining;' and is, full surely, beshone by the Heavenly lights, if we *can* get to the other side of it! More of such fine possibilities I might add. . . . But I forbear; feeling well enough how visionary these things look; and how aerial, high and spiritual they *are;* little capable of tempting, even for moments, any but the highest kinds of men. Few Noble Lords, I may believe, will think of taking this course; indeed not many, as Noble Lords now are, could do much good in it. Dilettantism will avail nothing in any of these enterprises;

the law of them is, grim labour, earnest and continual; certainty of many contradictions, disappointments; a life, not of ease and pleasure, but of noble and sorrowful toil; the reward of it far off,—fit only for heroes!"

> " While earnest thou gazest,
> Come bodings of terror,
> Come phantasm and error,
> Perplexing the bravest
> With doubt and misgiving.
>
> " But heard are the Voices,—
> Heard are the Sages,
> The Worlds and the Ages :
> ' Choose well, your choice is
> Brief, and yet endless :
>
> " ' Here eyes do regard you,
> In Eternity's stillness ;
> HERE is all fulness,
> Ye brave, to reward you ;
> Work, and despair not.' "

POSTSCRIPT.

SINCE the foregoing pages were in type I have read Mr. Ruskin's 'Master's Report to the Guild of St. George,' and it contains such a frank expression of sympathy with Carlyle's earnest appeal to whatever Aristocracy of Worth, titled or untitled, might remain in the country; and at the same time affords such a sorrowful confirmation of Carlyle's anxious forebodings, that I can hardly feel I am taking a liberty in extracting from it the following words :—

"The St. George's Guild was instituted with a view of showing, in practice, the rational organisation of country life, independent of that of cities.

" All the efforts, whether of the Government or the landed proprietors of England, for the help or instruction of our rural population, have been made under two false suppositions: the first, that country life was henceforward to be subordinate to that of towns, the second that the landlord was, for a great part of the year, to live in the town, and thence to direct the management of his estate. Whatever may be the destiny of London, Paris, or Rome in the future, I have always taught that the problem of right organisation of country life was wholly independent of them; and that the interests of the rural population, now thought by the extension of parliamentary suffrage to be placed in their own keeping, had always been so, to the same degree, if they had only known it.

"Throughout my writings on social questions I have pointed to the former life of the Swiss (represented with photographic truth by Jeremias Gotthelf), and to the still existing life of the Norwegians and Tyrolese, perfectly well known to every thoughtful and kind-hearted traveller in their respective countries,—as examples, nearly perfect, of social order independent of cities:—but, with Carlyle, I have taught also that in the English, French, and Italian natures there was superadded to the elements of the German and Norwegian mind, a spirit of reverence for their leaders in worldly things, and for their monitors in spiritual things, which were their greatest strength and greatest happiness; in the forfeiture of which by their nobles, had passed away their own honour; and on loss of which, by the people, had followed inevitably the degradation of their characters, the destruction of their arts, and the ruin of their fortunes.

" The object principally and finally in my mind in founding the Guild, was the restoration, to such extent as might be possible to those who understood me, of this feeling of loyalty to the Land-possessor in the peasantry on his estate; and of duty, in the lord, to the peasantry with whose lives and education he was entrusted. The feeling of a Scottish clansman to his chief, or of an old Saxon servant to his lord, cannot be regained now, unless under the discipline of war; but even at this day, an English hereditary owner of land, or any man who, coming into possession of land, would therefore set

2 B

himself to bring up upon it the greatest number possible of grateful servants, would find instantly that the old feelings of gratitude and devotion are still in the hearts of the people; and, to be manifested, need only to be deserved.

"I thought when, following Carlyle's grander exhortation to the English landholders in 'Past and Present,' I put these thoughts with reiterated and varied emphasis forward in connection with a definite scheme of action, at a time when, for want of any care or teaching from their landlords, the peasantry were far and wide allowing themselves to be betrayed into Socialism, that at least a few wise and kindly-hearted Englishmen would have come forward to help me; and that in a year or two enough would have understood the design to justify me in the anticipations which at that time, having had no experience of the selfishness of my countrymen, I allowed to colour with too great aspect of romance the earlier numbers of 'Fors Clavigera.' That during the fifteen years which have now elapsed since it was begun, only two people of means—both my personal friends, Mrs. Talbot and Mr. Baker—should have come forward to help me, is, as I have said in the last issue of 'Fors,' I well know in great part my own fault; but also amazing to me beyond anything I have read in history in proof of the hard-heartedness incident to the pursuit of wealth. Friends I have, whose affection I doubt not,—many; readers, becoming friends without profession, more. A week rarely passes without my hearing of, or receiving a letter from, some one who wishes to thank me for making their lives happier, and in most cases also, more useful. In any appeal to this direct regard for me I have found answer justifying my thought of them. They subscribed a thousand pounds to give me a Turner after my last illness, and with four hundred more paid the law costs of my defence against action for libel. I am grateful to them, but would very willingly have gone without my Splugen, and paid my own law costs, if only they would have helped me in the great public work which I have given certainly the most intense labour of my life to promote. Whereas, one and all, their holding back has shown, either, that they think me a fool in such matters,—or that they were apprehensive of any action which might in the least degree give insight into the corruption of our modern system of accumulating wealth."

Carlyle never had a more faithful fellow-labourer than Mr. Ruskin, however distinctly they may have differed in many practical details ; nor one upon whose self-devoted efforts he looked with more wondering interest. I recollect especially how he once spoke to me on the subject ; it was about the time of the fifteenth number of 'Fors Clavigera,' (published March 1st, 1872,) which number he afterwards posted to me, first having marked, very carefully and emphatically, the note explaining where they might be obtained. I shall not easily forget how earnestly and even affectionately he applauded Mr. Ruskin's fearless onslaughts upon all manner of delusions which were corrupting the very life-blood of our social existence ; and how he hoped that his ' sun arrows ' might pierce, and stir into nobler life, many hearts which he himself had been unable to reach. And now, after fourteen years have passed away, the above is what Mr. Ruskin has to report, as to the visible results of his earnest efforts ! Well might Carlyle say, " Imminent perdition is not usually driven away by words of warning. Didactic Destiny has other methods in store ; or these would fail always."

THE END.

PRINTED BY WILLIAM CLOWES AND SONS, LIMITED, LONDON AND BECCLES.